Benjamin Seebohm

Memoirs of the Life and Gospel Labours of Stephen Grellet

Third Edition

Benjamin Seebohm

Memoirs of the Life and Gospel Labours of Stephen Grellet
Third Edition

ISBN/EAN: 9783337279899

Printed in Europe, USA, Canada, Australia, Japan

Cover: Foto ©Raphael Reischuk / pixelio.de

More available books at **www.hansebooks.com**

MEMOIRS

OF THE

LIFE AND GOSPEL LABOURS

OF

STEPHEN GRELLET.

EDITED BY

BENJAMIN SEEBOHM.

"The fields in many parts I have visited are white unto harvest, so that sometimes I have wished that I might have the life of Methuselah, or that the sun might never go down, that I might do my share of that great work which is to be done in these nations."—S. GRELLET, p. 133.

THIRD EDITION ABRIDGED,

By R. and E. R. Alsop.

LONDON:

EDWARD MARSH, 12, BISHOPSGATE STREET WITHOUT.

—

MDCCCLXX.

LONDON:

BARRETT & SONS,

MARK LANE.

NOTICE TO THE READER.

In the perusal of the biography of Stephen Grellet, the reader can hardly have failed to observe, to how large an extent his native country, and other parts of continental Europe, were the scene of his Christian interest and loving labours: in connection with this view, the desire has often been expressed that this valuable work should be made accessible to the inhabitants of France in the form of a good translation. The Memoir itself, originally in two volumes, appeared to be too diffuse for the purpose ; but it was thought that, by careful abridgment, the spirit and identity of the original might be retained : so that, while acceptable to the English reader, it might serve as a basis for the desired translation. The subject was laid before our friend Benjamin Seebohm, who entered into the proposal and fully approved of the publication of such an abridged edition ; but as the state of his health precluded his giving attention to it himself, he cordially encouraged Robert and Christine Alsop to undertake it. We trust that the single volume now presented to the public will be found to include all the most interesting portions, and will be perused with pleasure and profit by many who may not be able to obtain the larger work.

The translation has been confided to G. de Félice, of Montauban, an eminent Protestant writer, who has heartily devoted himself to the labour ; and ere long we hope that this valuable piece of Christian biography may have a wide circulation on the Continent, before the personal remembrance of this devoted servant of the Lord shall have entirely passed away.

Stoke Newington, 1870.

PREFACE

TO THE FIRST EDITION.

LITTLE need be said by way of introduction to the "LIFE OF STEPHEN GRELLET." It is properly an Autobiography—he speaks for himself. Not much more has been done by other hands than collecting, arranging and selecting from the materials furnished by his own pen.

Under a sense of his own nothingness, and an aversion to say anything relating to himself, he had long been deterred from a review of his early life and subsequent history, and "in now attempting," he says at the beginning of his narrative, " to give some small account of the merciful dealings of the Lord with me, for my near relatives and friends, it is very far from my desire to perpetuate my memory to another generation ; but rather," with an eye to the advancement of the Redeemer's kingdom, "to encourage my fellow-pilgrims, whilst they may mark some of their own footsteps in the path which I have trodden from my youth up, to lift up their heads in hope ; for, in proportion as the tribulations of the Gospel have abounded, so its consolations have much more abounded by Christ. My soul magnifies the Lord, and my spirit rejoices in God my Saviour, for He has done great things for his servant!"

Bradford, Yorks., 1860.

CONTENTS.

CHAPTER VIII.

CHAPTER IX.

CHAPTER X.

CHAPTER XI.

CHAPTER XII.

CHAPTER XIII.

CHAPTER XIV.

CHAPTER XV.

CHAPTER XVI.

CHAPTER XVII.

CHAPTER XVIII.

CHAPTER XIX.

CHAPTER XX.

CHAPTER XXI.

CHAPTER XXII.

CHAPTER XXIII.

CHAPTER XXIV.

CHAPTER XXV.

CHAPTER XXVI.

CHAPTER XXVII.

CHAPTER XXVIII.

CHAPTER XXIX.

CHAPTER XXX.

CHAPTER XXXI.

CHAPTER XXXII.

CHAPTER XXXIII.

CHAPTER XXXIV.

CHAPTER XXXV.

LIFE

OF

STEPHEN GRELLET.

CHAPTER I.

CHILDHOOD AND COLLEGE LIFE.

FRENCH REVOLUTION—REMOVAL TO DEMERARA—ARRIVAL AT NEW YORK.

ETIENNE DE GRELLET DU MABILLIER* was born on the 2nd of Eleventh Month, 1773, in France, in the city of Limoges, capital of the modern department of Haute Vienne, and situated in the beautiful district of Limousin. He was the fifth child of GABRIEL MARC ANTOINE DE GRELLET and SUSANNE DE SENAMAUD.

His parents were wealthy, and ranked high among the nobility of that district. During Etienne's childhood, his father GABRIEL DE GRELLET, resided on his patrimonial estate. He was owner of extensive porcelain manufactories, in the neighbourhood of Limoges, as well as proprietor of some iron works. For some years he was comptroller of the Mint, and, at one time, formed part of the household of Louis XVI. As the intimate friend and counsellor of the

---

* This was the proper name of Stephen Grellet, in his own country, the affix "du Mabillier" being derived from an estate owned by his father before the Revolution, when, with most of his property, it was confiscated.

B

king, he was accustomed to attend service with him in
his private chapel. A title was conferred upon him for the
benefits he had rendered to his country, especially by the
introduction of the manufacture of superior porcelain ware.
His porcelain works were afterwards purchased by the king,
just before the French Revolution, but, on account of that
event, never paid for.

The ancestors of SUSANNE DE SENAMAUD, Etienne's mother,
had resided at Limoges for many generations; and their
standing in the world was among the first class of the inhabitants of that part of the country. They were remarkable
for their longevity, three of the family lived to above 90
years, and she herself died at the age of 93.

In religious profession the family of Grellet were Roman
Catholics. It was the religion of their ancestors on both
sides, and, whilst some of the present generation had chosen
secular pursuits, there were others who, in accordance with
the system of their Church, had quitted the blandishments
of the world for the seclusion of the convent. One sister of
Gabriel de Grellet had long since taken the veil, and resided,
as a nun, in the convent of the Visitation at Limoges;
another sister and her aged aunt, had, with still more ascetic
devotion, submitted to the severer discipline of the convent
of Clairetés.

Thus was the childhood of Etienne cast among the con-
flicting influences of rank, and wealth, and the luxuries of
life, on the one hand, and, on the other, of the quiet and
mysterious example of a voluntary withdrawal from the
external world, and all its attractions. But of his early
days, spent under the parental roof, he has told us but little.

Whilst at home, he was educated with his brothers and
sisters, under the care of tutors who resided in the house.
"My parents were desirous," he tells us, "to give their
children such an education as should make them accomplished in the eyes of the world;" but, though trained in

the precepts of a high toned morality, they received little
direct religious instruction.   The simple truths of Holy
Scripture were not the food of their early childhood,—the
" principles of the doctrine of Christ" were not taught them,
and they had scarcely " so much as heard whether there be
any Holy Ghost."

A quick susceptibility to religious impressions seems,
nevertheless, to have marked the youthful days of Etienne de
Grellet, and early indications of the work of Divine grace
upon his heart were not wanting.   When quite a child, his
thoughts on the omnipotence of the Divine Being, the Creator
of all things, so deeply affected him that he never afterwards
lost the recollection of it.   At the early age of five or six,
the efficacy of prayer to an omnipresent and omniscient God
was remarkably confirmed to him.   His juvenile powers had
been overtasked by a long Latin exercise ; he was quite
disheartened.   Alone, in his chamber, he looked abroad upon
the glories of the external world, and remembered that it was
God who had created them all.   The thought arose in his
heart—" Cannot the same God give me memory also?"
He knelt down at the foot of his bed, and poured out his
soul in prayer to the Lord.   His petition was immediately
answered.   On reperusing his lesson, he found himself
master of it; and henceforward, he was able to acquire
learning with increased facility.   Even in his old age, he could
look back to " happy days," when his childish heart was
deeply affected, and remember, " with grateful emotion,"
places in his father's house, where, " on his knees, with his
eyes flowing with tears, he had poured forth his supplications
unto God."   He had learnt to repeat the Lord's Prayer.
" O how was my heart contrited," he exclaims, " while
uttering the words, ' Our Father, who art in heaven.' "   To
be permitted thus to look up to his God, to call him Father,
and to consider himself as his child, filled his young soul
with the tenderness of reverential awe.

But, in a religious point of view, his external advantages were at this time very few. "I had none," he remarks in his Autobiography, "to instruct me,—none to whom I thought of unfolding my heart. My proneness to vanity soon dissipated all serious thoughts, my fondness for play gained the ascendancy, till the Divine visitation was renewed."

After a few years of home tuition, young Etienne and his brothers were sent to several successive colleges. The last he was at was that of the Oratorians, at Lyons. Unlike the previous one, in which "great corruption and levity were introduced among the pupils, this was a well ordered institution, and afforded many advantages to the students."

Etienne now applied himself vigorously to his studies, and obtained several prizes for his proficiency in Latin. He here laid the foundation for that general knowledge, and moral fortitude, which marked his future character. It was during his tarriance at this college also, that he was again "favoured with the Lord's gracious visitations to his soul." To this he afterwards refers "with instruction and gratitude," and, commemorating the Divine goodness, he exclaims, "O the heart-meltings I have witnessed,—fervent were some of the prayers I then put up when on my knees, my cheeks bedewed with tears."

"As we were educated," he continues, "by Roman Catholics, and in their principles, we were required to *confess* once in every month. I had chosen for my confessor one whom I thought to be a pious and conscientious man; and, as I could not understand how it was possible for a *man* to forgive my sins, I asked him what he could say to satisfy my mind on that point, for I considered that God alone could forgive sins; a doctrine, however, which I had never *heard* of. He, seeing further than many other priests, told me that he considered himself invested with such authority, only so far as that, if I was sincere, and truly penitent in the sight of God, he was the instrument through whom information was given me that my sins were forgiven. This rational answer gained him much of my confidence and respect. He bestowed a fatherly care over me."

Amongst the "*religious openings*" he had at Lyons, one left a deep impression; and the remembrance of it helped to sustain his spirit under many subsequent exercises and trials.

"I thought I saw," he says, "a large company of persons, or rather purified spirits, on one of those floating vessels which they have at Lyons, on the Rhone, occupied by washerwomen. They were washing linen. I wondered to see what beating and pounding there was upon it, but how beautifully white it came out of their hands. I was told I could not enter God's kingdom until I underwent such an operation,—that unless I was thus washed and made white, I could have no part in the dear Son of God. For weeks I was absorbed in the consideration of the subject— the washing of regeneration. I had never heard of such things before, and I greatly wondered that, having been baptised with water, and having also received what they call the sacrament of confirmation, I should have to pass through such a purification ; for I had never read or heard any one speak of such a baptism."

When, some years before, along with some of his companions, he received confirmation according to the rites of the Romish Church, he was bitterly disappointed, he tells us, that, "contrary to what he had been led to expect, after the bishop had performed the ceremony, he found his heart not at all changed; that his sense of sin still remained; that his propensities to evil were, that very day, as strong as ever ;" and "thus," he adds, "*at a very early age, I learned that neither Priests nor Bishops could do the work for me.*"

Before leaving the university, he joined with other collegians in preparing for participating in what is called the Sacrament of the Lord's Supper. Earnest were his prayers that he might do it worthily ; his heart was sincere, "and," he writes, "the Lord condescended to evince himself near to me under that shadow. This feeling continued while I

remained at the college, and some time after I had returned
to my father's house. But then, going into company, and
having an opportunity of giving full sway to my vain and
volatile disposition, I soon lost these religious convictions.
I sought after happiness in the world's delights. I expected
to find it. I went in pursuit of it from one party of pleasure
to another; but I did *not* find it, and I wondered that the
name of pleasure could be given to anything of the kind."

Before Etienne had completed his sixteenth year, the
political horizon of his country was changed, and with it the
horizon of his hopes.

Nearly allied to the nobility, and by all natural ties and
sentiments bound to their cause, the family of Gabriel de
Grellet shared their reverses during the great revolutionary
struggle which now swept over France. Their estates were
confiscated, and he and his wife were thrown into prison, and
had a very narrow escape of their lives.

In the early stages of the fearful conflict, Etienne was too
young to take a very prominent part; but there was much
to rouse his feelings, and to stir the youthful ardour of his
spirit. At the commencement of the Revolution, he tells
us, the inhabitants of the kingdom generally took up arms;
one scene of distress after another kept him continually
afloat. The many provocations which the nobility and their
adherents had to endure, and for which he admits they had,
in some instances, given too much occasion, would have
driven him to extremities, had it not been for what he gratefully recognises as a " Divine interposition," which preserved
him; for, at that time, in the summer of 1791, he was
violently seized with the small-pox. During this illness he
was brought very low.

"The Lord," he writes, "was pleased afresh to visit my benighted
soul. The state from which I had departed was clearly set before
me, and the misery into which I must be plunged, if the thread
of my life should then be cut off. After much *secret* sorrow, for

no man knew how it was with me, the Lord was pleased to lift up the light of his countenance upon me, and to enable me again to enter into covenant with Him. In adorable mercy He preserved my life, and relieved me from the apprehension of being totally blind, the disorder being much in the eyes. But, alas ! soon I forgot his works, turned his mercy into wantonness and became more and more estranged from Him." ·

Soon after his recovery, the nobility in general were retiring from France into Germany, to join the standard of the French Princes, and to unite with the armies of other Continental Powers to bring about a counter revolution, and restore the king. It was concluded that Etienne, and some of his brothers, should join them. Towards the close of 1791, therefore, he writes, "I left my dear father's house, and bid him, as it proved, a lasting farewell, having never seen him since." The brothers now proceeded to join the Royalists. After stopping a few days at Paris, they passed on towards Germany. Many were the dangers to which Etienne was exposed. In recurring to these, and the narrow escapes he had, he remarks :—

"I shudder when I remember the state of insensibility I was in. I was not the least moved when surrounded by people and soldiers, who lavished their abuse upon us, and threatened to hang me to the lamp-post. I coolly stood by, my hands in my pockets, being provided with three pairs of pistols, two of which were double-barrelled. I concluded to wait to see what they would do, and resolved, after destroying as many of them as I could, to take my own life with the last. No thought of eternity was then before me—no sense of remembrance that there is a God."

After a short detention, he and his brothers pursued their way to Coblentz, then the rendezvous of the nobility, the French Princes being there. The winter and spring were spent in military preparations for the approaching campaign in France. Both morally and physically it was a time of much exposure to Etienne.

"Everything about me," he says, "and the very nature of the work I was engaged in, was highly calculated to destroy every fibre remaining of those tender impressions I had heretofore received; but my gracious Lord did not wholly forsake me. I was preserved from those gross evils that are too generally attendant on an army. But O! the height of my infatuation! I attributed my preservation to my own reasoning powers. Divine light would, nevertheless, at seasons, pierce into the inmost recesses of my benighted heart. I was fond of solitude, and had many retired walks through the woods, and over the hills. I delighted to visit the deserted hermitages which formerly abounded on the Rhine. I envied the situation of such hermits—retired from the world, and sheltered from its many temptations; for I thought it impossible for me to live a life of purity, while continuing among my associates. I looked forward wishfully for the time when I could thus retire; but I saw also that, unless I could leave behind me my earthly-mindedness, my pride, vanity, and every carnal propensity, an outward solitude could afford me no shelter.

"Our army entered into France the forepart of the summer of 1792, accompanied by the Austrians and Prussians. I was in the King's Horse Guards, which consisted mostly of the nobility. We endured great hardships, for many weeks sleeping on the bare ground, in the open air, and were sometimes in want of provisions. But that word *honour* so inflamed us, that I marvel how contentedly we bore our privations. And what was it all for? To contend for an earthly crown! To satisfy our vain and proud minds!"

Towards the approach of winter, owing to various political changes, the Princes' army was obliged to retire from France, and, soon after, was disbanded. Etienne had been present at several engagements; he had seen many fall about him, stricken by the shafts of death; he had stood in battle array, facing the enemy, ready for the conflict; but, being in a reserve corps, he was never actually called out to the murderous onset; he was thus preserved from "shedding blood," having "never fought with the sword, or fired a gun."

Though, at the time, he might consider it as a "misfortune," he was wont, in after days, to recur to this circumstance with peculiar thankfulness to Him, who had so especially called him into the service of the Prince of Peace.

Numerous incidents connected with his personal history "which would alone fill a volume," and the well-known events of the Revolution, with the barbarities of Robespierre's reign of terror, are passed over in silence, or but slightly touched upon, in his Autobiography. After recording the retreat of the Princes' army, he simply remarks, that he and his brothers "went to Amsterdam." From other sources we learn, that, being made prisoners of war, they were ordered to be shot. The execution of the sentence was each moment expected, when some sudden commotion in the hostile army gave them an opportunity to make their escape. They took the route of Brussels, and thence reached Holland in safety.

The young brothers soon met with kind friends in Amsterdam; but it now became a matter of serious consideration what course to pursue. Etienne and his brother Joseph finally concluded to go to South America. Through the kind assistance of a republican General, a friend of the family, they obtained a passage on board a ship bound for Demerara, where they arrived in the First Month of 1793, after a voyage of about forty days.   .

They were provided with letters of introduction from their friends in Holland to some of the principal planters, who received them with much hospitality. Mercantile pursuits soon occupied their attention, and during a residence of two years in the colony, which then belonged to Holland, they had an opportunity of seeing much of the horrors of slavery, and of becoming intimately acquainted with the ruinous effects of that iniquitous and anti-christian system, both upon the coloured and the white population.

Such was the impression made upon Etienne by the scenes of cruelty and anguish he witnessed, that, many years after, the sound of a whip in the street would " chill his blood," in the remembrance of the agony of the poor slaves ; and he " felt convinced that there was no excess of wickedness and malice which a slaveholder, or driver, might not be guilty of."

The state of society in Demerara was deplorable.

" It was a place of much dissipation," he remarks. " I do not recollect, during the whole time I was there, that I saw anything, in any one, that indicated a feeling of religious sensibility. There was no place of worship ; no priest of any kind, except one who had been there a few years, who was a dissolute drunken man. It was of the Lord's mercy that I, and the whole land, were not destroyed like Sodom and Gomorrah. At that time, the prince of the power of air, who rules in the hearts of the children of disobedience, had obtained such a victory over me, that I had become one of the number of those infatuated ones who call good evil, and evil good,—darkness light, and light darkness,—to so daring a pitch as to say—*There is no God !* I not only thought that there was no God, and consequently no religion : that all the profession of it was but priestcraft, invention, and deceit : but so plausibly had I compassed myself with sparks of my own kindling, that I thought I saw a way to steer my own course. I had become a complete disciple of Voltaire, and writers of that class.

" How low, how degraded, did I see man to be ! And yet I could dare to think I had reached to that state of philosophy, and correctness of reasoning, that would enable me to rise from that sink of corruption, and live a virtuous life,—even concluding that it was this that preserved me from giving way to many of the vices, which flowed like a torrent about me. This was my situation when the Lord himself interfered to release me from that land, and to open a way for my emancipation from a bondage, far more to be dreaded than that of the poor slaves whom I commiserated.

" In the forepart of the spring of 1795 there was a report that a French fleet was coming to take possession of the colony. The consequences of falling into their hands, and the fear of seeing the same cruelties there, that were committed in France, induced my brother and myself to conclude to leave the country imme-

diately. An American vessel being on the eve of sailing for New
York, we took our passage in her.

"Thus in the space of two days we took our departure. A
few hours later would have prevented it : for, in the evening, as
we were going out, we saw a fleet standing in ; which, we did not
hear till some time after our arrival in New York, were the
English and not the French. However trivial this circumstance
may seem, it has often appeared to me as one that stands very
prominent in the days of my pilgrimage. I have viewed it as the
Lord's interposition to rescue me from the thraldom into which
I was plunged : these bonds, very probably, might have been
rendered still stronger, had I stayed till the English took possession
of the colony."

During the passage they had several narrow escapes.
After relating some of these, he concludes :—

"Thus did Divine Providence repeatedly interfere, and prevent
my sinking into everlasting misery. But such was the obduracy
of my heart, all that time, that I do not recollect to have felt any
emotion of gratitude."

CHAPTER II.

SAFELY arrived, after all their perils, in the United States
of America, the two brothers made a short stay in the city
of New York. They soon concluded, however, to retire to
Long Island, "where they could live more privately and
agreeably, till they might hear how it was with their parents,
and what were their wishes respecting them, either to remain
in America, or to return to them, if they thought it safe for
them to do so." They settled down for the summer at
Newtown. Here, as had been their former practice, they
sought the best company the place could afford. It was "a
maxim given them by their dear father, when taking their
last leave of him, always to choose the company of their
seniors in age, and their superiors in rank and abilities, in
preference to their inferiors." This led them to visit at the
house of Colonel Corsa, whose wife was a Franklin. They
were people of standing in the world, and the colonel had
served in the British army. He had a daughter who spoke
French, and the two brothers being entirely unacquainted
with the English language on their arrival, this was a great
inducement to cultivate intercourse with that family. One
day the conversation at the colonel's turned upon William
Penn, and the daughter saying that she had his works,
Etienne's curiosity was excited. He had heard of him as
statesman and politician, and expected to find something
relating to these things in his works. He took the volume,
a large folio, to his lodgings, and, with the help of a

dictionary, began to translate it. The subject which first engaged his attention was, however, of so different a nature from what he had anticipated, that he soon laid it aside, without proceeding far in the attempt to make out its contents.

Stephen Grellet, for so, dropping his French name, we shall henceforward call him, had now nearly completed his twenty-second year. His standing in society, his early training, and the character of his youthful experience in life, had been of a peculiar kind. Through the influence of surrounding circumstances, the serious impressions which marked some of his early days had given place to sceptical opinions, and he was now a professed unbeliever. But an important crisis was at hand. Through one of those remarkable interpositions which, for special purposes, sometimes distinguish the exercise of the Divine sovereignty, and the direct operations of the Holy Spirit, the thick veil of darkness was removed, the evil heart of unbelief was taken away, the faith and hope of the Gospel dawned again on the soul, and the objects and pursuits of life were completely and permanently changed. His own words will best describe the simple facts connected with the great turning-point of his life—his conversion :—

"Through adorable mercy, the visitation of the Lord was now again extended towards me, by the immediate openings of the Divine light on my soul. One evening, as I was walking in the fields alone, my mind being under no kind of religious concern, nor in the least excited by anything I had heard or thought of, I was suddenly arrested by what seemed to be an awful voice proclaiming the words, 'Eternity! Eternity! Eternity!' It reached my very soul,—my whole man shook,—it brought me, like Saul, to the ground. The great depravity and sinfulness of my heart were set open before me, and the gulf of everlasting destruction to which I was verging. I was made bitterly to cry out, 'If there is no God, doubtless there is a hell.' I found myself in the midst of it. For a long time it seemed as if the thundering proclamation was yet heard. After that I remained almost whole days and nights, exercised in prayer that the Lord would have mercy upon me, expecting that He would give me some evidence that He had heard my application. But for this I was looking to some outward manifestation, my expectation being entirely of that nature.

" I now took up again the works of William Penn, and opened upon ' No Cross, No Crown.' The title alone reached to my heart. I proceeded to read with the help of my dictionary, having to look for the meaning of nearly every word. I read it twice through in this manner. I had never met with anything of the kind ; neither had I felt the Divine witness in me operating so powerfully before.

" I now withdrew from company, and spent most of my time in retirement, and in silent waiting upon God. I began to read the Bible, with the aid of my dictionary, for I had none then in French. I was much of a stranger to the inspired records. I had not even seen them before, that I remember ; what I had heard of any part of their contents, was only detached portions in Prayer-books.

" Whilst the fallow ground of my heart was thus preparing, my brother and myself, being one day at Colonel Corsa's, heard that a meeting for divine worship was appointed to be held next day in the Friends' Meeting-house, by two English women on a religious visit to this land, to which we were invited. We felt inclined to go. The Friends were Deborah Darby and Rebecca Young. The sight of them brought solemn feelings over me ; but I soon forgot the servants, and all things around me ; for in an inward silent frame of mind, seeking for the Divine presence, I was favoured to find *in* me, what I had so long, and with so many tears, sought for *without* me. My brother, who sat beside me, and to whom the silence in which the forepart of the meeting was held was irksome, repeatedly whispered to me, ' let us go away.' But I felt the Lord's power in such a manner, that my inner man was prostrated before my blessed Redeemer. A secret joy filled me, in that I had found Him after whom my soul had longed. I was as one nailed to my seat. Shortly after, one or two men Friends in the ministry spoke, but I could understand very little of what they said. After them D. D. and R. Y. spoke also; but I was so gathered in the temple of my heart before God, that I was wholly absorbed with what was passing there. Thus had the Lord opened my heart to seek Him where He is to be found.

"My brother and myself were invited to dine in the company of these Friends, at Colonel Corsa's. There was a time of religious retirement after dinner, in which several communications were made. I could hardly understand a word of what was said, but as D. D. began to address my brother and myself, it seemed as if the Lord opened my outward ear, and my heart. Her words partook of the efficacy of that 'word' which is 'quick and powerful, and sharper than any two-edged sword, piercing even to the dividing asunder of soul and spirit, and of the joints and marrow, and is a discerner of the thoughts and intents of the heart.' She seemed like one reading the pages of my heart, with clearness describing how it had been, and how it was with me. I was like Lydia; my heart was opened; I felt the power of Him who hath the key of David. No strength to withstand the Divine visitation was left in me. O what sweetness did I then feel! It was indeed a memorable day. I was like one introduced into a new world; the creation and all things around me bore a different aspect,— my heart glowed with love to all. The awfulness of that day of God's visitation can never cease to be remembered with peculiar interest and gratitude, as long as I have the use of my mental faculties. I have been as one plucked from the burning—rescued from the brink of a horrible pit. O how can the extent of the Lord's love, mercy, pity, and tender compassion be fathomed!"

Religious convictions had now taken deep hold of his mind, and he carefully sought to cherish them. An anxious inquirer after "the right way of the Lord," he became still further confirmed, by evidence clear and satisfactory to his understanding, that what he had experienced "was really the work of the Lord's Spirit, and not the fruit of an exalted imagination." He now felt it to be his duty to unite with Friends in their meetings for divine worship. Quakerism was, at that time, very imperfectly understood, and little appreciated even by many Christian professors of other denominations;

much ignorance and prejudice still prevailed in regard to it.
It was by no means generally thought to be a creditable
thing to assume the character and appearance of a Friend.
Stephen Grellet boarded with a Presbyterian family; and
some of those about him, observing that he was disposed to
embrace the principles of Friends, began to reproach him.
Notwithstanding the natural intrepidity of his character, he
hesitated. He did not go to meeting when he felt that he
ought to go. Strong convictions for the sin of disobedience
were the consequence. Great were his sufferings, under what
he believed to be the heart-searching influence of the light
of the Holy Spirit. It was a time of great humiliation and
searching of heart, but it proved the means of confirming him
in a more unwavering and decided course of action afterwards.
From this time he went straight onwards.

"I was brought," he says, "to resignation to endure the world's
reproaches, or anything it might be suffered to inflict, if the Lord
would but again lift up the light of his countenance upon me.
The following First-day I went to meeting, though it rained hard,
and I had about three miles to walk. Divine mercy was pleased
to be near, and, as a tender father, the Lord condescended to
instruct me.

"I continued diligently to attend meetings, which were held in
silence. Very few persons assembled there, and I had no communication with them at all for some time. I have frequently
considered since that it was a favour that my lot was cast in a
place where I had no outward dependence to lean upon. In religious meetings, as well as out of them, my single concern was to
feel after the influences of the Holy Spirit in my own heart. As
my acquaintance with these increased, so did my exercises. The
axe of God's power was lifted up against the root of the corrupt
tree. As wave follows wave, so did my exercises. Yet I must
testify of the Lord's unspeakable love extended towards me; it
was great indeed. The sense of it was so much with me, that I
do not know whether tears of joy and gratitude have not flowed
as plentifully as those of grief, which latter have not been few.

"My dear brother, seeing how my face was turned, began to

unite with some of the people about me in reproaching the way
in which the Lord led me, which added much to my grief. He
could not bear to hear me tell of the Lord's work, as it was upon
me.   In my absence, however, I found after a while, that he read
in William Penn's works.   This encouraged me to hope that a
seeking disposition was awakened in him, though he tried to shake
it off. On First-day morning, when my prayer had been renewedly
put up in secret for him, he called me back, after I had set out to
go to meeting, saying he would go with me.   How thankful did I
feel ! Very few words passed between us by the way.   The
earnest petition of my heart was unto the Lord, that the power
of his love and presence might be so displayed, as to convince my
dear brother, and bring him to bow to his righteous sceptre. My
prayers were heard.   It was a memorable meeting,—held in
silence, however, as usual,—never to be forgotten. Very soon
after sitting down, great was the awfulness and the reverence
that came upon me.   It was succeeded by such a view and sense
of my sinful life that I was like one crushed under the millstones.
My misery was great ; my cry was not unlike that of Isaiah,
' *Woe is me, for I am undone !* ' The nearer I was then favoured
to approach Him ' who dwelleth in the light,' the more I saw
my uncleanness and my wretchedness.   But how can I set forth
the fulness of heavenly joy that filled me when the hope was
again raised that there was One, even He whom I had pierced,
Jesus Christ the Redeemer, that was able to save me ? I saw
Him to be the Lamb of God that taketh away the sins of the
world ; who was delivered for our offences, and raised again for
our justification ; who is our propitiatory sacrifice, our advocate
with the Father, our intercessor with God. I felt faith in his
atoning blood quickening my soul, giving me to believe that it
was He who could wash me from my many pollutions, and deliver
me from death and destruction, which I felt to be my just desert,
for my many sins and transgressions. On my earnest petition
being put up to Him, the language was proclaimed, 'Thy sins
are forgiven ; thy iniquities are pardoned.' Floods of tears of
joy and gratitude gave vent to the fulness of my heart !

  "Then I thought I heard again a sweet language saying, 'Proclaim unto others what the Lord has done for thy soul.' Apprehending that this was a requisition of *present* duty, I began to

plead excuses, from the consciousness of my inability to perform the service. 'Thou knowest, O Lord, that I cannot speak English so as to be understood,' was my answer, 'and what am I, that I should proclaim thy name?'

"There was not the least feeling then in me to flinch from doing, or becoming, whatever the Lord would require of me but a sense of my inability and unworthiness. I have since seen that this was more to prepare me for a future day, than a command for a present offering. My spirit continued so prostrated before the Lord, and encircled with his love and presence, that I was insensible to what passed around me. The meeting concluded, and the people retired, without my noticing it, till my brother, speaking to me, drew my attention, and I saw that we two only were left in the house.

" My gratitude was great when I found that my brother had partaken of the heavenly visitation. From that time he attended meetings diligently, and was a great comfort to me. But during all that period, we had no intercourse with any of the members of the religious Society of Friends."

The " disciple of Voltaire" now stands before us as the practical Christian — the humble believer in Jesus, the Emmanuel, the Lord our righteousness, "that liveth and was dead, and is alive for evermore." How wonderful the change! Incomprehensible to the natural man—but not on that account the less real—it was a living comment upon the words of Jesus, " the wind bloweth where it listeth, thou hearest the sound thereof, but canst not tell whence it cometh, and whither it goeth; so is every one that is born of the Spirit;"—it was a beautiful illustration of the declaration of our blessed Lord, " when He, the Spirit of Truth, is come, He will guide you into all truth; for He shall not speak of himself; but whatsoever He shall hear, that shall He speak; and He will show you things to come. *He* shall glorify *me*; for He shall receive of *mine,* and shall show it unto you." Under the presence and power of the Holy

Spirit, the transition from the mazes of infidelity to the humble and believing reception of the truth as it is in Jesus, in the love of it, was, in this instance, both rapid and complete. It was peculiarly marked as the Lord's own work; human instrumentality was but little made use of. In the course of a few months the young convert had acquired an entirely new position. God had not only "revealed his Son in him" as his own Saviour, but, as has been seen, the call "to preach Him" among his fellow-men, had, at the same time, been distinctly heard. And he was "not disobedient to the heavenly vision."

"He is a chosen vessel unto me, to bear my name before the Gentiles, and kings, and the children of Israel; for I will show him how great things he must suffer for my name's sake," was the word of the Lord to Ananias, whilst he was hesitating to bear the required message to the praying Saul of Tarsus; and in the case of Stephen Grellet, not altogether dissimilar, it was instructively manifest that God's ways are not as our ways, nor his thoughts as our thoughts." He "who commanded the light to shine out of darkness," had shined in his heart, to give him "the light of the knowledge of the glory of God in the face of Jesus Christ," and henceforward his Christian character is seen steadily maturing in the richness of a deep personal experience, while, in the progress of the work of Divine grace in his heart, he was prepared, during a long course of years, to partake largely of the blessing of those, who, "with open face beholding, as in a glass, the glory of the Lord, are changed into the same image, from glory to glory, even as by the Spirit of the Lord."

He felt as one "alive from the dead," and his Christian walk bore evidence that "the life which he now lived in the flesh was by the faith of the Son of God." He continued to frequent the "little silent meetings" at Newtown, and to unite with Friends in their simple mode of worship. Though in his secluded abode on Long Island, he had very little opportunity of associating with its members, by careful investigation he became increasingly convinced of the rectitude and scriptural soundness of the Christian principles and testimonies of the religious Society of Friends, and he felt it to be his duty entirely to carry them out in practice. Great was his love for the Saviour, in whom he had joyfully believed, and proportionately earnest was his desire to follow Him in all things. There was something quite characteristic in the tender conscientiousness with which he brought his views of Christian simplicity and self-denial to bear upon his daily walk in life, especially in connection with the costliness of some of his own habits, and the privations endured by others.

" It was a time of much scarcity of provisions in France," he remarks ; " great was the distress of the inhabitants. My dear mother wrote to me that the granaries we had at our country seat had been secured by the revolutionary party, as well as every article of food found in our town house. My mother and my younger brother were only allowed the scanty pittance of a peck of mouldy horse-beans per week. My dear father was shut up in prison, with an equally scanty allowance. But it was before I was acquainted with the sufferings of my beloved parents, that the consideration of the general scarcity prevailing in the country, led me to think how wrong for me it was to wear powder on my head, the ground of which I knew to be pride."

The expensive habit was, of course, relinquished; his Christian consistency was rendered more complete, and his money saved for better purposes.

Being convinced of the propriety of the practice of Friends in making use of the singular pronouns *thou* and *thee*, when addressing a single person, and in avoiding complimentary appellations, he says :—

" I took up my cross in that also, though it exposed me to much ridicule. Being about to write to my parents, the cross became great, chiefly because this way of speaking was then adopted by

the Revolutionist party in France, from whom my parents, with
most of the nobility, were suffering so much. But I was under
the necessity, with plainness and simplicity, to make use of the
language I saw to be my duty, leaving every consequence to the
Lord. This tended not a little to strengthen me to bear the various
railings and frowns of the world. Some who before had courted
my company now turned away ; and this became a blessing to
me, for it tended quickly to make the separation greater between
me and the world.

" By letters from our dear parents, we learnt that it was their
choice that we should, for the time being, at least, remain in this
country, seeing that the troubles in France continued great, and
that our lives would be exposed by returning to it. Our parents'
were in constant jeopardy. Their estates were under sequestra-
tion, and it became necessary for us to turn our attention towards
engaging in some kind of business. Our means began to be low,
and yet our feelings for the sufferings in which our beloved parents
might be involved, caused us to forget ourselves, strangers in a
strange country, and to forward them a few hundred dollars we
had yet left.

" I did not find it easy to obtain suitable employment, but I
sought right direction of the Lord. We first came to New York,
where I stayed about two weeks. I was much refreshed with
the company of some valuable Friends. I considered it a special
privilege to sit with them in their religious meetings.

" It was concluded that I should go to Philadelphia, and my
brother, meeting with a situation, continued in New York. Our
separation was painful, having partaken together of many trials,
and feeling much united in our religious exercises. I arrived
in Philadelphia in the Twelfth Month, 1795, and met with a very
kind reception from many Friends. I found fathers and mothers
in a spiritual sense. They, having a feeling of the exercises
that were upon me, were tender of me,—and they were so with
judgment.

" I had several offers to engage in commercial concerns, both
in Philadelphia, and from my European friends, particularly in
Holland, from whom I received proposals to place me in an
extensive way of business with the West Indies and Holland.
But, keeping my eye single to the Lord, whose direction I sought,

I could not be easy to accept any offer of this kind; for I saw that if I did, the sense of life in me, that was very tender, might easily be destroyed. I therefore preferred, for awhile, the occupation of teaching the French language. I engaged in it, it is true, much in the cross; but, having repeated evidence that it was a *right* engagement for me, it became easy to submit to it. I was at first concerned lest it should not be sufficient to procure me a living. For, from the complexion of things in France, I could not entertain any expectation that I should receive pecuniary means from that quarter. After many anxious thoughts on this head, one, day, as my mind was gathered in reverent silence before the Lord, the language was strongly impressed : 'Seek first the kingdom of God and his righteousness, and all things needful shall be added.' The evidence that it was the direction of Omnipotence, whose promise is sure, was so clear, that no doubt remained. I was closely engaged in my school, and though I scrupulously paid every requisite attention to it, yet during the intervals, my mind was wholly relieved from anxious thoughts about it. The one thing needful only absorbed me, whilst walking in the streets or sitting in the house. My mind was, at seasons, so taken up with the sense of the Lord's love, that it seemed as if I could have continued days and nights swallowed up in it. But though the love of God thus filled my heart, yet most of the time it was clothed with deep conflicts. Every step of my past life was retraced. I suffered deeply not only for the evil I had done, but also for the good I had omitted to do,—not only for the great loss I had sustained myself, but also for the harm I saw that my example might have done for others."

During the winter of that year Deborah Darby and Rebecca Young (afterwards Byrd), who had been the first instruments through whom " the Gospel's refreshing streams had reached his heart" at Newtown, visited the families of Friends in Philadelphia, and S. G. had frequent opportunities of being with them. They were made the means of confirming him in the knowledge of Christ, and he thankfully acknowledges the benefit derived from their company and labours in the Gospel.

A year had not passed since the hand of the Lord was effectually laid upon him, when He who had "called him by his grace," was pleased so remarkably to "reveal his Son in him." And "one of the exercises which *now* lay with much weight upon him, was the continued apprehension that it was required of him publicly to testify of the Lord's wondrous works and mercy towards him, in the assemblies of the people."

"I saw," he tells us, "my unworthiness to engage in such a solemn service, and felt myself to be altogether a child, that was only beginning to breathe the breath of life. Though I had made some progress in the knowledge of the English language, I knew how defective I was, and especially unqualified to act in the capacity of an ambassador for Christ, in the congregations of the people. How great was the Divine condescension in those days of my deep probation! As a father answereth his child, so the Lord condescended to answer all my pleadings and excuses; to give me also a sense of the source from whence all power, strength, and ability flow. He showed me how He is mouth, wisdom, and utterance to his true and faithful ministers; that it is from Him alone that they are to receive the subject they are to communicate to the people, and also the *when* and the *how*. It is He who giveth the seeing eye, the hearing ear, the understanding heart, and enableth the dumb to speak. I saw how, at the day of Pentecost, the disciples of our Lord, who were born again, 'not of corruptible seed, but of incorruptible, by the word of God, which liveth and abideth for ever,' were taxed with opprobrium, when the fruits of that new birth, through the everlasting Spirit, were brought forth in them, and every one heard them in their own tongues, speaking of the wonderful things of the kingdom of God. But what depth of knowledge they were endued with, after they had received the Holy Spirit! The mere touching upon these things may suffice to bring some of my fellow servants to consider the Lord's gracious dealings with them. My desire for them is that they may come to the state of the child,—the weaned child,—that they may come to Christ, and learn of Him; for though there may be much instruction in the sciences of the world, yet Christ is the only teacher in the things of God. Great was the Lord's condescension in instructing me, his poor servant, and deep were the impressions made on my mind, in attending to the immediate teaching of the Holy Spirit.

"Meeting after meeting I was under the pressure of concern to stand up and speak a few words ; but the sense of the awfulness of the engagement prevented me, time after time, till the Lord's displeasure was felt to be kindled against me. O the depth of my baptisms, in those days ! My disobedience did not, however, proceed from any outward considerations, or even the crosses involved to the natural man. I was brought too low to have thoughts of this kind ; and, I think I may say, my love for my dear Master was so great, that no sacrifice or suffering would then have been thought too much ; but I could not believe that such a poor creature as I was, such a great sinner as I had been, could be fit to engage in such a solemn work. My condemnation was, that after repeated evidences of the Lord's will respecting me, I should still continue to be of a doubtful and fearful mind. It was on the 20th of First Month, 1796, the third day of the week, that I first opened my mouth in the ministry. For some days after this act of dedication, my peace flowed as a river, whilst mine eyes were like fountains of tears of gratitude, in that the Lord had so mercifully continued to bear with me."

Stephen Grellet had not, at this time, made application for membership in the Society of Friends. Though his advancement in the school of Christ was unusually rapid, he was not precipitate in his movements—Christian prudence and caution marked his steps.

"Friends saw," he observes, "the tender and exercised state of mind in which I was, and dealt with me with much feeling and affection. Even whilst acting towards me the part of nursing fathers and mothers, their wisdom and care were manifest, neither to lay hands suddenly on me, by encouraging me to become a member of their Society, nor to discourage me, whilst not yet one, from bearing among them the testimonies the Lord gave me for his Truth. My spirit was so absorbed in the one thing, that for some time I did not much think of seeking for an outward fellowship with a people to whom I was closely united in spirit; but, when the concern came before me to apply to become a member among them, which was not till the summer following, I was brought under close exercise that I might take a *right* step.

" The ground of my faith, the nature of the testimonies I had already borne publicly, and what I apprehended I was convinced of, were closely considered. For I saw that it would not do for me to become a member of that religious Society unless I was established in their Christian principles, and was convinced also that these principles were consistent with the Truth as it was in Jesus. It was not till I was brought to see and feel again the foundation upon which they stand, even the eternal rock—Christ Jesus, that I could feel satisfied to join them in outward fellowship. The first rudiments of the Christian religion, the fall of man, my own fallen and sinful condition, redemption and salvation by Christ alone, the true Christian baptism, the supper, Divine inspiration, worship, ministry, &c., were again fully brought into view. At last, feeling with satisfactory clearness that Friends were the religious Society the Lord would have me to unite with in Christian fellowship, I made application at the *North Meeting*, to be received by them, which they accepted in the fall of the year 1796. "I have been a little particular in describing my exercises and the weight attending me, before I applied to become a member, as I have often felt since, that much responsibility attaches to us who have joined this Society on the ground of convincement; for if we do not come in at the right door, that is, both of conviction and conversion, we cannot profit the people we come among, neither can we be much profited by them ourselves. No man, nor any religious body, can save any. Salvation cometh from God alone."

CHAPTER III.

STEPHEN GRELLET had now become a member of the religious
Society of Friends. In the maturity of early manhood, he
had taken a deliberate but a decided step, and he appears,
at once, to have found a permanent resting-place for his soul,
in uniting himself to a Church which, in common with other
professors of the Christian name, gives its "hearty assent
and consent to all and everything" appertaining to the fundamental truths of the Gospel, as contained in the inspired
records of Holy Scripture, yet differs, more or less, from
most, as to the mode and extent in which it believes itself
required, under the government and guidance of the Holy
Spirit, to carry these principles out in practice.

There is no trace in his most private memoranda at this
time, or ever afterwards, of the least misgiving as it regards
the position which he had felt it right to assume. Neither
the reminiscences of his early connection with the Papal
system, nor the different phases of scepticism and infidelity
through which he had passed, appear to have left the
elements of doubt or hesitation upon his mind. Born of the
Spirit, and become a "child of God by faith in Christ Jesus,"
he had counted the cost; without attempting to do the work
by halves, he had consecrated himself entirely to the service
of his Redeemer, and he had already received, and publicly
exercised, a gift in the ministry of the Gospel. The love of
God was remarkably "shed abroad" in his heart. He had felt
the preciousness of "the blood of Jesus Christ his Son, which
cleanseth from all sin;" and, deeply impressed with the truth

that the "sons of God" are "led by the Spirit of God," it soon became the characteristic bent and concern of his mind to "walk in the Spirit," and to bring forth the "fruits of the Spirit." Peculiarly marked as had been his previous course, and very unusual as were the developments of his after life, the providence and the grace of God were signally displayed in his being brought into connection with a Christian community which, according to the usages of the primitive Church of Christ, allows such full scope to the operations and leadings of the Holy Spirit, and admits of the free exercise of every spiritual gift, in whatever direction the rightly authorised ambassador for Christ may be called to labour. His life soon became, and for a long course of years continued to be, emphatically "A MISSIONARY LIFE," in a sense in which probably no other religious Society could have recognised it, or made way for its full development and practical carrying out.

The horrors of the French Revolution continued, and whilst humbly endeavouring to pursue the path of Christian duty, as it had been opened to him in the new sphere in which he moved, Stephen Grellet's tender and susceptible heart was frequently brought into much conflict on behalf of his beloved parents.

"The accounts which I received in those days," he remarks, "of the distracted state of my native country much afflicted me. My dear parents being in prison, I expected every day to receive the mournful tidings of their having met with a cruel death, among the many victims who fell a sacrifice to the ferocious spirit that had overspread the nation, having been informed also that some of those who heretofore had professed to be the most intimate friends of my dear father, and others to whom he had rendered many services, were now his greatest enemies and persecutors. This brought me to test the ground of my religion, which is love divine —love even to enemies. My prayers were put up for his persecutors, and, through adorable mercy, I found that, though I abhored the spirit that influenced them, I could pray for them, and desire their salvation as my own."

After remarking upon the comfort and efficacy of prayer under the trying circumstances in which his beloved parents were placed, he continues :—

" And here it may be proper also to state, that they were preserved from an untimely death, and delivered from the hands of unmerciful men, though my dear father was several times on the very eve of being taken to the guillotine, and my mother also. It was finally concluded that they, and others, should be put to death the day following the death of Robespierre, when, that very morning, instead of being led to execution, as proposed, the prison doors were opened for their liberation."

The summer of 1797 was rendered interesting in the life of Stephen Grellet, by his first entrance upon some of those services in the Gospel of Christ, for the good of his fellow men at a distance from his own home, which, in after days, claimed so much of his time and Christian devotedness. Though not yet recorded as a minister, he felt it to be his religious duty "to visit in the love of the Gospel, and to distribute Testaments and religious books among the poorer classes of the inhabitants about Little Egg Harbour, Barnegate, and the sea-shore in New Jersey, and in the Pines.

On his return from this visit, he found that some cases of the yellow fever had made their appearance in the city, and many of the inhabitants had retired into the country to escape the infection.

" I visited some of the sick," he writes, " and felt much for the people. The Lord was pleased to prevent the spreading of the contagion. Many testimonies were borne, during the forepart of the year, to bring the people to a sense of the Lord's mercy, in having restrained the hand of the destroying angel ; forewarning them also of what was impending over the city, if they did not return to the Lord, and break off their sins by sincere repentance. This concern was heavy upon me for months, so that sometimes it seemed as if I must go through the streets of that great city, and declare to the people what the Lord was going to bring upon them because of their iniquities ; for, when He had a little shaken his hand over them, instead of receiving the warning, they had returned, during that winter, to all their follies and vanities. But after a while, being present at several meetings when powerful and clear testimonies were borne on this subject, the concern of my having to proclaim the same through the streets was removed from me, for which I felt humble gratitude. Yet my secret exercise for the inhabitants continued."

Thus, " walking humbly with his God," was the mind of Stephen Grellet prayerfully observant of the " signs of the times;" and prepared to recognise the hand of the Lord in those public calamities which are permitted to visit cities and nations, for purposes too little regarded, even by those who bear the name of Christ; and who would not willingly be suspected of calling in question the reality and minuteness of that providential superintendence which takes cognisance even of the falling sparrow. To the thoughtful reader, these indications of character will appear to have an interesting bearing upon the sequel of this narrative.

Steadily pursuing the path of Christian dedication, Stephen Grellet had continued to exercise his gift as a minister of the Gospel, to the satisfaction of the Church ; and in Third Month, 1798, he was duly recorded as a minister of Christ, by the Monthly Meeting for the Northern District, in Philadelphia, of which he was a member. Such an event could not fail to be deeply interesting to him.

" It brought my mind," he says, " under renewed concern that I might be so preserved in watchfulness, and humble walking before the Lord, as in no wise to wound his great and blessed cause, which I believed He had condescended to call such a poor unworthy instrument, as I felt myself to be, to espouse. Earnest were my secret supplications that my life and conversation might comport with the station of an ambassador for God—a minister of the Lord Jesus Christ ; one prepared to hold out to others what he has actually known of His redeeming love and power, speaking none other things than what he has himself tasted and handled of His divine and saving word of life. In those days my mind dwelt much on the nature of the hope of redemption through Jesus Christ. I felt the efficacy of that grace by which we are saved, through faith in Christ and his atoning blood, shed for us on Calvary's mount; and the excellency of the blessed gifts, which, in consequence of this the meritorious sacrifice of himself for sinful man, are offered to the believer in his name, especially that of the outpouring of the Holy Spirit. It was my soul's chief concern to draw the attention of the people to this saving work and experimental faith, and I felt that the best testimony I could bear to the efficacy of the Redeemer's love, was to evince, by my life, what He had actually done for me."

Not long after this important change in his position, as a fully recognised minister of Christ, he believed it required of him again to travel in the service of the Gospel. After giving a short account of this journey, S. G. says :—

"I returned home, after an absence of about three weeks and a half.

"Hearing that the yellow fever had again made its appearance in Philadelphia, the great exercise under which I had been for its inhabitants returned with weight, and I felt it my duty to go back to the city. O how thankful did I then feel that I had not wilfully departed from the Lord's pointings of duty, last winter, by not proclaiming through the streets the coming of that visitation of mortality among them. If I had wilfully departed from the Lord's command, it would then, I think, have been too hard for me to bear.

"A few days after I heard of the appearance of the fever, while I was yet in Jersey, as I was sitting in a room, with my mind retired before the Lord, I was seized with a violent pain in my back, head, and bones, accompanied with a great shaking; but my mind continued perfectly calm in the Lord's presence. After having remained some time in that state, considering why it was so with me, a secret language was proclaimed : 'This is the manner in which those who are seized with the yellow fever are affected ; thou must return to the city and attend on the sick ; and thus also shall the disease take hold of thee,' or words very similar.

My spirit bowed in prostration before the Lord, and said, 'Thy will be done.' Then I felt again free from pain. I proceeded immediately to Philadelphia, keeping these things, however, to myself.

"My friends of Woodbury, Haddonfield, &c., among whom I passed, endeavoured to dissuade me from going to the city, representing what dangers I should encounter; but my mind was perfectly calm and serene. When I came into it, the sight was solemn. That great city, but a few days before full of inhabitants, was now nearly deserted; its heretofore crowded streets were now trodden by a few solitary individuals, whose countenances bespoke seriousness or sadness. On reaching the friend's house where I made my home, I found it shut up, like most of the neighbours'; but, obtaining the key, I opened it, and resumed my former abode, though alone, in it. Several of my friends were urgent that I should go and stay with them, but I could not be easy so to do. Under the impression I had that I should have the fever, I was unwilling to expose any of my friends to take it from me.

"I went about for some time, visiting the sick and dying, and assisting in burying the dead. My friend, E. G., was a faithful colleague in the solemn work, which, however, awful and gloomy, was yet attended with much peacefulness. My feelings were much awakened, both on account of strangers and Friends. How sweet and peaceful was the close of some, so that I could have joyfully exchanged my situation for theirs; but how great the contrast with others! Some joyfully and smilingly departed, in the fulness of the hope which the Gospel inspires; whereas others experienced the agony and horrors of death—throwing their arms around me, to keep hold of a living object, crying out in bitterness, 'I cannot die! I am not fit to die!' The horror of the scene is yet present with me. O that those who live in pleasure might pause awhile, and contemplate the awful subject! Do not leave it to a sick-bed, or a dying hour, to make your peace with God. Rather, I beseech you, improve diligently your opportunity in time of health, and, whilst the Lord's visitation is extended to you, make your calling and election sure, through Jesus Christ!

"In those days former friends were deserted; yea, even the wife was left by her husband, and the husband became a stranger to his wife—seeking their safety in flight, leaving their sick to the care of a strange nurse. The dead bodies were conveyed to the grave, in most instances, with no other convoy than the hearse and driver. This was the case even with those who, weeks before, might have been attended by hundreds. Most of the places of worship were shut up. I think, for awhile, none in the great city were left open, but the Meetings of Friends, to which many of the sober people who could leave the sick often came; and we had solemn meetings, for the Lord's presence and power were with us.

"The evening of the 25th of the Eighth Month, having been much engaged that day, in providing for about ten Lascars (East India men), discharged from a ship, and left destitute, without friends in a deserted city, and also with some of my dear friends who were ill with the fever, as I was in my chamber, exercised before the Lord on account of the sick, some of whom were near their end, and actually dying at that very time, about eleven at night, just as I had lain down, my spirit being gathered in the Lord's presence, I felt myself seized with the same kind of pains I had upon me when in New Jersey; and the language was heard: 'This is what I told thee thou must prepare for.' My soul was as it were swallowed up in the love of God, and perfectly contented in the will of the Lord, though I did not see the end of this dispensation. After remaining about an hour in that state, feeling my strength fast declining, and being alone in the house, I went down stairs to unlock the front door. Had I deferred this a little longer, it is probable that I should not have had sufficient strength to do it, for it was with difficulty that I went up stairs again. My friend, E. G., not seeing me the next day at the usual time came to the house. He soon brought me a physician and a nurse. The former paid me but a few visits; for he took the fever and died five days after. The disorder so increased upon me that, my extremities having become cold, my coffin was ordered, and I was even returned among the daily deaths to the board of health, as a 'French Quaker.' But my dear Master had some further work for me to do, before I could be prepared to enter into his Divine rest.

"During the whole of that sickness I continued entirely sensible, and whilst death seemed to be approaching, and I had turned myself on one side, the more easily, as I thought, to breathe my last, my spirit feeling already as encircled by the angelic host in the

Heavenly Presence, a secret but powerful language was proclaimed on this wise : ' Thou shalt not die, but live—thy work is not yet done.' Then the corners of the earth, over seas and lands, were opened to me, where I should have to labour in the service of the Gospel of Christ. O what amazement I was filled with ! What a solemn and awful prospect was set before me ! Sorrow took hold of me at the words ; for it seemed as if I had had already a foot-hold in the Heavenly places. I wept sore ; but, as it was the Divine will, I bowed in reverence before Him, interceding that, after I had, by His assistance, been enabled to do the work He had for me to do, and the end of my days in this probationary state had fully come, I might be permitted to be. placed in the same state in which I then was, pass through the valley and shadow of death strengthened by his Divine presence, and enter finally into those glorious mansions, at the threshold of which my spirit had then come. I saw and felt that which cannot be written. Suffice it to say, that from that very time the disorder subsided. My strength, by degrees, returned, and, in a very few days, I was able to be removed to my kind friends, E. and M. G., where I felt quite easy to go. Their brother was then ill in the house, and died a few days after ; I was able to minister to him to the last. Soon after this, five of that family were taken sick, and, for awhile, some of them were so ill, that going from one to the other, I hardly knew which of them would die first. My health was yet very slender, yet I think I was about a week without undressing to go to bed. For part of this time there were only two of us to care for them ; no nurses could be obtained. The precious seasons, however, which I had by the sick beds of my friends, sitting under the canopy of the Lord's presence, often changed these scenes of mourning into joy. They all recovered, and, the sickness in the city continuing, I resumed my visits to the sick and the poor.

" One circumstance I may not omit to notice, as a confirmation of what the Lord had showed me, respecting the exercises I must prepare for during the residue of my pilgrimage. At a meeting I was able to attend, soon after my recovery, Arthur Howell mentioned me by name, and said the Lord had raised me up, having a service for me to the isles and nations afar off, to the east and west, the north and south. I had been careful to keep to myself the view I had had of these things, on what seemed to me a death-

D

bed. I knew, therefore, that this was a confirmation of the word of the Lord to me, which, like Mary of old, I hid in my heart."

The fever continued to prevail in the city, and the mortality was rather on the increase, when the usual time for holding the Yearly Meeting of Philadelphia drew near. Only a few families of Friends, who were able to entertain company, remained in the city.

On the appointed day, the 22nd of the month, however, more Friends than could have been expected, under such circumstances, arrived, "with their lives offered as a sacrifice, should the Lord be pleased so to permit." Though the number assembled was comparatively small, they were "owned of the Lord, and much blessed together, in their meetings."

Towards the close of 1798, the propriety of changing his place of residence, and joining his brother Joseph at New York, was brought under Stephen Grellet's serious considera-tion. A residence of more than three years in the city of Philadelphia, in the midst of a large circle of valuable Friends, . had been much blessed to him.

He felt deeply sensible of the advantages he had enjoyed in the bosom of such a Church, and, when the prospect of joining his brother at New York was brought before him, it is no wonder that he should have looked upon it with very mingled feelings. He thus first notices it in his journal :—

"First Month 24th, 1799. My spirit, for several months, and lately especially, has looked earnestly for the pointing of Truth, as it regards my removal from this place, where my soul has been so often replenished with the Lord's heavenly bread, and where I have almost daily opportunities to improve in the assemblies of his people, to join my beloved brother Joseph at New York. The prospect feels trying ; yet if I know my own soul, I have no will in it, only desiring to be in my right place.

" Second Month 6th. This morning, in my retired, silent sitting, I have felt the love and sweet presence of my dear Master in a more especial manner than I have done for some time. I have been fully satisfied of the rectitude of my proceedings in preparing for moving to New York."

CHAPTER IV.

AFTER having taken up his residence at New York, he was engaged, with his brother Joseph, in mercantile concerns in that city. But he had been "bought with a price," and he deeply felt that he was "not his own." The "love of Christ constraining him," he could not "live unto himself, but unto Him who died for us, and rose again."

"I was not long able," he writes in his Autobiography, "to devote much attention to business. My mind became much enlarged in Gospel love for the inhabitants of this land; but it distressed me that I could not feel any distinct prospect of the parts where the Lord would have me to go in his service. I greatly wondered why an exercise of that nature should come so heavily upon me. I was brought to such a state that, to obtain peace, and the lifting up of the Lord's countenance upon me, I could have given up to go to the ends of the earth.

"Some time after this, I heard that my dear friend John Hall was coming from England, on a religious visit to the United States, and the impression was made strongly upon my mind, that I must stand prepared to join and accompany him in that service. I cried earnestly unto the Lord that, if it was indeed his will that I should engage in such an extensive work, He would condescend to give me some strong evidence of it, and that, as a proof of it, He would give to this dear friend to see it himself, with clearness. He arrived at New York early in the Tenth Month. I visited him soon afterwards, when he took me aside and told me, in a solemn manner, that I was the identical person that he had seen, whilst at sea, prepared of the Lord to be his companion in the service of the Gospel here.

"After weighing carefully the subject, and seeking for the Lord's direction, I concluded that I would accompany him as far as Philadelphia.

"Leaving my small temporal concerns under the care of my dear brother and partner, and resigning myself to my dear Master's putting forth and blessed protection, and to the guidance of his Spirit, I went back to Philadelphia, to join my beloved friend John Hall."

After giving particulars of their visit to the meetings of Friends in Maryland and Virginia, S. G. says:—

"The 28th of First Month, 1800, we came into the pine woods of North Carolina.

"It took us till the 10th of Second Month to visit the meetings of Friends in that quarter. They were, as many had been in Virginia, attended by slaveholders, with whom the Lord enabled us, at times, to expostulate on behalf of the poor oppressed; and He gave us place in their minds, though we delivered plain truths, and showed them how contrary the fruits of oppression are to pure and undefiled religion before God. Very satisfactory, also, were some of the meetings we had with these poor afflicted people. The tenderness and the sensibility of some have often convinced me that of a truth God is no respecter of persons; Christ has died for all, He is near unto all, and his blessed Spirit would lead into all truth those that obey Him."

Alluding to the many hardships they had to go through in their journey, S. G. says:—

"The 3rd of Third Month we came into the upper parts of Carolina to the Spring Meeting. On our way there we met with many difficulties, bad roads and high waters; several times we had to cross the waters in canoes, having two lashed together, two side wheels of our carriage being in one, and the opposite ones in the other, the horses swimming beside them. The country being thinly settled, and meetings far apart, we found it difficult sometimes to obtain any kind of accommodation; but the Lord supported us under all, to the praise of his great name.

"We had a refreshing meeting at Spring; it was a large one.

The following interesting circumstance was there related to me by John Carter, a near relative of the Friend who had been an instrument in raising up that meeting from a decayed state, and on that account had called it Spring Meeting. A number of years ago, it had become much reduced, through the unfaithfulness of some of its members, and the death of others. A young man of the name of Carter became religiously inclined, so as to feel disposed to open the meeting-house, and to repair there, though alone, on meeting days. He had continued to do so for some time, when one day a great exercise came upon him, to stand up and audibly to proclaim what he then felt to be on his mind, of the love of God, through Jesus Christ, towards poor sinful man. It was a great trial of his faith, for nothing but empty benches were before him. He yielded, however, to the apprehended duty, when, shortly after having again taken his seat, several young men came into the house, in a serious manner, and sat down in silence by him, some of them evincing brokenness of heart. After the meeting closed, he found that these young men, his former associates, wondering what could induce him thus to come alone to that house, had come softly to look through the cracks of the door at what he was doing, when they were so impressed by what he loudly declared, that they came in. Some of them continued to meet with him, and became valuable Friends. The meeting increased by degrees to the size it now is. Thus is the Lord pleased to make the faithfulness of one a blessing to many.

"After attending the Quarterly Meeting of Deep River and several meetings in that quarter, we came to Rocky River, to David Wertell's, an aged and faithful Friend. It was late and cold when we arrived at his house. Informing him of our wish to have a meeting the following day, he said he would take all necessary care about it ; but as he did not leave us till we retired to bed, I concluded we should have a very small meeting. I saw no more of the dear Friend till next day as we were passing through the thick woods going to meeting. Wondering at the crowd of people we met in what appeared a wilderness, and meeting with David near the meeting-house, I asked him why we had not seen him the whole morning? He said he had been riding all night and morning, giving notice of the meeting; he then very cheerfully said, 'I feel now much refreshed, and have just been getting my breakfast under this tree.' He had ridden over a considerable circuit that night, and we found a large concourse of people in the house, with whom we had a solemn good meeting.

" We continued diligently engaged in visiting the meetings through the Quarterly Meeting of New Garden.

" After travelling about one hundred and fifty miles through a wilderness country, with hardly any other provisions than what we carried with us, for ourselves and horses, we came into South Carolina, and attended the Quarterly Meeting held at Bush River."

They met with many difficulties in their journey in Tennessee, and he says :—

" When encamping during the night, which we did several times, we kept up a good fire to protect us from the panthers, bears, and wolves. The latter were numerous. Sometimes it seemed as if a hundred of them were howling at once round about us."

Returning within the limits of Virginia, on the 24th of Fifth Month, he remarks :—

" The slaves in that part of the country are treated with more cruelty than I have seen elsewhere. I felt deeply for them, whilst beholding their ragged and emaciated condition. I saw the anguish of some of them, whilst passing through the market place of Lynchburgh, as they were publicly selling them like so many cattle. O the distress they manifested when separated from their nearest relations ! At a public meeting we had in that place, the Lord enabled me to plead the cause of our poor oppressed fellow-men."

After several months of close labour in those parts they came to Chichester, from whence they proceeded with the work before them, and were diligently engaged in visiting many meetings in those parts, till the time of holding Baltimore Yearly Meeting drew them to that city. Here Stephen Grellet remarks :—

" On the 11th of Eleventh Month began the Yearly Meeting of Baltimore, to which we went in lowness of mind, having carefully waited to know that this service was required of us ; for it was at the peril of our lives, the yellow fever prevailing in that city : about fifteen hundred persons had already died of it. But, having apprehended that the Lord had a service for us there, we were favoured with resignation to his will, confiding in his all-sufficient power to enable us to walk unhurt by 'the arrow that flieth by day, or the pestilence that walketh in darkness.'"

Of this Yearly Meeting S. Grellet writes :—

"The several sittings were attended by the Lord's baptising power. He graciously owned them by his Divine presence. The meeting concluded on the 16th, under great solemnity. Our spirits were bowed before the Lord, in much brokenness, for the favour He had vouchsafed us, day by day, keeping us above fear, under the sense that our lives are in his all-powerful hand. We cannot but notice, with humble admiration and gratitude, that from the beginning of the Yearly Meeting to this day, the number of deaths has considerably decreased. Before the opening of the meeting, they were from twenty to thirty per day ; during this week they have only been from five to six, and to-day there is only one death. 'Bless the Lord, O my soul, and all that is within me, bless his holy name.'"

Under this "grateful sense of the Lord's goodness," they left Baltimore, and had many meetings on their way to Philadelphia.

"Here," he remarks, "feeling my mind, for the present, released from further religious service, I took an affectionate leave of my dear friend John Hall, and returned to New York, after an absence of thirteen months, during which I travelled about five thousand miles. We were very nearly united in our religious exercises and services. Our travelling together, as fellow servants of the Prince of Peace, attracted the attention of the people in many places, bringing many of them to our meetings to see the Englishman and the Frenchman united in promoting the cause of righteousness and truth on the earth, whilst their respective nations were waging such destructive wars against each other. We heard some of them feelingly comment on the peaceable spirit of the Gospel."

Whilst "fervent in spirit, serving the Lord," Stephen Grellet was not "slothful in business": but, returned from a long and arduous engagement in visiting the Churches, he now applied himself with diligence to his temporal affairs. Keeping his eye single, in these concerns also, to his Divine Master, he was preserved from undue carefulness, and corroding anxiety. The believing remembrance of the gracious promise, so forcibly applied to his own heart in years past, that "if he sought first the kingdom of God and his righteousness, all things needful should be added," was often a comfort and encouragement to him, in his efforts to provide things honest in the sight of all men.

"I was not permitted, however," he writes, "to remain long thus engaged: for the love of the Gospel strongly drew me towards the Eastern, and parts of the Northern States. Feeling that it was a service which He, to whom I had made the offering of myself and my all, required of me, I spread the concern before my friends at their Monthly and Quarterly Meetings, and obtained their respective certificates of unity."

His beloved friend and former companion, John Hall, being led in the same direction, they again united as fellow-labourers, and, leaving New York together, in the Fifth Month, 1801, proceeded to Long Island.

"We visited," Stephen Grellet continues, "all the meetings of Friends, and had several also among the inhabitants. Our blessed Lord and holy Helper enabled us to labour among them in the service of his Gospel, and in this to obtain a considerable degree of relief under our various exercises."

From Long Island they returned to New York, to attend the Yearly Meeting in that city, after which they proceeded to New England Yearly Meeting at Newport.

"It was held," Stephen Grellet remarks, "under much solemnity, throughout its various sittings, and the business was conducted in brotherly love and harmony. Going thence towards the Island of

Nantucket, we attended all the meetings on the way to New Bedford, the Lord enabling us to preach among them the glad tidings of the Gospel of his salvation, and the offer of his free grace to all, through our holy Redeemer, our Lord and Saviour Jesus Christ."

After giving particulars of the places they visited, S. G. says :—

" We continued our journey through those eastern parts, as far as beyond the river Kennebec, the farthest settlement of Friends at that time, having many precious meetings with them, and with those of various other Christian denominations.

" We then went through Connecticut, into the State of New York, and after visiting the meetings through the several Quarterly Meetings in those parts, we returned to the city of New York on the 16th of Twelfth Month.

" I travelled in that journey about four thousand miles. My soul can again sing His praise, on the banks of deliverance."

On his return to his own habitation in the city of New York, Stephen Grellet applied himself, with his accustomed diligence, to his outward concerns. During his absence these had very much devolved upon his brother Joseph. The two brothers had " kept very much together during the various vicissitudes which had attended their chequered path," and, strongly attached by the ties of natural affection, they felt "doubly dear to each other in being closely united also in Christian fellowship." It was therefore no small trial to Stephen Grellet when in the next year, 1802, his brother felt it right to return to their dear parents in France.

Only a few months after his brother had left him, Stephen Grellet was again called from home, in the service of his Lord, " his mind being drawn forth in the love of the Gospel to visit the meetings of Friends, and the people of other religious denominations in Jersey." Of this journey he remarks :—

"I proceeded through all the meetings of that State, and having accomplished what I had in prospect, I was favoured to return to

New York in the Eleventh Month. I had with gratitude to acknowledge how bountifully my Divine Helper had dealt with me, during that journey. In my weakness and poverty He had sustained me, given a little ability to perform the service He had for me, and also cared for my small temporal concerns, so that they had been as prosperous as if I had stayed at home. Thus it is good for us to commit our all to Him whose power is over all, and from whom every blessing flows."

Stephen Grellet was now permitted to remain at home for more than a year.

During the latter part of 1803, the city of New York was again visited with the yellow fever. The mortality was not very great, many of the inhabitants having removed into the country on its first appearance. But as he was one of those who continued in the city, he had a fresh opportunity of mingling with the afflicted, and sympathising with them under such an awful dispensation.

CHAPTER V.

HIS MARRIAGE—DEATH OF HIS FATHER—RELIGIOUS VISIT TO THE
STATES OF NEW YORK AND VERMONT, CANADA AND PENNSYL-
VANIA—YELLOW FEVER IN NEW YORK—ILLNESS OF HIS WIFE.

THE commencement of the year 1804 was marked by the
interesting event of Stephen Grellet's marriage to Rebecca
Collins, daughter of Isaac and Rachel Collins, of New York.
They had been acquainted for a considerable time, and "care
having been taken fully to feel after the Lord's approbation in
this important step, they were united in the marriage covenant
on the 11th of First Month, 1804." It might be truly said
that their union was "in the Lord"; and, through a long course
of years, in an eminent degree, attended by his blessing.

Not long after this change in his social position, Stephen
Grellet received the affecting intelligence of his beloved
father's decease, after a short illness, towards the close of
1803. A two years' imprisonment, and all the anxieties and
sufferings connected with the revolutionary struggles in France
had impaired his health. He had concluded to retire into
Holland, and had made preparations for leaving the city of
Limoges, and France, when, as S. G. remarks, "the Lord
was pleased to order that his removal should be far more
distant, even to that world of spirits, where sorrows for ever
end. The afflictions he endured, were, through adorable
mercy, sanctified to him. The last years of his life, his
nature was changed; mildness and kindness were his characteristics. Even whilst in prison, under the iron rule of
Robespierre, he would encourage his fellow-prisoners, to
patient submission to the Lord's will. He was a man of
great integrity, much beloved by his family and friends."

After his decease, his widow relinquished the idea of leaving her native land, and continued with some other branches of the family to reside at Limoges.

Fully capable of appreciating and enjoying the comforts and blessings which had so recently been conferred upon him, through the happy matrimonial connection which he had formed, Stephen Grellet did not allow the endearments of home to interfere with his devotedness to the service of his God and Saviour, and in the Seventh Month of the same year, he entered upon an extensive religious engagement, in regard to which he says :—

"Having for a considerable time past felt drawings of Gospel love towards the meetings in New York and Vermont States, and parts of Canada, I made the necessary preparations for that journey, arranged my outward concerns, and my Monthly Meeting giving me their testimonial of unity, I left home the 7th of the Seventh Month, 1804, committing myself, my beloved wife, and my all, to the Lord's protection."

This journey occupied four months, and, on his return to New York, he concludes his narrative thus :—

"My spirit was humbled before the Lord, my blessed Helper, for his many preservations, and sustaining mercies, vouchsafed during that journey. He had often made a way for me to get forwards, when there appeared to be none—blessed be his name and magnified be his power for ever !"

An interval of six months had scarcely elapsed before Stephen Grellet believed it to be required of him by his Divine Master again to leave his home, on a similar embassy to the Churches in Pennsylvania.

In the meantime, he had felt at liberty to attend to his outward affairs, and his exertions in this respect were blessed. He had, however, declined to engage in various extensive and lucrative concerns in business, which were presented to his notice under very promising aspects, "feeling constrained," as he says, "by the limitations of Truth, from entering into any temporal pursuits, which were likely to occupy attention beyond a very limited period." He felt that, if it be needful for those who are engaged in an outward warfare "not to entangle themselves with the affairs of this life, that they may please Him who hath chosen them to be soldiers," it must be infinitely more so for those who are enlisted under the banner of Christ, and have become soldiers in the Lamb's army, to be the Lord's freemen, disentangled from the love and the spirit of the world, and given up to the willing service of their God and Saviour. "O Lord!" he exclaims, in the prospect before him, "the service of a minister of Jesus Christ—how solemn! Their sufficiency is in thee alone! Thou alone art their help, and their strength!"

With views like these, "his mind had been brought under much exercise for Friends and others, chiefly in Pennsylvania;" and, apprehending that "love of Christ constrained him again to resign his all to the Divine requiring," he obtained the usual certificates of unity from his friends, "arranged his temporal concerns so as to leave nothing behind that would prevent his thoughts being wholly directed to the work his blessed Master sent him to do," and proceeded on the visit, of which but few details can here be given. S. G. says:

"I left home the 17th of Sixth Month, 1805. My beloved wife and her father went with me for a few days. My valued friend, Henry Shotwell, an Elder in good esteem, obtained a minute to bear me company during the visit. At Rahway, my dear wife and her father left me, to return to New York, after having committed one another to the Lord, under whatever trial He might see best to permit. A sense that a cup of this sort might be mixed for us, rendered this parting solemn and very affecting."

Proceeding with his companion, they diligently pursued their journey, having many meetings; and on the 28th, at Millford, S. G. remarks:—

"28th. Travelling hard these days past, besides having meetings daily, together with the present warm season, when the water in these low countries is very bad, has materially affected my health. I had two meetings before me, which rendered the prospect very gloomy ; but I was enabled to cast my care on Divine help. Though far from well, I left my bed in time to go in the forenoon to Cold Spring Meeting. I was appalled on beholding a large gathering of people. I cried to the Lord for his Divine help. My mind was prostrated before Him, and I felt the quickenings of his power, strengthening me every way, so that under his putting forth and commission, I preached the everlasting Gospel to the people. Many minds were baptised and contrited under the power then felt. The meeting holding late, and the other meeting, which was to be held in an Episcopalian meeting-house, being at some miles distance, I had to repair to it pretty speedily, trusting in the all-sufficiency of the Lord's eternal power, to be my strength and my help. There also I found a great concourse of people of various denominations. Soon after sitting down among them, I felt the Lord's power upon me, and under it I had again largely to proclaim the Gospel of Christ, and on bended knees to offer prayers, thanksgivings, and praises to his Divine and Eternal name, who is for ever blessed in himself, whom all his works do bless and praise, as also my soul has done this day.

"Help was in a remarkable manner extended to me, so as to be able to proceed the next day twenty-five miles to William Matthews', at whose house I had a meeting that evening.

"The two following days I had meetings among the people called 'Nicholites,' at North-west Fork and Centre. They are some of the same people I visited some years ago in Carolina. Silence, solemn silence, was what, by my example, I had to direct them to. It is safe for us to follow Divine guidance, and I believe that this silent testimony, when of the Lord's ordering, often speaks to the attentive mind a volume of instruction.

"5th of Eighth Month. At the Bayside meeting, Maryland, many slaveholders were present, who make a great profession. I showed the inconsistency of slavery and its various features, with the spirit of Christianity."

During this journey S. Grellet appears to have suffered from depression and prostration of strength, with serious forebodings, and he remarks on the

" 10th. *Very unwell* last night; my strength is much reduced, and yet I have two meetings appointed to-day at some distance from one another. My inward as well as outward conflict is great. O Lord, my God, forsake me not !"

Through many difficulties, however, they proceeded on their journey through the western parts of Pennsylvania, till the 8th of Ninth Month, when S. G. says :—

" Had a meeting at Williams Port, in the Court-house. On our first sitting down my mind was brought into much conflict, under an apprehension that the yellow fever had made its appearance in the city of New York ; this language passed through it, 'one of thy near relations is taken with it'; at which my soul was bowed before the Lord. I remembered my feelings in parting from my dear wife and her father at Rahway, and I endeavoured to feel after that submission and confidence which is our only refuge and strength in trouble. After having thus made a fresh surrender of my all to the Lord's will, I was prepared to enter into feeling for the meeting, which was largely attended by the most respectable inhabitants. The Lord's power rose into dominion, and under it I was able to minister to the people, many of whom were tender in spirit, when, on bended knees before the sacred presence, I offered prayers, intercessions, and praises."

On the 9th he further remarks :—

" My mind continues to feel for the distressed in New York, though I have not yet any outward information of the yellow fever having begun its ravages among them ; but, under the strong impression that some of my near relatives are taken down with it, I am ready to conclude it may be right for me to return home, and methinks I hear the sound of retreat.

" I now recrossed the mountains, and on the 12th came through Reading to Exeter. Here I heard that the yellow fever was in fact prevailing in New York.

" Pottsgrove, 13th. This was a remarkable time for me, for after sitting a while in the meeting, it seemed as if I was following some of my near relatives to their grave, and I saw with clearness that it was right for me to return homewards with all speed.

It was a trial to me, as I had had some prospect of having a few
more meetings in these parts ; but I felt that the same power that
had put me forth in His service, now called me back from it ;
therefore my soul bowed before the Lord, in adoration.

"I proceeded that afternoon and the following days, with all
speed, towards New York. On the 15th of Ninth Month I reached
Rahway, by noon, and there heard that my wife's mother was very
ill with the epidemic. Thus confirmed in the correctness of the
impressions made upon me, I pursued my journey, and after crossing the North River that afternoon, I met with a person who
gave me the heavy tidings that my mother-in-law was deceased,
and that the family were in Westchester (twelve miles farther),
where they had retired when the fever made its appearance in the
city, and that my dear wife was sick. About nine at night I
reached the house. I found the family in great affliction but
supported under the stroke ; and now our solicitude was excited
on account of my dear wife, for she had a heavy load of disease
upon her. It is remarkable that on the evening of this my speedy
return to her, her mind was so sensible of my being near, that she
told her sister, who was near her bedside, that she saw me as if I
was in the chamber. Her sister thought her flighty, through the
fever ; but she replied, 'It is a reality ; I see him near ;' though
at that time she had every reason to conclude I was about two
hundred miles distant."

It is scarcely possible to read this simple record of facts,
without noticing the beautiful *coincidence* between the dispensations of Providence and the leadings of the Holy Spirit,
which at once illustrates and confirms the reality of both.
Arrested in the midst of his ministerial labours in a remote
part of Pennsylvania, by a guidance as precise as it was
direct, Stephen Grellet was most opportunely brought home
to his nearest connections in life, at a very critical moment,
and under circumstances of peculiar need. His steps seemed
clearly "ordered by the Lord," and his feelings of thankfulness mingled with those of sorrow. His tender solicitude was
kept alive on behalf of his beloved wife. She continued very
ill several months after his return, and her life was repeatedly

in imminent danger—her complaint having assumed the character of a low nervous fever, from the effects of which her health did not recover for some years. Though accustomed to bow in humble resignation to the Divine will, this dispensation proved the more trying to Stephen Grellet, on account of the prospect of distant scenes of labour which had long been opening to his view. Even during this season of domestic affliction, a concern to visit his native land, in the service of the Gospel of Christ, was gradually ripening in his mind.

CHAPTER VI.

First Visit to Europe.

VOYAGE—ARRIVAL AT MARSEILLES—QUARANTINE—VISIT TO CONGENIES, ETC. ETC.

AMIDST a variety of minor religious services at and about home, and the needful attention to his domestic and social duties, nearly eighteen months had passed away before Stephen Grellet felt the " necessity laid upon him " to take active measures for accomplishing the long contemplated visit to his fatherland ; but in the spring of 1807, " believing that the time was fully come to resign himself to the Lord's requiring," he once more "settled all his temporal affairs " to set himself at liberty for the work to which he was called.

We take the following extracts from his journal :—

"First-day. 14th of Sixth Month, 1807. At sea. I have embarked this day on board the ship *Brunswick*, Captain Beadle, bound for Marseilles. I came on board the ship at noon, directly from meeting, which, through the adorable mercy and continued kindness of my dear Redeemer, was a season of Divine favour. I was on my feet, engaged in proclaiming the Gospel to a large number of Friends, when messengers came at two different times to summon me on shipboard.

" It was a solemn parting between my beloved wife and myself ; but the Lord gave strength, in humble submission, to be resigned to his will, and to follow Him wherever He may be pleased to send me. Lord, for thy sake and thy Truth, my dear companion and thy servant have offered one another to thee ; keep her by thy power, comfort her by thy presence ; fulfil the promise thou hast made to thy servant, ' My presence shall go with thee and I will give thee rest.'

"Several of my friends and near relatives came with me on board, so far as Sandy Hook, and have left me at ten o'clock this evening, to return with the pilot. Now I am left a poor solitary one, none on board but the crew of the ship, and some of *them*, being in a state of intoxication, appear very unfit for duty. O thou, Lord, the faithful and never-failing friend, be with me, lead me by thy Spirit!

"Soon after I penned the above the wind blew hard and increased to a storm, which caused a very rough sea."

After describing this fearful storm, and the feelings which attended his mind during the prevalence of it, S. G. says :—

"26th. Yesterday and last night the storm was again raging, but my mind was kept in calmness. I have seen how those ancient worthies and faithful contenders for the faith of Jesus could rejoice in great tribulation. Amidst the tossing and confusion occasioned by the storm last night, my mind was introduced into a state of quiet, when my covenant was renewed with my God. How sweet it is thus to covenant with the Lord! Then, with cheerfulness, our all is resigned into his hands.

"First-day, 28th. I have felt much for the crew of the vessel, but way has not yet opened for our coming together to unite in the act of divine worship.

"First-day, 5th of Seventh Month. This forenoon I have had a meeting for divine worship with my shipmates, the captain kindly making suitable arrangements for it, and, as the weather was fine, none were left on deck but the man at the helm. It has been a solemn and instructive season to us, wherein the Lord enabled me to offer prayers and intercessions for our little company, and for the preservation of our near relatives and friends whom we have left behind.

"14th. We have passed to-day before Cadiz, so near that we could look into the streets of the city. We went through a British fleet which blockades that port. One of the frigates boarded us. The lieutenant treated us politely. He says they have been several months on that station, and they do not know how much longer they may continue. To see so many

engines of destruction brought many considerations before my
mind. Sad indeed are the consequences of the fall of man:
' Glory to God in the highest, and on earth peace, good will
toward men,' is not naturally his soul's anthem. With what
perseverance and apparent cheerfulness do men endure hardship
and many difficulties in the service of an earthly prince, shedding
their own blood, and that of thousands who have never done them
any personal injury, and that to obtain earthly glory. Be stimu-
lated, O my soul, in the service of the King Eternal, waging war
against sin, and bringing to thy fellow-men the glad tidings of
salvation through faith in the Redeemer's love.

"24th. This afternoon we saw a ship coming towards us. I
apprehended she was a suspicious vessel ; she had another in
tow, and as she came alongside of us, we saw her full of rough-
looking men, with swords or cutlasees in their hands, and other
weapons. The captain thought they were Algerines. They
ordered us on board their ship, and our seamen were in the act
of lowering our boat, to obey their summons, when, discovering
an English frigate in chase of them, they immediately made all
possible sail to escape with their prize, which was probably some
merchant ship they had lately captured, the crew of which they
reserved for slavery ; this, very probably, would have been also
our portion, had the frigate been a few moments later in making
her appearance. When our poor seamen saw the danger we were
in, some of them made doleful lamentations at their prospect of
slavery. My own mind was preserved calm ; for I remembered
what occurred to me some months ago, in New York, whilst in
a religious meeting, my mind solemnly gathered before the Lord ;
I then felt that there was a possibility of my being taken, during
the passage on that sea, by some of the Algerines, or Morocco
powers, and carried into slavery by them. My spirit bowed
reverently before the Lord, in confidence that He might, if it was
his good pleasure, deliver me from the hands of merciless men,
and every other evil ; but if He had a service for me among those
people, I bowed in humble resignation to whatever He might suffer
to come upon me, praying that it might only turn to his glory
and the salvation of my soul. Thus, while these men were by
the side of us, I was waiting to see what the Lord had for me
now to do for his great name. I thought I could willingly pro-

claim to them the Gospel message of redeeming love, or suffer among them for the sake of Him who has suffered and died for us, 'the just for the unjust, that He might bring us to God.' But after this day's fresh interposition of Divine power to deliver, my soul has ascribed blessing and praise unto Him.

"First-day, 26th. I had again a meeting with my shipmates. The hearts of some of them appear to have been made soft, by our great deliverance from the pirates.

"28th. We came yesterday in sight of Marseilles, and having taken in a pilot this morning, at three p.m., he has brought us safe into port, in that part where the shortest quarantine is required, which is fifteen days.

"29th. Hearing of the Lazaretto where I might go to perform my quarantine, I have removed to it. This afternoon John S. Mollet came to see me; he is a Swiss, but now resides in Marseilles. Through various deep trials he had come to some knowledge of the Truth as professed by our Society. It is a comfort to see him, and he will be a help to me in becoming acquainted with pious persons in these parts.

"7th of Eighth Month. Curiosity to see a Quaker frequently brings persons of various ranks and conditions to see and converse with me. Several priests have also come. I have daily to maintain my Christian testimonies, and to open the principles of Truth.

"25th. I came out of the Lazaretto last Seventh-day. John Malvesin, brother-in-law to J. S. Mollet, had kindly invited me to make his house my home whilst in Marseilles. Last First-day J. S. Mollet and a few others sat together with me, to worship Him who is a Spirit, and will be worshipped in spirit and in truth; the Lord pouring forth of his Spirit upon us, enabled us to approach Him to offer up our prayers to Him. I have been with some persons with whom I have been comforted. Dear Mollet and A. E. Kothen, a Swede, have awakened minds.

"First-day, 30th. I have had a meeting at my kind friend J. Malvesin's. The Lord was with us: Kothen was much affected, under the power accompanying the Gospel I had to preach among them.

"31st. In the course of the week I have had several religious opportunities, some private and others more public, among the people here, and I am now looking towards Languedoc.

"John S. Mollet proposes to accompany me there.

"Congenies, 10th. I left Marseilles early yesterday for this place, after having a refreshing opportunity, in the Lord's presence, with some of those whose hearts He has visited by his Spirit in that city. There is in these parts a small body of people professing with Friends. They appear to have existed long before they had any knowledge of our religious Society in England, and to have embraced some of the same Christian principles and testimonies. I have seen ancient records in manuscript, by which it is shown that at various periods they suffered great persecutions under the Papal powers, some of them being tortured, and put to death, amidst excruciating torments. Among these sufferers were several very young persons—delicate young women, who, like the ancient martyrs, were enabled to endure, through faith in Christ Jesus, whatever cruelty could devise, rather than yield to Popish superstitions and idolatries. They suffered considerably also in common with the other Protestants; I have seen copies of some very interesting letters,* which they wrote to these their fellow Protes-

---

* These no doubt had reference to the "Wars of the Camisards," which produced the "Troubles in the Cevennes," so graphically described by M. Court, their historian. After the revocation of the Edict of Nantes by Louis XIV., in 1685, the most cruel and protracted persecutions commenced against the Protestants of France. They raged with great violence in Languedoc. About the beginning of the eighteenth century, a little band of Protestant peasants, wearied out by the sufferings to which they and their fellow-professors had long been subjected, took up arms to rescue some of their brethren from the tortures they were enduring, and the cruel death about to be inflicted upon them by the Romanists. After having succeeded in this object, they retired to the mountain fastnesses for safety, whence they defended themselves against their papal persecutors. Their number gradually increased to a little army of mountaineers; and under the name of Camisards, they carried on for several years a bloody warfare against their oppressors. Great excesses were committed on both sides, and the expostulatory letters, of which Stephen Grellet here speaks, were probably among the remonstrances addressed to the Protestant warriors, by those of their own persuasion, who disapproved of their violent proceedings, and which, in the opinion of Court, "firent d'abord cesser les massacres, et furent la véritable raison pour laquelle les Camisards donnerent alors la vie à quatre ou cinq curés qu'ils avoient eu à leur discrétion." The following extract from one of these admonitory epistles may not be uninteresting or inappropriate here:—

"Nous savons que les violences qu'on vous a faites pour vous forcer d'aller à la messe, et d'envoyer vos enfans à l'école de

tants, when some of the latter took up arms to repel by force the
sword stretched out against them at the instigation of the Church
of Rome, during the war in France against Protestantism.   They
expostulated with them on account of the inconsistency of their
conduct with their Christian profession, showing them how far
they were from being gathered under the Standard of Christ, the
Prince of Peace—whilst in their warlike proceedings they did
unto others, when they had an opportunity, the very things they
complained that they did unto them—they plundered, they destroyed ; whereas servants of the Lord must not fight, but must
be even like their Master, render good for evil, love them that
persecute them, and not avenge themselves.   Thus they maintained a faithful testimony against war ; they objected to oaths

---

l'erreur; que les soldats qui vous environnent, qui veillent sur toute
votre conduite, qui fondent sur vous comme des loups sur des agneaux,
quand vous vous assemblez en secret, pour prier Dieu ; en un mot, que les
cruautés qu'on exerce contre vous sans pitié et sans relâche; que la
perte de vos biens et les mauvais traitemens de vos personnes ; que les
chaines, les prisons, les gibets, les roues ont enfin lassé votre patience,
et vous ont inspiré des sentimens de désespoir et de rage.

"Nous avouons même que dans de longues et excessives tribulations
comme les vôtres il est bien difficile de resister aux mouvemens impétu-
eux de la nature, qui s'élèvent malgré nous dans le fond de notre cœur,
et nous portent à rendre le mal pour le mal, nous vous plaignons de ce
que vous êtes dans une si terrible épreuve ; mais vous êtes chrétiens et
chrétiens réformés ; et si vous n'avez pas entièrement oublié ce que les
ministres apostoliques de la parole de Dieu vous ont autrefois enseigné,
vous pouvez vous souvenir qu'ils vous préchoient sans cesse, que l'hypo-
crisie et le mensonge ne conviennent pas aux enfans du Dieu de vérité ;
que les violences de vos ennemis n'excusoient pas les vôtres, et que
leurs crimes ne vous autorisent pas à en commettre de semblables.

" Peut-être vous flattez-vous que ces désordres feront cesser les maux
qui vous accablent ?   Peut-être vous imaginez-vous que ceux qui brulent
les églises, et égorgent de sang-froid les prêtres, détruisent la superstition
et l'idolâtrie ?   Peut-être attendez-vous de là votre délivrance et le
rétablissement du pur service de Dieu ?   Aveugles que vous êtes, avez-
vous oublié qu'il n'est jamais permis de faire le mal, afin qu'il en arrive du
bien? que vous n'êtes pas sous l'ancienne loi, qui étoit rigoureuse,
suivant une lettre meurtrière, qui ordonnoit d'exterminer les idolâtres et
les lieux consacrés à un culte défendu ? mais que vous êtes sous la loi
nouvelle dont l'Auteur dit, qu'il ne veut pas la mort du pécheur, mais
qu'il se convertisse et qu'il vive ; c'est du bras de Dieu, et non du vôtre,
qu'il faut espérer la fin de votre captivité; tâchez de l'obtenir par la
sainteté de votre bonne vie, et non par les œuvres de ténèbres que vous
faites."—*Histoire des Troubles des Cevennes, ou de la Guerre des Camisards, par M. Court. Vol. I. p.* 173.

also and recognised silent worship, and a ministry that proceeds
from the influence of the Divine Spirit and depends not on human
acquirements. They did not know of the existence of our Society
in England and in America, till the time of the American Revolution and the war which in consequence arose between England
and France. A Friend of Falmouth, in England, had shares in
several vessels. The other owners, not being members of our
Society, concluded to arm those vessels. He remonstrated in vain
against it. These ships made several prizes upon the French. His
portion of the prizes was given him, but as he could not conscientiously take an active part in the war, so neither could he share in
any emolument arising from it ; on the restoration of peace, therefore, he sent one of his sons to Paris, who, by public advertisements
in the papers, &c., stated that the owners of certain vessels that
had been captured by the vessels in which he had a share, should
on their application to him, receive their respective portions of
the proceeds of the prizes ; at the same time giving his reasons
why, as a Christian and a member of the religious Society of
Friends, he could not share in gains arising from war. This statement coming to the knowledge of the little body here, they deputed
a few of their number to go to London to confer with Friends
there. They rejoiced to find that the Lord had so large a body,
both there and in America, maintaining the same religious testimonies as themselves. After that period they were visited by
some of our Friends. G. Dillwyn, Sarah Grubb, Mary Dudley,
and their companions, were the first : then William Savery and
David Sands, and Richard Jordan. But these Friends, not speaking the French language, at least very imperfectly, had not a very
full opportunity of becoming acquainted with them.

"17th. I continued diligently engaged among the little flock
in the village. I have had religious opportunities in every one of
their families, also several meetings for divine worship among
them, and with the inhabitants at large, who are Roman Catholics
and Protestants. Several among the little flock here speak in the
ministry. Louis Majolier may be considered among them as a
father and a pillar."

S. Grellet visited those professing with Friends at Codognan,
St. Gilles, Vauvert, &c., and had meetings with them, as well

as large gatherings with the inhabitants. On the 24th of Ninth
Month, he writes :—

"Louis Majolier accompanying me, we went to Fontanés, to
Samuel Brun's, his father-in-law. He and his wife are valuable
aged Friends. There are three more families in the village, and
we had that evening a good refreshing meeting with the inhabitants. Next day had another precious meeting at Paradon's, two
miles beyond St. Hypolite. It being First-day, and notice having
gone before, people came to it from six to twelve miles distance.
Many very tender seeking persons reside on these mountains,
where the Lord has had a precious seed for ages ; they have greatly
suffered in the times of persecution. The same evening I had
another very large meeting in the town of Ganges. The streets
round the house, were thronged with people, but they were very
quiet. The Gospel flowed freely towards them, and many hearts
were open to receive it. It was a time to be had in lasting remembrance ; for the Lord's grace and power were exalted, and many,
with tears, acknowledged it.

"The following morning, we returned to St. Hypolite, where
also, feeling my mind engaged to have a meeting, a place was
provided. It was thought sufficient to contain the people, being
a pretty large room ; but it seemed as if all the inhabitants of the
town had turned out. The whole house was filled, and a very
large number stood in the street, in a quiet becoming manner. I
had taken my seat near the window, a very convenient place to
be heard both in the house, and in the street. For some time I
sat under great distress of mind, yet at the same time, the love
of God through Christ flowed in my heart towards the people.
Abiding under it, I felt the Lord's power to rise over all, believing
that whatever trial might come upon me, He would support me
even unto death. Then I thought I felt His word of command to
preach unto the multitude Christ, with his attributes and Divine
offices, when, on hearing some bustle through the crowd towards
the door, Louis Majolier, who sat by me, whispered to me, 'The
Commissary of Police is coming.' I so felt the Lord's power, that
I answered him, 'Fear not, only be quiet.' The Commissary then
drawing near to me said, 'Are you the person that is going to
preach ?' I replied, 'It may be so, please to sit down.' On which,

taking me by the collar of the coat, he said, 'You must follow
me to the Mayor;' when I answered, 'I may not detain thee long,
please to take a seat a little while,'—on which I began to speak to
the people, as the Lord gave me.   He stood amazed, keeping hold
of me as I spoke, till at last he said, 'I go and make my report,'
and then he retired.   I continued preaching to the people, who
all kept quiet, not moved at all by what passed.   Indeed, on the
contrary, when the Commissary, on his way to the door, passing
by some soldiers who were in the meeting-room, ordered them to
go and take me, they answered, 'We cannot disturb a man thus
engaged.' I continued about an hour to speak to the people, as the
Lord enabled me ; for He was with us, his love and power were
felt by many, whose spirits were greatly contrited ; the Divine
witness reached their hearts.   Having taken my seat, and now
feeling myself clear, the meeting concluded, when I judged it
expedient to go immediately to the Mayor's office, to see if he
wanted anything of me ; several persons accompanied me.   Not
finding him there, I was proceeding to his house, when I met the
Commissary, who began to threaten me with imprisonment and
with heavy fines upon those who were at the meeting.   We went
together with him to the Mayor's house ; he not being then at
home, we waited a considerable time for his return.   In the meanwhile, many people, out of concern for me, others from curiosity,
were gathered about to see the end of this.   At last, when the
Mayor returned, the Commissary went to him to make his own
representation, which prepossessed him against us, so that when
we came in, seeing me with my hat on, he put on a pretty angry
countenance ; but I, in a mild, respectful manner, gave him some
of my reasons for thus appearing covered.   I had hardly given
my explanation, when, with a placid countenance, he said, 'I know
something of the Society of Friends, and their manners.'   Then,
making me sit by him, in presence of the people now collected,
he inquired into the object of my present engagements, which led
to the unfolding of the religious principles of our Society, and
various Christian testimonies ; after which, in presence of all, he
read audibly the translation in French of my certificates, and
heard my account of the care extended by our Society towards
their ministers, when thus going abroad as ambassadors for Christ.
He said after that, 'I am sorry you have been disturbed ; had I

been here it would not have been so. If you wish to have any more meetings, I shall have care taken that every arrangement be made, and nobody will disturb you.' I accepted his civility, and we parted ; his heart was open towards me. I left with him several books, in French, on religious subjects which he kindly accepted; and the next day on my way to Quissac, another town, a messenger sent by his wife, overtook me, requesting that if I could spare some more of our books for some of their friends, it would oblige her. The name of the Mayor is Laperouse.

"At Quissac, where I arrived that afternoon, the people were very ready in making way for my having a meeting among them, and as no room large enough to accommodate them could be found, it was concluded to have the meeting out of doors. It was a fine, screne evening. They made choice of an orchard surrounded by high walls, which they seated, placing lanterns in the trees, in which also many persons had taken their station. There were thought to be about one thousand five hundred persons collected. I have seldom known a more solemn stillness prevailing in a religious meeting than we witnessed there. It was a time of very precious visitation of the Lord to this people ; the Gospel descended upon them as the dew upon the tender grass. The Lord has a precious seed in these parts. These are the plants I had felt so much for when in America, which the Lord now enables me to visit ; making me, his poor servant, an instrument in his hands to water them.

"I returned through Fontanés, and had another refreshing season with a few there, and then came back to Congenies, having during the last six days travelled mostly on foot; for we had but a small mule for three of us. The weather was very warm, but the Lord has strengthened me for the service, and is also my soul's rejoicing. I returned to Congenies in time to have an evening meeting with Friends and others."

A few more days were spent in communion with those bearing the name of Friends in those parts. S. G. writes on the 6th of Tenth Month :—

"Proposing to depart from Congenies to-morrow, I have spent the day in paying many solemn parting visits, and this evening I have had one more meeting with this little flock. Our spirits were contrited together, and once more refreshed in the Lord's presence, prostrated before our blessed Redeemer, in gratitude, that to the last we were favoured to feel the extension of his love. This is a hard parting to many of us, to some of the dear young people especially, in whom I hope the seed of the kingdom of Christ has taken some root. May the Lord water it, and cause it to bring forth fruit to his own praise ! "

Stephen Grellet now felt at liberty to leave Languedoc, and early next morning proceeded on his way to Montpellier. Many of the inhabitants of Congenies, and most of the "little flock," who had been, more especially, the object of his Christian labours, accompanied him some distance on the road ; "the dear people seemed as if they could not part with him, and, having once more supplicated before the sacred footstool, imploring the Divine blessing upon them," he left them, "looking after him, as long as they could see him." On arriving at Sommieres, in the midst of an annual fair, he could neither obtain accommodation at the inn, nor a conveyance to take him forward on his journey. Having, therefore, given directions for his baggage to be sent after him, he set off on foot, "staff in hand, like a poor pilgrim," and reached Montpellier, a distance of about twenty miles, late in the evening. He spent one day in that city. "Through the medium of D'Encontre, the professor I met with at Vauvert," he remarks, "I was introduced to a few religious persons, and have had a solemn and satisfactory meeting among some of the people."

CHAPTER VII.

BRIVES—THE SCENES OF HIS YOUTH—HIS CHRISTIAN FAITH—
INTERVIEW WITH HIS MOTHER—HIS RELATIVES—LIMOGES—
BORDEAUX—RETURN TO NEW YORK.

From Montpellier Stephen Grellet passed over the Cevennes;
"travelling night and day, about two hundred and fifty miles,"
he reached Brives, the place where his mother then resided.

His visit to the little company of Protestants who profess
with Friends, and the inhabitants of the small towns and
villages about Nismes and the hill-country a little to the
south-west, though attended with difficulties and trials, had
been a deeply interesting one. He had had "large and
precious meetings" among them, had "freely visited them
in their families," been the means of confirming many in the
faith of Christ, and of encouraging the little community who
bear the name of Friends in the support of a Christian discipline among themselves; he had enjoyed much of the comfort
of love, and of the help of mutual confidence and brotherly
openness, in his intercourse with that simple hearted people;
and he had taken his leave of them, though not without much
Christian solicitude, yet with the cheering hope that the Lord
had a seed among them which He would preserve and bless.

It was an interesting point in his Gospel mission, when,
passing away from these more Protestant districts, he entered
upon almost exclusively Roman Catholic ground, and now
returned to the scenes of his youth and early manhood. He
had left them about fourteen years before, in the ardour of

military excitement, in the midst of the great revolutionary struggle—nominally a Roman Catholic, but in reality an unbeliever : he came back a humble disciple of the Lord Jesus, a preacher of the faith he sought to destroy—a Protestant, and a member of the religious Society of Friends.

That Christian community, it is well known, taking its stand upon "the foundation of the Apostles and Prophets, Jesus Christ himself being the chief corner-stone," recognises no authority in matters of faith and worship, but that of God; upholding the Holy Scriptures of the Old and New Testaments, as the only *Divinely authorised record* of doctrines to be believed and duties to be practised, it absolutely rejects the idea of authority in the mere traditions of men. Holding that the true Church is confined to no particular denomination of believers, and depends only on her glorious Head, Christ Jesus the Lord, who rules the Universe for her sake, governs her by his Spirit, and blesses her by his gifts, it acknowledges no right of human interference with the consciences of men, except by the diffusion of *" The Truth."*

Giving no countenance to the assumption of apostolical succession, or the continuance, under any form, of the sacerdotal office, or the setting apart of a distinct class of men exclusively to minister in holy things, with a right to claim support from the temporalities of others, and to exercise dominion over them, that Society expressly maintains, on the contrary, that Christ himself is the supreme ruler in his Church, and that, under the guidance of his Spirit, all the Lord's children enjoy the right of self-government; and, considering *all* the living members of the Church as Priests of the living God—all capable of receiving and using the gifts of the Spirit—it sanctions no ministry in the Churches, but that which flows from the pure and immediate operations of the Holy Ghost.

Not admitting, for one moment, or on any plea whatsoever, the religious worship of any other being but the Eternal

Jehovah—Father, Son, and Holy Spirit,—that Society emphatically proclaims that "God is a Spirit, and must be
worshipped in spirit and in truth"; enjoins simplicity, sobriety,
and order, in all the assemblies for the purpose of that
worship; and, calling for the prostration of the soul before
the Majesty of Heaven, in the silence of all flesh, and for the
offering of spiritual sacrifices acceptable to God by Jesus
Christ, it repudiates all the pomp and parade of external rites
and ceremonies, the spurious aid of architectural display, and
the delusive charm of musical excitement; it lights no
candles, and burns no incense upon any visible altar, bows
down to no graven image, adores no saint, and recognises
no object of religious homage in the Virgin Mary.   Totally
rejecting the notion of works of supererogation, it performs
no pilgrimages to any sacred shrine, knows nothing of the
miraculous power of relics, is an utter stranger to the imagined
flames of purgatory, has no indulgences, no auricular confession, no sacerdotal absolution, no masses for the living, no
prayers for the dead.   Acknowledging no mediator between
God and man but Christ, no justification of the sinner but
through faith in his blood, no sanctification of the believer
but by his Spirit, it has no sacraments but that of the washing of regeneration—the baptism of the Holy Ghost and
fire—and that of a participation, by faith, in the body and
blood of our Lord Jesus Christ, the Saviour of the world—
no hope of eternal life but through the one offering whereby
He has perfected for ever them that are sanctified.

As a member of such a community, and an accredited
Minister of such a Church—so entirely opposed to the Papal
system, and to every kind and degree of hierarchical or
ecclesiastical domination anywhere—Stephen Grellet could
not fail to appear in striking contrast with those who now
surrounded him, in the heart of a Roman Catholic country;
it was not strange that peculiar exercises and conflicts should
await him, on mingling with them in social and religious

intercourse, both in the intimacies of private life, and on more public occasions.

On entering the borders of his fatherland he writes :—

"My conflicts in approaching Brives were great, so that I have entered this place with a great weight resting upon me.

"The meeting with my precious mother was an affecting one. We had not seen each other since the year 1790, and many eventful circumstances have occurred during that series of years. Her sufferings, and those of my dear father, during the Revolution, were great, more so than I had heard of before.

"I am here entirely surrounded by Roman Catholics, and am a public spectacle among them. Every part of my dress, speech, and conduct is narrowly considered, and gives rise to various inquiries. Never have I felt more forcibly the necessity of constant watchfulness, and to have my every action so wrought in the light, that, in the light of Truth, which bringeth conviction to the heart, I may answer their inquiries. My services among these people are of a different character to what they have generally been hitherto. There is no door open as yet for public meetings among them; indeed they do not understand the nature and object of them; but I have interesting and solemn seasons in private circles. In almost every company to which I am introduced, their inquiries lead to the unfolding of some of the principles and doctrines of the Gospel, and the nature of pure religion, and the true worship of God. Thus I have to set before them how unsafe it is to trust the salvation of a never-dying soul to what their priests can do for them, to prayers to their saints, &c., the short and only sure way being, with sincere repentance for our sins, to come to Christ Jesus, the only Saviour, who has given himself for us to save us from sin, and not that we should continue to live in sin.

"I find amidst much darkness some spiritually-minded persons. Their hearts rejoice at the glad tidings of salvation, and they are often much affected. Several of these are among the nuns. In one convent their superior with gladness gives me opportunities for unfolding the truths of the Gospel of Christ to the nuns of her convent. If the priests encouraged them in the right way, by example and precept, instead of setting a stumbling-block before them, bright instruments might arise from among them. I marvel indeed

how, under their present circumstances, I can have so open a door
with them : for the priests have endeavoured to represent me to
them as a very dangerous person, who is out of the pale of the
Romish Church. But these pious persons say, that it is the true
and everlasting Gospel that I declare to them, and therefore their
confidence in their priests is shaken.

"This has been the case with my beloved mother. She felt
such concern on my account, thinking that, according to the
representations of the priests, I must be finally lost as a heretic,
that she had them to say masses on my behalf, and paid also
money that prayers might be put up on my account : not satisfied
with that, she urged me to accompany her to her confessor, a
monk in whom she placed great confidence, hoping he would
convert me. To satisfy her, I yielded to her request. But great
was her disappointment, when she saw that, instead of using the
arguments she expected, to convince me, he gave way to bitter
invectives and reflections, because I would not fight, refused to
take oaths, &c. I brought forward clear Scripture passages, as
authority, from the positive commands of Christ the Lord, whom
we are to obey in all things, adducing also the Apostles, and the
practices of the primitive believers. Then he gave way to anger,
so that he could proceed no further, and being worked up into a
passion, I left him in that state. After we got out, my beloved
mother lifted up her hands in astonishment, at conduct so unbecoming the Christian professor ; and from that time her mind
has been much more open to receive the Truth. Like the noble
Bereans, she peruses and searches diligently the Scriptures, a copy
of which I have given her, to know if these things are so.

" I continued at and about Brives thus engaged, amidst many
secret and more public trials, till the 6th of Eleventh Month. I
then went to Limoges, the place of my nativity. My being here
awakens feelings of gratitude, for the mercy and power of redeeming
love, which has, I trust, brought me out of that state of darkness
and alienation from God, under which, in this place, the blessed
Saviour so long bore with me. It also brings to my view the
many sufferings that my beloved parents have endured, even from
persons who have been amongst their greatest intimates. I felt
nothing but love, Christian love, towards them, and in this I have
visited several of them ; one of them, the Mayor of the city, who

F

had been among the greatest persecutors of my family during the
Revolution, told me, in allusion to those days, 'we have in your
absence acted more like ferocious beasts than men—much less as
Christians.' I now only stayed two days in Limoges.

"On the 9th, I went to see my beloved sister De Boise ; and
there, or in the neighbourhood, I stayed till the 27th. I had some
interesting religious meetings.

"I returned to Limoges on the 28th, where, my dear Master
opening a door for preaching the unsearchable riches of Christ, I
continued till the 14th of Twelfth Month. I had many public as
well as private religious seasons, so that many of the priests became
much alarmed. It being the time when some of their renowned
orators who had come from a distance preach every day, I was
made the subject of discourse, in their large church (St. Peter's).
Their Church was represented as in the most critical state it had
ever been in ; it was said that Buonaparte had sent for me, from
the remote parts of America, to undermine and, if possible,
to destroy, their holy religion. Such representations excited the
public curiosity still more, and brought many more to the meetings I had. Others also pay me private visits, some from curiosity
only, but others from a disposition to come to the knowledge of
the Truth. Among these some of the nuns that I have visited,
have manifested great tenderness ; but it is very hard for them to
be emancipated from the influence and fear of their priests. I
have had several conferences with some of the latter, but very few
of them to satisfaction, for want of their keeping in Christian
temper. One of them, however, must be excepted—the teacher
of theology in the Priest's Seminary. I was also with another
who, before the Revolution, was their renowned preacher. During the Revolution, before the rude lawless multitude, he publicly
reviled and blasphemed the Divine character of our Lord Jesus
Christ, trampled upon the Christian religion, turning it into
ridicule, and told them, ' these forty years have I been deceiving
you and myself,' and then gave way, with the multitude, to acts
of vileness and profanity, defiling their altars, and setting up the
goddess of reason (as they called a young woman) upon them. I
did not know then who the man was. There was a company
present of about forty persons, when in a mild, becoming manner,
he inquired into my views on the nature of the fall of man,
and of his restoration through Jesus Christ, baptism and their

various sacraments, the eucharist, &c.; also, into the nature of true Gospel ministry and worship, what constitutes the true Church of Christ, &c. After I had distinctly answered him on every one of these important subjects, and some others, he told the company present, in a solemn, impressive manner, 'You have heard this day more true Gospel divinity than you have ever done before, or, may be, ever shall again.' I find that this man, after having gone such a length in infidelity, saw his errors, and the errors of the Church of Rome, which he had so zealously espoused before. Therefore, though pressed by the clergy to resume his former duties, and even to accept greater preferment, he declined ; he also refused to deliver, at the bishop's request, his manuscripts of sermons, that they might be preached again ; stating that they were written when his mind was in darkness, and understood not the great truths of Christianity, as he now beheld them.

" I returned to Brives the 14th of the First Month, 1808. My mind being not yet at liberty to leave those parts, I continued thereabouts till the 23rd, having some large meetings. I then went to Bordeaux.

" I have of late been greatly depressed on account of the condition of this nation ; the almost uninterrupted wars in which it has been involved for some years past, together with the oppressive system of the conscription, have brought obvious desolation and distress over the face of the country. In many places comparatively few men, besides those in public offices, are to be seen, except those maimed by the war, or the aged, so that females have to perform, out of doors, a great part of the laborious work that generally devolves upon men. My heart is also often made sad in beholding the bands of young conscripts, marching towards the army, now preparing to invade Spain.

" Here, in Bordeaux, a large number of handsome young men from Poland, of the first families of that nation, are training for the new war. I have been with some of these young people who appear to have received a religious, guarded education. How must their parents' hearts bleed to have them now thus circumstanced ! Day and night my mind is turned towards Buonaparte. O could I plead with him ! could I bring him to feel and see, as I do, the horror and misery he is accumulating upon man, and the vices and immoralities he causes poor unwary youth to be involved in ! I have made several trials to procure passports to go to Paris, but cannot obtain them, yet I have not told anybody the concern I feel for the Emperor. If this is a service that the Lord has for me, He is all powerful to open a door for it—into his hands I commit myself.

" I have found here a few pious Christians, with whom my soul has been refreshed in the Lord."

Stephen Grellet's labours in his native land were brought to an earlier close than he had looked for. Under the restrictions of Napoleon's military rule, he was not allowed to proceed to Paris, as he wished to do ; and no further service appearing to be required in other directions, he felt at liberty to leave France, and to take his passage in a vessel ready to sail from Bordeaux to America. He says on the 14th of Second Month, 1808, " I have embarked this day on the ship *Eliza*, Captain Skidy, to return to New York," and on the 24th of Third Month he again writes :—

" New York. Yesterday afternoon I was favoured to land here safely, my heart prostrated with gratitude before the Lord, who has restored me to my dear wife and friends, and preserved me amidst so many baptisms. I found my beloved wife still feeble, but able to go with me to meeting."

Stephen Grellet had been absent more than nine months ; a few weeks after his reunion with his family and friends, he adds the following memorandum :—

" 19th of Fourth Month. Since my return home I have frequently looked back on the Lord's merciful and gracious dealings with my soul, during the last few months of deep and peculiar exercises and dangers, both by sea and land. He has indeed fulfilled the most gracious promise He made me, on my going out. He has been with me, to help, protect, and deliver his poor servant. What shall I say now, O Lord, under the sense of these thy favours ? Return to thy rest, O my soul ! for the Lord hath dealt bountifully with thee ;—the Lord is thy strength and salvation, He has been thy shield, thy buckler, thy rock, and thy refuge. Enable me, O Lord, to the end of my days, to be thine, and to serve thee with my whole heart."

CHAPTER VIII.

NEW YORK YEARLY MEETING—DEPUTATION TO VISIT SUBORDINATE
MEETINGS—ELIAS HICKS—RELIGIOUS VISIT TO THE SOUTHERN
AND WESTERN STATES—DEATH OF THOMAS PAINE.

PEACEFULLY returned from an interesting visit to his fatherland, Stephen Grellet was soon called upon to mingle again
in religious exercise with the assembled brethren of his own
Church, and to unite with them in active exertions for the
promotion of the Redeemer's cause within its borders.

At the Yearly Meeting of New York held in the Fifth
Month, 1808, he was appointed as one of a Committee to
visit the Subordinate Meetings.

Soon after the conclusion of the Yearly Meeting, the Committee thus appointed engaged in the work. They found it a
deeply interesting, but "a laborious and arduous service," and
the mind of Stephen Grellet, deeply imbued with the knowledge and love of the Saviour, and watchfully turned to the
Spirit's teachings, whilst earnestly concerned that souls might
be "won to Christ," or be confirmed in the Truth as it is in
Him, could not fail to be keenly alive to everything that had
the least tendency to lead away from Him, or to lessen in the
view of others the beauty and loveliness of his character, and
the completeness of his Divine attributes.

"I became introduced," he says, "into very deep and painful
trials; for Elias Hicks, one of our Committee, frequently advanced sentiments repugnant to the Christian faith, tending to
lessen the authority of the Holy Scriptures, to undervalue the
sacred offices of our holy and blessed Redeemer, and to promote a disregard for the right observance of the First day of
the week. Though his assertions were often so covered that
few understood him fully, I frequently, fervently, and earnestly

laboured with him. He promised that he would be more guarded ; but vain promises they were ; and several times I felt constrained publicly to disavow the unchristian doctrine that he advanced. My distress was great when in my native land amidst popish superstition and darkness ; but now it seems greater among my own religious Society, as few appear to be sensible of the threatening affliction that I see gathering upon us ; the cloud becomes darker. I think it is three years since, when, at a public meeting in this city, after he had advanced some such sentiments, I felt it my place (in that meeting) to open and explain the subject, how, as a religious Society, we had uniformly received and maintained the fundamental Christian truths, in harmony with clear Christian doctrine."

Though, at that time, comparatively a young man, associated in religious service with men of much longer religious standing, it is interesting to see the simple records of his early course as a minister of the Gospel, how clearly Stephen Grellet was enabled to detect the subtle fallacies of an acute but shallow thinker, in the incipient stages of that departure from the " Truth as it is in Jesus, according to the Scriptures," which twenty years after was so fearfully developed. As a faithful watchman, Stephen Grellet early saw its character, and anticipated its results ; true and steadfast in his allegiance to the cause of the Redeemer, he bore unflinching testimony to the eternal glory of His name, and sought to vindicate the doctrinal soundness of the Christian community of which he was a member.

After returning from this engagement in the service of the Church, he resumed his ordinary occupations amidst the comforts of home. It had, however, been given him in the behalf of Christ, not only to " believe on Him, but also to suffer for his sake," and his time and talents were still devoted to his cause.

" During the winter," he remarks, " I endeavoured to engage in some little temporal business : but I was not permitted to

pursue it many months. For believing that my blessed Master
called me in the service of his Gospel, once again, to the Southern,
and some parts of the Western States, I made the necessary
arrangements for such a journey. My dear wife, concluding to
stay, during my absence, at her father's, who had now removed
to Burlington (New Jersey), we broke up house-keeping, and,
with the unity of my friends, and their testimonials of approbation, I left home on the 18th of Third Month, 1809. My
wife accompanied me as far as Burlington, which place we
reached in time to attend their meeting, on the 23rd. I sat it in
silence, but in this silence my mind has often been refreshed,
and encouraged faithfully to follow the Lord in all his requirings."

Thus cheered by the good presence of the Lord, and having
left his beloved wife under the care and protection of her
earthly parent, he committed himself and his all into the
hands of his Heavenly Father, and proceeded on his mission,
in obedience to His will.

In the course of this engagement he visited several of the
Slave States—Virginia, North Carolina, Tennessee, and
Kentucky; and had large meetings both with slave-holders
and with their slaves. He was deeply tried in thus being
brought into contact with slavery, in relation to which he
remarks :—

"I was under great exercise because of the oppression under
which the poor slaves are kept; and I was engaged, in some
places, to describe to the people the nature of that religion which
is pure and undefiled before God ; and to contrast it with the
fruits of slavery brought forth among them. At Georgetown, my
holy Helper strengthened me to bear to them the good tidings of
great joy, which shall be to all people, testifying to the Saviour
which is Christ the Lord. D. Madison, the President's wife, and
her sister, invited me to their house. A physician, a tender-spirited
man, related to me the following circumstance. A few weeks
ago he was sent for by a planter, to visit one of his slaves. On
entering the miserable cabin in which the sick man was—the

slave-holder accompanying him—he saw the poor slave stretched
on a little straw. On examining him he found him in an
apparently unconscious and dying state. The master who was
not aware of his low condition, began, in very alarming language,
to upbraid and threaten him, using very coarse epithets ; he said,
' By pretending to be religious and going to your meetings, you
have got this sickness ; but as soon as you are better I will cure
you with a thousand lashes.' The physician told him, that from
all appearances, the poor man had but a few moments to live ;
upon which, the slave suddenly raised himself, lifted up his eyes,
and stretching forth his hands, said in an audible voice, ' I thank
thee Lord Jesus, my blessed Redeemer, for all thy mercies to thy
poor servant ; now receive my spirit into thy kingdom ;' and
then expired. The scene was awful ; the slave-holder stood
speechless and amazed ; amidst his threats and reproaches, his
poor slave was taken out of his power ; he could oppress him no
longer ; his spirit had triumphantly quitted its afflicted tenement."

Towards the end of this journey he had a severe illness. On
his recovery he remarks :—

"Fairfield, Ohio, 4th of Ninth Month, 1809. My travelling
in my Gospel embassy has been interrupted through a heavy
illness. My health appeared to be sinking by degrees, till at
last, the symptoms of the fever prevailing here at this time of
the year were evidently upon me.

"The fever soon increased to such a degree that those about
me gave up all hope of my recovery. I was fully aware of my
situation, but under a sense that I had come here in the service
and at the command of my blessed Redeemer, I felt sweet comfort in committing myself to his Divine disposal and care, now in
sickness, as He had strengthened me to do in the prosecution of
the work of his Gospel. I had again a full view of what I had
beheld of the joys of God's salvation through Jesus Christ, when
near the gates of death with the yellow fever in 1798 ; but I have
seen also, that the end for which my days were then lengthened
is not yet answered, that though I have been extensively engaged,
as it was shown me then that I should be, in the service of
the Gospel of my blessed Master, very wide and extensive fields

are yet before me, both in this and in distant nations : therefore
I have said, ' Lord, thy will be done ! do with me and for me as
is good in thy sight, only bestow upon thy poor servant the
blessing of preservation, that through life, and the sufferings
attending, I may glorify thee, as also by my death, whenever the
work thou hast for me is accomplished."

He returned to Baltimore on the 17th of Tenth Month,
and says :—

" Burlington, 17th.   I arrived here this evening, where, through
Divine mercy, I am favoured to find my beloved wife restored
from a severe illness ; we are permitted to unite together in
celebrating the excellency of the Lord's power and mercy, who
has preserved us both on a bed of sickness, and supported us
under our several probations."

After spending a few days at Burlington, Stephen Grellet,
accompanied by his wife, proceeded to Philadelphia, and
thence to the meetings composing Concord, and parts of the
Western Quarterly Meetings, in most of which he found " an
open door for his labours in the Gospel."   During the course
of this journey they experienced a remarkable preservation
from drowning.   Going down a steep hill, at the foot of
which was a deep mill-race, S. G. was unable either to stop or
turn the horse, but horse and carriage, with himself and wife,
and a young female friend who was riding with them, were
suddenly precipitated into the water.   With characteristic
presence of mind and prompt exertion, he succeeded in rescu-
ing both his companions and the horse from their perilous
situation, when a few moments' hesitation or delay would
probably have caused the death of all.   In recording the
event, he remarks, " This preservation of our lives induced
us renewedly to adore and praise Him in whose hands we
are, and to desire, with an increase of faith and confidence,
to commit ourselves wholly to his Divine guidance and
almighty protection.   Certainly we have abundant   cause

to put our trust in the Shepherd of Israel, who sleepeth not
by day, nor slumbereth by night."

Having completed his religious engagement, he returned
to New York just eight months after he had left home;
"strong emotions of gratitude and praise filling his heart,
whilst once more united with his little family in private devotion, to wait together upon, and to serve their blessed Lord,
and holy Redeemer."

On account of his wife's health they had resided, for some
time previous to his last journey, out of the city, at the
village of Greenwich. At the same place lived the notorious
Thomas Paine. An authentic account of the last days of
such a man may have some historical value and interest, and
S. G. thus notices his decease :—

"I may not omit recording here the death of Thomas Paine.
A few days previous to my leaving home on my last religious
visit, on hearing that he was ill, and in a very destitute condition,
I went to see him, and found him in a wretched state ; for he
had been so neglected, and forsaken by his pretended friends,
that the common attentions to a sick man had been withheld
from him. The skin of his body was in some places worn off,
which greatly increased his sufferings. A nurse was provided
for him, and some needful comforts were supplied. He was
mostly in a state of stupor, but something that had passed between
us had made such an impression upon him, that some days after
my departure he sent for me, and, on being told that I was gone
from home, he sent for another Friend. This induced a valuable
young Friend (Mary Roscoe), who had resided in my family,
and continued at Greenwich during part of my absence, frequently to go and take him some little refreshment suitable for
an invalid, furnished by a neighbour. Once, when she was there,
three of his deistical associates came to the door, and in a loud,
unfeeling manner, said, 'Tom Paine, it is said you are turning
Christian, but we hope you will die as you have lived ;' and
then went away. On which, turning to Mary Roscoe, he said,
'You see what miserable comforters they are.'

"Once he asked her if she had ever read any of his writings, and on being told that she had read but very little of them, he inquired what she thought of them, adding, 'from such a one as you I expect a correct answer.' She told him that when very young his 'Age of Reason' was put into her hands, but that the more she read in it, the more dark and distressed she felt, and she threw the book into the fire. 'I wish all had done as you,' he replied : 'for if the Devil has ever had any agency in any work, he has had it in my writing that book.' When going to carry him some refreshment, she repeatedly heard him uttering the language, 'O Lord! Lord God!' or, 'Lord Jesus! have mercy upon me!'

"It is well known that during some weeks of his illness, when a little free from bodily pain, he wrote a great deal ; this his nurse told me ; and Mary Roscoe repeatedly *saw* him writing. If his companions in infidelity had found anything to support the idea that he continued on his death-bed to espouse their cause, would they not have eagerly published it ? But not a word is said ; there is a total secrecy as to what has become of these writings."

CHAPTER IX.

SECOND VISIT TO EUROPE.

AGAIN fixing his abode at New York, Stephen Grellet was permitted, for about two years, to remain very much at home. During this interval of comparative repose, his ministerial labours were chiefly confined to the city, and his own Monthly and Quarterly Meetings. As he had been accustomed to do, under similar circumstances, he again "engaged in a small way of business, to make provision for his family," and also, as he says, "to obtain, through the Divine blessing upon his endeavours, the needful supplies to defray the expenses of travelling in the service of the Gospel."·

In perfect accordance with the good order established in the Christian community of which he was a member, he might have availed himself, for the latter object, of the willing aid of his friends. But, with characteristic disinterestedness, he declined to do so. Hitherto he had been enabled, even in this respect, to "minister to his necessities" from his own resources, and he felt it to be a privilege both to spend and to be spent in the work of his Lord.

"He has so blessed me," was the grateful record of this devoted servant, "that to His praise be it acknowledged, I have gone on my own charges throughout all the extensive religious journeys I have to this time taken; though some of these have been expensive; my journey through France, and crossing the sea, especially so; and on this continent I have lost three horses. But I have only thus returned to my blessed Master, in his service, what He has bountifully bestowed upon me. My friends in New York would have paid my passage across the sea, but I could not be free to consent to it."

In connection with these remarks, it will be recollected that the religious Society of Friends have long borne an open testimony to the spirituality and freedom of the Christian ministry. Resting upon the experience and example of the Primitive Church, and the authoritative teaching of the New Testament, they continue to maintain that there can be no right appointment to the sacred office, except by the call of our Lord Jesus Christ, nor any true qualification for the exercise of the gift, except by the direct and renewed influences of the Holy Spirit. Hence they hold that what is " freely received" should be " freely given," and that therefore the ministry of the Gospel must be essentially gratuitous and free, without money and without price,—without " hire," and without " pay."*

But whilst precluded by these fundamental views of Christian truth, from providing any pecuniary compensation for preaching the Gospel, they fully recognise, on Scriptural grounds, the justness of the claim of the preacher, for the supply of his outward wants, upon those who hear him,

---

* Bearing upon this point, and the Saviour's charge to the disciples, it is interesting to meet with sentiments like the following in an eminent modern author of the Lutheran persuasion :—

"The direction, in a certain sense admonitory, freely to give what was freely received, does not refer to the working of miracles alone, indeed only in a *lesser* degree to this, for none but a Judas Iscariot would ever conceive the idea of being paid. It embraces all that they have to impart, the exercise of their power to heal and their preaching of the kingdom at once, indicating *both* as grace to be freely offered. No gift of God's grace is to be bought and sold with money.—(Acts viii. 20.) Or as Tertullian says, 'nulla res Dei pretio constat.' A comprehensive and most pregnant position, which cannot be too much laid to heart by God's ambassadors even to the present day ; condemning all improper methodical and commercial stipulations in preaching God's grace, all payment that surpasses the limits of their need—(ver. 10), and all those unbecoming perquisites which are ungracefully attached to the direct ministration of the word and sacraments."—*Stier on the Words of the Lord Jesus ; translated from the German by Pope and Fulton. Vol. II. p. 10.*

whilst actually labouring in the cause of the Gospel, and
expending his whole time and strength for their benefit.
During the progress and continuance of such undertakings,
the Ministers of the Gospel cannot be expected to provide
for themselves; and it is well known to be the prevailing
practice of the Society to pay the expenses of their journeys,
and to maintain them during the course of their labours;—
"the workman being worthy of his meat."

Stephen Grellet cordially accepted both these views,
though, like the Apostle, in regard to the latter, as we have
seen, he did not wish "that it should be so done unto
him." He "coveted no man's silver or gold," and when he
felt himself constrained, by the gentle influence of his
Saviour's love, to visit the Churches that are scattered
abroad, and to proclaim to his fellow-men the unsearchable
riches of Christ, he did it in the spirit that sought not *theirs*
but *them*, and "so labouring," both in his temporal and in
his spiritual concerns, he sweetly realised the truth of the
words of the Lord Jesus, "it is more blessed to give than
to receive."

In the early summer of 1811, he entered upon a second visit
to Europe, and thus adverts to it in his Autobiography :—

"Since my return from my religious visit to France, I have
been under almost continual pressure of mental exercise in the
prospect that I should soon have to return to Europe to labour
more extensively among those nations, in the work of the Gospel
of our holy Redeemer; and it having appeared to me last winter
that the time had come for me to prepare to enter upon this
important service, I accordingly settled my outward concerns,
and submitted my religious prospect to the serious consideration
and judgment of the Friends of my Monthly, Quarterly, and
Yearly Meetings, who gave me their certificate of tender sympathy and near unity. On the 23rd of Fifth Month, 1811, the
First day of the week after a solemn meeting, I went on board the
Orbit, Captain Bool, bound for Liverpool. My dear wife and
I were strengthened to part with one another, under a solemn

covering of the Lord's presence, and enabled to resign ourselves
and one another to his Divine guidance and safe protection.
O Lord ! preserve thy servant in the way in which he goes, into
which thou hast called him, so that, by keeping an eye single to
thy holy directions, he may faithfully follow thee, and do the
work thou hast assigned him."

The voyage was a favourable one, and Stephen Grellet
arrived at Liverpool on the 22nd of the Sixth Month, 1811.
He thus writes :—

" I remained in Liverpool till the 3rd of Eighth Month, having
several meetings with Friends in that large commercial place, and
several also among divers classes of the inhabitants.

" During the time I have been at Liverpool, Paul Cuffee, a black
man, owner and master of a vessel, has come into port, from Sierra
Leone on the coast of Africa. He is a member of our Society,
and resides in New England. The whole of his crew are black
also. This, together with the cleanliness of his vessel, and the
excellent order prevailing on board, has excited very general
attention. It has, I believe, opened the minds of many in tender
feelings towards the poor suffering Africans, who, they see, are
men like themselves, capable of becoming, like Paul Cuffee,
valuable and useful members both of civil and religious society."

The Slave Trade had indeed, at this time, been for some
years abolished, both by England and the United States ; but
it was still carried on, with all its cruelties and horrors, by
the subjects of several powers. In countries where the im-
portation of slaves from Africa was no longer allowed, the
desolating and widely extended effects of the *internal* slave
trade were still perpetuating the complicated miseries of this
dreadful traffic. Slavery itself still continued to prevail to an
undiminished extent, and with all the variety and enormity
of the evils and calamities inseparable from the inhuman
system ; while the notion of the inferiority of the African
race, and the prejudice against colour, had scarcely begun to
give place to more enlightened views, or to yield to the
righteous influence of Christian principle. Though some

check had been given to the iniquitous trade in the blood and
bones of our fellow men and coloured brethren, for whom
Christ died, they were still a down-trodden people everywhere,
whose sufferings no tongue could tell. Stephen Grellet was
one of those who deeply felt for the cause of the oppressed—
"the wrongs of Africa." The simple circumstance of the
arrival of Paul Cuffee with his coloured crew, in the port of
Liverpool, could not fail to touch a chord to which his heart
must vibrate; he welcomed him as "a man and a Christian."

Leaving Liverpool on the 3rd of Eighth Month, Stephen
Grellet proceeded northward, and visited the meetings of
Friends, had much service with others in Cumberland,
Westmoreland, and Northumberland, and then went to Edin-
burgh. Having meetings in various places on the way, he
reached Inverness, and says:—

" I felt my mind released from further service in the north
of Scotland, and we came back southward over the Highlands,
having meetings in many of the towns and villages among the
Highlanders.

"I came to Glasgow the 26th of Tenth Month, and had several
meetings there; a very large and satisfactory one in the Traders'
Hall. Feeling much for the poor weavers in the villages and
towns thereabouts, I had some baptising meetings in several
places. I found individuals in most of them who have known
the Lord Jesus Christ as their Saviour and teacher, and their
only hope of glory. Some of them sit together in silence,
feeling after the motions and quickenings of the Divine Spirit,
to enable them to worship the Father of spirits, in spirit and in
truth.

" I proceeded after that to Greenock and other towns till I
came to Portpatrick; the Lord very graciously making way for
me to preach the unsearchable riches of the Gospel of Christ. I
found through Scotland, in various places, some strongly entrenched in Calvinistic notions, among whom I had deep exercises
and close labours. I had frequently to enlarge among them, on
the universality of the love of God, through Jesus Christ; his

meritorious sacrifice for sin, yea, for the sins of the whole world ; that these are faithful sayings worthy of all acceptation, that Jesus Christ came into the world to save sinners, and is the propitiation for the sins of the whole world, that He would have all men come to the knowledge of the Truth and be saved : that in order that we might know those deep things of God, which none can know but by the Spirit of God, He has bestowed the visitations of his Spirit upon all ; the grace of God, which brings salvation, having appeared to all, teaching us, &c. &c. Thus I often earnestly pressed upon them the necessity to pay close attention to the in-speaking word of God in their hearts,—to obey the teachings of the Divine Spirit, and to seek to have fulfilled in them the very precious Scripture promises, 'they shall be all taught of God'; and the words of Christ, 'every one therefore that has heard and learned of the Father cometh unto me.' By so doing they would understandingly read the Scriptures, and escape being of the number of those, who search the Scriptures, which testify of Christ, but will not come to Him, that they might have life."

On the termination of his religious services in Scotland, Stephen Grellet felt "drawn in much Christian love and interest" towards Friends and others in Ireland, and at once entered upon a general visit to that island.

"The 17th of Eleventh Month, 1811. Accompanied by my valued friend, John Robinson, of Glasgow, and William Hall, we left for Donaghadee in Ireland."

This journey, of which many interesting particulars are given, occupied him till the beginning of the Fourth Month, 1812.

Among the many instances in the life and experience of this faithful servant of the Lord, in which, by following the leadings of the Holy Spirit, he saw clearly the line of his duty, and was enabled to accomplish the work which his Lord gave him to do, we cite the following :—

"I reached Lisburn in time to attend their Quarterly Meeting. Thence I went to Dublin, where I continued some time visiting

Friends in their families, and having several meetings among
them, and other people. Suffering humanity has a strong claim
upon my feelings, and led me into many of the abodes of wretchedness and misery, poor-houses, prisons, &c. I suffered deeply
among them, but found, in some instances, that the door for
preaching the Gospel is open among the poor. I had a memorable
meeting among the seamen. My mind was under considerable
exercise towards them, but I did not know that they were then
in so peculiar a position. On imparting my concern to Friends,
after the close of one of their meetings, they cordially united in
it ; when a friend stated, that though he felt great unity with
the concern he did not see how it could be accomplished ; for
orders from the Admiralty in London had arrived, to impress
as many of the seamen as possible, and that in consequence
not one was now to be seen either on board the vessels or
on the quays ; adding that he would go out immediately and see
what could be done. It was then near twelve o'clock. The
Friend went directly to the Admiral of the Port, with whom he
was acquainted, and told him of 'the religious concern I had
towards the seamen. The Admiral answered, ' It is a hard thing
that you ask me ; here, read what dispatches I have to-day from
London ; the impression of men is now going on in the city part
of London, heretofore exempt from it, but,' added he, 'if your
friend can have his meeting this evening, I give you my word of
honour that no impressment shall be made to-night.' Now, that
was the very time I had it on my mind to have the meeting.
Friends, therefore, had public notices printed, in which, with the
approbation of the Admiral, his promise that there should be no
impressment that night was inserted. The notices were distributed
at the houses seamen are known to frequent, and where they had
concealed themselves. The ground floor of a large warehouse was
prepared and seated for the occasion. The meeting was appointed
for seven in the evening, and, contrary to the apprehension of
some, the sailors turned out in large numbers, so as to crowd the
place. After the meeting had been settled in much stillness,
there was a bustle near the door, towards which the attention of
the sailors was directed with much anxiety. It was the Admiral,
accompanied by some of his officers. Fears were entertained that
he was not true to his promise ; but he marched quietly through

the seamen, came to the further end, towards me, and took his seat in front of them, as if to proclaim ' you see me in your hands before you ; you need not fear.' We had a solemn meeting ; many of those weather-beaten faces were tendered, even to tears. When the meeting concluded, the Admiral, under much feeling and religious tenderness, expressed his sense of gratitude for the Lord's favour extended that evening, and his hope that many of them would be lastingly benefited by this religious opportunity. The meeting separated under that solemnity, and, agreeably to the promise of the Admiral, no impressment took place that night in Dublin. But the succeeding days, throughout England and Ireland, it continued very rigid, this being the time when France threatened an invasion."

Rather more than five months had been spent in Ireland, and Stephen Grellet now crossed the Channel into Wales. The Half-year's Meeting for the Principality was about to be held at Brecon, and, having a few meetings by the way, he proceeded to that place.

" On the 5th of Fourth Month, 1812," he writes, " I landed at Holyhead, after a rough but short passage, during which I again suffered much from sea-sickness. O Lord ! direct my steps aright through this Principality, and, as heretofore, fulfil very graciously thy word of promise, in which thou hast enabled thy poor servant to believe : ' I will teach thee, and instruct thee in the way which thou goest ; I will guide thee with mine eye.'

" On the 14th began the Half-year's Meeting, where I was comforted among some valuable Friends, who belong to it. I had also a satisfactory meeting with the inhabitants of Brecon, and another with a considerable number of French officers, prisoners of war on parole ; I spoke to them in French ; some of them were brought under the power of the Spirit of God, and many of them came to me after meeting, in much love and good-will ; and some of them bore excellent testimony to the blessed principle of light and truth in the soul. ' What a blessed thing would it be,' they said, ' were men more obedient to it ; then there would be an end of wars and fightings.'"

After a large good meeting at Llandilo he afterwards went to Haverfordwest and Milford Haven. Thence, " having one or two meetings every day, and very close exercises in some of them," he returned along the coast of South Wales, by way of Carmarthen, Swansea, Neath, Cardiff, and Newport, and crossed the Channel to Bristol.

"30th of Fourth Month. I arrived at Bristol in time to attend the Week-day meeting. The next day I was at a funeral; on First-day I attended their two meetings; the following days I was at Frenchay and Thornbury, and returned to Bristol to their Third-day Meeting; my mouth was closed at all these meetings. I believe this was the service the Lord required of me. May I ever be preserved under the guidance of his blessed Spirit. There is a time to speak and a time to keep silence. I then went to Bath, and had a meeting with Friends, also in silence. In the evening a large one was held for the inhabitants, in which, through the Spirit of Christ, our holy, Head, I was enlarged in preaching the glad tidings of his glorious Gospel."

From this time Stephen Grellet was closely occupied in holding meetings on his way to the Yearly Meeting. He makes the following remarks:—

"Seventh-day, 30th. This forenoon the Yearly Meeting closed and that for Ministers and Elders was held in the afternoon. With grateful and reverent acknowledgment I may join with many dear and valuable Friends, anointed servants of the Lord, in believing that the blessed Head of his Church has condescended to be with us, during this yearly solemnity.

"Sixth Month, 6th. I continued in London to this day attending several meetings, some of which were held under great solemnity and the prevalence of the power of truth."

He continued about a week in the neighbourhood of London, after which he attended the Quarterly Meetings of Essex, Suffolk, Norfolk and Norwich, and had many meetings in Lincolnshire.

Having completed his visit to the Eastern Counties, Stephen Grellet passed over into Yorkshire, and pursued his religious labours through some of the northern parts of the nation.

Seventh Month 27th, he went to Hull, where he stayed two
or three days ; having religious service in several families, as
well as meetings with Friends and others in that populous
town ; also visits to the inmates of the poor-houses.   Respecting the latter he writes :—

"I feel my mind frequently drawn in Gospel love and very
near sympathy to visit that portion of my afflicted fellow-men,
and have had in several places some very interesting and solemn
seasons with them.   In some instances I have been forcibly reminded of the description of Lazarus, given by the Evangelist.   I
also see this Scripture fulfilling, 'To the *poor* the Gospel is
preached.'   The stream of this precious Gospel has repeatedly
flowed in a wonderful manner in the meetings that I have had
among them.   Prisons also are places to which my mind is often attracted.   How can it be otherwise, than that the abiding sense I have
of the great love and mercy of God in Christ Jesus, even towards
me, who, like the Apostle, may well call himself, 'the chief of
sinners,' should constrain me to feel and judge, that if love and
mercy have thus wonderfully been extended towards me, they
flow also to the inmates of prisons ; for Christ has died for all
men—He has come into the world to save sinners, yea, the chief
of sinners.   O how powerfully did the Apostle feel the force of
this, when he exclaimed, 'It is a faithful saying and worthy of
all acceptation, that Jesus Christ came into the world to save
sinners,' &c.

"I have now a great exercise upon me, because of the accounts
received, that war has been declared between England and
America, that there has already been considerable effusion of
blood, and that free intercourse between the two countries is interrupted.   In consequence of this, it is very difficult for me
to receive letters from my beloved wife, or to forward her mine.
The accounts also of the destruction of human life by the belli-
gerent nations on the European continent are truly awful ;
torrents of blood do indeed flow, both in the north of Europe,
and in Spain and Portugal ; prisoners of war from Spain continue frequently to be sent over to this island.   Under these
most afflictive circumstances, which so awfully develop the depravity and sinful state of the human heart, how can I but feel

myself most imperatively called upon, with all diligence and
faithfulness, to preach Christ the Redeemer, and the only Saviour
from all these evils, entailed on man by sin ; to direct all men
to Him, the Prince of Peace ; and to his Spirit, who would lead
into all Truth, if they can be prevailed upon to turn to Him with
full purpose of heart. My heart yearns towards the nations on
the continent ; deep is the travail of my soul for them, and
frequent are my prayers for their rulers, that the Lord may so
change their hearts, that He himself may come to reign in them,
so that they may be induced to beat their swords into plough-
shares, their spears into pruning-hooks, and neither learn nor
make war any more."

In the course of his journey in the north of Yorkshire, he
relates the following circumstances, after giving particulars of
meetings held at Scarborough, Whitby, &c.

"A few days ago, I had a meeting in the forenoon at Pickering ; on my way thence, to a large village some miles distant,
where I had appointed a meeting to be held in the evening, we
overtook a man on foot, going the same way. A Friend who
accompanied me, being alone in his chaise, invited him to take a
seat by him. He soon recognised him as the person whom he
had noticed in the preceding meeting, much affected by the testimony of the Truth that was proclaimed. My friend's attention
had been so attracted towards him, that he tried to speak to him
after meeting, but, in the crowd, he had lost sight of him. Now
the stranger, after alluding to that meeting, was melted into tears,
and then broke forth somewhat in this strain : 'What is the
matter with me ? what is all this ? I have never known anything like it. I was going towards Scarborough, and on my way
I felt an irresistible power turning me towards Pickering about
six miles out of my way, a place where I had no business, neither
had I been there before. Arriving there this morning, I heard
of the meeting, and thought that I must attend it ; but I was so
unwilling to do so, that after going to the door, and looking into
the meeting-house, I tried to go back again, but I felt constrained
to go in and sit down. O, I heard such doctrine there, delivered
with such awfulness and power, reaching my very heart, as I had

never heard before; my secret actions and thoughts were set before me; a heavenly flame was kindled in me,' &c. &c. Then he stated that at the conclusion of the meeting he retired as speedily as possible into the fields, out of sight, to give vent to his tears, and having heard of the meeting that evening, he was now on his way to it. It was another solemn meeting; blessed be the Lord for ever and ever."

In some parts of this journey S. G. mentions having two meetings almost every day; and at Newcastle, which he reached the 24th of Eighth Month, he writes:—

"At Newcastle a great concern came upon me, on account of the poor and labouring classes of the community, the colliers especially, and those employed in furnaces and glass-houses, many of whom endure great hardships and very severe privations. The love of Christ constraining me, I yielded to the prospect of duty to have meetings among them. It was a laborious service, especially those meetings held in the evening, and which were mostly out of doors, for there were no places found large enough to accommodate the people. Great solemnity was our covering, on those occasions; under the Lord's power many hearts were made tender. Truly many of these persons manifested that though poor in the world they are rich in faith. I entered deeply into the sufferings of those who pass most of their days in working in the deep and damp coal-mines. Coming out of them after sunset, they took a very short time to refresh themselves, so as to be at the meeting in due season. Sometimes great destruction of life occurs in these mines, by explosions from various causes; thus many are left widows, or fatherless. It was but a few days before I was at one of the collieries, that a large number were destroyed in one of the pits by the foul air; many of their widows and relatives attended the meeting I had in that neighbourhood; it was a large and solemn one; Divine love was in an extraordinary manner experienced to be over that assembly, when many felt the oil of joy poured forth upon them in lieu of the mourning under which they had been bowed, and, for awhile at least, they exchanged their spirit of heaviness for the garment of praise. The solemnity and stillness which prevailed in the meeting continued over the people after it concluded. My good and blessed Master was pleased, in a very particular manner, to strengthen me for the special services of these days,—praised be his name !"

Near the conclusion of this part of his services he writes:—

"I came to Undercliffe, near Bradford, to my very valuable friend, Sarah Hustler, one of the Lord's anointed servants, to whom I am very closely united in the bonds of the Gospel. Day by day the Lord has so graciously extended fresh qualifications to his poor servant, to suffer or perform the portion of service assigned, that I may truly say,

> "' In cares, and fears, and doubts,
> Which oft assail my mind,
> When they are left to thee, O Lord,
> The best relief I find.' "

From Bradford Stephen Grellet passed on to Liverpool, where he arrived on the 5th of Tenth Month. "Again much refreshed every way, at the hospitable house of his dear and kind friends, Isaac and Susannah Hadwen." We make a few extracts from his memoranda :—

"Through the populous parts of Lancashire and Yorkshire I had extensive services among the people at large, especially the weavers, for whose accommodation many meetings were held in spacious meeting-houses of the dissenters. The distress generally prevailing in these parts, for want of employment, and on account of the scarcity of food, draws forth my very great sympathy.

"At Chesterfield, besides having meetings with Friends, and with the inhabitants, I had one with about two hundred French prisoners on parole. One of them, an interesting young man, came afterwards to see me ; he loves the Truth, as far as he has come to the knowledge of it.

"Through these counties, as well as others, I frequently met with French prisoners, chiefly officers ; the men, both soldiers and sailors, being confined in large prisons. I have had the comfort of finding some in a tender state of mind, and several of them have become public professors of Christianity, being convinced also of the errors of popery, war, &c. At Lichfield, where a large number of these, my countrymen, are stationed, many of them attended the meeting held in the large Town Hall. It was a very solemn season. Several of these prisoners are of high rank—generals, colonels, &c. Three of the generals, one of whom had been at college in France with a first-cousin of mine, came to see me after meeting, and expressed, on behalf of the other officers, their gratitude for the opportunity given them to become acquainted with some of those excellent Christian doctrines to which they had been so great strangers. May the Lord bless the days of their captivity! I sometimes admire the ways of the Lord, who thus enables me to preach, on this island, the Gospel of peace and salvation by Christ, to a greater number of persons of such a character as these than I might have had an opportunity of doing in France; and now to do it at a time when they are, for a while at least, out of the hurry and excitement of warlike movements, and when suffering and reflection have tended to soften and humble them."

Though he had been several times at Birmingham, where he had had considerable service, Stephen Grellet now felt himself again strongly attracted to that place; arrived there, he remarks :—

" When I came to Birmingham I felt the exercise which had been upon me, for a particular class of the inhabitants, greatly increased. I had overwhelming sorrow also, because of the horrors of the war on the continent, where torrents of blood flow. I felt as if I was among drawn swords and bayonets. Then, deeply feeling the guilt of those who are the means of putting into the hands of the warriors the weapons of destruction, it appeared to me that those who manufactured them are sharers in the guilt. I felt it was the Lord's requiring, that I should have a meeting with as many of these as could be convened together. After consulting with Friends, who most feelingly entered into my exercise, they endeavoured to their utmost to promote my object. The large meeting-house of the Independents was considered the most eligible. The minister of that congregation entered so fully into my religious concern, that he not only relinquished his usual service on First-day evening, but announced my meeting at the close of his own in the forenoon. The concourse of people was very great, the house was crowded, and many remained out of doors. Awful and solemn was the weight that was on my mind on that occasion, and earnest was my secret prayer that the Lord would prevent the end, for which that multitude had been called together, from being frustrated ; the crowd in the house was so great, and those out of doors so numerous, that I feared for the consequences. The all-gracious and powerful God was pleased, after a while, to bring that multitude, both in and out of doors, into silence, and to cause a Divine solemnity to spread over us. He gave strength and qualification through his Spirit, to proclaim what the Christian religion is : what should be the manner of life and conversation of the professors of it. It leads, it calls to love and peace ; it is pure and undefiled, and enables to bring forth the fruits of the Spirit. These were contrasted with the fruits of the flesh ; and the cause of war was unfolded, its awful and dreadful consequences—misery, wasting, and destruction. In these are deeply concerned, not only those actually engaged in the field of carnage, but those also who give countenance, and are in any wise auxiliary to it, as the manufacturers of arms and engines of destruction. I spread before them the consideration, whether a greater trust in God, and love to Him and man, would not lead to the pursuit of a kind of business in which his blessing might be expected, and by which his glory may be promoted ; and if, as enjoined by our blessed Redeemer, we loved one another as He loved us, all our works and labour would not tend towards the advancing of his kingdom, and the coming of that day, when men shall beat their swords into plough-shares and their spears into pruning-hooks, and they shall learn war no more. The meeting concluded in stillness, and the people separated in a manner which gave some evidence that the power of the Truth had been felt by them.

" At Northampton a meeting was appointed on a First-day evening, in Friends' meeting-house. My kind friend, Isaac Hadwen, went to see if the house was properly lighted, and though it wanted about half an hour to meeting-time, he found the house full, and as many more out of doors ; in the fulness of his heart happening to say, 'what a pity that we have not a house capable to accommodate the people,' a young woman within hearing answered, ' O I dare say my father would take pleasure in opening his house to you ; ' whereupon, without waiting for an answer, she hastened away and soon returned, stating that very shortly her father's meeting-house would be prepared for the people. It was the house that Dr. Philip Doddridge formerly occupied. I found a great company collected; not one-fifth could have got into Friends' meeting-house. There was a precious seed among that people; their spirits feel near and dear to me. The minister of the chapel and his family attended; he appeared to be a man of a pious mind.

"Passing through Cambridgeshire, and being with Friends and others, I came to Stilton, near which are the barracks, wherein are confined about six thousand French prisoners, mostly soldiers, who are guarded by a body of English troops. Baneful indeed is the scourge of war; with deep anguish of spirit I have visited this portion of my fellow-men; my heart yearns with love towards them, who are indeed very interesting to me. In the conversations and religious opportunities I have had with them, many evinced sensibility, under the chastening hand that has been upon them. Some of them have been prisoners for nine years, and many, I find, have been brought up tenderly, even in affluence, having been conscripts that were forcibly taken from their homes, bands of whom I saw in France, fifty or more chained together, dragged as sheep to the slaughter. Some of them inquired what had brought me to this island, and what induced me to visit them in their affliction? On being informed of the nature of my mission, in the love of Christ to these nations, and what has prompted me now to visit them, and that I had it also in contemplation to go over to France to visit our countrymen in the love that seeketh the happiness and salvation of all, they replied, 'Our souls are full of gratitude to the Lord, who has put it into your heart thus to think of us, and feel for us.' I could not have them collected together, the rules of the prison not allowing it; but I had several satisfactory opportunities among them, in the wards where they are confined, a hundred or more together.

"O that the light of the glorious Gospel may so break in upon them, and the power of Truth so come over them, that though their bodies should remain many more years in captivity, their souls may be liberated from the bondage of sin and corruption."

Stephen Grellet now proceeded to visit the meetings of Friends in Essex and Hertfordshire, till on the 25th of Twelfth Month, he once more came to Higham Lodge, the residence of his dear friend William Dillwyn.

CHAPTER X.

RELIGIOUS ENGAGEMENTS IN LONDON—THE WEST OF ENGLAND—
RETURN TO LONDON.

STEPHEN GRELLET now came to London, to the home of " his dear friends, Joseph and Rachel Smith." Here he remarks :—

" I soon felt the heavy Gospel bonds awaiting me in this metropolis to be rapidly fastening upon me. The depth of exercise into which I was introduced on account of the various classes of its inhabitants, is indescribable. Rich and poor, but especially the last, including not only those in the city at large and in the various poor-houses, but also the inmates of prisons, &c.

" I was enabled again to offer myself and my all to the Lord and his service, not in that great city only, but also to go on the European continent, or wheresoever He might call me, or his Spirit might lead me. Great peace and quietness I felt after this full offering was made.

" Having felt deeply for the sufferings of a large portion of the labouring class in this city, I believed it to be my duty to have religious meetings among them ; great numbers are out of employment, in consequence of the stagnation of business, caused by the desolating war which the various European nations are waging against each other ; and the distress is greatly increased by the general scarcity of bread throughout this country. Many efforts are made to administer some relief to the poor sufferers. Friends generally are active and very liberal in these deeds of benevolence. One of them has sent to London from his own purse, the enormous amount of seventeen thousand pounds sterling, besides what he has bestowed for the same benevolent object in his own neighbourhood and other places. But this liberality is not confined to Friends. I have been delighted in hearing of the charities bestowed by many in the various ranks of life, according to their ability.

"The first meeting I had among the distressed was held in the Friends' large meeting-house at Devonshire House, for the weavers of Spitalfields, where thousands of them are out of employ. They came in such numbers that they stood in the house as close as they could crowd, and many could not get in. Under the apprehension that they had been called together to have bread distributed, some of them became very noisy, so that, for a time, it appeared as if our object of having a religious meeting would be frustrated; but my beloved friend, William Allen, well known to them by frequently handing out bread and other kinds of provisions to them, told the people that the meeting had been called for a religious purpose—a meeting for divine worship—and therefore requested them to act accordingly, so that, through the Lord's favour, they might be partakers of the benefits designed. Stillness soon prevailed over the dense crowd, and the Lord's power was manifested over us. The earnest prayers that were put up for this people were heard. The Gospel of Christ was preached to the poor. He fed them with good things, even the consolations of his Spirit; many of them were broken into tears, and the solemnity and quiet was not interrupted at the conclusion. Some of them said, 'It is a precious gift we have had this evening.' My beloved friend, William Forster, was my co-worker in the Gospel of Christ.

"After that I had several other meetings among the poorer class in London, held in the parts mostly inhabited by them.

"Feeling my mind now led towards the people of high rank, and the nobility in the West-end of London, and my much valued and beloved friend, Mary Dudley, having a similar prospect, we entered together into the service, and had meetings among them.

"My next field of religious labour was more particularly among the young people of our own Society, for whom I felt much, and I had several meetings with them. Many of them I believe received the testimony I had to bear among them in the way in which it was delivered."

Stephen Grellet had long felt much concern on behalf of the Jews resident in London; and in the course of his interesting labours in the service of Christ, a meeting was now held with them in Devonshire House Meeting-house, Houndsditch, which was well attended.

The reader cannot but be struck in the perusal of these extracts, which might be greatly extended, in observing the truly catholic spirit of this ambassador for Christ; how his sympathies were excited on behalf of all classes and conditions of men.

We insert the following particulars of some of his engagements :—

"After passing days and nights under deep exercise on account of the degraded and vicious portion of the inhabitants of this great city, I felt that I had a service towards them, but I could see no way to discharge it. I earnestly besought the Lord that He would open a way for me, and then spread this important concern before my dear friends in London, Ministers and Elders. They deliberated upon it with much feeling and care ; and, believing it was a service required of the Lord, they encouraged me, with simplicity and faithfulness, to attend to it. Friends' Meeting-house, in St. Martin's Lane, was considered the most eligible place to hold such a meeting, being very near to neighbourhoods resorted to by pickpockets, thieves of various descriptions, and abandoned women. It was a very arduous task for Friends to have to send notices of the meeting to such, but they did it faithfully. For the accommodation of that class of people, many of whom spend their nights in revelling, &c., and do not go out much in the day, the meeting was held in the evening, the 19th of First Month, 1813 ; but to have a concourse of such people brought together so late as seven o'clock, p.m., tended greatly to increase my fears of the consequences. My confidence, nevertheless, was in the Lord, that He would over-rule all to his praise and glory. The meeting was very generally composed of the class of men and women towards whom my mind had been directed. I was brought under great dejection and distress on beholding before me so many fellow-beings, of both sexes, in whose countenances so much vice and depravity were depicted ; some of whom, perhaps, had never been in a meeting for worship, and were strangers to religious sensibility. My soul was also greatly moved in observing that they were mostly young people. I wept bitterly over them ; but the love of Christ, who came to save sinners, 'to seek and to save that which was lost,' filled my soul, and prepared me not only to proclaim against sin, and the consequences of living and dying in sin, but also to preach Christ the Saviour of sinners.   O, it was a solemn time indeed ; the Lord's power was over us ; the lofty heads, the proud looks, were brought down.   I have seldom known such brokenness, and so general, as it was that evening.   The meeting remained in the same state during the silence after I had sat down, a silence only interrupted by the sobbings or deep sighs of some of them.   At the conclusion, the people retired in the same quietness.   O what a display of the Lord's power and mercy !   Surely our hearts can but overflow with gratitude to Him our blessed and sure Helper.

"The chief police magistrate in London, hearing of that meeting through some of our Friends, sent me word that, if I wished to see that class of people more generally throughout the city, he would take measures to have them all collected, when full opportunity would be given me to have meetings with them.   I acknowledged his kind offer, but could not accept it, though I told him I should be obliged by his giving me free access to the several prisons in London, having felt much drawn towards that class of poor, wretched humanity.   My request was readily granted, and I engaged very soon in the arduous and very trying service.

"The Compters* were the prisons I visited first ; there is one in each district of the metropolis.

"After that I proceeded with a visit to Newgate, which occupied some days, having religious opportunities in the many separate apartments, where the miserable inmates are confined.   Several were under sentence of death.   In one cell there were four together, who were to be executed the ensuing morning ; one of these particularly drew forth our tender feelings, my dear friend William Forster being then with me.   His wife, with two children, came to see him for the last time, when we were there.   One of the children was a boy, about eight years of age.   The sight of his father under heavy irons brought the child into a state of great terror and distress.   The grand-parents of this child were

---

* These Compters have since been abolished.

poor weavers, people of piety. We visited them the day after
the execution of their son. We were much instructed in beholding that, in their very deep grief, they were sustained by the
comforts of the Christian religion. The Lord Jesus was their
refuge and strength under their great and sore trouble. They
produced a letter written by the poor prodigal the night previous
to his execution, addressed to his wife, and to his parents. After
describing his heart-felt sorrow and deep repentance for his crime,
and the hope that, notwithstanding his great unworthiness, the
Lord Jesus Christ, who had mercy on the penitent thief on the
cross, would condescend to be merciful to him, he most earnestly
begged his aged parents to forgive him also. He described his
evil life as being the consequence of his disobedience to them ;
and particularly in having disregarded the due observance of the
Sabbath, so contrary to their parental entreaties. Having begun
to do so in the afternoon, it had led him into evil company, and
step by step he had become the companion of thieves. He most
earnestly entreated his wife to guard very particularly the children
from such dangerous and ungodly practices, and to spend the
afternoons and evenings of the Sabbath in attending religious
meetings, and reading the Bible and books of devotion. We found
in the boy above mentioned so much sensibility, that our interest
in him became excited ; some kind friends assisting in having him
sent to school.*

"The visit to that part of Newgate which is occupied by the
women prisoners had very nearly been frustrated. The jailor
endeavoured to prevent my going there, representing them as so
unruly and desperate a set that they would surely do me some
mischief ; he had endeavoured in vain to reduce them to order,
and said he could not be responsible for what they might do to
me ; concluding that the very least I might expect was to have
my clothes torn off. But the love of Christ constrained me, and
I felt persuaded that He who called me to this service could again
make way for me and preserve me. Very earnest was my prayer

---

* The boy behaved so well, that he was subsequently placed at a
boarding-school, and afterwards as an apprentice with a Friend. The
letter of his poor father, above alluded to, was preserved and given to
him on his coming of age. He married and settled respectably in life.

to have undoubted evidence that this was a service that the Lord required of me, feeling that my having visited the men was not a reason why I should visit the women also. My request was granted, and the path of duty being clear before me, I proceeded to the prison. When I came to the small yard, the only accommodation for about four or five hundred women, I found there some who immediately recognised me, as having seen me in the Compters, and who appeared much pleased at my now coming here. They told me that no preparation had been made to receive me, but that they would immediately do what they could towards it. Owing to the darkness of the morning the prisoners had been unusually late in getting up, and many of them had not yet risen. They occupied two long rooms, where they slept in three tiers— some on the floor, and two tiers of hammocks over one another. They had the whole soon rolled up, and all the women came together in one room. When I first entered, the foulness of the air was almost insupportable ; and everything that is base and depraved was so strongly depicted on the faces of the women who stood crowded before me, with looks of effrontery, boldness, and wantonness of expression, that, for a while, my soul was greatly dismayed ; surely, then, did I witness that the Lord is a refuge and strength, his truth is a shield and a buckler. The more I beheld the awful consequences of sin, and the more deeply I felt the greatness of the depravity into which these poor objects had been plunged by the devices of Satan, the more also I felt the love of Christ who has come to save and has died for sinners. As I began to speak, under the feeling sense of this redeeming love of Christ, their countenances began to alter : soon they hung down their heads ; their haughtiness and proud looks were brought low, and tears in abundance were seen to flow ; great was the brokenness of heart manifested on this occasion. I inquired of them if there were any other female prisoners in the place, and was told that several sick ones were upstairs. On going up, I was astonished beyond description at the mass of woe and misery I beheld. I found many very sick, lying on the bare floor or on some old straw, having very scanty covering over them, though it was quite cold ; and there were several children born in the prison among them almost naked.

" On leaving that abode of wretchedness and misery, I went to

H

Mildred's Court, to my much valued friend, Elizabeth J. Fry, to whom I described, out of the fulness of my heart, what I had just beheld, stating also that something must be done immediately for those poor suffering children. The appeal to such a pious and sensible mind as dear Elizabeth possesses, was not in vain. She immediately sent for several pieces of flannel, and had speedily collected a number of our young women Friends, who went to work with such diligence, that on the very next day she repaired to the prison with a bundle of made-up garments for the naked children. What she then saw of the wretchedness of that prison induced her to devise some plan towards the amelioration of the condition of those poor women, and, if possible, the reform of their morals, and instilling into their minds the principles and love of the Christian religion, &c. &c., as had been done, to some extent, on behalf of the boys."

In thus following Stephen Grèllet through his Christian labours among the haunts of vice and infamy, and the abodes of crime and misery in the British capital, in 1813, it is interesting to be able so distinctly to trace their connection with the origin of those systematic efforts for the amelioration of the condition of some of the most wretched of our fellow-men, the permanent effects of which are too well known and appreciated to need comment. In the memorable interview with Elizabeth Fry, as well as in many of his services in the metropolis, he " had, much to his comfort, the company of his beloved friend, William Forster; " and what passed at Mildred's Court first prompted Elizabeth Fry to those " visits to Newgate accompanied only by Anna Buxton" (afterwards the wife of W. F.), out of which ultimately arose that persevering devotedness to the temporal and eternal interest of the poor prisoners and outcasts, which has been so full of blessing to thousands, in various parts of the world. S. G. then proceeds :—

" I afterwards visited all the other prisons in London, and also the several poor-houses. Whilst during the day I pursued the above engagements in prisons, poor-houses, &c., I had in the evening, in some parts of London, several meetings of a character nearly resembling that I had in St. Martin's Lane, with the vicious and degraded portions of the community. Several of my very valuable friends accompanied me in these visits also."

Abounding, as Stephen Grellet thus did, in the work of the Lord, his labour was not in vain in Him, and on being permitted afterwards to see some of its results, he remarks :—

" Thus, though my labours have been attended with deep suffering and mental distress, I have cause, with reverent gratitude, to bless and praise the Lord, in that those humiliating and trying services have tended to the relief of many poor sufferers, and I hope also to reclaim many from the paths of vice and misery."

After these engagements Stephen Grellet visited the West of England. This journey occupied him about three months. On returning to London he writes :—

" I came back through Devonshire, Somersetshire, and Oxfordshire, to London, the middle of the Fifth Month, with a heart reverently prostrated before the Lord, who, both in that great city and out of it, amidst very laborious services in his Gospel, has, in such a merciful manner, helped and sustained me, the poorest of his servants. Surely there is great encouragement to trust in the Lord, in whom there is everlasting strength.

" Since I landed on these shores, I have travelled more than eight thousand miles by land, and have had two hundred meetings more than days in that space of time. I landed feeble in body, and yet my health has not prevented me a single day from prosecuting the Lord's work, and He has richly supplied all my wants."

CHAPTER XI.

SECOND VISIT TO EUROPE.

DEPARTURE FROM ENGLAND—ARRIVAL IN FRANCE—DETENTION AT MORLAIX—RELIGIOUS ENGAGEMENTS IN PARIS—VISIT TO LIMOGES—BRIVES—HIS MOTHER—MONTAUBAN—TOULOUSE—MONTPELLIER—CONGENIES, ETC.

NEARLY two years had been spent in paying a general visit to Friends and others, in Great Britain and Ireland, and the time had arrived when Stephen Grellet felt it to be his duty to prepare for carrying into effect his prospect of religious service on the continent of Europe. After more than forty-five years' enjoyment of the blessings of peace, during which many meliorating agencies of a civil, moral, and religious kind have been in operation, it is not easy to realise the contrast between 1860 and 1813, or fully to appreciate the characteristics of the earlier period. At that time there were neither railroads nor telegraphic wires; the freedom of *friendly* intercourse between the different States of Europe had long been interrupted; superstition and infidelity, vice and wickedness had spread to an alarming extent; religion was driven into seclusion, and with many, Christianity had become little more than an empty name; international feuds and jealousies had rendered the system of police and passport regulations exceedingly annoying, and painfully restrictive to individual liberty; travelling was difficult, and often dangerous. Though Napoleon had been compelled to retire from Russia, the French war was still raging with unabated, if not with increased fury, and great excitement prevailed abroad. To go forth, under such circumstances, and alone, "as an ambassador of peace to the nations, while the sword bereaved on every hand," was no small trial of faith and faithfulness. But S. G. knew Him in whom he had believed, and doubted not the safe guidance of his Spirit; he had counted the cost, and did not flinch in the day of trial; the sacrifice which he had "bound to the horns of the Altar," was not withdrawn.

The attendance of another Yearly Meeting in London, previous to entering upon such a service, was a matter of peculiar interest to him. After the conclusion of it he thus writes :—

"I now endeavoured to find out some way, whereby I might pass over to France ; the weight of the work the Lord has laid upon me in that land pressing heavily. Truly, in my measure, I can say, 'I have a baptism to be baptised with, and how am I straitened till it be accomplished!' O Lord! enable thy poor servant to glorify thy excellent name, into whatever suffering, or even death, thou mayest see meet that he should be introduced. My friends have kindly undertaken to make enquiries, or be on the watch, should any opportunity present for my getting over to the continent."

In the meantime, he was engaged in various religious services in and about the metropolis, visiting the sick and afflicted, and having solemn meetings with some of the most degraded classes. The efforts of Friends in London having been successful in making arrangements with the Lords of the Admiralty for a safe passage, S. G. left London on the 14th of Sixth Month, 1813. Their vessel, however, striking on a rock at the entrance of the river at Morlaix, although after great danger S. Grellet was permitted once more safely to reach his native country. At Morlaix he had some service —especially with individuals who had come for the celebration of a public fête, and testified against the superstitions of the Church of Rome. He also visited his fellow-passengers at the hospitals and other English prisoners. He proceeded to Paris on the 18th of Seventh Month.

On his arrival in Paris, he was pleased to meet his brother,

Peter de Grellet, with his wife and family; but in reference
to the object of his mission, " very dull prospects were before
him." The police regulations were very strict; he was
closely watched, and had to exercise great care in all his
movements. His religious services were, to a great extent,
of a private character. His dress and deportment naturally
led to inquiries, and these not unfrequently afforded opportunities for explaining the Christian principles of the Society
of Friends, and of drawing attention to the great Truths of
the Gospel upon which they are based. He was generally
treated with " great civility " ; and amidst all the discouragements which attended his solitary path, he could make the
grateful acknowledgment, " The radiant beam of faith, now
and then, opens something like a crevice through the thick
cloud which surrounds me. It is a great thing to walk by
faith, and not by sight, to *live by faith*." He proceeds :—

" Soon after arriving in the capital of France, I went to see
Pomier Rabaud and Goep, one a member of the Lutheran Church,
the other of the Reformed. I had brought letters for them from
England ; they are both men of piety, especially the last ; Rabaud's
father was eminently so ; during the great persecution against the
Protestants, he underwent great sufferings for his faithfulness to
the testimony of Jesus, and for many years continued a zealous
preacher to the persecuted Protestants, scattered over the mountains of the Cevennes. The constraining power of Gospel love
and the Spirit of Christ were what he felt to be his call to the
ministry, and his labours, with his piety and faithfulness, were
greatly blessed. I heard many bear testimony to this, when I
was on those mountains a few years since. Through the medium
of these two men, I was brought to an acquaintance with several
more of both denominations; also with some Roman Catholics,
who were dissatisfied with what they had discovered of popish
impositions and superstitions. I have had very interesting conferences with them, and also some private and more public
religious opportunities, when sometimes most of the Protestant
clergymen in Paris were present. On one of these occasions they
manifested an inclination to inquire into the various principles

maintained by the Society of Friends, particularly respecting divine worship, the Christian ministry, the 'ordinances,' faith in and salvation by our Lord Jesus Christ, &c. I was helped of the Lord to open these various subjects according to clear Scripture doctrine, so that Truth brought conviction to their minds, and constrained their assent. I told them, it is of the greatest importance that our hearts should be converted to the Truth and not our understanding merely convinced ; for if the Truth reaches no further than the understanding, it can never produce fruits unto eternal life.

"I have visited some of their Protestant schools, in which they begin to extend care towards the moral and religious education of the children. I had religious opportunities in some of them, when the children were brought into great tenderness. At the close of one of these, Goep appeared sensibly to feel the power of heavenly love that had been over us, and he earnestly desired, in a few broken expressions, that the children might treasure up, and often recur to such an unlooked-for extension of Divine favour to them. I have been particularly delighted in visiting their schools for girls, set up under the special care and oversight of females of rank, whose minds having been brought under religious concern on their own account, now feel the same for the rising generation.

"I have been visited also by a Jewess, the wife of a man of great wealth ; she has become convinced of the truths of Christianity, but does not see her way to unite with any form of worship, or ceremonies, or creeds, which do not harmonise with the pure and simple truths that she finds unfolded in the Holy Scriptures. She is in a very tender frame of mind, and appeared to have a heart open to understand and receive what I felt it my place to communicate to her.

"The fact of my being in Paris becoming known, induces many to come and see me. Some of these, now on a visit in Paris, reside in various parts of this country, and as I hand them books treating of the great truths of Christianity, in several languages, a door is opened for the knowledge of the Truth to become extensively diffused."

His stock of tracts becoming diminished, Stephen Grellet

reprinted some of them. On this account he had frequent intercourse with the Inspectors of the Press and the Commissary of Police. He says :—

" They could not reconcile our upholding the peaceable spirit that the religion of Christ inculcates with the warlike spirit that animates France and their rulers. I have endeavoured to answer all their questions, and also to proclaim the redeeming love, power, and mercy of the Lord Jesus Christ. I told them that I had nothing to do with politics ; my business as a servant of Jesus Christ—the King eternal and immortal, the Supreme Ruler in heaven and earth—was not to induce men to join this or that party, but to invite them all to come to Christ, so that through his Divine mercy they might, by his grace, become heirs of his kingdom, which stands in righteousness, peace, and joy in the Holy Ghost—a kingdom where no enmity prevails, and wars are not known ; 'Glory to God in the highest, on earth peace, and good-will towards men,' being the song of its inhabitants.

" Apprehending that the time of my departure from Paris was at hand, I endeavoured to make preparation for it, by obtaining the requisite passports, and by having also some private and more public religious opportunities, with those pious persons with whom I have become acquainted. I have been mournfully affected in finding so few Bibles among them, even among the Protestants ; but there is a prospect that an edition of the New Testament, put forth by Francis Leo, will soon be out of the press ; it is now being stereotyped. I have succeeded, however, through Soulier, an aged and pious Protestant with whom I became acquainted in the South of France a few years ago, to discover in an upper room, a parcel of Bibles in sheets, of Martin's edition, printed some years since, but which have remained neglected. I have obtained about two hundred of them, had them bound, and sent in separate parcels to various parts, through which I expect to travel on my way southward."

Leaving Paris he proceeded to Limoges, and the scenes of his earlier days : and having spent some time amongst his relatives in those parts, he extended his travels to the South of France, to revisit the little community who profess with Friends in Languedoc. He left Paris on the 15th of Eighth Month, 1813, and arrived at Limoges on the 20th. He was once more among his relatives and those pious persons whom he had visited before, respecting some of whom he says :—

" Though, in many respects, under the yoke of superstition, they nevertheless possess genuine piety, and love the Lord Jesus Christ in sincerity and truth.

" I had several religious opportunities in families, and some-times thirty or fifty persons collected together at private houses ; public meetings in a country like this could not be held, neither would the people understand what they are called together for. There are here some very tender spirits : they are Roman Catholics, and there is not perhaps one Protestant within fifty miles.

" The Mayor here, having been my companion in early life, manifests much kindness towards me, and gives me free admit-tance to the prisons, poor-houses, &c., which I have visited. I distributed in them some copies of the Scriptures, which were received with gratitude. In one of the prisons I had all the prisoners collected in the yard ; some of them, under the sensible feeling that the Redeemer's love was extended to them, were very tender in spirit, which they evinced by their tears ; visits like these, they said, they had never known nor heard of before."

Leaving the place of his nativity he reached Brives, the residence of his mother, late in the evening of the 29th of Eighth Month. He remarks :—

" I am much comforted in being permitted to be again with my beloved aged mother, who, since I was here, has, under the teachings of the grace of God, made further advances in vital Christianity ; the scales of superstition that were once upon her eyes have now fallen off ; her hope and confidence are no longer in the priests, or the Pope, but in the Lord Jesus Christ alone ; her delight also is to read the Scriptures, a copy of which (in French) I left with her on my previous visit. Among the pious persons I visited soon after my coming here were the nuns of the hospital, with whom I had such precious seasons of the

Lord's favour six years ago. Their aged and venerable Superior
continued in the greenness of the Divine life, manifesting
Christian meekness and humility. Some of the nuns accompanied me through the several wards of the hospital, where
various opportunities presented for religious communications,
under feelings of Gospel love : some of these were with the inmates of the several wards. collected together ; others were more
private, near their sick-beds. There was an entrance for the
word preached in the hearts of many of the poor sufferers ; I
left some Bibles for their perusal. On returning to the aged
Superior I found that, Cornelius-like, she wished that her
household should share with her in the consolations she hoped
for from my visit. She, therefore, had all the nuns collected ; we
were soon brought into solemn silence before the Lord, who
baptised us together by the one Spirit into the one body. Then
was my heart enlarged among them in the love of Christ, who
was preached to them as the only Saviour and the Bread of Life ;
they were directed to enter into the temple of their hearts,
sanctified by the Spirit, and there to offer up to God the
worship well-pleasing in his sight in spirit and in truth. That
baptism which constitutes the new creature was set before them,
and also the Bread of Life, on which the new-born child of God
lives. As he is not born of man, nor of the will of man, but of
God, so none of the doings or workings of man, can minister
living bread to him but Christ alone, even through faith in His
name. The next day a nun from another religious order, who
sometimes visited my mother, accompanied me to some of the
prisons, which she attends once every week. At the close of two
of the religious opportunities I had during that visit, and which
were peculiarly solemn, to the contriting of many of the prisoners,
that nun, under much feeling, entreated them to lay up in their
hearts this visitation of Christ's love to them, who was reveal-
ing himself to seek and to save such as are lost. There was
something particularly pleasing to my mind thus to hear a nun
as my co-worker directing sinners to Christ as the only hope of
salvation.

"Shortly after this I received a message from the nuns stating
that one of their priests, on coming to the hospital, had seen the
copies of the Scriptures I had left with them, and had manifested

great displeasure, finding fault with them for having received them, and had taken them away; 'but,' said the nuns, 'he has not seen the other books and tracts you have given us, and we shall take great care to keep them out of his sight.'"

His memoranda proceed :—

" I left Brives the 7th of Ninth Month for Toulouse, stopping on my way to visit some piously-inclined persons at Cassades, Cahors and Montauban. At the last place I was much distressed on finding to what an extent the principles of infidelity have prevailed in the Protestant college there ; several of the principal professors openly teach and preach doctrines repugnant to Christianity ; so that popish superstition on the one hand, and infidelity on the other, threaten to destroy all sense of true religion. There are a few, nevertheless, preserved even in this Sardis, to whom the name of Jesus is precious. In the college itself, . . Bonard, one of the professors, with whom I had been acquainted on my preceding visit to France, testifies boldly that Jesus is the Christ, and that there is no salvation by any other name than his. There are also a few pious individuals who resort to Him, and who show, by their life and conversation, that there is a manifest difference between those who know, love, and endeavour to serve the Lord Jesus Christ, and those who love and serve Him not.

" I came to Toulouse on the 10th, and, amidst very deep conflicts, I was comforted amongst a few precious spirits, awakened children of the Lord. It is beyond comprehension how man can be capable of giving way to such an excess of depravity, mirth and folly amidst so much suffering and distress, as there is publicly exhibited in this city. It was but a few days since, that, after a battle between the English and French armies, such a number of wounded soldiers were brought in, that the streets were strewed with them, till places to remove them to were prepared : and so numerous were the amputations that, in several parts of the city, piles of legs and arms, like heaps of wood, were to be seen ; nevertheless, in the sight of all this, there are public diversions, and great wantonness ! How terrible is the scourge of war ! What misery and sin are annexed to it ! My soul is exceedingly sorrowful, my eyes and ears also deeply affect my heart.

"The 12th of the month I came to Alby; this place was formerly inhabited by Protestants who suffered so greatly during their severe persecution that it appears as if they had been totally destroyed; now popish darkness and irreligion seem to have an undisturbed reign. I felt much distress in that place, from which I proceeded to Rodez, where I remained some days. I again found there a little door opened for religious intercourse with some Roman Catholics of tender and pious spirits, acquainted with vital Christianity. Here, also, I visited the prisons and the hospital, in all which I found individuals who had been softened under their afflictions, and who were thus prepared to hear of Jesus the Saviour of penitent sinners, and the comforter of the afflicted who flee to Him for consolation; great brokenness of heart, accompanied with many tears, was manifested by many of these poor sufferers, at the several meetings I had among them. In the prisons I had also the company of some other persons, who appeared to partake of the visitations of the dear Redeemer's love, and the offers of his mercy, that were graciously extended. In the hospital, several of the nuns accompanied me; they appeared to feel great interest in my religious movements in the place, having, of their own accord, collected together those of the inmates who were able in some of the wards. It was remarkable to behold the silence and solemnity prevailing on such occasions among persons totally unacquainted with our religious Society, and our views and practices connected with the holding of our meetings for divine worship. I had also a precious season among the nuns; I am persuaded that many of them are very near the kingdom of God, and they might become bright and shining ornaments to the Church of Christ were it not for the ascendancy that the priests, their blind guides, have obtained over them."

At Rodez he had much satisfaction in being with his brothers Peter and Joseph. In a letter to a Friend from this place he remarks:—

"I requested a religious opportunity with my brothers and their families, and my mother and uncle, which was readily granted. The Lord has very mercifully owned us together. My dear connections have never been more precious to me, and I believe the Truth has never been more endeared to them."

Leaving Rodez at ten o'clock in the evening of the 20th, he travelled day and night over a mountainous and very rough country, and reached Montpellier on the 23rd of Ninth Month. Resuming his memoranda, he says :—

" It was a trying parting from my dear mother ; it may prove a final one. I parted from her with a grateful heart, believing that she has received the Truth in the love of it, and that all her comfort is in walking in it, though she may continue in the observance of some externals.

" At Montpellier I found my dear friend, Louis Majolier, waiting for me. He had come from Congenies to meet me, and began to be under some discouragement at my non-appearance ; but our meeting at last was grateful to us both. Some of the pious families I am acquainted with at this place I found under heavy affliction on account of the death of their sons in the army ; and now, others of their children are being marched off also to the place of slaughter, or perhaps worse—to the sink of vice and immorality. Our meeting, both in private and collectively in a religious capacity, was solemn. The Lord is near and very gracious to the contrite in heart and the broken spirited ones.

" Accompanied by my beloved friend, Louis Majolier, I came to his hospitable house at Congenies on the 25th. The next day being First-day, I had two meetings among them, which were numerously attended : Friends and others had some expectation that I should be with them that day, and on that account they had come to Congenies from ten different towns or villages many miles distant. The overshadowing of the Father's love, and the melting influence of his Divine Spirit, were felt in such a powerful manner that the whole assembly, even the children, were broken into tears.

" Louis Majolier accompanied me after this towards the Cevennes, having two, and sometimes three meetings a day on our way thereto, and some of them were very mercifully owned by the Lord's presence. To one of the meetings in the mountains the people came from miles distant ; the Mayor and the chief magistrates were among the number present, as well as the principal inhabitants. The testimony of Truth appeared to be received with gladness, and the Gospel, like a refreshing shower upon the tender grass, distilled down among them. After meeting, many of their old people, bathed in tears, taking me in their arms, desired that the Lord's blessing might rest upon me, and upon the labour of love bestowed that day upon them. The inhabitants of these mountains are generally Protestants.

" At St. Hypolite, where six years ago I had a memorable meeting, I had now another highly-favoured one ; the Commissary of Police, who had been so rude before, now treated me with all kindness and civility. He took upon himself to have a place prepared for a meeting that I appointed ; he made choice of a very spacious, convenient building, had it properly seated, and during the meeting he took his seat by me. The place was crowded with Protestants and Papists. Though nearly all unacquainted with our religious Society, great silence and solemnity prevailed over that numerous company from the first of our coming together, and it proved to be a season of peculiar visitation from the Lord, by the extension of his love towards the people ; many of them appeared to be sensible of it. O that fruits may be brought forth to the Lord's praise and glory ! At the close of the meeting, an old popish priest, residing in that town, came to me and expressed his gratitude for the favour and mercy that the Lord had granted us that day, and added, 'that since the Lord Jesus Christ had thus chosen me for his instrument to preach his glorious Gospel of life and salvation, I should go and proclaim it throughout all their towns and villages, seeing what great good may be done thereby.'

" I stated in a few words what the duty of a servant of the Lord is—that he is not to direct his own steps, but in simplicity and faithfulness to go only where the Lord sends him, and to speak that only which he is commissioned to do. To which the old man with tenderness assented.

" I returned to Congenies the 5th of Tenth Month, and on the 9th I went to St. Gilles on foot. I found those professing with us at that place in a low state, but on the 12th I had a satisfactory meeting with them. I had appointed that evening a meeting at Nismes ; notice of it was sent there by a pious Moravian, named Jalabert Blanc, who also undertook to have proper information of it given to pious persons in that city. As I could not procure any conveyance to take me to Nismes, I had to perform that journey

also on foot, which prevented me from getting there as early as
had been anticipated ; finding on my arrival that the hour at
which the meeting was appointed had come, I went directly to
the house. About eighty persons, some of them Moravians, soon
collected ; silence and great solemnity prevailed. The blessed
Redeemer rendered us partakers of his gracious promise to the
two or three gathered together in his name. Whilst we were thus
assembled, two officers of the Gendarmerie (police) with some
soldiers came in and took their seats ; the meeting continued
some time in solemn silence before the Lord ; many present were
worshipping the Father of Spirits in spirit and in truth. Some of
them evinced that they were prepared to offer unto the Lord the
sacrifices of a broken heart, and of a contrite spirit. He gave me
a solemn testimony to bear to his blessed Truth, and to the great
love of God to us through his beloved Son Jesus Christ, our
blessed Redeemer. Towards the close of the meeting solemn
prayers and supplications were offered up on bended knees to the
Lord God and the Lamb, through the Spirit. The whole assembly
were broken into tears, and with the most tender affection, took
their leave of me. The officers of police came with the others to
shake hands with me, having also tears in their eyes. After I
had come into the street they followed me, and one of them, who
was the lieutenant of the gendarmes, drew very politely towards
me, and after making several apologies, told me they had been
sent by the Prefect of the Department to apprehend me, and had
orders to bring me before him. They stated that they had been
in search of me for some days—had been as far as the Cevennes,
but that I was gone from the several places I had been at before
their arrival there ; at last, having heard that I was at St. Gilles,
they had rode all night to meet me there, and had been much disappointed on finding I had left that place also ; they hoped to
have overtaken me on the road, but being again disappointed,
were going to make their report ; when, hearing of the meeting,
they thought they might there hear of or perhaps find me. Now
they could bless the Lord for having permitted them to attend
such a meeting, and so sensibly to feel the visitation of his redeeming love, adding how trying it was therefore to them to be
under the necessity of taking me to the Prefect. I encouraged
them to do their duty, and said that I was ready to follow them

immediately. They were somewhat reluctant to proceed before giving me an opportunity of taking some refreshment, for they saw how exhausted I was after the exercise of such a meeting, and the fatigue I had endured from walking all the way from St. Gilles, after a meeting there ; but as it was then past nine o'clock it was thought best not to put off going to the Prefect. He, at first, gave me a rough reception, because of the many and large meetings he had been informed I had had through the country, and threatened what should be done to me, but that for the present I must go to prison, and wait till he could send to Paris a statement of the whole case. I told him that the Minister of Police was not ignorant of those meetings, for I had given him in Paris a full statement of the nature of my religious engagements in other places where I had been, and what I proposed to do as I travelled through the nation, &c. The Prefect, after a while, took the officer aside to inquire of him what had passed in the meeting. I heard the officer give him a pretty accurate short statement of it, concluding with these words, ' I have never heard any one speak in such a manner before ; the whole assembly was melted into tears.' After further consultation, I was told that I might go for the night to my hotel, but must return next morning at nine o'clock. It was pretty late by that time, but though spent in body, my spirit was refreshed of the Lord ; the joys of whose presence, wherein there is life, had been in a gracious manner dispensed to me that day, and I felt great peace in resigning myself to his will, whatever He might permit to be done unto me. I went to the Prefect the next morning at the time desired. I was now received with more civility ; many inquiries were even made with apparent interest into the nature of the Christian testimonies of our religious Society, and of my object in having such meetings, ' to which,' he said, ' the people are flocking in such crowds.' On finally parting, he manifested good will towards me."

Having thus narrowly escaped the walls of a prison at Nismes, S. G. took a short journey to Montpellier, and had several religious interviews with pious individuals and families there, " the Lord refreshing them together." From this little digression he returned to Congenies, to mingle

once more in Christian sympathy and fellowship with those
of his own religious profession in that neighbourhood,
before leaving the South of France to pursue his mission
elsewhere. His heart had been again enlarged among them
in the love of the Gospel, and he had laboured abundantly,
both publicly and from house to house, to establish them in
the Truth as it is in Jesus, and " to set in order the things
that were wanting." He was now about to take his final
leave of them. The day before his departure " Friends
from different parts met together," and after a meeting for
divine worship in the morning, an interesting conference on
the affairs of their little community in the afternoon, " their
hearts overflowed with gratitude towards their Heavenly
Father, thus mindful of them." " Mine also," he remarks,
" has overflowed, in that the Lord has given us proofs that
He has not forsaken that people—that He has yet a seed
among them, which He cherishes and visits." On the 18th
of Tenth Month, he remarks :—

"This morning I have taken a solemn farewell of Friends who
have come generally to Majolier's. The Lord's power has broken
in upon us in a remarkable manner. A most solemn silence
covered us. Truly the spirit of prayer and thanksgiving was
upon us. It is indeed the end that crowns all. I had at last
to tear myself from the arms of these dear friends, some of them
following us even to Nismes."

CHAPTER XII.

SECOND VISIT TO EUROPE.

MARSEILLES—NICE—GENOA—TURIN—GENEVA—LAUSANNE—BERNE—ZURICH—ST. GALLEN.

QUITTING Languedoc and the Cevennes, Stephen Grellet went to Marseilles, with the prospect of going to Italy ; and he was now brought into great conflict in looking towards the accomplishment of this service. It was a time of war ; he was alone ; the roads were much infested with robbers ; and he was not easy to join the caravans of ordinary travellers, accompanied by armed men. But " offering up his life and all to the Lord," he was afresh animated to put his trust in Him, and to be faithful in his service. His " path of religious duty appeared clear towards Italy," but he felt restrained from taking the accustomed route through Mont Cenis, &c. Without going a long distance round, there was no other course, except a very difficult one over precipitous mountains, by way of Nice.* " After deep conflict, and earnestly praying to the Lord for direction," he believed it right to choose the latter apparently impassable road, " assured that the Lord could carry him through all, he reverently bowed before Him, and, trusting in his Divine guidance," he left Marseilles on the 30th of Tenth Month, and reached Nice in safety. He writes :—

" At this place my distress has been great. My heart is deeply affected by all I hear and see. I do not know when I have seen so many Romish priests together as here, or so much levity as is exhibited by that class of men. They have been celebrating

---

* The Corniche Road was not then made.

' The Feast of the Dead,' and truly they appear dead to God and his truth. On the other hand, I hear of the numerous bands of brigands that frequent the road I am going to travel. But, surely, the Lord is a refuge and strength in time of trouble ! Blessed be his holy name ! I have found Him so again at this time. My faith in his gracious promise, that through fire and water He would be with me, has been renewed, and therein strength has been given again to commit myself and my all to Him.

" The first place I came to was Mentone, a very beautiful little town at the foot of the Alps, whose summits are covered with perpetual snow. The narrow valley in which the town lies is by the side of the Mediterranean Sea.

" The heat of the weather would be unbearable, were it not that the air is very pleasantly tempered by the ice and snow above. The orange trees are abundant in that valley ; they grow to the size of our apple trees, and are planted like our orchards ; they are continually blossoming and bearing fruit.

" I had a letter of introduction given me by Kothen, at Marseilles, for Maurice Berea, a friend of his, a pious Roman Catholic, who resides at his country-seat, near the town. I went to see him, and met at his house several persons who, like him and his wife, are piously-minded. To be in company with such, especially after what I had suffered at Nice, on account of the gross darkness and irreligion, was truly refreshing to my spirit ; I felt free to accept the pressing invitation to tarry the night with them. In the evening, the whole family being collected together, we had an opportunity for religious retirement, and for the worship of God. He condescended to open the spring of the ministry of his Gospel among us, to our mutual refreshment and edification, and the contriting of our hearts before Him. There was present a popish priest, an old Dominican friar, who appeared astonished at what he heard and saw, but he did not attempt to show any opposition. The next morning M. Berea accompanied me back to the town. He is in the meridian of life, and a man of bright parts ; but from a sense of religious duty he has withdrawn from the world's pursuits, to live in retirement in this sequestered but beautiful and fertile spot, covered with vineyards, olive, lemon, orange, almond, fig and other trees ; the hedges lined with pomegranates, myrtle, rose, green-aloes, &c."

"I now proceeded toward Genoa, through Savona. The Lord was pleased to bring me safely through that journey, notwith-standing the dangers and difficulties attending it ; neither did I meet any of the robbers so 'much talked of, and though I had very coarse accommodation, I generally met with civility from the people. I found that the road, as it had been described, lay over high rocky mountains, by the side of great precipices, and so narrow that a mis-step of the mule would have precipitated us to a great depth. Sometimes even that narrow path was covered with rolling stones, and so steep that it was like ascending or descend-ing a staircase. I was favoured to pass all this without injury, though once or twice my mule stopped short, refusing to go for-ward, till my guide, who had kept behind, coming in sight, had only to speak and the mule went on.

"The scenery before me was frequently very grand, so that with admiration I could not help crying out, 'Great and wonderful are Thy works, Lord God Almighty,' &c. Surely his works do praise Him. A project is being carried out to render this road even superior to the one through Mont Cenis ; should they complete it, it will be one of the finest roads in Europe.

"Soon after my arrival at Genoa, I became acquainted with the Swedish Consul, a pious man ; he introduced me to several others like-minded with himself; among those he brought to my lodgings to see me was an Italian, to whom the Consul had given the perusal of the short account of our Christian principles that I had presented to him, with other books of a religious kind. He was so delighted to find in that tract sentiments so in accordance with the convictions made on his own mind, by the secret but powerful operations of the Divine Spirit, that he came to me with a very full heart, rejoicing that there were others convinced of the same Gospel truths. We had a very affecting and interesting time together, the Consul also being present.

"The way was now opened for my having several small meet-ings, composed of from fifty to sixty persons, Protestants and Papists, generally of pious, seeking minds, so that the Lord's baptising power, and the comforts of his Divine Spirit, endeared us to one another, and refreshed us together in his presence. I had also a precious meeting with some of the Waldenses, who have retired from the valleys of Piedmont, and reside here ; there are bout one hundred.

"Some of these meetings were held at my hotel, the owner of which, being himself a pious man, and one of the Waldenses, the people were more free both to attend the meeting and to see me in private.

"During my tarriance at Genoa, I was introduced into very close exercise of mind and trial of faith. Deep had been my concern on account of various parts of Italy—Rome, Naples, &c.—places that I had felt for in years past, with an apprehension that I should be required to visit them in Gospel love. I thought that the time had come for me to engage in that service, especially as I was then in Italy. Finding, however, that it would be impracticable to go by land to Rome, on account of the numerous bands of robbers that attacked travellers even when escorted by large companies of soldiers, I concluded to try to go there by sea, by way of Leghorn. As I was going to engage my passage for that port, my mind was introduced into unutterable distress—gross darkness seemed to be before me, whilst a bright stream of light was behind; I stood still for a while, and found I could not go forward. I returned to my lodgings, and in my chamber poured forth my soul unto the Lord, entreating Him to direct me aright. He knew it was in obedience to his will that I had come to these nations, and that to his Divine guidance and almighty protection I had wholly committed myself and my all. He very graciously condescended to be near to me in my distress, and to hear the voice of my supplication. He gave me to see, and strongly to feel, that to Rome, Naples, &c., I should indeed go; that I had baptisms there to be baptised with, but that the time for it had not yet come, and the language of the Spirit was to proceed with all speed for Geneva and Switzerland. My soul was greatly humbled and tendered before the Lord, who thus condescended to instruct his poor servant, and to direct him in the way in which He would have him go. I remembered with awful reverence and gratitude the gracious promise made me, before I left America, when, contemplating the extent and magnitude of the Lord's work to which I was called, my soul was dismayed : 'I will teach thee and instruct thee in the way in which thou goest, I will guide thee with mine eye.' Now I saw how wonderfully my blessed Lord and Redeemer fulfilled his Divine word, and He also renewed a little faith in the safety of his guidance and almighty protection.

"I soon agreed with a person to take me in a carriage to Turin, for which I set off the next day, the 13th of the Eleventh Month.

"I arrived at Turin late in the evening of the 16th. I had letters from Genoa to some pious persons here, to whom I have paid, or from whom I have received, some interesting visits, and I have had several religious opportunities with them. One of these, Vassally, formerly a priest, is in an inquiring state of mind ; several others manifest much tenderness of spirit ; among them are two physicians and some professors of the university. Through the medium of these, many persons met me at my lodgings for religious intercourse, who made many inquiries respecting our Christian principles and doctrines. Several of these, like Vassally, have been priests, but their eyes having been opened to see the inconsistency of popish superstitions, they could no longer, with peace of mind, officiate in that capacity.

"On coming to Turin my mind was turned with a strong Gospel love towards the Vaudois in the valleys of Piedmont, not far distant. I did not know but that it might be a suitable time for me to discharge the debt of love which I have long felt I owed them ; but, seeking for the Lord's direction, my way has appeared totally closed. I have felt as if I must proceed with all speed for Geneva, the impulse on my mind was as if I must flee for my life ; surely the ways of the Lord are above our ways ! vain would it be for poor man to inquire why or wherefore it is so ? At least I found it so with me. Under the conviction that my only safety was in simple obedience to the Lord, I have said, 'Thy will be done,' and I have accordingly taken my passage in a carriage going to Geneva."

After travelling five days and nights, he arrived in that city, and remarks :—

"As I proceeded on my way, I felt that I was leaving a heavy weight behind me, and that a bright light shone on my way forward ; such peacefulness accompanied me that I did not feel any weariness from the journey ; the consolation of the Lord was so richly extended to me that my soul was poured forth in reverent gratitude before Him, surprised, nevertheless, in having

een thus driven to Genoa, and now brought to Geneva ; surely
he Lord has wise designs in all this, though I do not understand it."

It was soon manifest that there was, indeed, "a cause"
for this visit to the "city of Calvin, of Farel, and of Beza,"
and that it was peculiarly well-timed : Geneva had sadly
fallen from its ancestral faith, and proved how vain are
historic names, orthodox creeds, and Scriptural formularies
when the Spirit ceases to animate the lifeless form. The
clergy at that time were, with scarcely an exception, Socinian ;
and there is ground to believe that S. G.'s labours amongst
them were permanently blessed. He writes :—

"Soon after my arrival, I called on some individuals for whom
I had letters. Among these were Vaucher and Duby, both
professors of theology at the university here. After a pretty
long conference together, during which they appeared to take
great interest in the object of my thus travelling in these nations
in the love and service of the dear Redeemer, they made various
inquiries into the nature of our Christian profession, and told me
that that evening there was to be a general meeting of all
their clergy. After very serious consideration, I found it would
be my place to attend that meeting ; I felt it nevertheless a great
cross, being very sensible of my want of qualification as a man to
appear thus alone among so many wise and learned men and high
professors. The weight of exercise and distress, however, under
which I had been at Montauban, and other places, on account of
the principles of infidelity I found disseminated by some of
the clergy among the Protestants, together with a desire I had
often felt to have an opportunity to plead with them on this
account, came forcibly before me, and I thought that it might be
in part for this purpose that the Lord had brought me here with
such haste. About the time of their meeting, Vaucher and Duby,
accompanied by Picot, their President, came to wait upon me. I
found fifteen of their ministers collected together, with the three
Professors of Theology. I felt among them like a poor stripling,
but was favoured in calmness to have my mind stayed upon God.
They were informed of the invitation given me to sit with them

on this occasion; but I thought it proper to request them to proceed with the business for which they had met, as they would have done were I not present. They answered that they could meet at any time to transact their business, but that they might never have another opportunity of having me among them, and therefore desired to know if I had any objection to answer a few questions they felt disposed to ask me, not for disputation, but for information. I told them that I was willing to answer all their inquiries with Christian candour; indeed, I felt the love and power of the Redeemer to be over us; his gracious promise to his disciples that it should be given them what to say or to answer, when they should be brought before kings and rulers for his sake, was very sweetly and encouragingly brought to my remembrance. They inquired concerning the qualification requisite for a minister of the Gospel,—the nature of divine worship,—what renders a man a true member of the Church of Christ, of baptism and the supper; then passed on to perfection, election, reprobation, and dwelt very particularly on redemption and salvation by our Lord Jesus Christ. I endeavoured to answer them in as concise and clear a manner as the Lord enabled me to do on all these and some other very important subjects. Among the questions respecting the Divinity and Godhead of the Lord Jesus Christ, one of them said, 'If Christ is from eternity, why is He called the first-born of every creature?' This fully opened a door for me to testify to the Lord Jesus Christ in his various offices and attributes, being true God and true man also, who is from ever-lasting to everlasting. It also prepared my way to speak of my great distress at Montauban, and particularly to lay before them the great responsibility which rested upon them on account of the infidelity which was thus promulgated by men who had been sent there from the university. They heard all I had to say in answer to their various questions with becoming attention; seriousness and solemnity prevailing over us during the whole time that we continued together, upwards of three hours. At the conclusion they said: 'This has been to us a season of instruction and edification.'

"Thus has the Lord been pleased to help his poor servant, and to magnify the great and adorable name of Jesus, my Saviour.

"A wide field was now set before me for religious labours among serious individuals, both among the wealthy inhabitants of this city and those in humble life. I found several companies of these in the practice of meeting frequently together for religious edification. I had some very solemn and tendering seasons with them ; a number of these meetings were also held in the houses of some of the Protestant ministers. Among others I had several at Moulinié's and Demalleyer's. I was several times much comforted with Mary Ann Vernet and her family, where several more of that class met us ; some of these evince that they have learned in the school of Christ, and are well acquainted with his law, written in the heart.

" Eight of the ministers called at one time upon me, wishing to have further information on certain subjects, particularly the ministry, spiritual worship, baptism and the supper.

" My dear Master has given me much service among that class of men. After I had, in simplicity and sincerity, once more set before them the consequences of the baneful principles of Socinianism, several of them said they were almost persuaded ; I would they were altogether so. My dear Master has enabled me clearly to lay before them what is the dispensation of the Gospel. Blessed be the Lord for this renewed help of his Holy Spirit to testify of his Truth and power among the great and wise.

" During my tarriance here I have had a little unfolded to my view why the Lord has led me about in such a remarkable manner,—to deliver me from the bonds and snares that were devised against me. I now learnt that the Prefect of Nismes wrote to the Minister of Police at Paris respecting me, as he told me he should do. He received an order from him to have me arrested, and sent to Paris. In consequence he sent his gendarmes after me to Marseilles, expecting that I was still there ; but finding that I had left that place for Italy, they did not think I could have attempted to go there by that difficult road through which the Lord directed my steps, but that I must have followed the highway through Chambery and Mont Cenis ; and finding that I had not passed through Chambery, they reported to the Prefect that they could not discover where I had gone ; and again, why I have been prevented, in such a remarkable manner, in going towards Rome, or even among the Waldenses, and felt myself constrained to come here with such speed, is now explained as being a very merciful interposition of my blessed Master, under whose guidance I desire to be kept. The armies of Buonaparte have met with signal defeats in Germany, at Leipzic, and in several other places, so that the survivors of this once large army are hastily retiring, some over the Rhine to France ; and the army of the King of Naples to Italy, by way of the Tyrol, the Simplon, &c. ; so that I had hardly left Italy when they began to arrive, closely pursued by the Austrians. A delay in Italy of a ew days longer, might have shut me up there, as there is no possibility, at present, for anybody to pass away from their lines ; neither could I now escape from Chambery. Thus have I been delivered from twofold dangers,—from being carried to Paris as a prisoner for the testimony of Jesus, or shut up in some corner of Italy. Bless the Lord, O my soul ! trust for ever in the guidance of his Divine Spirit, who alone can and ought to direct thy steps, and all thy movements, especially in the service of the ministry of the Gospel, to which He has called thee."

More than a week had now been closely occupied with religious engagements in and about Geneva, and kindly furnished by his friends there with introductions to pious individuals in various parts of Switzerland and Germany, Stephen Grellet left that city. Proceeding by Lausanne to Berne he writes :—

"Berne, Twelfth Month 12th. On my arrival here, I found the inhabitants in much anxiety and distress ; parts of the army of Italy, in their retreat, have passed through this place, and left a contagious fever, which in many instances proves to be mortal. A number of persons attacked with it did not survive more than a day or two. I was several times much affected on being told in the morning of the decease of pious persons whom I had been with at meeting the preceding evening. Great seriousness prevailed, and our meetings were solemn baptising seasons, attended by many pious persons, rendered still more serious under the present aspect of things."

At this juncture he was himself taken ill with the prevailing epidemic, and for several days his recovery seemed doubtful. In reference to this he says :—

"Several pious persons I had become acquainted with came to my inn, very kindly, to minister to me. They thought there was but little prospect of my surviving the attack ; but my mind was preserved in great calmness, in resignation to the Divine will, feeling at the same time a renewed confirmation, that the service for which the Lord has sent me into Germany must be performed, and that I should be enabled to surmount all difficulties and dangers to which I might be exposed. That sickness was a season when my faith and confidence in the Lord were renewed. My strength soon returned, after the fever left me : and a door being set open before me for religious service, I was enabled, with diligence, to attend to it, both in private families and smaller or larger meetings. As many of these were held among persons who spoke the German language only, I was obliged to make use of an interpreter. In this service, L'Orsa, a pious Protestant minister, very kindly assisted me, translating for me from the French, which he did with much feeling, and at times with great tenderness of spirit.

"I left Berne on the 24th of Twelfth Month. As I was passing through the gates of the city, I met the advanced posts of the Austrians coming in, and the whole way to Zurich I found the Austrians on their march to France. They treated me with civility ; but finding the towns crowded with soldiers, and the inns occupied by them, I travelled night and day without stopping, except to take some refreshment. I have found here in Pestalozzi (a banker of Zurich) a very kind and faithful friend ; he has devoted much of his time, during my tarriance in this city, to going about with me, and acting as my interpreter both in families and in larger congregations ; as I have had several meetings and the mass of the people understand the German only.

"In the widow of the late Lavater, and in many branches of her family, I have found genuine piety. One of the daughters, married to George Gessner, one of their clergymen, has been largely taught in the school of Christ, and is well acquainted with the influences of the Holy Spirit. Gessner also is a man of piety, who sees beyond forms and shadows. I have had several precious religious opportunities with them and their numerous relatives ; their hearts were open to hear the testimony of Truth. Gessner has

also opened his house for more public religious meetings. This
has been the case also with Antistes Hess, an aged man, the head
of the clergy in this canton ; he is green in old age, and of a
very tender spirit. On one occasion, when, at his request, I had
given him an outline of the views entertained by our religious
Society, respecting the new birth, the Christian baptism, the bread
of life on which the renewed man feeds, on worship, ministry,
the Church of Christ, faith in our Lord Jesus Christ, his various
offices, redemption and salvation by Him, together with the gift
and operations of his Divine Spirit, he, with much tenderness,
expressed his gratitude in that the Lord has raised himself a
people among whom the standard of Truth is lifted up, and the
Gospel in its purity is proclaimed. ' I have read and diligently
studied the Scriptures,' said he, ' in Greek, Hebrew, and Latin,
but it is in the school of Christ only, through the teachings of
that Spirit by which alone the things of God can be known,
that I have learned that those things you have now set forth are
true.'

" This place was crowded with Austrian and Hungarian troops ;
many of the officers put up at the hotel where I had taken my
lodging. I felt it to be my duty to take my meals with them at
the public table ; I thought there was a service for the Lord in
it ; I soon found it was the case, for my dress, manners, and
language, attracted their attention, and drew forth their inquiries
into my religious principles, in respect to war, in an especial
manner. I was much gratified to find among that class of men,
the Hungarians particularly, so much sensibility as they manifested. ' Thankful should we be,' said some of them, ' were the
nations gathered into the peaceable spirit, which the Gospel of
Christ inspires, and your religious Society maintains ; we should
not then be, as we now are, marching to the slaughter to kill and
be killed.'

" During the time I stayed at Zurich, I continued to take my meals
in like manner : and as the troops daily went forward, and others
arrived, I had an opportunity to proclaim the Gospel of peace
and salvation to a considerable number of the military officers.
Their anxiety for information, and their attention to my answers
to their inquiries, were such that I frequently rose from the table
without having had time to eat more than a very few morsels.

"In some of the meetings I had, I was engaged to press upon the people to attend faithfully to the teachings of the Holy Spirit in their hearts; for it is the Spirit of Truth who not only brings the repenting sinner to Christ, the Saviour, but also 'leads into all Truth.' I also earnestly pressed upon them to repair often to the house of prayer, with faith and confidence in our Lord Jesus Christ, who has promised that 'whatsoever ye shall ask in my name, it shall be done unto you.' After one of these opportunities, Lavater, a physician, brother to the late Lavater, told me, 'I have good reason for being fully convinced of these great and important truths, that you have delivered. Once I did not believe in them, and even ridiculed them; but the Lord was pleased to convince me of their reality, in the following manner:—My son, my only son, was very ill; I had exerted all my medical skill upon him in vain, when in my distress I wandered out into the street, and seeing the people going to the church where my brother, Lavater, was to preach, I went also; he began with that very text that you have mentioned, "whatsoever ye shall ask in my name, *believing*, it shall be done unto you." He dwelt very particularly on the nature of prayer, in whose name, and to whom it is to be offered; he described also the efficacy of that faith, which is to be the clothing of the poor supplicants. I attended very closely to what my brother said, and I thought I would now try if it was indeed so; for my solicitude for the recovery of my son was great,—my prayer for it was earnest; I thought also that I believed the Lord Jesus had all power to heal him if He would. Now,' said he, 'in my folly I dared to limit the Almighty to three days, concluding that by this I should know that He was indeed a God hearing prayer, if my son was restored within that time. After such a daring act, all my skill, as a physician, seemed to be taken away from me. I went about looking at my watch, to see how the time passed, then at my son, whom I saw to be growing worse; but not a thought to minister anything to him arose. The three days had nearly passed away, when with an increase of anguish, and also a sense of the Lord's power, I cried out, "I believe, O Lord! that thou canst do all this for me, help thou my unbelief;" on which some of the most simple things presented to me, to administer to my son; so simple, that at any other time I should have scorned

them ; yet, believing it was of the Lord, I administered them,
and my son immediately recovered. Now,' said the doctor, 'I
felt fully convinced that the Lord heareth prayer, and that there
is an influence of the Spirit of God on the mind of man, for
I have felt it.' These are very nearly the words of the doctor.

" During my continuance at Zurich the seat of war was brought
so near, that the distant sound of heavy artillery could be heard,
both towards Basle, and on the other side of the lake. Very
mournfully was my spirit affected, in daily seeing so many of my
fellow-men marching to the field of battle.

" The armies of the Allies are passing through this land to
enter into France, so that I am now in the midst of them. Poor
France, where I have just proclaimed the glad tidings of God's
salvation, and the day of his vengeance also, is now going to be
the theatre of war—herself drinking of the cup of blood she has
so plentifully administered to the other nations."

On the 1st of First Month, 1814, Stephen Grellet left
Zurich, and proceeded to St. Gallen. At this place ended
his labours in the Helvetic Republic. He left it with deepened feelings of Christian interest in its inhabitants.

CHAPTER XIII.

Second Visit to Europe.

MUNICH — LANDSHUT — OETTINGEN — STUTGARD — FRANKFORT—
NEUWIED—BARMEN—MINDEN—BREMEN—RETURN TO ENGLAND.

From Switzerland Stephen Grellet passed over into Bavaria. That country was then in a very interesting state, as it regards the spread of vital religion. Towards the close of the last century, many persons had been quickened, under the influence of the Holy Spirit, to a deep and serious concern for the salvation of their souls ; and it was a well-known fact that there existed, in some parts of Germany, a multitude of Christians, of the Roman Catholic persuasion, who were distinguished from others of the same communion, by a profound acquaintance with, and a sincere attachment to, the fundamental doctrines of Christianity. Persons of this character were particularly numerous in Bavaria. A religious awakening had taken place, not only amongst the members of the different flocks, but amongst their pastors also—nearly forty priests were known to have been brought under its influence. It was there that, forty years ago, Feneberg and Winkelhofer had taught, and it was there that Sailer was still pursuing his useful labours ; whilst many priests of less note, once his pupils, were preaching the Truth ; which, though obliged to avoid much publicity, they desired to spread. From Bavaria sprang Lindel, Gossner, and Boos*—those three faithful witnesses, who were driven

---

* See a valuable memorial of Boos, translated from the *Archives du Christianisme.—Christian Observer*, September, 1827.

by persecution from place to place; and who, wherever they turned their steps, did not hesitate to proclaim that Gospel which had brought peace and salvation to their own souls. They were not proscribed for having taught any particular heresies; but for having declared, with much force and fulness, the fundamental truths of Christianity—the natural corruption of the heart of man, the impossibility of salvation by works, the need of the Spirit's influence, and the free grace obtained for sinners by the expiatory death of Jesus Christ.

Sailer continued at his post, in Landshut, surrounded by many difficulties; Gossner was preparing his translation of the New Testament for his Roman Catholic brethren, at Munich; and Boos, not long before his banishment, was still patiently enduring severe persecution, in the midst of "some thousands of spiritually-minded persons in his own parish in Austria," when Stephen Grellet visited those parts.

On leaving Switzerland, he says:—

"We crossed the Rhine at Rheineck, on my way to Munich. On getting into the diligence, I was agreeably surprised to meet with J. Graff, of Geneva. He was from home when I was in that city; but his wife, one of the pious individuals whom I had visited there, had written to him respecting me; and, recognising me by my dress, he at once saluted me with warm affection. Little did I think how providentially he had met with me, to render me particular services."

For want of a required visé to his passport, he was subjected in this journey to great difficulties with the police; and in all probability he would have been sent back to Berne, had he not in so remarkable a manner met with J. Graff. Through his kind offices he was allowed to proceed to Munich, simply on his undertaking to deliver himself up to the authorities immediately upon his arrival. He proceeds thus:—

"Matters thus settled, Graff left me with much affection, marvelling with me at our providential meeting, when he could

thus serve me. I presented myself to the Minister of Police as
soon as I arrived at Munich. At first he appeared somewhat
excited at my appearing before him with my hat on, but a very
few words of explanation sufficed. He treated me with courtesy,
and at once removed everything in the way on account of my
passports ; he became, moreover, a means of introducing me to
serious persons of the first rank there, among whom were several
of the Ministers of State, particularly the Minister of Finance ;
in whose palace I have had a very full opportunity, in a religious
meeting, to proclaim the blessed Truth. The meeting was attended by a pretty numerous company ; to some of them I might
perhaps seem like Paul at Athens, in the Areopagus ; but some
others were sober, and manifested religious sensibility.

"The Baron Pletten, Director-general of the Posts, has been
very attentive to me, accompanying me in a visit to some pious
persons, and being my interpreter also in several meetings among
Protestants and Roman Catholics. Some priests, among the
latter, having become convinced of many of the errors of Popery,
have withdrawn from that Church. There are about forty of
these in Bavaria I am told. Three in this place endured much
persecution, and two have been obliged to leave the district.
Gossner is the only one remaining at present, but there are a
number of Papists who join with him ; among these are several
nuns. I have found much spiritual-mindedness among these
people ; they appear very earnest in their desire to come to the
knowledge of the Truth, and to walk in it. The Lord's presence
and power have been in a contriting manner with us in some of
the meetings I have had with them. Persons like-minded, hearing of it, have come from fifteen to twenty miles distance.

" Gossner is engaged, under religious concern, in the translation
of the New Testament, which he thinks might be of much
service among many of the Papists, who are desirous to read the
sacred volume, but are prejudiced against the edition of Luther.
He has nearly completed his translation, but does not know
where he can obtain the means to print it. My mind being
introduced into deep feeling on the subject, I have put him in
a way to have an edition of six thousand copies executed,
which I hope may be ready for circulation in a few months.

" I have become acquainted with the Physician to the Crown

K

Prince, the son of the King, who, hearing of me through him, has sent me a request to visit him. I accordingly went to the palace, and found him in a tender spirit, and under religious concern for his soul. He proceeded to unfold the exercise of his mind, and whilst mentioning the deep distress in which he had been, the big tears dropped down his cheeks; 'Many a time,' said he, 'under strong convictions for my sins, I have formed resolutions to pursue a different course of life, but the very next temptation has overcome me; none of my resolutions prove sufficient to preserve me.' I directed him to the Lord Jesus Christ, as the only sure refuge and helper—the only Saviour—able to save to the uttermost all that come to Him, with a penitent heart and in faith. We parted under feelings of solemnity. The next day I received a letter from him: after alluding to the feelings that have attended him since I was with him, with a little faith that the Lord Jesus Christ might condescend to become his helper, he said that that evening he had been with the King his father, and that on speaking of me to him, he had expressed a desire to see me himself, and that accordingly he would expect me that forenoon, at eleven o'clock. The Prince requested me to stop a few moments with him, before I went into the King's apartment.

"Though I had felt some desire to have an interview with the King, particularly in reference to the severe persecution under which many of his subjects have suffered, because from conscientious motives they have abjured Popery, and the threatening of the Pope's nuncio that they would proceed to greater extremities against them, I had been much discouraged from making an attempt to see him, on account of the great obstacles which, as I was told, were in the way. But now, receiving an invitation from the King himself, I felt prepared to accept it. I went first to the Prince, as he requested. He told me that he wished to know what reception his father would give me, and therefore requested that I would see him again, before I left the palace. On my entering the King's apartment, I found he was alone, and waiting for me. He came towards me as I entered, having his head uncovered; I saw at once that he was not well pleased to see me with my hat on, but after a very few words had passed between us, his countenance brightened up. At first he had many inquiries to make relative to the object of my travelling, the nature of my religious engagements, and respecting several of our religious testimonies ; that against war, in an especial manner. He also wished to know the result of my observations in the visits I had made to their prisons. Having answered his inquiries, my way was open for introducing the subject of liberty of conscience, and the sufferings that had been inflicted on several of his subjects on that account. He very soon threw the blame on the Pope, his nuncio, and the bishops, &c. 'They are continually teasing me on that account,' said he ; 'I am tired of them, and will let them know it.' This very interesting topic led me to make some remarks of a religious character, under which the King's mind appeared to be impressed ; and at last, when I was about to withdraw, he put his arms round my neck, and bid me farewell. We had been together above an hour.

" The Prince was delighted at my account of the reception the King, his father, had given me. I do hope that the powerful convictions that he has received, and the impressions that, through the love of Christ, have been made upon him, will prove lasting.

" Among the visits made me by pious individuals, are those of two very interesting young men, the Baron Gumpenberg and the Prince Oettingen. They both give evidence, especially the young Prince, that the visitation of the Redeemer's love is very peculiarly towards them. The Prince is in a very tender state ; may the Lord bless the work that He has begun.

" 16th of First Month. I came to Landshut, my principal object being to visit Sailer, a very remarkable Roman Catholic priest, and valuable in the Lord's hands in extensively promoting the work of reformation from Popery. He is well known for his learning, but more especially for his great piety ; he is also a teacher in Theology,—has educated many young men for the priesthood, and has a number now under his care ; he has endeavoured, as he told me, to direct them especially to the school of Christ, and to the influences of the Divine Spirit, under whose teachings alone, as he stated, the things of God can be known. The fruits of his teaching appear, in that the greater number of those priests who have of late deserted Popery, received their education under his care. I found that he, like Gossner, has in his hands several books of Friends, which he said he often peruses.

" He accompanied me in visiting several persons spiritually-minded, like himself, some of whom joined us afterwards in a religious opportunity, which I had with the students at this university. Several priests also attended.

" 18th. Late in the afternoon I left for Braunau, in a sleigh with post-horses, the snow being deep and the weather very cold.

" I found Braunau crowded with the Austrian soldiers, on their march forward ; but my object in coming was chiefly to endeavour to find and to visit some of those pious persons who have become dissatisfied with their popish profession. I could not well reach their villages but by going on foot over the snow. The first village I aimed at was Kirchberg, the residence of Langenmeyer, one of those enlightened priests, who has endured much persecution ; and heavier trials appear impending, as they threaten to send him to Vienna. There are several others of the popish clergy in that neighbourhood like-minded with him. He told me of thirty-one, five of whom met us. Truly this is a seed of the Lord that I am called to visit in their distress, and to water from the spring that flows from his Divine presence. They have amongst them many persons to whom their labours of love have been blessed, and whom they are gathering to Christ as their only bishop, high-priest, and hope of salvation. They had them collected together, and the Lord gave us to feel the refreshings from his Divine presence. Langenmeyer was my interpreter of what the Lord gave me to communicate to them. Such were the consolations received of the Lord that day, that I was refreshed in body and mind, though I had travelled the whole of the night before, had close religious labours that day, and had walked about twelve miles."

Stephen Grellet then proceeded direct by Ratisbon to Nuremberg, and from thence to Oettingen, where, he says :—

" I had letters from Sailer to the President von Ruosch, and for the Princess Dowager of Oettingen. The President would not allow me to stay at an inn ; both he and his valuable family treated me with the kindest hospitality. I found in the palace my dear Master's presence, for to some of its inhabitants the Lord

Jesus is precious—they know him as a Saviour. Among these, besides the Princess Dowager, is her sister-in-law, the Princess Jeanette ; the Baron Braun also, and the Princess Amelia, wife of the young Prince. The latter is only eighteen years of age, but she manifests stability of character, and an advancement in religion beyond her years. With these, and several others, together with the pious family of President von Ruosch, I had such solemn and baptising religious opportunities, as reminded me feelingly of the interviews which William Penn relates to have had with the Princess Elizabeth and the Countess de Horne. It is surprising how way has been made for me among that company. I spent most of an afternoon with the Princess Jeanette and the Baron Braun, in serious conversation. I left the palace in peace."

Three weeks had now been spent in the midst of a body of Christians in Bavaria, who, in the bosom of the Roman Church, fully confessed, by their faith and practice, the grand fundamental principles of the Reformation. On renewing his labours amongst them, S. G. writes to a friend in England :—

" The fields in many parts I have visited are white unto harvest ; so that sometimes I have wished that I might have the life of Methuselah, or that the sun might never go down, that I might do my share of that great work which is to be done in these nations. There is a most precious seed in these parts, and in places where I have not actually visited it. O did our Society stand faithful, what a blessing they might become ! Many are ready to gather to the standard of Truth, from among all the various denominations and ranks. I have been with rich and poor, princes and princesses, Protestant ministers and Popish priests, all speaking but one language, not upholding forms and ceremonies, but Christ and his Spirit. I have visited various of those Romish priests in Bavaria of whom we had heard, and have found them to be spiritually-minded men. I am nearly united to some of them. A few have married, and have answered those who have come to visit them on that account, out of the Scriptures, and the practice of the primitive Church ; and they continue Romish priests still, much beloved by the people, among whom they exercise a good influence. Many of the people desire to have the Scriptures, but have it not yet in their power to obtain them. Some of their priests told me, that they believe it to be their duty to remain in their places for the sake of the people about them, and to help others to come into the same spirituality. I am not able to give them any other advice than closely and faithfully to follow Him who has begun a good work in them, and will lead them safely. They feel very precious to me, and I know they rejoice in the visit which Gospel love has led me to pay them. My life seems interwoven with theirs. Some think I am a man of deep learning, whilst my greatest science is to know nothing—nothing but Jesus Christ, and Him crucified. It is He who is mouth and wisdom, when my mouth is laid in the dust."

In Bavaria Stephen Grellet had met with much that interested him, and called forth his sympathy and solicitude. He found it no easy thing to part from those to whom he had become so closely united in the bonds of Christian fellowship ; but the time had come to enter upon new fields of labour ; and now entering the kingdom of Wurtemberg, he writes :—

" I arrived at Stutgard on the 28th of First Month, 1814, where I met with several persons prepared, by letters from their friends of Geneva, to see me ; and I had several solemn religious meetings with them ; much Christian simplicity appears among them.

" I paid several visits to the Countess Seckendorf and her daughter, in their affliction. The Count, who was Prime Minister to the King, died only a few days since. He was a man of great worth, and, above all, of much piety ; and such are his bereaved near relatives.

"I have found the greater openness here, in consequence of a time of recent excitement, which appears to have been blessed. Dan, one of their clergymen, a man of great piety, found it his duty to proclaim against public places of diversion, showing how contrary these are to the precepts of our holy religion. His preaching had an awakening influence on many, and particularly on some

in high life; at which others became so displeased, that a persecution against him soon followed. They succeeded in having him
removed from Stutgard, to an out of the way place, among a
rough, depraved people. This proceeding had led many more
sensibly to feel his worth, and now to endeavour with faithfulness to act according to the doctrines he preached among them.
How frequently do we see that the efforts of men to prevent the
Lord's work only tend to promote it; this appears to be the case
in this place and neighbourhood.

"I then proceeded to Tübingen, where reside several persons I
felt desirous to see; some of these are professors of the university. They are full believers in our Lord Jesus Christ, and feel
it to be their religious duty to maintain their faithful testimony,
against the introduction into that university of principles repugnant to Christianity, as has lamentably been effected in many
other places. I found them in a tender but tribulated state, and
endeavoured to encourage them to uprightness and faithfulness.

"On my way to Tübingen, I turned out of the road, about twelve
miles, to visit Dan, in his sequestered abode. I found him in affliction. One of his family had just died in the house, and his wife
was ill with the same fever. The dear man was preserved in much
calmness and Christian resignation, waiting to see what the Lord
would further do for the refinement of his soul. Since his coming
here, a great reformation has taken place among the people, in a
place where irreligion and vice prevailed. Thus has the Lord
overruled for good the evil that had been intended against this
his pious servant.

"I went a little further to Ocksingen, where I met with a few
disciples of the Lord Jesus. Our religious intercourse was truly
pleasant. My spirit is often contrited when meeting here and
there with the Lord's children, who, like a little salt, are sprinkled
over the land. If these are faithful in their several allotments,
they may be like lights in the world.

"I had for a length of time felt my mind strongly drawn towards
Carlsruhe, and now, believing the time had come to go there, I
proceeded towards it, visiting a few places on the way. I arrived
at Carlsruhe, after being two nights on the road. I had letters
for Jung Stilling, a man extensively known in Germany by his
writings; and for his daughter, much respected by many because

she puts in practice what her father describes in his writings. I was introduced by that family to several serious persons, of various ranks in life.

"Many Prussian soldiers are here. I find among some of their officers much religious sensibility. The Baron de Lachevalery is under a very precious visitation from the Lord ; it does not appear as if he could long continue in his military career ; he longs to be under a better standard ; he does, indeed, already feel that there is a banner over him which is love. Another is General Stockhorn ; he was in a very broken state of mind : strong are the convictions of the Spirit of Truth upon him. I told him it would not do to struggle against them any longer : and queried whether he did not feel that the time had come to take off his military garments, to put on the meekness and gentleness of Christ, and to exchange his warlike weapons for the Christian armour.

" I met here the Baroness Krudener ; she is a remarkable woman, and has been an instrument of real good among several young women of high rank, particularly here at court. They frequently meet with her for religious purposes, and this has enabled me to have several religious opportunities with them. One evening, when the meeting was silently gathering, two of them came softly to me, and said, 'Do not be disturbed if we withdraw before the meeting concludes, for this week is our turn, as maids of honour, at court ; but we wished to stay at the meeting as long as we could.' Several of these young women feel such conscientious scruples that, when performing duty at court, they cannot join in the pleasures or pastimes of it ; and, when not needed, they retire to read their Bibles, &c. Much of the service that has been laid upon me in these meetings, and with others in private also, has been to direct them to the teachings of the Lord's Spirit in their own hearts, telling them that, to hear the language of the Spirit, silence on our parts and cessation from our own actings is necessary ; we must 'hearken and hear what the Lord has to say unto us.' The Lord is nigh to them that wait upon Him.

"What I saw and heard of the horrors of the war greatly afflicted me. Several bloody engagements have taken place not far distant from this. I was not released from this place till the 9th of Second Month.

"On my way to Frankfort I was greatly distressed several times,

on meeting with waggons loaded with wounded soldiers, that they
were carrying away from the field of battle fought near the Rhine ;
the blood ran down from the waggons. And in some of the towns
through which I passed I saw the poor wounded ones remaining
a considerable time exposed, before provision for their reception
could be made.

" I found in Frankfort a considerable body of Russians and
Cossacks, Prussians and Austrians ; these were part of the troops
that fought at Leipsic, Dresden, &c. They had many of the French
prisoners with them, and I have seldom seen more distressed-look-
ing beings—so reduced by disease and famine. It was difficult in
Frankfort to obtain provisions sufficient for the multitude. The
description given me by some Prussian officers of the road through
which the French army retreated is most awful. It was strewed
with the dead or dying ; many died in consequence of malignant
fever that broke out among them ; and they were the means of
introducing the fever very extensively through the country.

"My mind has been deeply afflicted on account of the inhabitants of this city ; their sufferings have been great ; bloody battles
have been fought within their walls ; they have even now before
their eyes the sad consequences of them ; yet few appear to lay it
to heart. I find a very small company only, with whom I can
assimilate in religious fellowship ; with these few, however, the
Lord has given us the consolations of his presence.

" I left Frankfort with a heavy heart for Neuwied, where I
arrived the 16th instant. Very solemn have been my feelings on
the way, attended with reverent gratitude to the Lord, who has
called me from darkness to light, and from the service of the
prince of darkness to that of his glorious and blessed Gospel.
Twenty-three years ago I passed through these parts as a military
character, in the same spirit that actuates those I am now among,
who have been the means by which torrents of human blood have
mixed with the waters of the Rhine. It is true that by the
Lord's tender mercy I was preserved from the shedding of blood ;
but nevertheless, I abhor myself in the remembrance of the spirit
by which I was then animated. O that I might be an instrument
of inducing many now to come and range themselves under the
standard of the Prince of Peace ! May it not be in good measure
for such a kind of service that the Lord has sent me into these

nations at this time? Day by day I have opportunities, at the
inns particularly, to be with many officers, when the way is often
made for me to preach Christ to them, and to unfold the nature
of his kingdom, and the peaceableness of it. Though I have been
thus very frequently engaged, I have once only met with an
opposing spirit. It was at Frankfort from the military Governor,
saying what he would do if Friends were sent to him as soldiers,
and should refuse to fight.

"The Moravians have a large establishment in Neuwied : and
here is also a people who go by the name of Quakers. They
maintain many testimonies similar to Friends ; that against war,
among others, on which account some of them have suffered
greatly. Their meetings for worship are conducted much like
those of our Society. I have visited these persons individually,
and had some solemn meetings with them. Peculiar circumstances greatly tended to contrite our spirits together, and bring
us to feel the uncertainty of time. This is a place through which
numerous bodies of the French, in their retreat, have passed. By
their plunders they have left great desolation behind them ; and
by the seed of diseases which they have spread, the destruction
of human life is continued. Perhaps there is not a family here
which is not mourning over the death of near relatives. It very
frequently occurs that, in the morning, we hear of the illness or
death of some that were congregated with us in a meeting for
divine worship the evening before. Very solemn in these meetings is the contemplation that some of us, in a few hours more,
may be gathered into the Lord's presence. O that we may be
found prepared to join his redeemed ones !

"I had also a good meeting with the Mennonists. Their pastor,
a pious man, who had taken a kind and Christian care to have
notice of the meeting given, died that evening, before meeting
time ; several of his family were also taken ill. Loud was the
warning to endeavour to stand in readiness, having our lamps
trimmed and burning. Amidst so much calamity, many hearts
are made soft, and my way is open among every class. I have
visited the clergy among the Protestants, and also the Popish
priests, who have all received me with cordiality, and appeared
to take in good part the messages that, in the love of God, I had
to deliver to them.

" I make my home in the family of one of those called Quakers, or Inspirants, which gives me an opportunity of hearing much of that people, and of their history. I am persuaded that if they had been faithful in the maintenance of the testimonies committed by the Lord to their forefathers, they would have become a great and good people ; their light would have been bright, and many might have gathered to it.

" My host has given me an awful account of the sufferings that prevail over the country generally, in consequence of the war. He has heard of and knows several travellers who have been plundered and wounded ; others have been killed. He has been himself stripped nearly naked, and so abused, that after reaching his house, he was for some time in a helpless state, and he has not yet fully recovered.

" On leaving these dear people, they put me over the Rhine in a small boat, and I took the public carriage for Cologne ; I should otherwise have had to ride many miles to effect it. My mind was greatly saddened on the way to that city and in it, because of the multitude of soldiers, many of whom have come from the further ends of Russia—Calmucks, Tartars, Cossacks, &c. Desolation and misery are over the land, and yet rioting, drunkenness and all manner of wickedness prevail. Thus vice and misery are mixed closely together ; at the sight of it my soul is overwhelmed with anguish.

" From Cologne I went over the Rhine again, and soon fell in with the advanced guard of about thirty thousand of the Swedes, who are marching into France to join the Allied armies, against that nation. Great order and sobriety prevail among the Swedish army, neither do I hear any of the inhabitants, through whose country they pass, complain of their conduct.

" I arrived at Elberfeld the 21st of Second Month. Here, and in the neighbourhood, I met with many persons of tender minds. They received me with Christian affection. ' In our great distress, and many bereavements,' said they, ' the Lord has sent you to minister to us the consolations of his Gospel.' My spirit greatly rejoiced, at seasons, before the Lord, whilst among that people, in that He very compassionately condescended to his afflicted ones, and caused the stream of his consolations, and the refreshings from his Divine presence, to flow among us during the meetings that we had together. Truly they were meetings for worship ; for our spirits were very reverently prostrated before the Lord, at his sacred footstool. It was given me most tenderly to enter into feeling with these people, under the grievous sufferings they have endured by the hands of unrighteous and wicked men.

" Through this part of the country many of the French troops passed on their retreat : desolation and destruction marked their steps. Who that has seen the horrors of war, its accompanying cruelties and vices, can plead for it ? Or who that has only heard of the wickedness and misery that attend, but must bitterly deplore it ? From my observations I may say, that the sight of the bloody field of battle conveys but one part, and perhaps the smallest part, of the woes and miseries that attend this horrible scourge.

" At Barmen I had a solemn and baptising meeting. Under the influence of the one Spirit, we felt that which unites in the true fellowship. I had a pious female for my interpreter, and she did her part with much tenderness of spirit and Christian dignity.

" I set off for Pyrmont in the evening of the 24th, and was three nights and three days on the road, which I found very difficult to travel. I went part of the journey by a sleigh, but the glaze of ice formed on the road was such that it was very dangerous in some places ; for on both sides of the road were deep gullies, ravines or ditches, so that it was needful to keep on the middle of the road. At one time, whilst thus situated, I saw a body of horsemen coming towards me. They might be about six thousand men. My driver tried repeatedly to bring his sleigh to the side of the road, but at every attempt it seemed as if we should be precipitated on one side or the other. The General, who was with his officers at the head of the troop, seeing my dilemma, very kindly gave the order for the horsemen to open their ranks, and to pass on the right and left ; whilst he himself saluted me very civilly. I could not account for this marked attention, but possibly he might be one of those officers whom I had met at inns.

" After my arrival at Pyrmont, a place of much resort on account of its mineral waters, I felt myself much straitened for a while. I had expected that a Friend there, who is well acquainted both

with the French and English languages, would act as my interpreter, but he was not in a state of health to do it. Several
services laid heavily on my mind towards those professing with
our religious Society, and others. I poured forth my soul to
the Lord, who I knew could open a way for me, where all
seemed to be closed up. As I was going to their meeting, and
saw a considerable number of strangers drawing towards it, a
great exercise came upon me, for I did not see how help was to
come ; but I endeavoured to possess my soul in patience, to see
what the Lord would do for his great name. On entering the
house I was told that very probably a youth, who was pointed
out to me, who understood English well, could act as my interpreter, should I need one. He was only about sixteen years of
age, and on my asking him whether he thought he could undertake the office, he replied that ' he would do his best.'

" I was brought under great weight in that meeting, but I also
felt the Lord's power to arise into dominion, with a little faith
that, in attempting to communicate to the company present
what I thought to be the word of the Lord to them, all would
be well ; I rose on my feet, and the dear boy stood by my side,
and interpreted for me into German, as I went on, with all readiness. I felt much attached to him, and he became my faithful
and kind helper through all the meetings I had at Pyrmont and
the vicinity, and in my visits to the families of those under our
name in that district. He went with me to Minden, and several
places thereabouts, where some professing with us reside. I had
meetings with them and with the inhabitants also.

" I left Minden for Bremen on the 14th of Third Month, and
suffered much on that journey from the severity of the cold, and
the badness of the roads ; an open farm waggon was the only
carriage that could be used. At Bremen I found in the senator,
John Volmers, a truly pious and interesting man ; several
branches of his family are so also. He would not allow me to
stay in any other place than his house ; and during the whole
time of my being at Bremen he was my constant attendant—a
helper by his spirit, and of great assistance as an interpreter.

" Here I have found a considerable number of honest inquirers
after truth ; others also who I hope have come to the saving
knowledge of it. Some of these give very precious evidence

that the love of God is shed abroad in their hearts. I had satisfactory and solemn meetings in this place; some were numerously attended.

"Volmers is one of the eight senators by whom this little republic is governed; but his standing in life does not prevent his sitting very lowly at the footstool of Christ. He is in the daily practice of religious retirement, and a small company unite with him in a silent meeting for worship; for none of them have believed themselves called publicly to minister to others, but each receives his instruction and consolation from the Lord himself, the true and great minister. They told me of a sailor who resided sixty miles distant, in Friesland, who went to England a few years ago, and being at Yarmouth, happened one day to pass by the meeting-house of Friends, as they were going in. He felt inclined to enter also. The meeting was held in silence; but such were the strong convictions made by the Spirit and power of truth on his mind, that since his return home he has continued in the practice of silently sitting down to wait on the Lord, though entirely alone. Having heard of the pious people at Bremen, he had sometimes come to sit with them, and they wished I could see him. What was their surprise, when, that very evening, shortly after we had sat down together and were gathered into silence, they saw him coming in. He had just arrived, and came immediately to the house. I could not help noticing the great reverence with which he sat, and the brokenness of his spirit during the meeting. The little intercourse we had with one another afterwards furnished me with an evidence that he is a disciple of Jesus.

"Visiting one day a person of rank, called Lady Mettapost, where I expected to meet none else but her, I was surprised to see a large company of ladies of rank coming in; we sat in silence for some time, during which, and under the testimony to the truth given me to bear, the hearts of many of these were contrited. This lady is an unmarried young woman, possessing a large estate, and has a liberal hand in administering to the needy: she frequents the little meeting at senator Volmers'.

"I left Bremen at five p.m., the 20th, for Osnabrück. On my arrival there I felt for a while much discouraged, for I knew nobody in the place; I had not even the name of any one; but

I concluded here, as I have done in other places, to wait on the
Lord, and feel after his guidance, knowing that if He has any
service for me, He can open a way for it. After a while I thought
it proper for me to go out, and walk in the streets. , I had not
proceeded far when I was met by a serious, respectable-looking
man, who, after attentively looking at me, addressed me with the
inquiry if I did not belong to the Society of Friends, and if I
had known John Pemberton ? He then gave me a short and very
interesting account of his religious visit to that city. His name
is Mertens, and he is pastor of the Lutheran Church. He took
me to several pious persons, rich and poor, and soon after
accompanied me to a meeting which he had very quickly put in
a way to be collected. It was composed, like the few families he
had taken me to visit, of rich and poor, Protestants and Roman
Catholics ; but all of a class that love the Lord Jesus, who makes
no difference between Jews and Gentiles, bond and free. It was
an unexpected meeting and a very solemn one. The Lord owned
us graciously by his Divine presence."

S. G. now felt that the right time had come for his return
to England, and, proceeding by way of Holland, he again
reached in safety the British shores. He thus writes :—

" Feeling my mind released from the great weight of exercise
under which I have been for the people on the continent, my
soul has been prostrated very reverently before the Lord, who
has been my saving help and strength day by day : night after
night—the everlasting arms have been underneath to uphold and
preserve me. During this winter I have been more than forty
nights on the road, many times amidst robbers and murderers. I
have repeatedly been where contagious diseases prevailed to a
high degree, so that the mortality was great ; often also I have
made but one scanty meal a day ; but amidst all these things the
Lord has borne me up, and delivered me,—yea, rendered hard
things easy. My health is now as good or better than when I
landed in France more than nine months ago. And, above all,
the Lord, my great and blessed Master, who called me to this
service in these nations, has opened a way for me to find and visit
a portion of his seed, and to proclaim the glad tidings of his salvation to thousands of the people, both rich and poor. Bless the

Lord, therefore, O my soul, and forget not all his benefits! O
Lord! bless thou also those pious ones whom thou hast enabled
me to visit! . O, bless the work of thy hands everywhere!"

Thus he concludes the account of his second visit to the
continent of Europe. Numerous letters followed him from
Gessner, Vernet, Gautier, &c., of Geneva; Langalerie of
Lausanne'; Hess, Schlatter, &c., of St. Gallen; Baron Gumpenberg, Gossner, President von Ruosch, Baron Pletten, the
Princess Jeanette of Oettingen, &c. &c., in Bavaria. These,
with others, all bore testimony to the value of his religious
visit and services, and the spiritual comfort and instruction
derived from them. With some of these interesting characters he kept up a correspondence for many years afterwards.

NOTE.—Dr. Steinkopff, the well-known and devoted disciple of our
Lord and Saviour, whose earthly course was finished on the 29th of the
Fifth Month, 1859, gave the following testimony respecting Stephen
Grellet, on his return from the extended journey on the continent of
Europe: " He is, properly speaking, a French gentleman; he is a native
of France, but at the time of the Revolution went to America, where he
became enlightened amongst the Society of Friends. He is now in England on a religious visit; when I saw him two weeks ago he gave me
some account of his travels on the continent, and it was indeed astonish-
ing to me to hear how he had escaped danger in many parts. Previously
to his going this journey I had an interview with him, when he told me
his intended route: I said, 'It is one of the most difficult you could
have formed.' I knew that if he gained a passport at all to visit some
parts of France, that it would be from one of the most strict police
officers on the continent, and much I feared for the safety of this excellent man; but when he began to tell me what his religious views were,
and I saw how his heart was bound to his duty, I believed that the
Lord sent him, and that it was his work; I could not doubt of its accomplishment. So it has proved. Stephen Grellet is now safely returned to England; after having passed through armies of Cossacks,
from whom he met with little or no insult. The blessing of the Lord
was with him, and I doubt not made him instrumental of much good.
This gentleman has all the vivacity of a Frenchman with the solidity of
the English."

CHAPTER XIV.

Second Visit to Europe.

DUBLIN YEARLY MEETING—RELIGIOUS ENGAGEMENTS IN THE
IRISH CAPITAL—LONDON YEARLY MEETING—VARIOUS RELI-
GIOUS SERVICES IN ENGLAND—FLANDERS—VOYAGE HOME.

It was not long before the "Peace of Paris" that, after an
absence of a little more than nine months, Stephen Grellet
again set his foot on British ground. He landed at Harwich
on the 1st of Fourth Month, 1814, and thus resumes his
journal :—

"I was favoured with a short passage from Holland to this
place. My soul felt the overflowing of the love and mercy of
my blessed Redeemer ; very graciously indeed has He dealt with
me, one of the poorest and most unworthy of his servants.
Here some of my beloved friends · from Ipswich, Richard D.
Alexander and others, met me. Several friends from London,
hearing of my arrival, have also come. My spirit has been refreshed in being thus met by my beloved friends, after so many
months' separation from them. Here also I have received letters
from America, after having been long without any from my
dear wife."

After visiting Ipswich and Chelmsford, he writes :—

"7th. I reached Tottenham this morning, in time to attend
their meeting ; my soul was made joyful in the presence of God my
Saviour. He has done great things for his poor servant : thanksgiving and praises were ascribed to Him on bended knees.

"14th. I have been in London attending their several Monthly
Meetings, and the Meeting for Sufferings ; silent travail of spirit
in them has been mostly my service. I feel it a favour that after
such long and constant engagements in another nation, I am permitted now, for a while, in silence and retirement, to commune
with my own heart before God, and to have my strength a little

L

renewed. My dear friend William Allen is urgent that I should make my home with him at Plough Court, when I am in this city, and I accept his invitation. He is a friend beloved by me; one whose life is spent in acts of benevolence, but who is designed by our gracious Lord to occupy a station in his Church, beyond that of serving tables. I look upon him as one of the Lord's anointed."

After a short tarriance among his friends in and about London, he crossed over to Ireland. We make a few extracts from his memoranda :—

"Dublin, 20th of Fourth Month. Accompanied by my friend John Pim, I left London on the 16th, and arrived here this morning, where my dear friends Jonas Stott and wife have again given me a most kind reception.

"I was engaged in having meetings till the 23rd, when the Yearly Meeting began. Several of the sittings were attended with much solemnity, for the Lord owned us by his presence; the Gospel stream also flowed to the refreshing of many.

"After the close of the Yearly Meeting, I felt my mind brought under deep exercise for several classes of the inhabitants of the city of Dublin; my baptisms on their account were very similar to those I passed through, some time since, in London. My beloved friend, Wm. Forster, joined me again in several of my very arduous services. We had two large meetings with the soldiers, who are in garrison in the castle; there are pious men among them, who strongly reminded me of Cornelius the Centurion. We held also several meetings among the most degraded portion of the inhabitants. O what a mass of woe and misery have I beheld! how great is the prevalence of vice and depravity among this people! I felt at times as if my spirit, together with my outward man, would sink under the weight of distress. My beloved friend, Wm. Forster, was under the necessity to let me pursue this humiliating service alone; it was too much for his tender frame to endure. This engagement, however, was attended with some consolation; for in several of those abodes, which at first resembled a Sodom, I found a Lazarus, poor, full of sores like him, but rich in faith; in others I have been with a weeping Mary, sitting at the Lord's feet; and many also of the meetings, held among such as seemed to be of the outcasts of society, have been much more quiet than could have been expected, and tenderness of spirit appeared in some of them.

"These visits kept me closely engaged till the 12th of Fifth Month, when I felt released from Dublin."

The Yearly Meeting in London was now at hand, and, taking his departure from Dublin, he travelled day and night, and reached the city on First-day morning, the 15th of Fifth Month, a quarter of an hour only before meeting-time, and proceeded immediately to the meeting-house, in Gracechurch Street, where he says :—

"I found a large number of Friends, many from the various parts of the nation having already come in to attend this yearly solemnity. It has been a good meeting : the Lord's presence, which is the crown of the assemblies of his people, was with us. The same Divine favour was granted us at the meeting in Devonshire House, in the afternoon, which was likewise very large. This evening I feel refreshed in body and mind, though when I left Dublin I was much worn down. O how great is the Lord's goodness ; may not such a worm as I am, unworthy of the least of the Lord's mercies, exclaim with David, 'all my springs are in thee !'

"30th of Fifth Month. The Yearly Meeting closed this evening. Various subjects of great importance have been under the very solid deliberation of this body, and though one of them particularly was of a trying nature, being an appeal by which the fundamental principles of vital Christianity were assailed, and these had to be unfolded and defended : it proved, by the Lord's help and strength, one of the most instructive and solemn seasons that even the aged present had ever witnessed.*

"I was brought under deep exercise for suffering humanity, on account of the cruel scourge of war, such as I have so awfully beheld during my late engagement in France and Germany ; my soul was poured forth with supplication to the Lord, that He

---

* This has reference to the case of Thomas Foster, so graphically described by J. J. Gurney.—*See his Memoirs, by Joseph Bevan Braithwaite. Vol. I. p.* 98.

might open a door for me to plead with the kings and rulers of the nations, that if possible a return of such a calamity might be averted. Whilst I was bowed under this exercise, I heard that there was an expectation that the Emperor of Russia, the King of Prussia, and others, perhaps, now in Paris, would come to London. On this information I felt as if the prayer of my soul might be heard, and that an opportunity was about to be given to plead before some of these crowned heads for the kingdom of righteousness and peace of our Lord Jesus Christ, which, if not now embraced, might never be offered again. It appeared also that this was a subject in which the whole of our Society now collected together, as a Yearly Meeting, were deeply concerned ; and that a step so important to humanity and religion would have much greater weight, if felt and proceeded in as the concern of the collected body. Accordingly, at a suitable time, I opened my concern to the Yearly Meeting. It brought great weight over Friends ; they felt it a duty to embrace the opportunity to uphold the peaceable principles of the Gospel before the rulers of the nations ; and the Yearly Meeting directed the Meeting for Sufferings to act in it, as soon as way should open to carry into effect this concern of the Yearly Meeting.

"A few days after this, the Duchess of Oldenburg, sister of the Emperor Alexander, who had arrived in London, came to one of our meetings with several of her retinue ; also the young King of Wurtemberg. They sat in a very becoming and serious manner. We had a precious meeting, and the Duchess appeared to feel it to be so to her. During this Yearly Meeting I received very interesting letters from several of those pious persons with whom I mingled in Christian fellowship in Germany. It is very sweet to have evidence that Jesus continues to be precious to them, and that several little companies have continued to meet silently together to wait upon and worship the Lord, from whom only is their expectation. One of these letters is from Gossner, in Munich, who tells me that his translation of the New Testament is finished, and ready for the press. Several of my beloved friends here have entered into a liberal subscription to enable him to have a large edition printed, and the money requisite for the purpose is forwarded to Gossner accordingly. I believe this is a work that will be productive of much good, especially to those numerous Roman Catholics who appear disposed to inquire into the reality of religion. The more their priests endeavour to prevent them from reading the Scriptures, the more eager they are to possess them.

"17th of Sixth Month. Since the Yearly Meeting I have been closely engaged in having meetings in this great city and its environs. The Emperor of Russia and the King of Prussia have come to London, and the Meeting for Sufferings has met to endeavour to carry into effect the concern of the Yearly Meeting. Friends felt deeply on the occasion, and were united in the sentiment that addresses to the Emperor Alexander and the King of Prussia should be prepared ; for which service a committee was separated. Our meeting together on the occasion was interesting. Dear Joseph Gurney Bevan took so much interest in it, that after hearing the views of Friends respecting the subjects which the addresses should embrace, he, though now blind and in great feebleness of body, nevertheless undertook to prepare these documents.

" The addresses having been prepared, were approved of by the Meeting for Sufferings. My dear friend William Allen and myself were amongst those nominated to present them. We had to seek and wait for suitable opportunities, which were difficult to obtain, so many persons, from various motives, crowding about these sovereigns. The King of Prussia was the first to whom we had access. As he did not understand English, but French, I presented to him the address, dear William Allen being with me, together with two other Friends. He received us very civilly ; according to the custom on such occasions, he had seen a copy of the address before, and he was prepared with a suitable reply ; among other things he stated, that there were some under the name of Friends in his dominions, and that they were good men. His attention having been particularly directed to the great misery, vice, and destruction of human life attending war, so contrary to Christianity, he intimated his strong desire that the love and the peaceable spirit which the Gospel of Christ inspires might pervade the whole world, and lamented the sufferings that have attended the last few years.

" We could not find an opportunity to be with the Emperor Alexander till the 21st of this month ; dear William Allen and

another Friend went with me to the Pulteney Hotel, at the time
appointed by the Emperor. He came to meet us at the door
of his apartment, took us by the hand in a kind manner, and said
that for a length of time he had wished for an opportunity to be
with us. Through the Empress, who was at Baden when I was
at Carlsrühe last winter, he said that he had heard of me and
of my visit there. Then he inquired into several of our religious
testimonies, principles and practices, to which dear William
Allen answered in English, which language the Emperor speaks
well. Whilst William was engaged in stating the nature of our
Christian principles, the Emperor said several times, 'These are
my own sentiments also.' He was very particular in his
inquiries respecting our views and practices in connection with
divine worship, the ministry, the influence of the Divine Spirit,
&c. He made several very pertinent remarks on these various
subjects, particularly on prayer; respecting worship, he said, that
God, who knoweth our hearts, cannot be pleased with, nor be
acceptably worshipped by the observance of outward forms and
ceremonies, or the repetition of words which the wicked and the
hypocrite could use, though continuing in their sinful practices;
but that a worship in spirit and in truth is the most acceptable
to God, who is a Spirit, and that before Him our own spirit
must be reverently prostrated. Respecting prayer, he said, 'I
pray every day, not in a form of words, but as the Lord, by his
Spirit, convincing me of my wants, enables me to do.' We
entered fully on the subject of our testimony against war, to
which he fully assented. He made several other inquiries of
a religious character, which having been answered, silence ensued, during which, feeling my heart warmed by the love of
Christ towards him, and under a sense also of the peculiar temptations and trials to which his exalted station in the world subjected him, I addressed a few words to him; his heart appeared
sensibly and tenderly affected; with tears, he took hold of my
hand, which he held silently for a while, and then said, 'These,
your words, are a sweet cordial to my soul, they will long remain
engraven on my heart.' We furnished him with a number of
Friends' books, which he received with pleasure, and on our
taking leave of him, having been together upwards of an hour, he
took each of us by the hand, and said, 'I part from you as from

friends and brethren ; feelings which I hope will ever remain with me.'

"After we had left, the Grand Duchess, his sister, sent a request to us to furnish her with books like those we had presented to the Emperor, which was cheerfully complied with. Here I may say that the Emperor and his sister, accompanied by Count Lieven, his Ambassador, came to one of our meetings at Westminster Meeting-house ; William Allen, who knew of their intention through the Ambassador, accompanied them. It proved a good and solemn meeting. The Emperor and Grand Duchess, by their solemn countenances and religious tenderness, gave evidence that they felt it to be so to them.

" I felt my mind much relieved after this service with these crowned heads, particularly as I had a full opportunity to lay before them the enormities of war, and to direct their attention to the peaceable Spirit of Christ ; Alexander, especially, appeared deeply to feel the subject, and to be sincere in his desire for the promotion of harmony, love, and peace throughout the world ; he told us that his concern had been great that the several crowned heads might conclude to settle their differences by arbitration, and not by the sword."

After these interesting interviews Stephen Grellet went down to the North of England, and attended the Quarterly Meetings of York, Durham, Westmoreland, and Lancashire, holding many meetings by the way, and in returning to London. He then visited the meetings in Sussex, and came to Tottenham the 4th of Eighth Month, much worn in body and mind.

He was now again brought into close exercise on behalf of some of his " suffering fellow-men," and about this time he writes :—

" I had hoped for a release from further religious services in this land, and to be set at liberty by my blessed Master to retire from this long and arduous field of Gospel labour, and to return to America to my beloved family ; but the Lord, whose sole right it is to direct my steps, has given me to feel that my bonds

in this great city of London and in some other places are not
yet loosed. My soul has bowed very reverently before Him, to
whom I have made the surrender of myself and all, and I said,
' Here am I, Lord, do with me whatever thou pleasest, only
condescend to uphold me and preserve me from bringing any
reproach on thy blessed cause, and be pleased in the end,
through thy Divine and unmerited mercy in Christ Jesus my
blessed Redeemer and Saviour, to receive me to thyself.

"Feeling attracted towards such of the poor-houses in London
as I had not visited before, I felt peace in yielding to that
service of love towards this portion of my suffering fellow-men.
My beloved friend, Mary Stacey, joined me in these visits.
Our spirits were much affected in beholding so many of our
fellow-beings brought low under affliction and infirmities. The
Lord graciously condescended to be near to us, repeatedly fulfilling
the saying that, ' to the poor the Gospel is preached ;' giving us
also joyfully to believe that to more than a few of the poor of this
world, the blessing annexed to the poor in spirit doth belong.

" I also visited again the houses of refuge opened to the poor,
destitute, and once degraded females. Many tears are poured
out there by some of them in the remembrance of the past, and
songs of joy also are heard, for the unmerited love and mercy of
a gracious Redeemer.

" Whilst thus engaged in feeling for and labouring among
suffering humanity, my concern towards the members of our
own Society did not abate : but I attended all our meetings in
and about London. The more I have mixed with persons of
other religious denominations, the stronger has become my
attachment to our own Society and the Christian principles
which we maintain. I rejoice greatly indeed in having met with
individuals, yea, many, in the several nations where I have
travelled, who are very near and dear to me in spirit, and who,
I believe, love the Lord Jesus in sincerity ; but I met with no
people, who, as a religious body, maintain doctrines and testimonies, so scriptural and agreeable to vital Christianity, as
does the religious Society of Friends ; and my great concern
and frequent labour for this people are, that they may not only
believe in these principles and Divine Truths, but also walk
uprightly and with faithfulness in accordance therewith.

At the conclusion of these services in and about London, his attention was once more turned to some parts of the continent, and "believing that he had a little further debt of Gospel love to discharge in Flanders," he "resigned himself to the Lord's requirings," and crossed over to that country. On his visit he briefly remarks :—

"We proceeded pretty directly to Ghent, where I continued some days, but found very little opportunity for service among the people, except with a few individuals : the inhabitants are strongly entrenched in Popery. I found much greater openness in Brussels and Antwerp, where I had several public and private religious services. My soul was made sorrowful under the feeling of the sufferings of the people in these parts during the war. I have mingled my tears with my bread.

"Whilst at Brussels," he informs us, "I heard an interesting circumstance respecting the Emperor Alexander when he was in that place. He had taken a walk through the streets alone, in plain garments, so that his rank was not observable by his dress. A heavy rain came on, which induced him to look for shelter. A tailor's shop being near, he went in, and entering into conversation with the occupant, inquired about his family, and how he succeeded in business. The tailor, by his answers, manifested that he was a pious and conscientious man, but under pecuniary embarrassment, not being able to pay the rent of his house and shop. Alexander left him without making himself known ; but, to the great surprise of the tailor, a few days after, a person came to him, and handed him the title-deed of the house he lived in, made out in due form to him. It was not till some time after that he found that his benefactor was the Emperor of Russia, and the same unknown person who had taken shelter in his shop.

"We returned to England by way of Calais, and hearing that there was a Cartel ship at Dartmouth, nearly ready to sail for New York, I felt my way pretty clear to go by her. My mind being now released from continuing longer at present in this land, the sound of the trumpet of retreat appears to be clear, and O what a favour to have a perceptible evidence of the Lord's guidance, both in our going out and in our coming in.

"The necessary arrangements having been made, and liberty from the government being given to take my passage in the Cartel, called the *Jenny*, Captain Myers, I left London on the 19th of the month, being accompanied by my dear friends G. and M. Stacey.

"We reached Dartmouth on the 25th, where several friends from London and other parts have kindly come to meet me, to bid me once more farewell in the Lord ; and truly we may say, that it is in the fulness of the love of the Gospel, and the precious fellowship thereof, that we part one from another."

After taking a solemn leave of his beloved English friends, S. G. went on board about eight a.m., on the 29th of Tenth Month, and the vessel set sail from Dartmouth a few hours after. They had thirty cabin, and seventy-five steerage passengers. Though the former paid a very high price for their passage, they soon discovered that the captain had very insufficiently provided for their wants, and found it needful, before leaving port, at their joint expense, to lay in a good stock of additional provisions of various kinds of their own. They had " a boisterous, uncomfortable voyage across the the Atlantic ;" the vessel proved leaky ; their beds were often wet, and the cabin floor was sometimes several inches deep in water ; they were frequently exposed to much danger, and their prospects were often gloomy. " Yet the Lord," writes S. G., " condescended very graciously to keep my mind in confidence and peace, trusting in Him amidst our various difficulties and perils. The evidence He had given me that the ship should carry me safely, continued as an anchor to my soul, even when my fellow-passengers were in great dismay."

"When in sight of the Jersey shore," he continues, " we had so nearly finished the provisions which could at all be eaten, that, on coming near Sandy Hook in the evening, we partook of our last scanty meal. That night was very stormy, threatening to blow us out to sea again. The captain at last thought he might succeed to reach Newport ; but to our great thankfulness, the wind altered ; a pilot came to us, and by ten o'clock we were

near the lighthouse. The account of our situation soon reached
New York, when some of our kind friends, officers of the Custom
House, several of whom knew me, went to some of the hotels, and
put in requisition some of the provisions they had ready prepared,
which they brought to us in a pilot boat, and through their kindness we made a good meal after a long fast. My soul was reverently
prostrated before the Lord for the preservation extended to us. His
own arm brought us deliverance. At seasons, when violent winds
and foaming billows assailed our very frail and shattered vessel, and
my fellow-passengers saw no possibility for us to escape a watery
grave, this gracious promise, 'Thou wilt keep him in perfect peace,
whose mind is stayed on thee, because he trusteth in thee,' was
revived. Thus did my gracious Lord uphold me, and deliver
me; for ever adored and praised be his Holy Name. How often
has He, in the course of these last three years and a half, greatly
magnified his name. He has been my refuge and strength, and has
never failed me. I have travelled during this engagement about
twenty-six thousand miles by land, besides several thousands by
water, and have had during that period nearly as many meetings
as days. I went out poor; I return poor—very poor in spirit;
and yet I can truly say that I have not lacked anything. It is
the Lord's doing, and to Him the whole praise and glory are
ascribed! On my arrival at New York I found that my beloved
wife was at Burlington. We soon met there, and rejoiced together
in the Lord for his great goodness to us both, exciting a desire that,
through his Divine grace helping us, we may stand offered up to
Him and his service to the end of our lives."

CHAPTER XV.

PARTNERSHIP WITH ROBERT PEARSALL—PROSPECT OF FURTHER
RELIGIOUS SERVICE—VISIT TO HAYTI.

On his return from Europe, Stephen Grellet again took up his residence in New York.

"I found it my place," he remarks, "as early as I could rightly do so, to engage again in some business, that, by the Lord's blessing on my exertions, I might have the means to defray all needful expenses, should my dear Lord and Master see meet to call me out again in the service of his glorious Gospel. I did not desire great things for myself, but I felt there is a blessing in being able to give, even a little only, to others, rather than be under the necessity of receiving."

Way soon opened for his entering into partnership with his brother-in-law, Robert Pearsall. They "endeavoured to conduct their business with all prudence, attending, in the management of it, to the restrictions of the Spirit of Truth. The Lord prospered them in their undertaking, and it was even becoming a lucrative one." But it was not long before an impression was made on S. G.'s mind that he must " stand loose from the world and every earthly object, and hold himself prepared for further service in distant parts of the Lord's heritage." In allusion to this, he remarks :—

" I had entertained a hope that I had accomplished in Europe the whole of the work that my dear Master had for me there ; and very sweet peace had continued to attend me, when I recurred to the deep and peculiar exercises, and the nature of my services there ; but now I beheld such a field of further labours in those nations, as well as in the West Indies, which I should have to enter, that my soul was dismayed at the prospect. The North of Europe, Norway, Sweden, Russia, parts of Asia Minor,

Greece, Italy, Rome, many parts of Germany and Spain, &c., were brought into view, as portions of the earth where I should have to proclaim the Lord's redeeming love and power. Strong and awful was the impression made on my mind, that I could not enter into my Master's rest till this work was accomplished. With this a little faith was given that Omnipotence can enable to perform what to man seems impossible. I bowed very low before the Lord, and through the aid of his Divine grace, I was enabled to say, ' Here I am, Lord ! do with me as thou wilt ; only go with me, and fulfil again thy blessed promise,—" I will teach and instruct thee in the way in which thou goest ; I will guide thee with mine eye." ' "

Whilst thus exercised in the midst of his outward engagements, and enabled to stay his mind on God in the prospect of what was before him in regard to the nations afar off, and the people of other religions denominations, his love and Christian solicitude were kept alive towards the members of his own religious Society. The insidious workings of the " spirit of error," assuming the garb of an " angel of light," deeply affected him. " The light of the Gospel of *the glory of Christ* " had shined upon his own heart, and with an eye sharpened by love to the Redeemer, he was very quicksighted in regard to everything derogatory to his Divine character and offices.

" I have deeply lamented," he remarks, in reference to these things, "because of the gradual ascendancy which the grand enemy of Truth gains over many minds. Some are carried away by a worldly spirit—others by that of Anti-Christ, under a specious appearance of sanctity. Attempts to detect it, or to proclaim against it, have no more place in the minds of many than had the endeavours of Lot to prevent his sons and daughters from falling in the overthrow of Sodom ; he seemed to them as one that mocketh. Nevertheless, I have felt it to be my duty to labour in love with individuals, and particularly with Elias Hicks."

Little more than a year had elapsed since his return to·

the bosom of his family, when, "for Christ's sake and the
Gospel's," he felt constrained to make preparations for
again leaving all.

In the fore part of the year 1816, the time appearing fully
to have come for him to go to St. Domingo, and pay a visit
in the love of Christ and his Gospel to the coloured population there, and having obtained the approval of his friends at
home, with the needful certificates, he says :—

"I left my temporal affairs under the care of my partner, and
on the 25th of Sixth Month, 1816, taking a solemn and affectionate leave of my beloved wife and dear friends, I went on
board the schooner *Remittance*, bound for Les Cayes, Hayti. My
dear friend, John Hancock, a member of New York Monthly
Meeting, accompanied me. His affection for me, and his love
for the cause of Truth, prompted him to make this free-will
offering."

They had a prosperous voyage, and only one fellow-
passenger. When the weather allowed, they held religious
meetings on board their vessel twice a week. These were
generally attended by all that could be spared from the
ship's duty. On landing in Hayti, S. G. remarks :—

"We were favoured to arrive at Les Cayes on the 17th of
Seventh Month. We soon became acquainted with some serious
characters, who have received us with much kindness. After
visiting some of them in their families, my way has opened for
an attempt to spread the notice of a religious meeting among the
inhabitants. It was for a time discouraging, because of the obstacles
put in the way by some Spanish priests and friars; but I felt it
to be my duty to pursue my prospect, and commit the result to
the Lord. A spacious place was provided, and the meeting was
largely attended. Among those present were the General-in-Chief
of the Department, several generals, and military and civil officers.
One of the Romish priests also attended, and after meeting several
expressed their gratitude in that the love of Christ had constrained
me to come and visit them, some saying their hearts were pre-

pared and open to receive such doctrines as I had communicated, for they were disgusted with their Romish priests, whose conduct they considered to be a reproach even to morality."

S. G. held five more meetings at Les Cayes, and visited Miraguane, Cavarillon, &c., and he had interesting service with the inhabitants, and distributed Bibles and Testaments as well as books and tracts, which were well received. He remarks :—

"I felt my mind pressed to go to Port-au-Prince also ; and on reaching that place we paid an early visit to the President, Alexander Petion. He had heard of our arrival, and was desirous to see us. He received us with much affability, and expressed his gratitude that the Lord has put it in our hearts to come and visit them on this island, and has prospered our way thus far. Petion is a large, portly man, of a rather handsome and pleasing countenance, a light mulatto, very plain in his apparel and simple in his manner of living ; in this he acts from principle, to give an example to his officers that they may not oppress the people to obtain the means of supplying the expenses of high life. He is also a very humane man, and is not known to have ever sanctioned taking away the life of any offender, even of those who have conspired against him.

"Eighth Month 11th. I have had several meetings for divine worship since my coming here. There appears to be a great openness in the minds of the several classes of the inhabitants ; some are drawn evidently by no other motives than those of curiosity ; but sincerity appears in others. The meetings hitherto have been held in private houses ; but the President was anxious that the meeting on First-day should be held in their large Romish church, that being the largest and most convenient place to accommodate the people of this town, and the country round. I endeavoured to set before the President the objections that some might have against it, the priests particularly ; but he could not see any difficulty in the way. 'The meetings that you hold,' said he, 'are meetings for divine worship, and for this very purpose the church has been built.' Moreover the chief priest came yesterday to see me, and said that he had no objection, nor did he think any one else would have. He appears indeed, to care very little about religion. His emolument, twenty thousand dollars a year, is his great object. He told me that he did not hoard up that money, *but expended it as freely as it came.* It was trying to me to have a meeting in that place, but I felt it my duty to see the people ; for this purpose I have come here, and therefore I agreed to have it appointed. It has been largely attended, many persons from the country coming to town. Great was the travail of my spirit for this large congregation. The Lord condescended to hear my prayer, and to reveal his power among us, and to cause the stream of his glorious Gospel to flow. The nature of pure and undefiled religion before God the Father was set before them, together with its fruits. The fruits of false religion were also described ; Christ, the Saviour of sinners, was largely preached ; and they were earnestly entreated to come to Him, who, by his Divine Spirit, reveals himself to be very near to seek those who are lost in their sins, and to save them. Much quietness prevailed among that multitude, and many appeared tender.

"12th. This evening I had a more select meeting, and a precious season it has been. The people now appear to understand the nature of silent worship ; a solemn silence prevailed over us. The company very generally were in tears, and feelingly united in the acknowledgment that was made, on bended knees, to the love and mercy of a gracious and compassionate Redeemer, and the prayers offered for his grace and Spirit to enable us so to live as to bring glory, and no reproach to his Holy Name.

"18th. I have had one or more meetings every day during this week. They were held in the several parts of this city, so that most, if not all the inhabitants have had an opportunity to attend them. This morning, being First-day, I had a meeting with about six thousand of the military, who were collected before the palace of the President, and stood in close ranks near the porch, where seats had been prepared for Petion and his chief officers, about two hundred in number. The President sat by me. I was enabled to preach the unsearchable riches of Christ, describing the nature and blessedness of his kingdom of righteousness, peace and joy in the Holy Ghost ; urging them to come and range themselves under the standard of the Prince of Peace, who would enable them to bring forth the fruits of peace. As the weather was very calm, and great stillness prevailed among the people (for many of the inhabitants had collected besides the soldiers), my voice was heard distinctly by all. About an hour after I had retired to my lodgings, the General-in-Chief, Boyer, with most of his staff, came in to express to me, on behalf of the military at large, their grateful acknowledgment.

" 19th. I had another large meeting this morning ; then we went by invitation to dine with the President at his country seat. He lives very abstemiously himself, drinks water only, and eats of but one kind of meat ; but keeps, however, a good table. There were about sixty persons present, besides his family. The whole was conducted with becoming seriousness, and a part of it to edification."

On the subject of education S. G. remarks :—

" The subject of a liberal education, coupled with a pious and guarded training, was held up to their view. They have indeed many schools, and the children make rapid progress, and are in no wise behind any white children in intellect and capacity.

" It has been very grateful to me to observe the eagerness with which some of the people have received the Scriptures ; I had brought several hundred copies with me, also a pretty large number of useful and religious books. Among these are many relating to our Christian principles, which are well received."

He then had meetings at Jacmel and Gonaives, and says :—

" Here, as has been the case in some other places, many of them have said, ' O if you could come among us once a year only, or let one of your friends come, we should not want to hear any one else, and should have done entirely with the priests.'"

And he continues :—

" The next meeting that I had was at Miraguane. It was held in the house of Colonel Auger, Commandant of the place. The power of truth was so felt by many that tears indicated the tenderness of their spirits.

" After that meeting we forded Little River, which was attended with some danger. We lodged at Colonel Adonis', the Commandant. He was stolen from Africa when very young. I

M

find many who were thus carried away from their homes. Some
moving accounts they give of the cruelties they beheld, and the
sufferings they endured.   One of them, whilst relating his sufferings, was moved to tears in the recollection of them, and added,
' but me must love them (his persecutors), and try to render them
good for evil, and pray for them.' That evening I had an interesting
meeting at the house of the Commandant, but instead of feeling
my mind relieved thereby, a great increase of exercise came upon
me, so that I requested to have notice of another meeting for the
next day spread round the country. The whole night, my
exercise was such that my soul cried deeply unto the Lord for his
saving help and strength. It was as if the weight of the mountains was upon me, and I felt so poor and empty, that I thought
I could never more advocate the cause of Truth. Early next
morning, First-day, I was greatly dismayed at beholding the
number of people who had already come into the town to attend
the meeting, whilst others were seen at a distance descending the
mountains round about. To accommodate such a crowd, it was
considered proper to hold the meeting in their large market-place.
About meeting-time, a regiment of soldiers on their march to
Port-au-Prince, also arrived in the town, and their officers brought
them all to the meeting. Several thousand persons it was supposed were collected. They stood very close round me, and
I was placed on the market-cross, or rather Liberty Tree, which
is planted in almost every town. The Lord very graciously
condescended to be near to support me on the occasion.   I
had been brought very low, but He is riches in poverty, as well
as strength in weakness. It was a quiet, solemn meeting.

" We came to Lansavone, and leaving that town early the next
morning, we got to breakfast at the house of a kind, serious man
named Denis, near the Great River. We had a satisfactory religious opportunity with his family, and by the time that we were
prepared to proceed on our journey, the waters of the river, which
were very high when we arrived, had considerably subsided, so
that with the assistance of our kind, new friend Denis, we were
favoured safely to cross, though the water came up to our saddles.
In the evening we reached Miraguane, where we had a meeting, and early next morning we proceeded towards Great Gonaives,
where we had a very precious meeting at the house of the Com-

mandant, Colonel Simmons. After the conclusion of it, we set off for Leogane, fifteen miles distant. A little before our arrival there it began to rain heavily, and continued to do so in such a manner that at ten o'clock in the evening a general alarm was sounded throughout the town, and everybody called out to work, to endeavour to put a check to the overflowing waters, now rushing into the town, threatening general destruction. The extensive plain round the town was like a sea; the water was from three to six feet deep, and torrents continued to pour down from the mountains. The streams flowing through the streets were like so many rivers. We had truly an awful night. Next morning the whole country around presented nothing but waste and desolation; the most beautiful, rich plantations had now not a sign of verdure, or of good soil left; all had either been carried into the sea, or was covered with stones and gravel, brought down from the mountains; houses and other buildings, horses and cattle, were in like manner carried away. It was supposed that the lives of many of the inhabitants had been destroyed. Heaps of large trees brought down from the mountains, against which many stones and much sand had accumulated, blocked up the roads. Had we been only an hour later, the preceding evening, we must have shared the portion of other travellers who were drowned. It was indeed reported that we were lost; two Spaniards, who were drowned, having been taken for us. The Lord graciously watched over and preserved us. I felt much for the people in their affliction, and the great bereavement of many, both by the loss of property, and that of their relatives. I had a very solemn meeting with the people of the town; their minds in affliction were prepared to receive and appreciate the consolations which the Gospel of our Lord Jesus Christ imparts.

"The next day I had two other meetings. That in the forenoon was held in the market-place; for the crowd who from various causes had come down from the mountains, was great; and many soldiers had been sent as labourers, to endeavour to assist the sufferers, so that several thousand persons were collected on the occasion. It seemed that day as if 'when the Lord's judgments are in the earth, the inhabitants of that part of the world were learning righteousness,'—seriousness prevailed over that numerous assembly, and the hearts of many were contrited. The meeting in the afternoon was more select, and the refreshing from the Lord's presence was sensibly felt by many.

"I frequently marvel in beholding how, among these descendants of Africa, who have had so few advantages compared to many of the Europeans, the Gospel stream *does flow*; and the word preached appears to have an entrance ; they receive it in the simplicity of their hearts, and in the love of it. I may also bear testimony to their general good conduct and honesty. One may travel among them with the greatest security. I have heard that very frequently large sums of money are sent over these mountains from one sea-port to another, and no attempt at robbery has been known. Very lately a man had six horses loaded with sacks of dollars, and one of the sacks had become so worn, that when the driver discovered it, it was nearly empty. On his going back he found the dollars scattered on the road for some miles, and people collecting them. They immediately gave him what they had picked up, and assisted in finding more. When the driver sat down to count, he found that only about ten were missing ; and then these men went further on in search, and at length brought him back every single dollar! We might in vain look for so much honesty among many of our white people.

" The 9th of Ninth Month we set off for Port-au-Prince, and the General very kindly sent one of his officers to conduct us through bye-paths across the country, the highway being rendered . impassable by the flood.

" 10th. At Port-au-Prince. I have had a meeting this evening with the more select company of this place, with whom I used to mingle. There appeared to be an increase of solemnity among them, and a deep ingathering into the sanctuary of the heart before the Lord. It appears they have continued to hold their meetings during our absence, and their dependence being then entirely drawn from men, and directed with single-ness of heart to the Lord, the Minister of the Sanctuary, they have become better acquainted with the operation of his Divine Spirit, and have made some advances in the root of religion.

" 11th. I have been several times with the President and chief men of this place ; for, apprehending that the time of my release from this part of the service that my blessed Master had for me is near at hand, I desire not to withhold from them any portion of the Lord's counsels which I feel towards them. The more I am with Petion, and the more I hear of him by those who during many years have had full opportunity to know him, even under the most difficult and trying circumstances, the more do I feel for him and respect him. I believe he is truly a great man ; there is that in him which leads me .to believe that it is his littleness in his own sight which exalts him.

" 12th. I had another meeting with the inhabitants of this city. It was again much crowded. To be generally heard, I had to raise my voice considerably, which much exhausted me ; for I was very unwell when I went to the meeting, and have felt so since ; it seems as if I were on the eve of having a heavy sickness."

According to the apprehension expressed in the foregoing memorandum, S. G. was seized with a severe attack of illness. On his partial recovery, about a fortnight after, he makes the following record in reference to it :—

"The disease made such rapid progress, that in a few days I was reduced to the greatest weakness : neither the physician nor those about me thought my recovery possible ; my limbs were already cold. I was very sensible of my situation, and that my life did now hang on a very slender thread, and that it was proper I should stand prepared for the moment of my departure, should the Lord order it to be so near at hand as it appeared to be. Accordingly I gave directions for my funeral, and circumstances attending my demise. My mind, through my dear Redeemer's love and mercy, was preserved in much calmness, and, in peaceful acquiescence with his Sovereign will, prostrated before Him. I marvelled if, in his Divine mercy and compassion, He would now indeed cut short my work in righteousness, and release me from the great weight of service which I have repeatedly felt for many of the European nations particularly. At the time when I was the lowest, my concern in Gospel love for these nations came upon me with force, and the language was proclaimed in my ear, ' Thou shalt indeed visit those nations ; the days of thy earthly race are not yet accomplished.' My soul bowed reverently before the Lord, and I said, 'Do with me, O Lord! according to thy Divine will.'

"The night of the 18th was a terrible one on this part of the island; there was a great hurricane with an earthquake. As it rained heavily, I was greatly exposed. I had at the time a high fever, and the rain fell upon me in torrents; my beloved companion, John Hancock, a most kind and faithful attendant on me by night and by day, removed me (for I was too feeble to help myself) to a corner of the house that remained a little sheltered from the weather; but considerations about myself were absorbed in feelings for the mass of the inhabitants, whose distress was great. All the vessels in the port were sunk, thrown on their beam-ends, or cast high up on the shore."

A week later, S. G. continues :—

"4th of Tenth Month. My strength returns slowly. I am now able to sit up a part of the day, though the fever is yet high, and perspiration is very profuse; I have, nevertheless, concluded to leave this island for New York, and have taken my passage accordingly. This afternoon I have taken a solemn leave of the people here, the President among others. They accompanied me on board the ship *La Franchise,* Captain Nuisan. She is a fine vessel and belongs to the President. There are fourteen passengers on board, besides my companion and myself.

"26th of Tenth Month. Favoured to arrive safely in New York, and to find my beloved wife in good health. We have united in thanksgiving and praises to the Lord. Though He has afflicted me sore in my outward man, his love, goodness, and mercy have been great, and the consolations of his Spirit are multiplied upon us."

The deep religious interest which S. G. had felt in the people of Hayti, did not cease after his return. He corresponded with Petion* and some of the chief men of the island, and, both by enlisting in their favour the efforts of English philanthropists,

---

* John Candler visited Hayti, many years afterwards, and found the following characteristic inscription on Petion's tomb:—

"Il n'a jamais fait couler larmes à personne, sauf à sa mort."

and by more direct influence, he was the means of rendering valuable aid in advancing the cause of general education, and of social as well as moral and religious improvement amongst them.

Bearing in mind the obstacles which must necessarily stand in the way of a people just emerging from the disqualifying influence of slavery, still suffering from the effects of long-continued struggles for political liberty, and surrounded by enemies to freedom, it is no disparagement to the African race, that by the side of the most cultivated nations, their advancement in the arts and habits, as well as in the enjoyments of civilised life, should be comparatively slow and fluctuating; but what has been already realised in their attempts at self-government, during the short period of their independence, is enough to encourage the hope, that, through the Divine blessing upon persevering efforts in a right direction, a brighter future awaits the free children of Hayti.

CHAPTER XVI.

Third Visit to Europe.

It was some months after his return from Hayti before Stephen Grellet fully recovered from the effects of his severe illness ; he was able, nevertheless, to devote some time to his temporal concerns, and "felt it to be his duty," as much as possible, to relieve his partner, upon whom, during his absence, the whole care of the business had rested.

In the spring of 1817 he took a journey into Pennsylvania, and attended the Yearly Meeting in Philadelphia. On completing his services in that city, he returned home to his own Yearly Meeting in New York. Soon after its conclusion he went to the Yearly Meeting of New England.

After his return from New England the prospect of another religious visit to Europe, alluded to in the last chapter, was brought before him with deepening interest, and under date of the 26th of Eleventh Month, he makes the following memorandum :—

"The weight of the service which the Lord calls for from me in Europe, becomes heavier and heavier ; my whole mind is at seasons absorbed by it. I greatly wonder that services of this kind should be laid upon me, in nations whose language I understand not, where I do not know that there is even a practicability to travel, and where numerous difficulties and great perils must necessarily attend me. Yet sometimes it seems as if I saw a plain path before me in Norway, Sweden, Russia, towards the Crimea, over the Black Sea, in Greece, Italy, &c., with a conviction that the Lord can remove every difficulty, and 'make of the mountains a way.' Many days and nights I have spent prostrated with much reverence before Him ; and now believing that, in simple faith and childlike submission, I must commit myself to his Divine requirings, I have found it my place to prepare to follow the Lord, wheresoever He is pleased to call me. My first step must be to wind up all my temporal concerns and retire from my business, which has become a prosperous one, whereby I have been enabled to defray the heavy expenses of my last journey, to provide for my beloved family, and to lay up enough to pay my expenses during the extensive service before me. The little substance with which the Lord has blessed me is offered to his service, and a promise made me years ago, 'that if I endeavoured faithfully to serve Him, He would provide for me everything necessary,' is renewed. Under these my exercises and deep conflicts my beloved wife is my faithful helper ; she very sweetly encourages me to follow the Lord in the paths of obedience in all faithfulness."

In due time he spread his concern before the Friends of his Monthly, Quarterly, and Yearly Meetings, who, by their certificates, commended him to the Christian notice and kindness of those among whom he might come, in the course of his service in the Gospel of our Lord and Saviour Jesus Christ." Soon after this he embarked on his third visit to Europe, in relation to which, he says :—

"17th of Sixth Month, 1818. Having settled all my affairs and taken a very solemn farewell of my beloved wife and child, giving up one another to the Lord's sovereign will and almighty disposal, even unto death, should it be so ordered that we should never meet again in this mutable state, I came this day on board the ship *Hercules*, Captain Cob, bound for Liverpool."

On again reaching the shores of England, he says :—

"Liverpool, 14th of Seventh Month. Through the Lord's favour we have landed here safely this morning. I am once more under the hospitable roof of my dear and very kind friends, Isaac and Susanna Hadwen. My beloved friends in this city receive me in the love of Christ, with hearts warmed by Christian affection ; to the Lord be the praise for this and every other blessing ! I feel it a great privilege to have the love of the brethren."

On his arrival in London he took up his quarters at William Allen's, who then resided in Plough Court, Lombard Street.

"London, 21st. I arrived here this evening, and have not delayed telling my dear friend William Allen, that I have thought for some time, that it was he who was to be yoked with me in the Lord's work among the nations, and have left the matter for him to consider. The Lord has laid upon him the same concern that I have upon me. He felt it before my arrival in this land ; the weight of it has been at times overwhelming to him ; he has so many things that hold him like strong bands that he does not know how he can be released ; but the Lord is all-powerful to remove every obstacle.

"26th. I have attended several meetings, and visited several families in affliction. In most of these services dear Allen has accompanied me. Great is the exercise of his mind, but I have rejoiced in the evidence that the Lord is with him. This evening, in company with his mother and daughter, and dear Rebecca Christy, we had a season of most solemn silence. It was felt to be precious, and was broken by dear William, prostrated on his knees, offering up himself and his all to the Lord, to go with me wherever the blessed Master may be pleased to send us, and to drink whatever cup He may prepare for us in the course of that service, be it even unto death. O ! it was a solemn season indeed ; my soul very reverently adored the excellency of the Lord's power and mercy in thus providing for me the companion after my own heart, towards whom my mind had been inclined for a length of time, though none knew it except my beloved wife. Bless the Lord, O my soul, and all that is within me, bless his holy name !"

In looking at the prosecution of his religious labours, Stephen Grellet's attention had been much turned towards the northern parts of the continent, and in allusion to it he remarks :—

"Dear Allen having now concluded to go with me, at least as far as Petersburg, and there to wait to know what the Lord may further require of him, uses every exertion to prepare to leave home, and he has also laid his religious concern before Friends, and obtained their testimonials of full approbation. I had been

under great apprehension as to how I could be of the least service
in the great work of my dear Lord in Norway and Sweden, for
neither dear Allen nor myself understand their language. I felt,
indeed, at times, the word of promise proclaimed in my spirit,
'The Lord will provide,' and I said, 'Good is the word of the
Lord ;' but yet, I was again full of fears and doubts. Now, to my
soul's wonder and reverent gratitude, it is given me to see that
the Lord's promises are indeed verity and truth ; they are yea and
amen for ever. Enoch Jacobson, a Norwegian, one of those I saw
during my last visit to this nation on board the prison-ship of war,
and who there became convinced of Friends' principles, having
heard that I proposed to return from America to visit Norway,
&c., has just arrived in London. He has come under the apprehension that he would find me here, and that it was his duty to
come and render me any service in his power. Surely this is the
Lord's doing ! My friends here unite with me in the acknowledgment of it. Blessed for ever be his holy name, who is glorious
in holiness, fearful in praises, doing wonders."

Thus provided both with a companion and an interpreter,
S. G. left London for Ipswich and Harwich, and embarked for
Norway.

Stephen Grellet now entered upon his third " Missionary
Journey " on the European continent. To have a fellow-
labourer in this important service so entirely " after his own
heart," greatly added to its interest and usefulness. It was
only recently that William Allen had become a public
preacher of the Gospel, and during the present engagement,
he had an opportunity of making " full proof of his ministry."
Banded together in the Lord's service, the Christian brothers
spent about two months in Norway and Sweden, and S. G.
thus notices their religious engagements :—

" Norway—Stavanger, Eighth Month 25th, 1818. Through
Divine favour we arrived here this day, i.e. William Allen, Enoch
Jacobson, and myself. We had a rough and tedious passage on

this North Sea. Our vessel being small rendered it more trying. This town contains about three thousand inhabitants, and the parish four thousand more. There are very few among them who cannot read, which is also the case throughout the district, and yet it is thought that fifty Bibles could hardly be found among them all; indeed money cannot procure them here; one young Lutheran minister has not been able to obtain a copy, and he very gratefully received one that we presented to him (for we have brought a quantity of the Scriptures with us). We had some satisfactory intercourse with this young man, and also with the senior clergyman, who unequivocally acknowledged his full assent to the Gospel truths that we felt engaged to communicate to them. Enoch Jacobson is already very useful to us.

"28th. Several of the dear people who became convinced of our Christian principles in the prison-ship in England reside here; we have visited them in their families, and had very solemn and interesting religious seasons with them. These people are here as shining lights, so that several pious persons in this place have joined them in silent, reverent waiting on the Lord. They meet together twice a week for the worship of God; they have no kind of vocal communication, so that their meeting together is truly and solely to wait on the Lord.

"We met with them at their usual week-day meeting; there were seven men and seven women, with a few children. We found them gathered into the same collectedness of spirit and state of solemn silence as we witnessed in our visit to their families. Surely this is a people that gather to Christ, whom they know to be their teacher. After we had sat a long time, and enjoyed together in the Divine presence a very precious fellowship of spirit in harmonious silent waiting on the Lord, dear Allen and myself were enlarged in vocal ministry, Enoch interpreting sentence by sentence. It seemed like dew falling upon the tender grass. After having briefly but clearly set before them the manner of life and conversation, which ought to distinguish the members of a religious community, and what are the cardinal portions of the Christian doctrine and precepts, which they must firmly believe and endeavour to act up to, we left them to consider these various matters among themselves, and to see who among them felt warranted to give in their names as members. Enoch told me that they proceeded in this concern under great weightiness and tenderness of spirit; eight only, out of nearly thirty, apprehended themselves prepared to make such a solemn profession; and yet several others are truly spiritually minded and conscientious men and women; but they wish to act with deliberation. We endeavoured to prepare a few rules of discipline suitable to their condition, which they have adopted, and have sent them for the consideration of those who profess with them in other parts of Norway.

"Several opportunities have presented for our being with many of the inhabitants of this place. Sometimes a large number were collected together. They received the truths of the Gospel that we felt ourselves called to proclaim, with religious sensibility. The two Lutheran clergymen have been to see us; their object appeared to be to obtain a few hundred copies of the Scriptures, which has been attended to, and we expect they will receive them in a few weeks.

"This part of the country is rocky and stony, but very picturesque; there are many small lakes. The people generally are very poor; they subsist mostly by fishing; they have often to pay very dear for the small portion of bread that they eat, and have several times been reduced to the necessity of eating the bark of trees, instead of bread. They cultivate a small quantity of oats or barley, in little patches here and there among the rocks. Their horses are small ponies, very strong for their size.

"The little company here who profess with Friends have hitherto held their religious meetings in one of their houses, which sometimes subjected them to interruptions. We have therefore obtained a commodious room which we have hired for one year·

"First-day, 30th of Eighth Month. Those professing with us came pretty generally to our meeting this morning, which was held in the new house. They were about fifty. It was a good meeting. In the afternoon we found a large company collected. Curiosity most probably was the inducement that brought many of them, but others, I am persuaded, came from better motives. The crowd out of doors, as well as in the house, was great, and yet no public notice had been given. The Lord's power came over us, and brought all into stillness; when, after a pretty long silence, my heart being warmed with Christian love towards that assembly, I addressed them in the words of the Apostle ; " After the way which they call heresy, so worship I the God of my fathers, believing all things which are written in the Law and in the Prophets, and have hope toward God, which they themselves also allow, that there shall be a resurrection of the dead, both of the just and unjust,' &c. &c. I unfolded to them the nature of true worship, in spirit and in truth ; who He is whom we are to worship. Then I set forth what the Christian Baptism and the Lord's Supper are, and earnestly besought them to come to be baptised by Christ's Spirit, so that they may have a right to partake of his Supper, even to feed on the Bread of Life, which if a man eat of he shall live for ever ; not like the manna of which the Jews did partake and are dead ; nor like that bread of which so many Christian professors so often partake, which they call the Lord's Supper, and yet continue dead in trespasses and sins. I proclaimed to them the glad tidings of salvation by Jesus Christ, and invited them to come to Him, their Saviour, who is so near us, that He is described in the Scriptures as, ' Christ *in us* the hope of glory.' I forewarned also the disobedient and the rebellious of the day of the Lord, who will render to every man according to his works. My dear friend William Allen had also very good service. The people were very attentive, and some very tender. In the evening the old clergyman, who had been at meeting, came to us, and in a very feeling manner expressed his gratitude for the opportunity given him of the Lord, to hear the great Gospel Truths that had been proclaimed that day.

" 31st. This forenoon we visited the prison and the schools ; the former is kept by an old woman. She had but one prisoner in it, and had so much confidence in him that the door of his cell was kept open. In the afternoon we had another meeting with most of those professing with us. We endeavoured to encourage them to keep near to Christ, their foundation ; that He may keep them, and enable them to maintain all their Christian testimonies with uprightness and faithfulness, that so they may be made a blessing to their neighbours and the nation. We assisted them in organising a meeting for maintaining good order and Christian care over one another, which is to be held every two months. We then took leave of them in much nearness of spirit ; fervent prayers also were offered unto the Lord for one another.

"Ninth Month 1st. Tanangar, three Norwegian miles from Stavanger. We went this morning on board a little vessel to take us to Christiansand. The weather was fine, but we had proceeded a little way only, when the wind blew vehemently, and with it such a high sea that the captain had great difficulty to put into this place for shelter. There are here a few fishermen's cabins ; their business is to catch lobsters, mostly for the London market. The storm being of long continuance, has given us an opportunity to walk a considerable distance round this place, and to visit the people in their solitary habitations. The country is very barren ; heaps of rocks and stones seem nearly to cover it. We left Bibles and Testaments in many of their families, who gratefully received them. We met a young man who resides on a small island at some distance. He was at Stavanger when we first came. We then gave him a Bible. The people on the little island have daily gathered about him whilst he read it to them ; and he expects they will continue to meet together for that purpose, chiefly in the evening, and on First-days."

Having been detained several days by stress of weather, they did not leave Tanangar till the 6th, on their way to Christiansand.

"9th. Christiansand. It has taken us two days to come here in our little vessel, which we have now discharged, as we expect to proceed by land.

"Accompanied by Peter Isaacson, a pious man to whom we were introduced, we have visited the Governor, who treated us with great civility, and is disposed to give us every facility he can in the prosecution of our religious or benevolent objects.

"We find in this place a people called Saints. Some of them are scattered over various parts of this land. There are conscientious and spiritually-minded persons among them.

"10th. We had this evening a meeting at the house of one of these 'Saints.' Above fifty had collected."

Leaving Christiansand on the 11th, they availed themselves of several opportunities for religious service, during a long and perilous journey of nearly ten days, to Christiania,

by way of Arendal, Brevig, Holmestrand and Drammen.
S. G. writes :—

"21st. Christiania. We arrived here early this afternoon, and
had this evening a small meeting at Canute's with those who
profess with us. Some of them I had seen on board the prison-
ship in England.

"27th. We have found here a wide door set open before us by
our blessed Master, who has also been pleased to give us a little
ability to labour in his Gospel among various classes. We have
had several meetings among those who profess with us, and have
also visited them in their families.

"This evening we closed our religious engagements in this
place by having meeting with them. Some of them are in
a tender state. May the Lord bring to perfection the work that
is begun among them !"

Having now completed their services in Norway, they left
Christiania about noon on the 28th of the Ninth Month, and
proceeded in a direct course to Stockholm, a distance of
four hundred and twenty miles.

They arrived at Stockholm on the 5th of Tenth Month,
and were detained in the Swedish capital more than three
weeks. On a review of the various religious services in
which they were engaged during that time, S. G. makes the
following memoranda :—

"20th. We have been closely occupied since coming to this
city, where we felt ourselves particularly concerned for the poor
and the suffering. It has led us to visit their various institutions
for the relief or retreat of these. We have had the acceptable
company of Phillipson, a pious man, whose time and large estate
are employed in acts of benevolence. He is the founder and
supporter of several of these establishments, and takes a very
active part in many others.

"We have visited all these establishments, and their prisons
also, having religious meetings in many of them ; Enoch Jacobson being our interpreter. We have had many religious opportunities also among the inhabitants ; some of these were held at
our lodgings, where we have a spacious room for the purpose.

"Soon after our arrival here, we waited on the Count D'Enger-ström for whom we had letters ; he is the King's Prime Minister. He told us that the King had been informed of our arrival in his dominions, and had expressed a desire to see us when we came to Stockholm. We told the Count that we should wait on the King whenever he requested us to do so. The Count has appeared to take much interest in the object of our religious engagements.

"22nd. Being informed by Count D'Engerström, that the King (Bernadotte), would receive us this evening at his palace at Ros-endal, a little out of town, we went there at the time appointed. The Count came to meet us on our arrival, and said he would present us to the King. We had requested that it might be a private audience, but the Count at once introduced us into a very spacious and richly furnished room, full of the King's great men, ministers, generals, &c. &c.—all in full court dresses—for we were actually brought into the court. I felt pretty low on finding myself in such company. What a contrast we were to them ; we in our plain simple garb, our hats on—they in their rich attire and many insignia of high rank. They treated us, however, with respect, and even with affability ; several especially, at whose houses we had been, and who had attended our meetings. Shortly after, we were introduced to a private apartment where the King was alone. He received us with kindness, entered with interest into the objects that have brought us into his dominions, and wished every liberty and facility to be given us to visit any place we may desire ; and requested us to impart to him any observa-tions we make, that he may administer help and relief where needed, adding, ' but you know that the King's name, which im-plies power, is not always attended with it ; on the contrary, I feel very often my impotency.' Having inquired what further stay we proposed to make in Stockholm, and finding that it was to be prolonged for a few days, he said he desired to see us again. He would soon let us know, and wished we might be more pri-vately together than we could be then.

"24th. The visits of pious or inquiring persons, have kept us closely engaged at our lodgings, early and late, when we were not holding meetings. Among them are several of the clergy : some appear dissatisfied with their various forms, which are but

N

little removed from Popery. An aged clergyman, who at first raised many objections against what we had advanced in support of the vitality and spirituality of real religion, and strongly advocated a man-made ministry, by the imposition of the hands and ordination of the bishops, brought to us afterwards two of his sons, who, having been educated for the ministry, now decline to be ordained, not apprehending themselves called of God to the sacred office, and finding difficulties in reconciling many practices and ordinances in their church with the Scriptures ; among others, worship, baptism, the supper, &c. In the presence of their father, the young men stated their objections, with great feeling, and religious sensibility. We endeavoured to unfold to them those various subjects, with others connected therewith, agreeably to scriptural testimony, the force of which they appeared to feel. The father, instead of raising objections, as he had done before, now appeared to unite with us, and on parting manifested much love and good-will, requesting some books that treat of those subjects more fully. One of the pious persons who has come to see us was once a renowned preacher, but during the last eighteen years of his life, he has withdrawn from all outward fellowship, and spends his time in retirement, in silent worship and prayer. He has given us an interesting statement of the Lord's gracious dealings with him, and of his experience of the quickening influences of His Spirit, who leads into all truth, and out of all error ; by whose teaching we must learn daily, things old and new.

"25th. The Count D'Engerström having sent us information that the King wished to see us at five p.m., in the town palace, we went accordingly. The Count was waiting for us, and brought us at once into the King's private chamber. He received us in a kind and friendly manner, and made us take seats by him, none being present with us but the Count. We had a very full opportunity with him, in the course of which we pressed the necessity of allowing liberty of conscience in his dominions ; and pleaded on behalf of the little flock of his subjects, who have embraced principles similar to ours, and who have in some instances been brought into suffering for maintaining their testimony against war, oaths, a hireling ministry, &c. The King, in a feeling manner, said that he had made himself acquainted with our

Christian testimonies, of which he spoke in a respectful manner, adding, ' I know you are a peaceable people, opposed to wars and the shedding of blood ; that under some circumstances you may perhaps parry a blow, but you cannot return it ; therefore, above any other people, you ought to be protected, and your Society shall have the utmost of my protection.' He feelingly alluded to the great responsibility he felt as King over this realm ; that if he was successful in doing any good, he was but a weak instrument in it ; indeed his power was very limited. He spoke, with much feeling, of the case of the poor Jews, who by the law of the nation are not allowed to reside in this country. He had several times tried to have this iniquitous law repealed, but his efforts have been in vain. He mentioned an occurrence that took place lately. A number of Jews were wrecked on the Swedish coast, when it was with the utmost difficulty that he, the King, had succeeded in allowing them to be landed ; but he could not protect them from being sent out of the kingdom as speedily as could be, though the poor sufferers had lost their all. Supplies were given them from the King's private purse. We were almost two hours together ; and on our parting, the King held us by the hand, and embracing us, seemed as if he could hardly let us go, following us with his eyes and uplifted hand till we were out of sight.

" 26th.   On our calling this morning on Count D'Engerström, who himself was much affected during our visit to the King yesterday, he took us to his cabinet, saying the King was willing that we should know how he spends some of his time. The kingdom is divided into many provinces, and these are so managed that a daily statement laid before him of what has occurred in each during the week, brings under his notice the state of all. These accounts are separated into several heads ; one of them relates to circumstances of a more private nature, such as the losses the poor may have sustained by the death of a horse or a cow ; a barn or cabin being destroyed by fire ; of peculiar distress by sickness, &c. These occurrences are read to the King every morning before he rises, and out of his own purse he administers assistance as the cases appear to require ; the Count produced to us the book of those private donations, which evince the King's great sympathy for his poor suffering subjects,

as well as his great liberality. After breakfast, other items of
what has transpired in each province, of a political nature, or
otherwise, are also brought before his consideration. In this
way he had been made fully acquainted with our movements
and engagements since our first arrival in Norway."

This second interview with the King of Sweden very
much brought their labours in that country to a conclusion.
They made and received a few more visits, in connection with
the object of their Christian errand, and took their departure
from Stockholm on the 27th of Tenth Month.

They took an affectionate leave of Enoch Jacobson, on
board the vessel that was to take them across the Gulf of
Bothnia to Finland. He had been " a kind and useful
friend, and a faithful and feeling interpreter and co-worker,"
without whose aid their services would have been much
hindered.

CHAPTER XVII.

Third Visit to Europe.

FINLAND—RUSSIA—PETERSBURG.

A FINE passage of forty hours across the Gulf of Bothnia brought them to Abo. Alluding to the favourable passage and the beauty of the scenery through which they passed, S. G. remarks :—

"Abo, 29th of Tenth Month. We arrived here early this morning. My mind was under too great a weight of feeling to enjoy the surrounding beauties. On the one hand, I was prostrated before the Lord in adoration and praise, for the help He has granted us through Norway and Sweden, the wide door He set open before us to proclaim his great and holy name; and, on the other hand, my spirit was brought very low under the weight and magnitude of the concern upon me for this vast empire of Russia, not knowing what may befall us here. O Lord ! all things are possible to thee ! Not by might nor by wisdom, but by thy Spirit only are thy servants to be directed ; their help is from thee alone !

"Finding ourselves now again among a people of a strange language, the Finnish, we concluded to hire a man, who was recommended to us as an upright and faithful person, who speaks French, Finnish, and Russian, and who is able to serve us in various capacities. We soon found his usefulness in showing us the way to persons we wished to visit, and for whom we had letters. The first of these was Count Steinhielt, Governor-General of all Finland.

"The Count Rosenblad, of Stockholm, had kindly given us a letter of introduction to him. He received us with Christian kindness, and at once offered to give us free access to every place we may wish to visit.

"30th. We became acquainted with a physician, named Hartman, a pious person, who is very serviceable to us. He speaks good English.

"In the afternoon we went to the prison in the castle, accompanied by the Doctor and the Secretary of the Governor-General. The castle is about two miles out of Abo. The approach to the prison is through an arched stone vault, which extends some distance. The chains and irons fastened upon the poor prisoners exceed what I have seen anywhere else, though I have visited many prisons. The Governor has it not in his own power to remove these fetters, but by his humane treatment, the prisoners are kept very clean, and the cells dry and well warmed in winter. We have taken a sketch of the fetters of these miserable sufferers, which, perhaps, may be of use at a future day, in endeavouring to procure some relief for them. One man has been confined in heavy irons for eighteen years. The worst of all is that many, under great bodily suffering, have minds as hard as the iron which nearly covers them.

"31st. I felt so distressed last night under a sense of the sufferings and misery which I had beheld, that I could not sleep ; my soul was poured out before the Lord that He would open the way for the mitigation of so much distress.

"1st of Eleventh Month. Yesterday we had a full opportunity with the Governor. We laid before him the heavy sufferings of the poor prisoners in the castle, and in the other prisons. He feels for them, and says that he has taken steps towards a change in their treatment, but has not yet succeeded ; he apprehends it has never yet come to the knowledge of the Emperor. We pressed it upon him to exert his influence for the relief of such great suffering. We have had a religious opportunity in his palace, with his family, and about fifty other persons. His wife and daughters are serious characters ; we proclaimed among them the redeeming love and mercy of God, through Jesus Christ, who would that all men, coming to the knowledge of the blessed truth, should be saved ; and who has also given to every man, for this very purpose, the manifestation of his Spirit.

"This evening we had another opportunity with about forty or fifty persons ; two of them were our fellow-passengers from Stockholm, a young nobleman from Russia, and a female ; it was to some satisfaction. The Archbishop sent us a request to visit him,

and wished us to take a family dinner with him. We accordingly
went to his house. The Archbishop received us at first in his
private apartment, but soon brought us into a spacious room, in
which were his wife and several branches of his family, who were
shortly after joined by many of the clergy.

"One of the first subjects introduced by the Bishop was liberty
of conscience. We were enabled with clearness to state that the
control of the conscience is a prerogative which the Lord has
reserved in his own hands; to Him alone it belongs, by his Spirit
and his Truth, to rule in the hearts of men; men may make hypo-
crites, constrain them to an outward profession, but they cannot
convert the heart. Water baptism and infant baptism were the
next subjects, which led to our fully setting forth the nature and
effects of the baptism of Christ. Then followed what constitutes
a member of the Church of Christ. The Christian worship and
ministry, out of which branched an allusion to the many ceremonies and practices that have found a place among different
religious denominations, for which there is no authority in the
Holy Scriptures, which, contrariwise, bear testimony against them.
The Archbishop gave unequivocal assent to many of our sentiments on these subjects, and several of those present united in the
same. They said that all the best forms and outward observances
are but a shadow of the substance, to which every true Christian
is to gather; 'none of these things,' said the Archbishop, 'will be
found in heaven; but love, which should be universal on the earth;
and love to God, which is to endure for ever, will prevail there.'
When we came to the dinner table, instead of sitting down at
once, the company stood in silence behind the chairs, and then,
without uttering a word, we all took our seats. I was seated
between the Archbishop and his wife, and took the opportunity
to ask him respecting their having thus stood in silence before
sitting down. He said that it is his regular practice in his family;
he considers it much preferable to the formal habit of uttering set
prayers, which often the heart does not feel; but that in silence
there is an opportunity for the heart to feel after and receive a
qualification for secret prayer to God. I felt my mind strongly
drawn, in the love of Christ, towards the company, and I was
endeavouring to wait for a suitable opportunity to express what I
felt towards them, when, after dinner, they all rose and placed

themselves again behind their chairs, and so continued for a while in silence. I then believed it was the proper time to communicate what I felt to be the Lord's message to them. Much seriousness and solemnity prevailed ; and, before we separated, the Archbishop expressed his gratitude that he and his brethren had had such an opportunity to be with us, which had been to their edification, and he desired that the Lord might prosper and bless the work to which He has called us, and bring us to the knowledge of thousands of his faithful servants, in the nations whereto He is sending us, and finally, by his redeeming grace, enable us to meet all together in the kingdom of his dear Son, our Lord Jesus Christ. The whole of this was expressed in French, which the company understood ; consequently it has been easier for us than when an interpreter is required."

They now took their departure from Abo, and arrived at Helsingfors on the 4th of Eleventh Month. They visited the prison, and had interesting intercourse with Count Heystan, the Commandant of the Fortress of Sweaborg, and also with Count D'Ehrenström, Governor of Helsingfors.

From Helsingfors they had a quick journey to Fredericks-hamm ; and on the 9th they came to Viborg, their last halting-place before entering into winter quarters in the capital of Russia.

Stephen Grellet and his companion arrived at Petersburg just at the setting in of winter. They remained there four months. The Emperor Alexander was absent in other parts of his dominions, and did not return to the capital till near the end of their stay. But, in the meantime, " a great door and effectual was opened" to them for their united labour to promote the advancement of the Redeemer's kingdom, both among the rich and the poor—the prisoner and the outcast. Their services were of a peculiar kind; but it was evident that the Lord was with them, and "preserved them whithersoever they went." S. G. makes the following memoranda :—

"Petersburg, 12th of Eleventh Month, 1818. On our arrival this afternoon, by the side of the Neva, opposite to Petersburg, we found that the boats that form their floating bridges here, had been removed a few hours before, for the ice was coming down in large masses. It was a considerable time before we could meet with anybody that would venture to take us across in a boat; but, as we could find no inn or shelter in which to pass the night, or even to have refreshments, we persevered in our endeavours, and towards evening succeeded in persuading some men to take us over the Neva in a small boat, which was effected, though not without danger and suffering from the cold. It was dark when we came to the Hotel de l'Europe. Among a people of a strange language, we feel ourselves strangers indeed.

"14th. We delivered letters that we had for several persons. It brought us to an acquaintance with some who manifest kindness towards us, and through whose medium we have obtained convenient private lodgings, at the house of an English woman, widow of a Russian officer, where we have now removed. It is a great accommodation to be in a house where they speak a language we understand.

"Daniel Wheeler and family reside at Ochta, a few miles up on the other side of the Neva. They came to Russia some months since. The Emperor Alexander had employed some persons to drain extensive morasses near this city ; but they did not understand their business, and sought only to make money, so that under various pretences they expended considerable sums ; which induced the Emperor, after his return from England, to desire, if possible, to have a member of our Society to undertake the management of such works, believing that he could rely on the faithfulness and uprightness of such persons ; and he wished also to have near him a man of religious principles, whose example might have a good influence on others. In consequence he wrote to the Prince Lieven, his Ambassador in London, who consulted with William Allen. During that period our dear friend Daniel Wheeler, who resided at Sheffield, had felt strong drawings of Gospel love towards Russia ; though he did not feel called upon

to go to travel as a Gospel minister, he yet thought that it was a
sense of religious duty that prompted him to go to that nation.
He was brought under very deep conflict of mind; when hearing of the desire of the Emperor that a member of our Society
would undertake the draining of those morasses, Daniel felt
immediately that it was for this very object that his mind had
been preparing, and accordingly, in due time, he removed here
with his family. Though his work has only been in operation
during last summer, his success and progress are such as to excite
the wonder and surprise of all. He holds religious meetings
regularly twice a week, in his own house.

"15th, First-day. We were prevented by the severity of the
weather, and other obstacles, from attempting to cross the Neva,
so as to attend the little meeting at Ochta, with Daniel Wheeler
and family; but dear Allen and myself sat down together, as
usual, to wait upon the Lord. This has been our daily practice
since we left England, and mostly twice a day; we have not been
prevented by travelling, often finding our carriage like a little
sanctuary, where the Lord's presence has been near, and our
spirits have been refreshed by Him.

"17th. We visited, yesterday, several persons for whom we
had letters. The Count Lieven, elder brother of the Ambassador
in London, came to see us; his family are Protestants; they are
from Livonia. He is at present under deep affliction; his wife,
who was a pious woman, died a week since; and his eldest son,
with the other branches of the family, have gone to accompany
her remains to Livonia, to be buried on his estates there. Feeling
much for the Count in his bereaved state, we went to see him to-
day. His only daughter was with him; they are in a tender
state of mind, prepared to receive the consolations of the Gospel
of Christ.

"Among those who extend great kindness to us, and are
helpful in many respects, are John Venning and Walter his
brother. They are benevolent men, and spend much of their
time in doing good.

"19th. We visited the Prince Alexander Galitzin, Prime
Minister of the Emperor. The Prince has a Christian spirit; he
received us with an open heart; he was prepared thus to welcome
us, as the Emperor had given him an account of the visit we paid

him when in London. 'The Emperor,' said he, 'is not here at present, and it will be some weeks before his return, but here is a letter I have just received from him, in which he says you were soon expected to arrive in Petersburg, and he charges me to treat you *as his friends*, and to detain you here till his return.' The Prince inquired into the nature of our religious prospects, and how he can in anywise assist us. We gave him our certificates, the reading of which pleased him much. After various inquiries of a religious character, his secretary, Papoff, a pious young man, being present also, we were brought in a simultaneous manner into a state of silent prostration before the Lord, an experience to which the Prince does not appear to be a stranger. In the love of Christ towards them I communicated a little out of the overflowing of my soul. Before we separated the Prince kindly offered us free access to whatever place we might feel ourselves disposed to visit, prisons, poor-houses, &c.

"We went to see the Princess Metchersky. She is a woman of superior mental abilities, greatly improved and directed to the right channel for usefulness by the grace and Spirit of the Lord Jesus Christ. As she is well acquainted with several languages— French, English, German, &c.—she has been much engaged in translating several works and tracts, especially into the Russian language, calculated to promote virtue and morality, and to set forth the spirituality of the Christian religion; she has them printed and widely circulated in this vast Empire. She was an instrument in the Lord's hands in fostering religious impressions in the mind of the Emperor, when he first came under the powerful convictions of the Spirit of Truth. As a proof that the Emperor is in the daily practice of reading the Scriptures, she stated to us that some years since they agreed to begin to read the Bible at the same time, one chapter of the Old Testament in the morning, and another of the New Testament in the evening; that, however far separated, they might both every day read the same chapter; and as they correspond, the Emperor in his letters often alludes to the particular religious impressions made on his mind by his reading that day; by which she knows that he continues the practice.

"First-day, 22nd. Accompanied by S. Stansfield, William Allen and I went over to Ochta, to Daniel Wheeler's, about five miles distant from our lodgings. We had to go pretty early, as at this time of the year the days here are very short ; the ice on the Neva being now very thick, we walked over it. There were about twenty persons at meeting, including the family of D. Wheeler.

"28th. I continue under deep mental conflicts. Some of the places I have visited, accompanied by dear Allen, have brought me the more deeply to feel and to suffer. We have been at nine of their prisons, called Segees. They are much of the character of the Bridewell at New York, or the Compters in London, except that men and women are more mingled together. Young females for very small offences, or taken only on suspicion, are night and day exposed to the vile company of hardened wretches. We have succeeded in obtaining the liberation of two of these young persons. Last Fifth-day we went to visit Kazadavloff, Minister of the Interior. We found there a large company, beside his family and their nephew and niece, the Prince and Princess Shabatoff. Among others, there were the Princess Metchersky, the Princess Tenbetokoy, Papoff, secretary to Prince Galitzin, Paterson, secretary of the Bible Society, &c. &c. Way was made for our having a religious opportunity, and the hearts of some appeared open to receive and acknowledge the testimony unto the Truth, which, in the love of Christ, we felt constrained to proclaim among them.

"30th. By appointment, we spent two hours this morning with the Prince Alexander Galitzin and Papoff. The heart of the Prince is open towards us in Christian liberty and fellowship, and we feel him as one baptised with us by the one Spirit. We had a precious season with them in silent retirement before the Lord.

"Twelfth Month 5th. During these last days we have mingled again in feeling with poor sufferers ; some because of their vices, others from other causes.' Whilst visiting the great and smaller prisons, we were deeply and sorrowfully affected. It would appear that sympathy with the sufferings of humanity in the nations that I visit, is one of the services laid upon me. O, that the Lord would soften and comfort their hearts under their deep sufferings, that, through sincere repentance and faith in Christ, they may know reconciliation and acceptance with God.

"We spent some hours this day at the Princess Metchersky's. I had a pleasant opportunity with a sister of hers, who spends much of her time in religious retirement and meditation, 'where,' as she expressed it, 'without forms or the aid of any shadow, He whom no man can comprehend nor make any likeness of, is to be worshipped in spirit and in truth.' We dined at John Venning's; the Prince Galitzin, Papoff and Paterson, were the only strangers besides us. The Prince related some interesting circumstances about the Emperor, strongly evincing his Christian benevolence and tender feelings towards the afflicted, and also showing his piety.

"First-day, 6th. We went over the Neva to D. Wheeler's, and attended their meeting. It has been a precious season to me. The Lord has lifted up the light of his countenance, and caused his face to shine upon his poor servant.

"9th. Yesterday and to-day I have been under sore distress from what we have seen and felt in the abodes of wretchedness and misery. The prison near the Admiralty is so filthy, and the air so impure, that it much affected us. The prisoners, by their emaciated countenances, show that they also suffer by it. Ten of them were fastened, two and two, to a long chain, marching out to Siberia; what sufferings must these poor creatures have to endure, during so long a journey, to be performed on foot, and in the severity of a winter like this. May the Lord be pleased to open our way, in due time, to plead for so many sufferers, that their distress may be relieved.

"14th. Our engagements have continued to be among the poor, and in visiting several schools. We had also a season of silent retirement in company with the Prince Galitzin, when, on bended knees, prayers were offered up to the Lord for the help and guidance of his Spirit in all our movements; 'Send forth thy light and thy truth, let them lead me and guide me,' was our earnest supplication. I felt low in the prospect of paying a visit to Michael, the Metropolitan of the Greek Church. The Prince Alexander has encouraged us in it, and kindly offered to make way for it. This afternoon was the time appointed for going there. We accordingly went to his residence, the monastery called 'Alexander Nevsky,' Papoff accompanying us. It is about three miles out of town, and is a great mass of buildings. The Metropolitan, to receive us, very

simply attired Quakers, had put on his rich pontifical garments ;
his apparel reminded us of the clothing of the High Priests under
the Mosaical dispensation ; under his large purple robe was a richly
embroidered garment ; he had a white tiara or mitre upon his head,
on the front of which was a cross made of emeralds, diamonds, and
other precious stones ; from a golden chain on his neck hung a fine
picture of one of their saints ; on his sides were several small and
large stars, and in his hands was a large string of amber beads ;
his beard was long and of a flaxen colour. He received us with
much affability, and made us sit down by him ; he soon began to
inquire of our religious principles and practices, and much approved
of our reasons for not conforming to the compliments, language,
and fashions of the world ; the account we gave him of the Christian discipline exercised over the members of our Society pleased
him much ; he inquired also into our manner of conducting our
religious worship ; our care and practice in the acknowledgment
of our ministers ; and what object they have in going abroad in
the service of the Gospel. We gave him the perusal of our certificates ; he then said that he had not heard of any people acting
on grounds so scriptural, and conformable to ancient apostolic
practice. We entered pretty fully on the important subject of
Divine inspiration, and the gift of the Holy Spirit, the manifestation of which is given to every man ; to all of which he assented.
We made several attempts to withdraw, but he evidently wished
to have further conversation with us ; ordered tea to be brought
in ; and finally, on parting, he accompanied us to the door of the
outer room, and, taking us by the hand, desired that we might
remember one another in our prayers. We went thence to see
Philaret, who is an Archbishop and Vicar of the Metropolitan.
His habitation is also in the monastery. His apartment is of great
simplicity, like the cell of a monk ; the little furniture in it cor-
responds therewith : his dress is the same that the Greek clergy
have worn for several ages—a black gown, black cassock on his
head, a long beard, and his long hair hanging on his shoulders.
He is a man of learning, acquainted with most of the ancient and
modern oriental languages ; but he bears the marks of great
humility ; he is considered a man of piety and spiritual-mindedness. We think, from what passed during the long opportunity
we had with him, and from what is told us by persons acquainted

with him, that he deserves such a character. He stated that the
knowledge of ancient languages may facilitate the understanding
of the words written, but that the Spirit of God alone can give a
right knowledge of the things of God; for they can only be
spiritually discerned. In a very modest manner, he said that he
should wish to know why we declined the practice, so general
among the Christian Churches, of partaking of the communion,
or, as he called it, the Eucharist. After stating to him what we
apprehend constitutes the real Christian, according to the defini-
tion given in the Scriptures, 'If any man be in Christ, he is a new
creature,' we described what this new birth or new man is; then
we proceeded to answer his question, showing what bread, living
bread, the Christian is to feed upon—in reality and not in shadows;
that to live on Christ, through his Spirit, is the only living bread
of the soul; it is the only food that nourishes it unto eternal life.
On which he said, 'We have had hermits amongst us, who, from
various causes, have lived entirely secluded from the world, to
whom it would have been impossible to participate in the outward
communion of bread and wine, or in any of the ceremonies in the
worship of God or other like practices, but who, nevertheless, in
their solitude did really feed on the Lord Jesus Christ by his Spirit,
through living faith in Him; they had no places of worship to
resort to, no man to minister to them, but the Lord Jesus Christ,
the Minister of the Sanctuary was their minister, and their worship
was in spirit and in truth.'. Philaret further said, 'All these forms,
ceremonies, and ordinances, that have been introduced into the
churches, though they be performed with ever so much sincerity
and devotion, can only be, as the law was to the Jews, "a school-
master to bring us to Christ." He is the end of all these things
and their substance.' Philaret has been a useful instrument of
much improvement among the clergy. The Emperor, who knows
his worth, places great confidence in him; to him, therefore, is
committed chiefly the selection of suitable persons, best qualified
by their piety and spiritual-mindedness, to fill important places in
the Greek Church; and at the head of their large schools, of which
there are several in the Empire, supported at the expense of the
Government, containing each from nine to twelve hundred pupils.
These are chiefly composed of the sons of the clergy; according
to their capacities or inclinations they pass from these schools to

the clerical office, or stations in the civil department; every one
intending for the priesthood must marry before he can be ordained;
but when he loses his wife by death, he cannot marry another; if he
chooses, he can retire to a monastery and thus become eligible for
a higher station in the Church than simply that of a priest. The
monks do not marry. Michael, the Metropolitan, was some years
since a priest in one of the Churches in this city, and was a man
of piety, concerned for the religious advancement of his parishioners,
and induced to preach to them in a language they could understand.
The general practice of the clergy has been to perform their public
service and read the Scriptures in the Slavonian language, which
very few among the people understand. After a while, Michael's
wife died. Some tried to persuade him to retire to a monastery,
for which he felt no inclination; but Paul, who was then Emperor,
and had much approved of his giving public religious instruction
by preaching, sent him word that on a certain day he should attend
at the monastery, 'Alexander Nevsky,' where he should take the
vows of a monk. Michael could only consider this message of the
Emperor Paul as an absolute order which he must obey, however
reluctantly: he went at the time appointed; Paul was there, and
as soon as the ceremony of being made a monk was ended, the
Emperor had the mitre and garments of a Metropolitan brought
in (that office was then vacant), and had Michael, to his great
astonishment, invested with them, and ordained to that station."

In a letter written to William Dillwyn dated 23rd of
Twelfth Month, 1818, after alluding to the conflicts and trials
they had to pass through, S. G. says:—

"Do not conclude from this that I repine in any degree, as
complaining of my allotted portion; for contrariwise, I may even
now, as frequently, through the mournful days of my pilgrimage,
'with the voice of thanksgivings and praises publish the Lord's
wondrous works.' They have been marvellously displayed on
our behalf, a poor solitary pair as we often feel to be, when going
from city to city, and from nation to nation.

"28th. We have passed, this morning, about two hours with
Prince Alexander Galitzin, which we generally do every Second-
day morning, from nine to eleven o'clock, for the purpose of
religious retirement, and to wait together on the Lord; or for

mutual religious edification. We have also frequent seasons of this sort with the Princess Metchersky, her sister, the Princess Sophia, and several others, both in high rank, and those of the poorer class. The Lord is no respecter of persons; He is good to all that seek Him, and to all that call upon Him.

"9th of First Month, 1819. The last few days we have been very closely engaged in visiting various extensive public institutions, mostly under the care of the Empress-mother. Among these are retreats for poor widows; hospitals; and a deaf and dumb establishment, an institution for about two thousand children, where every care in a moral and physical sense, appears to be bestowed.

"11th. The Emperor has now returned to Petersburg, and sends us word by the Prince Alexander Galitzin that, as soon as we can make way for it, he wishes to see us.

"24th. We received a note last evening, stating that the Empress-mother wished to see us at the Palace; but on our going there to-day, we found that the information of the very sudden death of her daughter, the Queen of Wurtemberg, has just been received: this affecting event is deeply felt by the Emperor, especially; she was a much beloved sister to him. When with him in England, she was the widow of the Duke of Oldenburg, and afterwards married the King of Wurtemberg. Amidst our various engagements we have visited a school, just established on the Lancasterian plan, for the benefit of the military, but which is designed to spread this system throughout the empire of Russia. We saw at that school young men, Russians, Calmucks, Tartars, Cossacks, &c., from various parts, who are preparing to teach that system in their several regiments, after they have acquired the knowledge of it; we were surprised at the quick intelligence they display; so that their progress in learning is very rapid. But we were much grieved on finding that some of the lessons given them to read or write are sentences taken from such authors as Voltaire, &c., and are of a very demoralising tendency: this induced us to go to the office where those lessons are printed, and on looking carefully over them we found among them impious and deistical sentiments; some very obscene, some from the ancient philosophers, and one out of Cicero: ' When life becomes a burden, it is magnanimity of soul to release ourselves from it.' We feel deeply the incalculable mischief that may thus be done, and are very anxious to do all in our power to prevent the evil. No time is to be lost.

"The more we have dwelt on the subject, the more sensible we are, that by the introduction of suitable lessons into these schools, the knowledge of the principles of vital religion, piety, virtue, morality and justice may be extensively spread over this vast Empire, and various vices and immoralities exposed and proclaimed against ; and that the knowledge of the blessed Truth, and of that salvation which comes by our Lord Jesus Christ, may be brought to those who are now totally ignorant of it.

"In order to meet this end without exciting the jealousy of the clergy, it is intended that the simple language of Scripture only shall be brought forward ; and having so far prepared our plan, we expect diligently to prosecute the work."

In carrying out this important concern, in which they were heartily joined by Dr. Paterson and his wife, and both the Vennings, these devoted servants "whilst closely engaged during the day," in their Gospel labours, "spent parts of some nights" in preparing a series of "Scripture Lessons" of a very comprehensive character. For this purpose they "cut up several Bibles,* taking a verse here and another

---

* Dr. Paterson, in his interesting *Reminiscences of Bible Circulation*, remarks :—"Prince Galitzin was highly delighted with the work, and said that if our friends had done nothing else but this in Petersburg, it was well worth while having come." Dr. P. adds : "Though humble in appearance, it was in effect a truly great and blessed work. As far as the Old Testament was concerned, the translation into the modern Russian had to be made on purpose, into the language of the people ; and to this day, with the exception of the Psalms, this is their only Bible. Blessed be God, it contains all the leading facts and doctrines, and duties of Divine revelation. The child who thoroughly knows it, may truly be said to ' know the Scriptures, which are able to make him wise unto salvation through faith in Christ Jesus.' We all loved these good men. Certainly, like myself, they had come to Russia, just at the right time. The way was not open sooner, either for prison or school plans, and a few years later it would have been shut. Thousands and tens of thousands have profited by their plans."

N.B.—Nine years have elapsed since the preceding note was penned ; and in that interval great changes have taken place as relates to the

there, and neatly pasting them in a book, arranged under different heads, so that it was obvious at first sight that the work contained nothing but Scripture." These lessons were not only adopted, by order of the Emperor, for the use of schools in Russia, but translated afterwards into many languages, and extensively used in different countries, leading the young to an acquaintance with the Holy Scriptures, which they could not easily have gained otherwise.

---

circulation of the Scriptures. A few years since the Synod resumed the printing of the Scriptures in modern Russ, commencing with the New Testament. The Old Testament has now been published as far as Esther, and the work is going forward.

The Bible Society have now an excellent depôt at St. Petersburg.

CHAPTER XVIII.

RUSSIA—PETERSBURG, CONTINUED.

THOUGH the Emperor had returned to the capital, they had not yet seen him. But they had subsequently two interviews with him, and also spent some time with the Empress and the Empress-Dowager. As the time of their departure drew near, they were indefatigable in the earnest pursuit of the object of their Gospel mission. Stephen Grellet goes on to say :—

" 10th of Second Month, 1819. We have been several times with Count Miloradovitch, the Military Governor of several provinces. He has kindly made way for our admission to several prisons. He inquired what we had observed amiss, that might be remedied. We told him that much might be done, but that there were certain things that should be attended to immediately. We remarked upon the great impropriety of confining men and women indiscriminately in the same apartments, and the demoralising effect it must have ; the soldiers on guard, being placed inside the wards, adding to, rather than diminishing, the evil. We represented the great filthiness of the prisons, which are full of the most disgusting vermin, and do not appear to have been cleaned for years. We suggested that as they have several large prisons, totally distinct, they might easily confine the women in some, and the men in others ; taking care to make an entire separation between the older offenders and the young prisoners, and those confined for small offences ; and to keep out of doors the soldiers on guard. To this the Governor replied, ' All this *can* be done.' On our being with him to-day, he said : ' *All these things have been done.*' The prisoners have been furnished with brooms, brushes, water, lime, &c. &c. ; they have themselves thoroughly cleansed their prisons, and care has been taken that daily attention shall be paid to cleanliness henceforth. The Governor seems disposed to have many other improvements made. Thus with gratitude to the Lord, we see a little fruit resulting from our painful labours among these sufferers. We have also succeeded in having many released, who had been in prison for months because their passports were irregular, or they had come to the city without them.

"The Governor has considerably reduced the number of places where strong drink is sold, confining these, as formerly, to cellars, where no seats are allowed. During the absence of the Emperor, the Minister of Finance, in order to increase the revenue arising from the consumption of strong drink, had allowed the sale of it in upper rooms, coffee-houses, &c., to the great demoralisation of the people, who would be ashamed to go into the cellars. The very day of the Emperor's return to Petersburg, the Governor said to him, 'Which do you prefer, the increase of your revenue, at the expense of the morals of your subjects? or their well-being, in not being enticed to evil?' The Emperor readily replied, 'that the well-being of his people was far more dear to him than his revenues.' On which Miloradovitch said, 'In your absence they have considerably increased the consumption of ardent spirits, by allowing them to be sold out of the cellars; and thereby drunkenness and vice have proportionably increased; but, if it is agreeable to you, I will have those places shut up.' 'Do so,' said the Emperor. That very evening the Governor had it done.

"Having told us that the Countess Potozka desired to be acquainted with us, he accompanied us to her palace. Her principal residence is in the Crimea, where she has large estates, with a numerous population upon them. She has established schools among her people, and appears to feel concerned for their moral and religious improvement. She told us that she has, for years, ceased to use formal prayers, but that she silently waits for qualification to approach the throne of grace, and to put up her prayers to the Lord, in whom is her only hope. She is in the frequent practice of religious retirement. It is on her grounds that John Howard was buried, near Kherson.

"On our return to our lodgings we found a messenger from the

Emperor waiting for us, with the information that he would
receive a visit from us at six this evening.   At the hour appointed
another messenger came to show us the way to the private apartments of the Emperor.   We found him alone, and he received us
with great affability, 'like old friends,' he said.   He made us sit
down on a sofa on each side of him, and recurred feelingly to the
visit we paid him in London, by which, he said, his mind was
encouraged and strengthened, under the trying circumstances then
attending him.   He made many inquiries of a religious character,
which evince his concern to obtain a saving knowledge of the
blessed Truth ; he has a good understanding of the Scriptures,
and clear views of that salvation which is through faith in our
Lord Jesus Christ, in whose grace and merits alone he trusts.
The influence of the Holy Spirit is a subject on which he appears
to delight to dwell, being, as he calls it, one of the corner stones
of the Christian religion ; for if a man has not the Spirit of
Christ, he is none of his ; and if the things of God can only be
known by the Spirit of God, then what hope of salvation can
a man have who is destitute of or disregards that Spirit ?   He
inquired of the nature of our various religious engagements since
we have come into Russia, and in what state we had found the
public establishments, particularly the prisons.   We were glad to
have the opportunity to acquaint him with the wretched situation
of several of these, and of the poor-houses also.   We alluded
especially to the prison at Abo ; we showed him the sketch, taken
there, of a man with his fetters upon him.   The Emperor was
much affected, and said, 'These things ought not to be ; they
shall not continue so.'   We also represented the case of the man
there who had borne these heavy chains eighteen years, for having
threatened in an unguarded moment to strike his mother.   The
Emperor appears to be much interested in the subject of public
education ; we therefore told him of the visit we made to the
Lancasterian school, and how greatly pained we had been in
noticing there, and at the printing office, that their lessons were
a selection of sentiments calculated to demoralise the people, and
bring them into a far worse state than that in which their ignorance
places them at present ; that on this account we had been induced
to begin to prepare a selection from the Scriptures, under the
name of 'Scripture Lessons' ; we then gave him a brief outline

of the contents of the little work. The Emperor remained a few moments absorbed in deep thoughtfulness, and then said, 'You have done the very thing that I was anxious should be done ; I had for a long time been contemplating how that mighty engine, general public education, might be used for the promotion of the kingdom of Christ, by bringing the people to the knowledge of the dear Redeemer, and to the practice of Christian virtues ; send me immediately what you have prepared.'

" The Emperor spoke in strong terms of his regard for Daniel Wheeler, and considered his coming to Russia as a blessing to the people. ' It was not,' he said, ' the cultivation of morasses, nor any outward object, that led me to wish to have some of your Friends come and settle here ; but a desire that, by their genuine piety and uprightness in life and conversation, an example may be set before my people for them to imitate, and your friend Wheeler sets such an example.' After this he said, ' Before we separate for the present, let us spend a short time in religious retirement together.' We were disposed to do so, for we felt the Lord's presence and power very near ; we continued for a time in solemn silence ; our spirits were contrited together :—after a while, feeling my mind clothed with the spirit of prayer and suppli-cation, I bowed before the Divine Majesty on my knees ; the Emperor kneeled by my side ; we had a humbling and grateful sense that the Lord condescended graciously to hear our prayers ; we continued a short time in silence afterwards—when we retired the Emperor expressing a desire shortly to be with us again. We were about two hours with him.

" 14th of Second Month. During the last few days, besides attending, as usual the meetings at Ochta, we had several others in this place, and have visited large establishments under the especial care of the Empress-mother, particularly her schools for young women ; one is for the nobility, and contains five hundred girls ; another is for the daughters of the burgesses.

" By appointment of the Empress-mother, we went to her palace ; Count Skotchinsky received us, and we were soon intro-duced to the Empress, in her private apartment. She was at first tenderly affected on seeing us, feeling keenly the removal by death of her daughter, the Queen of Wurtemberg, whom she knew we had seen in London. Having heard that in the course of my journey I intended to be at Stutgard, she requested I would not omit to visit her motherless grandchildren. We could but commend the order and care maintained in the schools under her patronage that we had visited, but stated that we greatly regretted that the education of the girls, among the mass of the people in this city, is totally neglected ; that we have not been able to hear of one single school for them, and that we found, on inquiry, the same neglect prevailed throughout Russia. To this, perhaps, might be partially traced the miserable, comfortless manner in which many of the people live, and the prevalent habit of drunkenness among them : we therefore urged the necessity for girls' schools, under the care of pious, well-concerned female teachers. We acquainted the Empress also with the great exposure of females in prisons ; how many girls, who were sent there for very trifling offences, even a simple informality in their passports, might enter the prison with virtuous habits, but leave it initiated in vice. We also told her that visits to those prisons by females, capable of advising and instructing such poor sufferers, might be highly beneficial ; to all which the Empress feelingly assented. Conversation on serious and religious subjects opened an easy way for us to draw her attention to things that pertain to the kingdom of God, and to eternal life ; and to represent to her how important it is, that by the grace of our Lord Jesus Christ, and our co-operating therewith, we be found prepared to appear before God in a state of acceptance, whenever He permits the slender thread of our lives to be cut. She was very serious : and on parting from us said, ' I wish to be kept fresh in your prayers.' The whole of our conversation was in French, which she speaks very well : as is generally the case with people of rank here.

" This evening our little meeting, held at our lodgings, was a refreshing season from the Lord's presence. He condescends to give us to see, with some clearness, the way through which we are to be directed when ready to depart hence ; dear Allen also sees with clearness, that his religious duty is to keep with me, at least till we reach the Grecian Isles.

" 26th. Among some of the interesting persons that we have met with the last few days, is the Baron Stackelberg ; he is from Revel, in Esthonia, a man of piety and great benevolence, and is the person who first set free the serfs on his estate. The improvement made by the peasantry in those parts, since they were liberated, is great. The first man to whom the Baron gave freedom has become pious and useful : the Baron considers him as his right-hand man, in the introduction and general care of the schools on his estates ; he has also an establishment for the purpose of training schoolmasters for other places.

"9th. We spent, as we usually do once a week, about two hours with Prince Alexander Galitzin. He told us that the Emperor had given orders for the immediate translation from the Slavonian into the Russian language, of those portions of the Bible in our Scripture Lessons that are not already translated, and to have those Lessons immediately printed. The New Testament in Russ is *now* printed, but the Bible is not yet done ; the translation not being completed. The Emperor being apprised that the time of our departure is near, has directed the Prince to have letters of introduction prepared for us, addressed to the Governors of the Provinces through which we travel, and to his Ambassadors in those nations where we may come, recommending us to them ; the expressions used by the Prince are, 'to recommend you, as being well known to him, the Emperor.' We have also called on the Metropolitan, and Philaret the Archbishop, to take leave of them. Our interview with the latter was truly solemn and very touching ; he unfolded to us, in much Christian freedom and tenderness, his religious scruples and exercises, and during a short time spent in silence, we witnessed the fellowship of the Spirit with one another, for the baptising power of Truth was over us ; he was much affected on parting, took us in his arms, and gave us a kiss of Christian love. After our return to our lodgings he sent us short letters to the several persons whom he knows to be pious and spiritually minded, on our way towards the South of Russia.*

"13th. Our departure appearing to be at hand has brought us under very close engagements during these last days ; we have

---

* Stanley visited him in 1857, and in his interesting " Lectures on the Eastern Church," speaks of him as "the aged, gentle, and saint-like Philaret," then the " venerable Metropolitan of Moscow." To him was intrusted the State secret of the will of Alexander I. He crowned both Nicholas, and Alexander II.—*Stanley's Lectures on the Eastern Church*, p. 489.

had many services of a public and more private character ; some
of these partings, which most probably are a final separation,
have been very solemn ; we rejoice that we can entertain the
hope, that we leave behind us a seed that the Lord has visited.
Many of our private opportunities are also tendering seasons ; the
one we had this evening with the Emperor was particularly
so.   Having sent us information that he would be pleased to see
us this evening, we went at eight o'clock, the hour appointed.
He again received us in his own apartment, to which we went by
a private door and staircase, without passing among the guards, or
the persons attending at the palace ; no one, anywhere, has
appeared to take offence at our keeping our heads covered.   He
received us with cordiality as before.   One of the first things he
said was, that the chains we saw on the prisoners at Abo were
now removed, and that the man we told him of, who had been
eighteen years loaded with fetters, was now liberated, and orders
were given for the better treatment of the prisoners generally.
He requested also, that in the course of our visit through Russia,
we would communicate directly to him, whatever we may notice
in the prisons or other places, that we may think proper to bring
before him.   The Military Governor had related to him what we
had said of the improvements that might be made in the prisons
in Petersburg, and he was pleased that the Governor had so
speedily attended to it ; he added that the Empress, his mother,
had given him some relation of the visit we had made to her, with
which she had been very much pleased.   She told him also what
had been said respecting the neglected education of the daughters
of the poor, which she had taken much to heart, and he also felt
so much the necessity of a speedy remedy, that yesterday he
made appropriation of money sufficient to establish and support
six schools for that class in this city, so that they might receive a
virtuous and religious education.   He said he had carefully
looked over the Scripture Lessons that we had prepared, and was
delighted with them ; that had we come to Russia for no other
service than this, it was accomplishing an important work ; that
he would have these Lessons introduced for the use of all the
schools in his dominions.   He also gave us an account of the
manner in which he was educated from a child, under the care of
his grandmother, the Empress Catherine.   The tutors placed over

him, he says, were men possessed of some good qualities, but
they were not Christian believers ; consequently his early education was calculated to estrange him from serious impressions, and
yet, after the manner of the Greek Church, he was trained up in
the habit of repeating some formal prayers, morning and evening,
but he disliked the practice of it ; several times, however, after
having gone to rest, he so strongly felt the convictions of sin for
the impropriety of some parts of his conduct during the day, that
he was constrained to rise from his bed, and on his knees with
tears to entreat the Lord's forgiveness, and strength to act with
more watchfulness.   These strong convictions continued with
him for a length of time ; but, by degrees, for want of attending
to them, they became more and more faint ; with dissipation, sin
gained more and more ascendancy over him ; but in the year
1812, the Lord's visitation in love and mercy was afresh extended
to him in a powerful manner.   It was about that time that
a pious person (it was the Prince Alexander Galitzin, who had
been brought up with him) recommended him to read the
Scriptures, and gave him a Bible, which he had not seen before. ' I
devoured it,' said the Emperor, ' finding in it words so suitable to,
and descriptive of the state of my mind.   The Lord by his Divine
Spirit was also pleased to give me an understanding of what I read
therein ; it is to this inward Teacher alone that I am indebted ;
therefore I consider Divine inspiration, or the teachings of the
Spirit of God, as the sure foundation of saving knowledge.'   He
said much more on these subjects in a feeling manner.   We
entered pretty fully into the nature of the peaceable kingdom of
Christ, and to what the Spirit of the dear Redeemer, who is
Love, would lead all those who are obedient to his dictates ; on
which he stated, how great his soul's travail had been that wars
and bloodshed might cease for ever from the earth ; that he had
passed sleepless nights on account of it, deeply deploring the woes
and misery brought on humanity by war ; and that whilst his
mind was bowed before the Lord in prayer, the plan of all
the crowned heads joining in the conclusion to submit to arbitration whatever differences might arise among them, instead of
resorting to the sword, had presented itself to his mind in such a
manner, that he rose from his bed, and wrote what he then
so sensibly felt ; that his intentions had been misunderstood

or misrepresented by some ; but that love to God and to man was
his only motive in the Divine sight. He was in Paris at the time
he formed that plan. We had spent a considerable time conversing on these very important subjects, when he said, 'We are
then going to be soon separated in this world, but I am a full
believer that, through the Lord's Spirit we may, though separated
one from one another, feel the fellowship and communion of
spirit ; for with the Lord there is no limitation of space.' He
requested that we would write to him as a Christian friend,
through Prince Alexander Galitzin. 'Finally,' said he, 'I have
'one more request to make, that before we separate, we silently
unite once more in waiting on the Lord, if so be that He condescend to give us a manifestation of his Divine Life and presence,
as He did on former occasions.' We were prepared to accede
to his request, for we felt in a precious manner the wing of
heavenly love to be stretched over us. The Lord was present
during a solemn silence that came over us ; our souls were very
reverently prostrated before Him ; He himself ministering to us
in a most gracious manner. After a while, in the love of Christ,
I felt constrained to impart a few words to the dear Emperor for
his encouragement ; that he may hold fast in the ways of the Lord
unto the end, fully relying on the efficacy of his Divine grace to
preserve him from all evil, and to strengthen him for every good
work. He was bathed in tears ; then dear Allen, on bended
knees, supplicated the Lord on his behalf, and that of his people.
The Emperor, who had kneeled by him, continued some time thus
prostrated after William had ceased utterance. Our separation
was solemn. It is very humbling and wonderful to me, to see
how the Lord has opened a way in these nations where I saw
none at all ; truly the promise, 'the Lord will provide,' has been
fulfilled in a remarkable manner ; besides, a door towards the
further labours of love that may be required of us in this Empire
is now open, so far at least as this can be effected by the good
will of the Emperor ; but to the Lord alone we must look to give
us an entrance into the hearts of those we may visit.

" 15th. Prince Alexander Galitzin sent us a message last
evening that the Empress Elizabeth, the wife of the Emperor,
wished to see us this forenoon, if we could possibly spare a little
of our time to her. The religious feelings I had towards her

five years since, when at Carlsruhe, were still with me, therefore, though closely engaged, we accepted the invitation. We went to the palace this morning, and she received us in her private apartment in a very modest manner, even apologising for her request to us to come to see her ; she had for some time wished for such an interview, but had been fearful to propose it ; what she had heard of my visit at Carlsruhe made her regret not to have seen me there, and now, what the Emperor told her of us, induced her to request this visit. Her heart was tender, and prepared of the Lord to receive what, in his love and counsel, we felt it to be our religious duty to impart to her ; she was bathed in tears. From what she told us it is evident that Jesus, the Saviour, is precious to her ; she is of a retired character ; is seldom seen in public when she can avoid it ; her dress generally is very simple ; when she goes out she has only a plain, two-horse carriage, with the simple cipher E upon it ; whereas all the nobles have generally four horses to their equipages ; the Empress-mother has six. The Empress Elizabeth told us how frequently she envied the humble station in life of those maidens who carry the milk about St. Petersburg, in order that she might live in privacy and religious retirement. This has been a very satisfactory visit.

" We dined at John Venning's ; none were present besides his family, and Prince Alexander Galitzin, Papoff, Paterson, and the widow of a clergyman, who is now the companion of the Empress Elizabeth. She is a pious woman, who has learned both in the school of affliction and in that of Christ ; the Empress is much attached to her. The Prince gave us several more interesting particulars respecting the dear Emperor ; among others, the peculiar circumstances attending the renewing of those religious impressions that of latter years have been of an abiding nature with him. When the information was received at Petersburg that the armies of Napoleon had entered Moscow, a general panic came upon the inhabitants, and they packed up their valuables to take their flight ; for they expected the French would soon march for that city. The Emperor was prepared to go with the body of troops collected there to oppose them. Prince Alexander Galitzin had at that time many men employed in repairing his palace, which he continued calmly to go on with, whilst so many

others were panic-stricken. Some envious persons told the
Emperor what he was doing, and that he must be a traitor. He
went to the Prince and queried, ' Galitzin, what are you doing?
what means all this? every one prepared to flee, and you are
building?' 'Oh,' said the Prince, 'I am here in as sure a
place of safety as any I could flee to: the Lord is my defence,
in Him I trust.' 'Whence have you such confidence?' replied
the Emperor; 'who assures you of it?' 'I feel it in my heart,'
answered the Prince, 'and it is also stated in this divinely
inspired volume;' holding forth the Bible to the Emperor. By
some inadvertent motion of the hand the Bible fell upon the
floor—open. 'Well, permit me,' said the Prince, 'to read to
you in that very place in which the Bible lies open before
us.' It was the 91st Psalm: on hearing which the Emperor
stood for a while like a man astonished. The army during
that time was marching out of the city. It is the usual practice on such occasions, or when the Emperor is to be absent
for a length of time, that the last place he leaves is their great
church. He repaired there. The portion of Scripture read there
was again the 91st Psalm. The Emperor sent for the Priest, and
inquired, ' who told you to make choice of that particular passage of Scripture this day?' He replied, ' that nobody had done
so, but that he had desired in prayer that the Lord would
direct him to the portion of the inspired volume he should
read to encourage the Emperor, and he apprehended that this
Psalm was the word of the Lord to him.' The Emperor proceeded some distance on his way; and late in the evening he
felt his mind under great seriousness, and desired that the
Bible should be read to him. When the person who came in
for that purpose began, he also read the 91st Psalm. The
Emperor, interrupting him, inquired, ' Who told you to read
this? has Galitzin told you?' He replied that he had not seen
the Prince, nor had any one told him what to read; but that
on being told he was sent for to read to the Emperor from the
Bible, he had desired that the Lord would direct him to what
was most appropriate for the occasion, and accordingly he had
selected this portion of Scripture. The Emperor felt astonished
at this, and paid the greater attention to what was read, believing
that this must be of the Lord's ordering: he was therefore very

solemnly and tenderly impressed, and from that time he concluded, morning and evening, to read privately a chapter in
the Bible. He was the next day with the Princess Metchersky,
at Tver. They agreed to begin the Bible together, and regularly to read it every day, so that they might both read the
same portion on the same day, and be able to communicate to
one another the particular impressions or reflections the reading of the day might have produced. The Prince tells us that
the Emperor has directed proof sheets of the 'Scripture
Lessons' to be regularly sent us, that we may see how the work
progresses.

"16th. Philaret has sent us a feeling Christian note, in which
he desires ' that the Lord may be with us on our way, as He was
with his two disciples on their way to Emmaus.' The Metropolitan has also sent us a Christian farewell. In the afternoon a
number of persons joined us at John Venning's. We had a
very precious and solemn religious opportunity together ; our
beloved friend, Daniel Wheeler, who was with us, closed it with
praises and thanksgivings to the Lord for the help granted to us,
his servants, for the important work in which we have been
engaged in this city ; humbly praying that He would be pleased
to bless the work to his own glory, be with us who go, and with
him also, now to be left behind."

At half-past six p.m. they got into a cabitzky, a kind of
large covered sleigh, and "having bid an affectionate farewell
to all those dear friends, who kept near to them to the last,"
they left Petersburg for Moscow and the South of Russia.

CHAPTER XIX.

THIRD VISIT TO EUROPE.

RUSSIA—NOVGOROD—TVER—MOSCOW.

DURING four months of the darkest season the little family of Daniel Wheeler, at Ochta, had been cheered and refreshed by the company of Stephen Grellet and William Allen, who were generally with them two days in the week. " They left us," says Daniel Wheeler, " with minds full of peace—beloved and regretted by all who had the happiness of becoming acquainted with them. The stream of Gospel love which was at seasons permitted to flow, when channels were open to receive it, has made, I believe, an impression on the minds of some, which will never be obliterated ; and which has clearly evinced whose servants they are ! They were, I think, of all men, most fit to move in such a work, in such a place, and under such circumstances.

After twenty-four hours travelling they came to Novgorod and thence to Tver, when S. G. remarks :—

"24th. We have had the pleasure of meeting the Princess Metchersky ; she is on a visit to her father and brother : the latter is the Governor of this province ; we had a letter from the Emperor for him ; he readily makes way for our admittance to such places as we desire to visit.

" We had a letter from Philaret for Athanasius, the Archimandrite, with whom was another Bishop, from a distance ; their hearts were open to receive the religious communication we made them : they accompanied us to their large school for the sons of the clergy, who were collected together ; several other persons came in also. I felt my mind concerned to draw their attention from outward observances, forms and shadows, to Christ Jesus, the eternal substance.

" The young men were serious. The Bishops acknowledged that the truth, as it is in Jesus, had been declared to them that day. In the evening the Archimandrite met us again at the Governor's; also his sister, the Princess Metchersky, and a pretty numerous company. Our minds were solemnised together, and the Lord gave us a fine opportunity to proclaim among them the everlasting truth: Christ, the only Saviour, the way, the truth, and the life, without whom none can come to the Father; they were tenderly entreated also to consider, if there is not a danger of having our attention turned aside from Christ, when we assiduously follow the many ways of man's device and invention, or are captivated by the spirit of the world."

Moscow afforded them a still wider field of usefulness, and many objects of deep interest claimed their attention. S. G. gives many particulars, from which we make a few extracts :—

" Moscow, 26th. We left Tver yesterday afternoon, travelling during the night, and arrived here this evening, one hundred and sixty-eight versts; the road is very bad by the deep snow and the great number of sledges upon it; we counted them as we passed during two hours and a half; they amounted to one thousand one hundred and thirty-three; but we are persuaded that during some other parts of the day, there were three times as many. The quantity of produce that goes down is immense; including beeves, sheep, fish, &c. The meat is frozen solid, and keeps so as long as the cold weather continues.

" 31st. The day before yesterday we delivered various letters of introduction. Among others those for the Governor and Minister of Police. We are again brought deeply into feeling for suffering humanity, for the inmates of prisons and poor-houses. Free access has been given us to these places. One of the officers of police who speaks French accompanies us, and interprets for us. The prison of the Tribunal is called the 'Hole,' and it is well named, for it stands in a hollow place, and is most gloomy; but cleanliness has of late much improved it. Another, called the Great Prison, is a large and commodious building, constructed on the best plan that I have seen anywhere, and kept very clean ; the prisoners are also clean in their persons, especially the women, who are entirely separated from the men ; the several degrees of guilt are also separated from one another. We had several tendering religious seasons among them, in their various wards."

Two days were spent in visiting schools, &c., and on the 3rd of Fourth Month S. G. writes :—

"3rd. We had a letter from Philaret for the Archbishop. He received us with kindness. We were greatly surprised, when he brought us into a spacious parlour, to find ourselves amidst a large company of the clergy, monks, &c. There were several Bishops among them, and two Archbishops ; also some Princes from Georgia, who are of the Armenian Church. These are hostages to this Empire. The Inspector-General of the Posts in the Empire, a man of religious sensibility, had come with us, and kindly acted as our interpreter. Various inquiries were made respecting our Christian testimonies and religious practices, to which having answered, way was opened for us to impart to them some impressions made on our minds. I felt much, especially for the Georgian bishops and princes ; seriousness prevailed over the whole company. At the conclusion of the meeting, one of the monks, who speaks French, came and sat near me, and alluding to some parts of my communication, said, 'All outward rites and observances are but forms, Christ and his Spirit are the substance ; this we must press after, without it nothing else can avail us.'

"4th. We held our little meeting together this morning, as is our regular practice, whatever other engagements we may have ; we often find these very profitable seasons, and good preparations for the work that our blessed Lord may require of us in the day ; we found it so this morning. We had accepted the invitation of Prince Sergius Galitzin, a distant relative of Prince Alexander, who had written to him about us ; we had besides, a letter for him from the Empress-mother. Many of his near relatives were with him, sisters, nephews, and nieces, I think thirty-four in all ; he is very wealthy and spends liberally his large income, in acts of benevolence ; he gave very lately two hundred thousand roubles

towards the further endowment of a hospital, founded by an uncle
of his. He is a pious man, like his relative. Our conversation
before dinner was altogether of a religious character, on topics
which appear to be uppermost in his mind ; not on speculative,
but substantial and practical religion. The young princes and
princesses paid great attention, and appeared to take a lively
interest in what was said ; they evince that the great and saving
truths of Christianity have often been brought before their view,
and that they are no strangers to the influences of the Divine
Spirit. Several in the company were melted into tears.

"5th. Visited the large hospital, founded by the uncle of
Prince Sergius, in which every comfort appears to be extended to
the afflicted inmates, even such as many of us have not in our
own houses. Near it is a retreat for poor and old persons, conducted in the most liberal manner. We next went to a large
hospital, called ' Peter and John,' founded and supported by the
present Empress-Dowager ; it is exclusively for persons who are
considered pious characters. From this we visited a comfortable
retreat for one hundred and forty-five widows, most of whom had
once been in easy circumstances ; children of these widows are
also taken in, and educated so as to fit them for business. Though
our engagement this day has been very laborious, we feel this
evening much comfort ; these visits have been so different from
those we so often make, where nothing but wretchedness and
misery is to be seen. We had also this day a number of religious
opportunities ; Christ the refuge in trouble, the Saviour of men
and the hope of eternal life, was proclaimed."

They again spent several days in visiting schools for both
rich and poor, as well as other institutions, and many private
individuals. S. G.'s narrative proceeds :—

"8th. In the evening we went to see the Countess Orloff ; she
is a young unmarried person of very large estates, and liberally
expends her wealth in acts of benevolence and charity. It is to
her and some others of that class, that so many charitable institutions in this city and other places are indebted for support ; but,
above all, the Countess has a pious, humble mind ; she is one of
those spirits with whom we could mingle in very near Christian

fellowship ; she knows what it is, like Mary, to sit at the feet of Jesus, to hear, through the Spirit, his gracious words. We had with her a season of edification.

"9th. The Civil Governor accompanied us six versts out of Moscow, to visit a large poor-house under his direction ; also a house of correction and a workhouse ; they are kept in good order and cleanliness. The Governor kindly acted as interpreter. These visits enable us to have access for religious services to several classes of the inhabitants, and some who come from various parts of the country whom we could not otherwise see, and to preach to them Jesus crucified for our sins, risen again for our justification ; pressing upon them to break off their sins by repentance, and to come with faith unto the dear Redeemer, who would have mercy upon them.

"19th. The last few days we have had some interesting opportunities with several persons. One of these was at the Military Governor's, and another with the chief Minister of Police. We have endeavoured, with these and the Civil Governor, to plead for some of the objects that attracted our special attention in our visits to the prisons, Segees, &c., and have succeeded in having several persons released from their bonds. We are preparing an account of some of these visits for the Emperor, stating to him what, in our apprehension, should speedily be attended to ; and that the severity of the law, or the latitude taken by the police, of sending to prison men and women, and some very young persons, for little irregularities in their passports, ought to be put a stop to. We do not doubt that the Emperor will immediately attend to it. We have met here much to comfort, but much also to afflict and depress us ; my soul has been plunged into deep exercise, so that during some nights my tears have flowed in abundance. The Lord is very gracious in my distress, and his promise is in the most consolatory manner renewed, that He will be with me.

"21st. We were again with the Prince Sergius Galitzin, and several of his family. In the evening we went to General Gourard's. We met the General at the door, going out, but we were introduced to his wife's apartments, where we found about fifteen females together. On our first coming among them, total strangers to one another, our minds were solemnised ; a feeling sense was given that the Lord's presence was there ; it seemed as if we had suddenly come into a meeting of spiritually-minded persons; very few words passed between us, but we were all gathered together into solemn silence and prostration of soul before God, evidently 'drinking together into the one Spirit.' We had continued some time in this state, when, the love of Christ, the dear Redeemer, constraining me, I began to speak as by his Divine Spirit He gave me utterance; we had a contriting season; indeed I have seldom known any select company of my beloved friends in religious unity and fellowship with me, when more of the Lord's baptising power has been felt, than we then witnessed together. After the conclusion of that solemn meeting, we gave some account of ourselves; for we were as great strangers to the company as they were to us; we handed to the mistress of the house the letters we had for her from the Princess Metchersky. Among those present were two Princesses from Georgia, sent to this Empire as hostages; another is the Countess Toutschkoff, and two of her sisters; the others were of the same rank. They are in the practice of meeting frequently together, silently to wait upon the Lord; they have become acquainted with the operations of his Spirit, and the power of Truth, under which they have witnessed the one baptism, and are also favoured at seasons to partake together of the one bread, even Christ the bread of life.

" The Countess Toutschkoff gave us an interesting narrative of the manner in which she was first brought to the conviction that there is a secret influence of the Spirit of God in the heart of man. The impressions made upon her were such that she can never doubt that it was the Lord's work. It occurred about three months before the French army entered Russia, the General, her husband, was with her, on their estates near Toula; she dreamed that she was at an inn in a town unknown to her, that her father came into her chamber, having her only son by the hand, and said to her in a most pitiful tone, 'All thy comforts are cut off, he has fallen (meaning her husband), he has fallen at Borodino.' She woke in great distress, but, knowing that her husband was beside her, she considered it as a dream, and tried to compose herself again to sleep; the dream was repeated, and attended with such increased distress of mind, that it was a long time before she could rise above it, and fall asleep again. A third time she dreamed the same; her anguish of mind was then such, that she woke her husband and queried,

'Where is Borodino?' and then mentioned her dream; he could
not tell her where that place was; they and her father carefully
looked over the maps of the country, but could not discover any
such place. It was then but an obscure spot, but has since become
renowned for the bloody battle fought near it. The impressions,
however, made upon the Countess were deep, and her distress great;
she considered this as a warning given her of the Lord, that great
afflictions were to come upon her, under which, she believed, that
his Divine grace and mercy could alone sustain her. From that
period her views of the world became changed; things that belong
to the salvation of the soul, hitherto disregarded, were now the
chief objects of her pursuit. She ceased to attend places of diversion, which formerly had been her delight; she looked forward to
see what the Lord would do for her; for she believed that she had
not had mere dreams, but warnings, through the Lord's Spirit, of
what was impending over her. At that time the seat of war was
far off, but it soon drew near: before the French armies entered
Moscow, the General Toutschkoff was placed at the head of the
army of reserve; and one morning her father, having her little
son by the hand, entered the chamber of the inn at which she was
staying; in great distress, as she had beheld him in her dream, he
cried out, 'He has fallen, he has fallen at Borodino.' Then she
saw herself in the very same chamber, and through the windows
beheld the very same objects that she had seen in her dreams.
Her husband was one of the many who perished in the bloody
battle, fought near the river Borodino, from which an obscure
village takes its name.

"The Countess said that the impressions made upon her, that
the Lord, through his Spirit, communicates himself to man,
became strongly confirmed; she was convinced that there is a
sensible influence of the Divine Spirit; she endeavoured to attend
to it; one thing after another was unfolded to her of the 'deep
things of God,' and those 'which concern the Lord Jesus Christ;'
and it was by this that she had become acquainted with the
nature of spiritual worship. This was the case also with her two
sisters, then present.

"The next day the Countess Toutschkoff came to our hotel,
bringing her son with her, and told me she came to request that
I would take this her only child and educate him as my own;

that however dear to her, and her only earthly treasure left, her love to him and her desire that he might become a child of God, enabled her to make the sacrifice; 'to see him in the way to become a true Christian was far more desirable to her,' she said, 'than to have him heir of earthly treasures, or to obtain ever so many worldly honours.' She strongly reminded me of Hannah bringing her son Samuel to be offered up to the Lord's service. But I did not see how I could then undertake so important a charge."

It was quite cheering to Stephen Grellet to meet with such a character, and to mingle with such a group of pious Christians in the heart of Russia. He afterwards had some correspondence with the Countess, and "her letters," he says, "displayed the same religious sensibility, and the same love for the blessed Saviour." This little fragment of her personal history and Christian experience doubtless presents some points of peculiar interest, as an instructive illustration of the variety of ways in which the Lord is pleased to deal with his children. In connection with narratives of this kind there is, perhaps, in some minds, a tendency to foster an unhealthy appetite or craving for the marvellous and exciting, which is to be carefully guarded against and repressed. But, on the other hand, there is a dread of admitting what is out of the usual course of man's experience not less morbid, and still more mischievous in its effects. The simple facts of the world's history so clearly attest the supernatural and the Divine, and certainly, the records of Christianity, both of the Old and New Testament, so abundantly assert and confirm it, that it is only "the evil heart of unbelief" which withholds the assent of the understanding and the judgment to evidence so conclusive as to the direct operations of the Divine hand. It is indeed only *in harmony* with the dispensations of Providence, and the gracious influences of "the Spirit who leads into all *truth*," that *real* sanctity of mind can be attained and preserved; and it may well be questioned whether infidelity in some of its forms, does not indicate a diseased state of mind, arising from a wilful disregard of the gentle operations of "the Spirit that is of God," bestowed upon the believer, "that he might know the things which are freely given to us of God," through our Lord Jesus Christ. Stephen Grellet's own experience had prepared him tenderly to sympathise with kindred spirits.

"27th. This evening we visited again at General Gourard's. The time of our departure from this place being at hand, we felt it on our minds once more to be with some of those spiritually-minded persons we had met there some days since. We found among those collected on the occasion several young women, who were not present before, but who are likewise under a precious visitation of the Lord's love; we had a solemn meeting together and, under a sensible influence of heavenly love, we took a solemn and probably a final leave of each other, with the joyful hope that through the dear Redeemer's mercy and love we may meet before the throne of God and of the Lamb, where there shall be no more parting.

"We are preparing for our departure; the snow is fast melting away; we have purchased a kind of carriage called britzka, without springs, but the most safe for the long journey we have before us. We were with the Prince Obolunsky, the Curator of ten Departments, in a religious opportunity in his family; several others were present.

"The Prince afterwards accompanied us to a school, for about three hundred men, sons of the nobility; we felt it on our minds earnestly to recommend them to apply themselves to the knowledge of the blessed and saving Truth, which would enable them to become possessors of the true nobility, and if their lives are spared, prepare them to abound in works truly noble, in the sight of God and man. We visited after that about two hundred persons at the University, where we had also a religious opportunity, with them and their teachers.

"29th. Amidst the necessary arrangements preparatory to our departure, we have received the visits of several persons who have come to bid us farewell; some have done so in great brokenness of spirit."

CHAPTER XX.

Third Visit to Europe.

A LONG and arduous journey southward now lay before them.
Stopping by the way in some of the towns on their route,
they visited the German colonies of Mennonites on the
left shore of the Moloshnaia, spent some time among the
truly *Christian* Malakans, and the neighbouring settlement of
the Duhobortzi, and then crossed the Steppe from Altona,
the last establishment of the Mennonites, to Perekop and the
Crimea. The letters of introduction with which they were
furnished through the kindness of the Emperor Alexander,
and the various civil and ecclesiastical authorities in Petersburg, opened the way for them wherever they came, and
" both in the palace and the prison " the Lord continued to
prosper their labour of love.

On the 1st of Fifth Month, 1819, S. G. continues his
memoranda, from which we make a few extracts :—

" We arrived at Toula on the 2nd of the month, late in the
evening. Our difficulties on account of the high waters were
considerable, and the road very rough besides ; we are sorely
bruised by it. Here we were several times with the Archbishop,
whom we find, as Philaret represented him to us, a spiritually-
minded man ; several of the monks here are the same. The
Archbishop accompanied us to their seminary, and to their large
school for the sons of the clergy, among whom we had an interesting religious opportunity ; some of those spiritually - minded
monks, for whom we had letters from Philaret, interpreted for us.
We endeavoured to direct the attention of those young men to

the influence of the Spirit of God, who leads into all truth, by whom alone the things of God can be known, and the worship acceptable to God can be performed ; much solemnity and seriousness prevailed over them before we left them.   The Archbishop entreated them to attend to the Gospel truths which had been delivered, saying that vain would be their improvement in scholastic knowledge if they did not learn and make advances in the school of Christ, as He instructs us by his Spirit. We had another memorable season with those at the head of this large establishment, and many of the monks who reside in the place ; some of them, of the younger class, were brought into great tenderness. We returned to the Archbishop's to take tea ; many priests and monks met us.   The Lord proclaimed silence over us, and gave us a solemn season in his presence ; Christ, the Shepherd and Bishop of souls, was preached to them ; it is his prerogative to feed and instruct his people ; his servants, even those who are Divinely anointed as his ministers, can only hand out to the flock the bread which the Lord first gives them for the purpose, and which He himself blesses ; neither can any availingly instruct the people but as the Lord himself commissions and qualifies them by his Spirit.

" Orlov, 6th of Fifth Month.   We came here this afternoon. We find in the Civil Governor a mild, serious man.   He lost one of his limbs at the battle of Borodino.   With his family, the Military Commandant, several of the officers and others, we had an unexpected religious opportunity.   The Commandant has considerable knowledge of our Christian principles ; the open door we found among them reminded me of those many seasons I had in Switzerland and Germany, years since, with the officers of the army that marched into France ; surely it is the will of God that all men should be saved ; and therefore, besides the operation of his good Spirit in their hearts, He commissions his servants to proclaim the Gospel of his salvation to all, to invite all to come to Christ, who has died for all ; accordingly, my blessed Lord calls me, his poor servant, to proclaim his name, and his redeeming love and power to all—in palaces and in prisons, to those secluded in monasteries, and to the soldiers.   O Lord, bless thy work, and prosper thou it !

" Here also we visited their schools, hospital, and prison."

Proceeding on their journey they visited Koursk and Biel Garvel : at the latter place they had interesting intercourse with the Bishop Eugenes and many of the clergy and monks, and paid a visit to a school of nine hundred young men, the sons of the clergy, several of the monks and priests accompanying them. S. G. remarks, 12th of Fifth Month :—

" Visits of this kind introduce me into great exercise, perhaps as deeply as any service I am engaged in. O ! how is my soul poured forth that the Lord's spirit of wisdom and counsel may be with me. The Lord and his Truth were proclaimed to them ; his worship and service set forth ; also the nature of the priesthood under the Gospel dispensation, and what constitutes a minister of Christ ; whence the qualification to exercise the solemn office, &c. &c. The Lord helped us, poor servants, to exalt his blessed name.

" 13th. Kharkov. We set off very early ; for which we were prepared, not having undressed these three days and nights ; we did not even take off our boots : but we feel very comfortable in the Lord, who is our strength. Way being made for us by the Governor, we proceeded in the work, which, almost from place to place, is called for from us. The Governor has not only kindly accompanied us throughout our close engagements, these two days [in which they visited schools for more than two thousand students], but has also acted as a faithful and feeling interpreter ; how great is the Lord's goodness in thus making a plain path for us day after day, and in providing such as can assist us in imparting to others, whose language we understand not, our religious exercise and concern for them. Those in high rank very generally speak French, but hardly any of the mass of the people understand any other language than the Russ.

" Ekaterinoslav, 18th. We had a very tedious and dangerous journey of two days and two nights to this place. Here resides Contenius, originally from Germany ; he also speaks French and Russian ; he is Superintendent of the Colonies of the Germans, Mennonites, Duhobortzi, &c., in the Crimea, and is a valuable, serious man. Senator Hablitz had given us a letter for him ; he appears very kindly disposed to render us every assistance in his power ; from religious motives he has devoted the last thirty years of his life to endeavours to promote the well-being of the several Colonies ; he has been to them an instrument of much good, as Prince Alexander Galitzin told us ; he is seventy years of age. On a visit to the Governor of this place, we met with the Governor of Kherson, which was a pleasant circumstance, as we have it in contemplation to be at that place.

"19th. Accompanied by that valuable old man, Contenius, who acts as our interpreter, we visited prisons, hospitals, and schools ; we had a satisfactory visit at Count ——'s, under whose super-intendence are all the schools in this province. In the evening we went to the monastery to see Macarius, for whom we had a letter from Philaret ; he is rector of the seminary for the sons of the clergy ; he is about my age ; we found him in his cell, a very simple place indeed ; one table and a few stools appeared to be the only furniture in it ; he is a man of great humility and reli-gious tenderness, and he felt his heart so open towards us, as to impart some of the exercises of his mind, and the ways in which the Lord, by his Spirit is pleased to lead him—paths which very few about him can understand ; he has been much tried about the various ceremonies attending divine worship in the Greek Church ; his views of baptism and the supper appear to be very similar to ours ; respecting the ministry, he said that formerly he endeavoured, and that with much care and labour, to prepare his sermons ; but when in the pulpit he attempted to preach them, he felt them to be so dry and lifeless, that his tongue seemed to refuse to perform its office, and he was obliged to stop ; when, under very deep abasement before the Lord, he felt the quicken-ing influences of his Spirit, constraining him to speak, as he then gave him matter and utterance : now, when he ascends the pulpit, his dependence is on the Lord alone, and he has nothing prepared beforehand. We spent some time in silence together, an engage-ment which the dear man appears acquainted with, and during which he shed many tears.

"21st. This morning we had a visit from an old man, eighty years of age, one of the people called Malakans ; they call them-selves Spiritual Christians. We had heard of that people, and hoped to meet with them, but did not know there were any of them in this place. There are about twenty families, and we appointed a meeting with them, to be held at our lodgings that evening. Macarius came in as the meeting was gathering; at first, we feared that his presence might mar the religious opportunity; for, during the reigns of Catherine and Paul, this people and the Duhobortzi suffered heavy persecution from the clergy and the Government. They did not, however, appear to be at all disturbed by his presence. We were soon all gathered into solemn, silent waiting and prostration of soul before the Lord; this is the manner in which these people meet together for divine worship in silence, which is not interrupted, unless some one present apprehends, under the sensible influences of the Divine Spirit, that he is required to speak as a minister among them, or to offer vocal prayer. The meeting was a solemn season; conversation with them afterwards made us desirous to know more of their religious principles and doctrines; we therefore appointed another meeting for conference with them, to be held to-morrow morning, at one of their houses. After they had retired, Macarius remained for some time absorbed in silent meditation, then, with a flood of tears, he cried out, 'In what a state of darkness and ignorance have I been! I thought I was alone in these parts endeavouring to walk in the light of the Lord, to wait for and sensibly to feel the influences of his Spirit, so as to be able to worship Him in spirit and in truth; and behold, how great has been my darkness, so that I did not discover that blaze of light here round about me, among a people, poor in the world, but rich in faith in the Lord Jesus Christ.' He left us much affected.

"22nd. Previous to our going to the meeting with the Spiritual Christians, we prepared a list of the principal subjects respecting which we wished to inquire of them. They were very free to give us every information we asked for, and they did it in few words, accompanied, generally, with some Scripture quotations as their reasons for believing or acting as they did. On all the cardinal points of the Christian religion, the fall of man, salvation by Christ through faith, the meritorious death of Christ, his resurrection, ascension, &c., their views are very clear; also respecting the influence of the Holy Spirit, worship, ministry, baptism, the supper, oaths, &c. &c., we might suppose they were thoroughly acquainted with our religious Society; but they had never heard of us, nor of any people that profess as we do; respecting war, however, their views are not entirely clear; and yet many among

us may learn from them; they said, 'War is a subject that we have
not yet been able fully to understand, so as to reconcile Scripture
with Scripture; we are commanded to obey our rulers, magistrates,
&c., for conscience' sake; and again, we are enjoined to love our
enemies, not to avenge ourselves, to render good for evil; therefore we cannot see fully how we can refuse obedience to the laws
that require our young people to join the army; but in all matters
respecting ourselves, we endeavour to act faithfully as the Gospel
requires; we have never any law-suits; for if anybody smites us
on the one cheek, we turn to him the other; if he takes away any
part of our property, we bear it patiently; we give to him that
asketh, and lend to him that borrows, not asking it back again,
and in all these things the Lord blesses us; the Lord is very good
also to our young men; for, though several of them have been
taken to the army, not one of them has actually borne arms; for,
our principles being known, they have very soon been placed in
offices of trust, such as attending to the provisions of the army, or
something of that sort.' Their ministers are acknowledged in much
the same way as ours; and like us, they consider that their only
and their best reward is the dear Saviour's approbation; therefore
they receive no kind of salary.

"Accompanied by dear Contenius we left Ekaterinoslav early in
the morning of the 23rd, for the colonies of the Mennonites, on the
Dnieper; we came sixty-five versts to the chief village of the fifteen
that form this part of their settlement; they are an interesting
people; much simplicity of manner, and genuine piety appear
prevalent amongst them. I felt my mind so drawn towards them
in the love of Christ; their Bishop, who resides in this village,
was sent for by Contenius to consult on the place and time to
hold a meeting; the dear man, who is very plain in his manners
and way of living, was at the time in the field behind the plough;
for neither he nor any of the clergy receive any salary. They
maintain themselves and families by their honest industry. They
are faithful also in the maintenance of their testimony against
oaths, public diversions, and strong drink. The Emperor exempts
them from military requisitions. The Bishop concluded that there
was no better place than their meeting-house, which is large. At
the time appointed, they came from all the other villages; the
house was crowded with the people and their ministers; much

solidity was evinced. The people settled at once into such stillness and retiredness of spirit, that it seemed as if we were amidst
our own friends, in their religious meetings. I was enlarged
among them in the Gospel of Christ; Contenius interpreted from
the French into German; dear Allen had an excellent communication to them, which I first rendered into French, and then Contenius into German; we also had access together to the place of
prayer."

They spent about a week in visiting these colonies, and
were much interested with the Malakans and the Mennonites;
but their visit to the colonies of the Duhobortzi was far from
satisfactory, because of the spirit of unbelief which prevailed
amongst them. He felt constrained to have a meeting with
them, and remarks :—

"No seriousness appeared over them at any time. O how my
soul was bowed before the Lord, earnestly craving that He would
touch their hearts by his power and love! I felt also much
towards the young people. I embraced the opportunity to preach
the Lord Jesus Christ, and that salvation which is through faith
in Him; 'If ye believe not that I am He (the Christ, the Son of
God), ye shall die in your sins.' I entreated them to try what
manner of spirit they are of; for many spirits are gone out into
the world; and 'hereby know we the Spirit of God; every spirit
that confesseth not that Jesus Christ has come in the flesh, is not
of God; but this is that spirit of Antichrist,' &c. Whilst I was
speaking, the old men appeared restless; they invited me several
times to retire to the house, but I could not do so till I had
endeavoured to relieve my mind of the great concern I felt for
them : many of the people were very attentive, and the Truth
appeared to reach their hearts. We then went into the house
with the old men ; they had a few things to say, but not to any
more satisfaction than yesterday. We left them with heavy hearts,
and returned to Altona.

" At five o'clock the meeting with the Mennonites began ; it was
very numerously attended ; the people came from several other
villages. O ! what a difference in our feelings with this people,
and those we were with in the morning ; then darkness encom-

passed us, but here was light, as in Goshen : the Lord's presence
was over us ; the stream of the Gospel of life and salvation
freely flowed towards the various ranks in life ; many in the
assembly were contrited before the Lord, and under a sense of
his redeeming love and presence we took a solemn leave of each
other.

"There are no post-horses to be had in these parts ; we therefore hired one of the Mennonites to take us with his horses to
Perekop. Early in the morning of the 31st, after a solemn
and tendering opportunity in the family where we had been so
kindly entertained, several others coming in also, we set off for
a long journey through the wilderness. Contenius, who had
become increasingly endeared to us, and whose services have
been so valuable, accompanied us about ten versts on our way.
At the entrance of the desert we took a solemn leave of each
other, under feelings of Christian love. This desert or steppe
extends all the way to Perekop and a great distance beyond, and
to the right and left ; the water is bad and brackish. Several
lakes of salt water occur. Large herds of cattle, flocks of sheep,
and many wild horses are met with on these steppes.

"A Mennonite, from Altona, overtook us in this wilderness ; he
was the bearer of letters for us, which had arrived after our
departure. One was from America, from my beloved wife ; in
ten weeks it had travelled from America to England, whence it
was sent to Petersburg, then to Moscow, to Ekaterinoslav,
then to several of the colonies on the Meloshnaia, and finally it
came to hand in this desert.

" Passing one day through a large village of the Tartars, where
we stopped to try to purchase some refreshments, the Chief
among them, who spoke Russ, pressingly invited us to his habitation ; he gave us a cup of tea, and said that, if we would stay
the night, he would have a sheep killed—a great treat among
them. We could not, however, accept his kind invitation. He
then took us to a school where we met a large number of boys.
Their master is a Mahometan priest. The boys sat cross-legged
after the Eastern fashion. They were writing with reeds instead
of pens, from right to left. Others were reading in the Alcoran.
We felt constrained to speak to them of the great love of God to
man, ' for God so loved the world that He gave his only-

begotten Son that whosoever believeth on Him should not perish, but have everlasting life,' &c. &c. Our Pole interpreted what we said into Russ, and the person who attended us into Tartar. The young men and their master were serious, and repeatedly expressed their approbation, by putting their hand on their breast, with eyes lifted up ; they manifested their love towards us on our going away, and our kind host kissed our hands three times, and then laid them on his forehead.

" Our road led us afterwards frequently in sight of the Putrid Sea. We met several herds of camels, flocks of large birds, and some large eagles. Wolves are very common on these steppes, and they are so bold that they sometimes attack travellers. We passed by a large one lying on the ground with an eagle, which had probably attacked him, by his side ; its talons were nearly buried in his back ; in the struggle both had died."

After a tedious journey over " the great steppe," they reached Perekop on the 2nd of Sixth Month, and once more had " the luxury of a good wash in pure, fresh water, which they had not enjoyed for some days ;" but, " finding very little to detain them there," they continued their journey the next day, " still travelling over the steppe." They arrived at Simferopol about noon on the 4th of Sixth Month, and it was not till that day that they saw, for the first time since leaving Abo—a journey of nearly two thousand miles—" the horizon bounded by a range of high hills, or mountains." The " face of the country had now changed ;" they were in the midst of the beautiful scenery of the Crimea.

———

Arrived at the chief scene of attraction in the Crimea, Stephen Grellet and his companion at once resumed their accustomed work. In the spirit of the Apostle, who—without giving up any Christian principle, or lowering the standard of Gospel requirements—was " made all things to all men that he might by all means save some," they freely

mingled in religious intercourse with all classes and denominations that came in their way, both among the rich and the
poor, " ready, as much as was in them, to preach the
Gospel " to all.   Of their interesting labours in those parts,
and the conclusion of their visit in Russia, at Odessa, S. G.
gives the following description :—

"Simferopol, 5th of Sixth Month.   This place contains four
thousand inhabitants, who are mostly Tartars and Turks ; they
have four mosques.   We find here some of the Spiritual Christians, called Malakans.   One of them, a nice and intelligent
young man, speaks some French.   They have Bibles and Testaments in some of the Eastern languages, but they find very few
of the Mahometans willing to read them ; they will read written
but not printed books.   One of the Malakans saying that he was
formerly among the Duhobortzi, I inquired of him how he had
become convinced of their errors ; he answered with great energy,
'I had the Bible put into my hands ; I read it, and is it possible to read the Bible, and not be convinced of the great errors
under which I was?'   We have had several very interesting religious opportunities with this people : they give us the same
answers to the questions we put to them which their brethren at
Ekaterinoslav did : they have also given us much information
relative to the great persecutions they endured previous to the
Emperor Alexander's interfering on their behalf : in some distant
governments his benevolent views towards them and his orders in
their favour have been evaded, so that some of their families are
yet separated by banishment.   We have several copies of the
New Testament in Russ just printed ; they were sent to us at
Ekaterinoslav.   These people are delighted with them ; one of
them read to the others in the Gospel of John.

"We set off early in the morning of the 6th of Sixth Month
for Baktchiserai.   The country is beautiful, rich and fertile, and
well cultivated ; there are very fine vineyards, and lofty trees on
the high ground.   This town is very ancient : it was the capital
of old Tartary, where their Khans used to reside.

"We took a police officer, a Tartar, who speaks the Russian
language, which very few here do, to accompany us to 'the

Fortress.' It has the appearance of a strong wall, from sixty to eighty feet high ; but it is a solid hard rock. The entrance is through an iron door. It is a place inhabited by Karaite Jews.

"The houses are two, three, and four stories high. The windows have blinds or bars, so that none of the inmates can be seen. We did not see a woman out of doors. Arrived there, we sat down in the market-place, for we were much fatigued by the walk and the powerful sun.   Some men, after a while, came to look at us, and soon after their High Priest approached, and invited us to go into the synagogue, speaking to us through the medium of our Tartar, who translated again to our Pole, and he to us.   His name is Isaac Covish. We were soon joined by other Rabbis and Jews. They have another synagogue near, one not being sufficient to contain them all.   They are about one thousand men, besides women and children.   They tell us that they have evidences from their records, that their ancestors have been on this rock for more than nine hundred years ; but, by their tradi- tions, they trace their coming here to the time when Titus came against Jerusalem. They differ much from other Jews.   Like that people *formerly*, they till the ground. They have gardens, vineyards, ploughed fields, &c. They take great care in the religious and moral education of their children.   Besides having the Law written on parchment, kept in the Ark, which they showed us, they have the Old Testament printed in books, and each of their children has a copy of it.   It contains nothing but the simple Scriptures : none of the Rabbinical additions, with which they do not unite.   They told me that our own Bibles are a very faithful version of theirs.   We have been told by the Governor and police officers at Perekop and other places, that these Jews are very exemplary in every part of their conduct ; they know no instance of any of them being ever brought before them for misdemeanour of any kind.   A very similar testimony is given of the Malakans wherever they reside, so far as we have been able to hear.   A large number of the Jews col- lected about us, and our conversation became of a more serious nature, chiefly with the High Priest ; he fully believes, he said, in the operations of the Divine Spirit, and that the Lord, by the prophets, bears a clear testimony to it ; among other pro- phecies he mentioned that of Joel ; he also holds the sentiment

that if all men were obedient to the teachings and guidance of
the Holy Spirit, there would be no difference between Jews and
Gentiles, for all would bring forth the same fruits—all would
bring the same acceptable offering unto the Lord. He was told
that he must then believe that the prophecy of Joel was now fulfilled, ' It shall come to pass in the last days, saith the Lord, that
I will pour out of my Spirit upon all flesh,' &c. &c., for we are
now living in these latter days ; this led us to speak of the coming
of our Lord Jesus Christ, and the prophecies respecting Him, the
manner of his coming, the end for which He came, &c. &c.
Among others reference was made to this Scripture testimony :
' The sceptre shall not depart from Judah, nor a lawgiver from
between his feet, until Shiloh come, and unto him shall the
gathering of the people be.' — *Gen.* xlix. 10. He well knew that
the sceptre had departed from Judah some time before the destruction of Jerusalem by Titus, that Christ had then come on
the earth, and in Him was so literally accomplished all that the
prophets had written of Him, that it might appear as if they had
given a description of what had already come to pass, rather than
of what was not fulfilled till many centuries afterwards. He remained silent and pensive for a length of time, then said, ' I know
not what to say.' We had some further serious conversation, and
on parting he desired that we might not forget to visit some of
his people further on in the Crimea, expressing his satisfaction
with our visit here."

On the 7th of Sixth Month they reached Sebastopol, at
which place, as well as at Simferopol and Theodosia, they had
extensive religious service with the inhabitants ; also in visiting the hospitals, prisons, and schools. S. G. continues his
narrative :—

" 12th. This morning early we set off for the German and
Swiss colonies. Governor Engel kindly gave us a Greek and a
Tartar to accompany us, and to interpret. These colonies lie out
of the public road. Heilbrunn, the first we came to, thirty-six
versts from Theodosia, is settled by emigrants from Wurtemberg.
The people were at work in the fields, but as soon as they heard
that we wished to see them, they repaired to the school-house,

used also for a place of worship. They have no minister among
them at present, but they nevertheless attend their meetings for
divine worship with great regularity. We understand that the
other German colonists hereaway are similarly circumstanced.
Our silent sitting together was very precious. They are acquainted
with spiritual worship. We had but little to communicate in the
way of ministry, but we were edified and comforted together.
They were very urgent that we should stay the night with them,
but we wished to go on to the Swiss. Some of them accompanied
us to Zurichthal. We were a motley group; the German, the
Russian, the Greek, the Tartar, the Pole, the English and the
French—all going the same way, for the same object. O that
people of all nations and languages may thus become banded
together, and harmoniously travel with each other in the one way
to everlasting life !

" The colonists here came from the canton of Zurich. Our
meeting for divine worship with them on First-day morning was
precious and solemn. We sat a considerable time in silence
together. Worship in spirit and in truth was performed. In
the afternoon we passed through Rosenthal, a large village of
Roman Catholics, on our way to Neusatz, another village of Lutherans, who came from about Stutgard. We lodged that night
among them, and appointed a meeting for the ensuing morning,
an invitation to which was extended to another settlement of the
same people. Next morning a deputation came from the Roman
Catholic village to request that we would not pass them by without having a meeting with them also. As we passed through
their village, my soul was strongly drawn towards them, but I
apprehended they might not be willing to attend a meeting appointed by us; now we felt prepared to accede to their request.
Like their Protestant neighbours, they have no priest among
them. One comes once a year only.

" At the time appointed we arrived at the Roman Catholic
village. As we entered it the steeple bell began to ring. We
expected that the meeting would be held in a private house, but
they told us that no place was more suitable, or better able to
accommodate the people, than their church. On entering it we
found a numerous company already gathered, for it is a large
village. They had lighted their wax candles on the altar, after

their usual manner, though the sun shone very bright. I did not
think much of this. My mind was under deep exercise for the
people, with earnest desire that they might come to the light of
the Lord, and be gathered to the brightness of his arising. We
took seats, facing the people, with our backs to the altar. After
we had sat a while in silence, we were several times a little disturbed by a man coming near to us to ring again and again the
bell of the steeple. I could not think what the man meant, but
at last he told me in Dutch, 'I do not think, sir, that anybody
else will come, for the whole village is here.' I was then about
rising from my seat; the interpreter stood by me. The Lord
enlarged me in his Gospel. The people were directed to Christ,
the Shepherd and Bishop of souls, the High Priest of our Christian
profession, who is very nigh every one of us, and ready to minister in the temple of the heart to every one that waits upon Him.

"15th. This is the third time we have come to Simferopol.
We found here five of the Malakans who have waited several
days for our return. They are a deputation from their brethren,
who reside at a considerable distance in the Government of Tam-
bov, where there are upwards of two hundred families who profess
with them. They inform us that most of them can read, and are
in the daily practice of reading the Scriptures in their families.
They confirm the account given us of their great numbers in
several Governments, especially in Astrakhan, the Caucasus,
Saratov, &c.

"16th. We left very early this morning for Perekop; but
some of the Malakans were at our door before daylight, waiting
to bid us farewell once more; they also brought us bread for our
journey; this is a very general practice in the Crimea, when
departing to go into the desert; to decline it would give great
offence to the givers. One of their old people, a venerable-look-
ing man, with his long beard and sheepskin covering, appeared
very desirous to go with us a little way; he got in and sat
between us; we could not converse with one another, but there
is a language more forcible than words; he held each of us by
the hand; big tears rolled down on his venerable beard; we
rode on several versts in solemn silence, till we came to a water
which we had to pass, when he took us into his arms with the
greatest affection, kissed us, and got out of the carriage; on look-

ing back we saw him prostrated on the ground, in the act of worship or prayer to God ; and, after he rose, as long as we could discern him, he stood with his face towards us, his hands lifted up ; we felt it, as he did, a solemn separation. May the Lord bless and protect that portion of his heritage, a people whom He has raised by his own power, and instructed by his own free Spirit. We visited at Perekop the prison in the fortress, and the hospital, and set off at noon, on the 17th, for Berislav, where we did not arrive till midnight. We crossed the Dnieper for the third time at dark ; the only accommodation we could obtain was a dirty yard, where we spent the rest of the night in our vehicle.

" 18th. We visited a small prison, in bad condition, and a hospital, and travelled again over the wilderness to Kherson where Count de St. Priest, whom we saw at Ekaterinoslav, at the Governor's, gave us an invitation to make our home at his house : he is the Governor of this part of the country. He kindly gave us his horses and carriage to take us to several places we wished to visit. They are now preparing to erect here a monument to the memory of Howard ; this is the place where he caught the prison fever, and where he died of it ; what better monument could they erect for him, than a prison conducted after the plans he has given. We intend to represent the whole of this to the Emperor. We returned to dine at the Governor's, and went afterwards to the seminary for the sons of the clergy. The Director and Rector of it are both pious men. The latter kindly acted as our interpreter to the pupils.

" The next day we had an interesting opportunity with about one thousand five hundred of the children of the soldiers. The system of mutual instruction has been introduced among the juniors. We presented them with fifteen sheets of the 'Scripture Lessons,' sent to us at this place from Petersburg, by order of the Emperor. We then paid a satisfactory visit to the Mayor, who had been our kind and useful attendant. He has a numerous family, in whom the parents have the satisfaction of seeing the fruits of their Christian care. We had a precious religious opportunity with them, and then set off for Nikolaiev. As we were leaving Kherson, two of the Greek priests, whom we had seen at the seminary, came to bid us farewell, and to bring us five loaves of bread for our use in the wilderness, to evince their love and good-will to us. With much kindness and tenderness they desired that the Lord's blessing might be on our labours of love, and bring us safe back to our respective families.

"22nd. Nikolaiev. Admiral Greig, Commandant-in-Chief of the Black Sea and of this place, received us with kindness. We had frequently been with his sister at Petersburg. We met at his house a pretty large company with whom we had a religious opportunity."

Leaving Nikolaiev on the evening of the 22nd, they reached Odessa the next day. Here they were detained by various engagements, and finally closed their religious labours in Russia. S. G. writes :—

"Odessa, 28th. We have been occupied these last two days in writing several letters ; one to the Emperor, to give him an account of the miserable condition of several of the prisons we have visited since we left Moscow. We have also made a particular statement of our visit to the Mennonites, and the Malakans. We have sent him an account of the religious principles of the latter, and a representation of the sufferings to which a few of them continue to be exposed, in some of the governments. We have also requested, on their behalf, that he would allow them lands to settle upon, near the Moloshnaia, or in that district, and that the same civil and religious privileges should be extended to them which he has granted the Mennonites. As they had hitherto been confounded with the Duhobortzi, we have pointed out the distinction between them. We have also once more conveyed to the dear Emperor, before leaving his dominions, our deep solicitude that, by the grace of our Lord Jesus Christ and faithfulness to the dictates of the Holy Spirit, he may walk in the Divine fear and counsel, and so fulfil the great and important stewardship given him as Emperor over this vast nation ; that he may promote the honour and glory of God and the happiness of his subjects, and finally obtain, through the redeeming love and mercy of God in Christ Jesus, the salvation of his soul, and exchange his earthly for a heavenly crown. We have also written to the Empress-Dowager, and sent her a statement of the great mortality in the foundling hospitals, and our painful concern at

finding that throughout, where we have travelled, the education
of the girls among the mass of the population is totally neglected.
The only places where we found a little attention paid to the girls,
were some of the Tartar towns, and there they only learned to
read. We have also addressed the Mennonites and the 'Spiritual
Christians.' Our epistle to these will, we hope, circulate extensively among these interesting people.

"The arrival yesterday of a French ship that touched at Constantinople, where the plague prevails, has spread an alarm here.
A man on board the ship died of this contagious disease since her
arrival; another is not expected to live, and several others are
sick. We are thus brought under very serious considerations; for
Constantinople is the place to which we had intended to proceed
from this place; earnest is our cry to the Lord that, as He has
thus far led us by his counsel in the way that He would have us
to go, He would direct all our future steps.

"After carefully weighing the subject before the Lord, craving his direction, we have felt it to be our right way to proceed,
as before contemplated, over the Black Sea to Constantinople,
believing that the Lord can protect us from the noisome pestilence, as He has done from many other imminent dangers. After
thus concluding we felt sweet peace, and have engaged our passage
on board a large British ship, the *Lord Cathcart*, loaded with
wheat, going by Constantinople to Malta. This evening we
hear that three more deaths, by the plague, have occurred among
the crew of the French ship, and that several others are attacked
with it.

"7th. We visited General Ingoff, who has all the colonies
under his superintendence; he was absent when we arrived here;
we are much pleased with him; he is a mild, serious man. We
afterwards went on board the ship, to have our baggage stowed
away; she is a large, fine vessel, lately returned from the East
Indies. This is a commodious port; many vessels from various
nations are here at present."

The next day they set sail from Constantinople. "I am
under no apprehension," says Stephen Grellet, "that I have
left Russia before the right time; I feel great peace in looking
back upon my various religious labours in that Empire."

CHAPTER XXI.

Third Visit to Europe.

CONSTANTINOPLE — DARDANELLES — SMYRNA — SCIO — ARCHIPELAGO
— ATHENS.

STEPHEN GRELLET had been permitted to leave Russia under very peaceful feelings. These continued to cheer him on his passage over the Black Sea, though, notwithstanding the fine weather, he was suffering from "very distressing sickness." The ground of his rejoicing was not that, through the Divine power, "the spirits had been made subject," but rather that, through the Redeemer's love, "his name was written in heaven." He felt himself "an unprofitable servant," yet in looking *back* upon the scenes of his past labours, he had the reward of grace—the "answer of peace."

In looking *forward*, however, to what yet awaited him, he was brought very low "under great pressure of exercise." It was "not the fear of going into the midst of the plague that distressed him :"—

"I feel confidence," he writes on board the *Lord Cathcart*, "that my life is in the hands of my Almighty Father and Protector, so that, in quietness and peace, I can resign myself into his Divine hands and keeping ;" "but," he adds, "I have a baptism to pass through, under a sense of the further service prepared for me in the nations to which I am going. I feel that I am but a worm. O Lord ! direct and assist by thy Spirit thy very poor and unworthy servant !"

"12th. I spent a night of watchfulness unto prayer, like Jacob, wrestling the whole night for the Lord's blessing, and towards morning, the light of his countenance has very graciously arisen upon me. My trust and confidence are renewed in Him, blessed and praised be his adorable name !

" At seven a.m. we discovered the entrance into the Bosphorus. We came down very rapidly, keeping close to the Asiatic side, and by six o'clock p.m. we anchored near the Seraglio.

"Constantinople, Seventh Month 13th. We landed at ten a.m. Thomas Nixon Black, a merchant here, for whom we had letters, kindly came on board to welcome us. He accompanied us up to Pera, where Sir Robert Liston, the British Ambassador, resides. He had heard from London that we proposed to come to Constantinople, and expected us. Both he and his lady, who looks like a serious, motherly woman, very kindly pressed us to make our home in their palace, which stands in a very airy situation ; but we declined their invitation, for we had previously accepted that of Nixon Black. We found that it would be unsafe to put up at any of the Turkish hotels, in most of which there are, or have been, some cases of the plague. Sir Robert Liston has had the kindness to send his Dragoman and a Janizary to bring our baggage from the ship. We dined with the Ambassador. He stood for some years in that character in Philadelphia, before Washington was built, so that both he and his wife are well acquainted with several of our friends in that city, where they frequently attended our meetings ; they are therefore not strangers to our religious principles. Among other persons we met there, is his chief Dragoman, an old Turk of good information. He communicates nearly daily with the Sultan. Most of the business of Ambassadors here is transacted through such a medium. He speaks good English and French, and evinces great liberality of sentiment. We received here a large supply of religious books, in different languages ; and a pretty good supply of New Testaments, sent us from Malta, in Greek, Latin and Italian.

" 15th. Among the serious persons that we met with, are Greeks, Armenians, Italians, some from Ragusa, also the old Dragoman and his son-in-law. They generally manifest a great desire to become informed of our Christian testimonies ; the Ragusans especially. We had religious opportunities with these persons to some satisfaction. We do not expect to have much to do among the Turks ; my chief concern is for the Armenians and Greeks.

While in Constantinople, they had much service in visiting prisons, &c., and also in the families of the different Ambassadors. On this subject S. G. remarks :—

"Sir R. Liston took us first to the Spanish Ambassador's, a particular friend of his ; he sent him word yesterday that he should take a late breakfast with him. On account of the great heat of the weather we left Constantinople very early, but there having been a fine rain during the night, it was cool and very refreshing. On our entering the apartment of the Spanish Ambassador's wife, we were greatly surprised. It seemed from her dress and manners, as if we were with one of our women Friends : the Ambassador himself is a grave man, and simple in his dress and manners. She told us that from a child she was brought up in simplicity of dress, which she likes ; it was, said she, her valued mother's maxim and practice to endeavour to adorn the mind with Christian virtues, and not the body with vain apparel, which disfigures rather than embellishes it. 'I have frequently thought,' she said, 'that could I have been in one of those nations where your Friends reside, I should have been one of your Society, for what I have heard of your religious principles has greatly endeared your Friends to me ; you are, however, the first that I have ever seen. My mother often spoke of your Society ; she had read some of your books, but never saw any of your members ; she dressed as plainly as I do.' We found, on conversing with her, that she has a claim to our Christian affection ; the tenderness of her heart rendered her very near to us ; she is acquainted with the sensible influence of the Divine Spirit. We were soon met by some of the other Ambassadors and their wives—the Austrian, the Neapolitan, and the French. It was pleasant to see the harmony that appeared to be maintained among these representatives of different nations ; had I anticipated such a meeting, I should have probably have passed under much exercise, but being thus brought without any agency of ours, I felt it my place to yield to whatever service might be designed by my dear Master on such an occasion ; all speak French well ; it was therefore easy to communicate to them what, in the love of the dear Redeemer, we apprehended ourselves required to do. We then went to the Russian

Ambassador, who kindly offered to serve us in all things that he can.

"21st. We have had several religious meetings in the palace of the British Ambassador, held in the large audience chamber; and some others at our own lodgings, where our generous host treats us with great kindness. We met with some valuable people among the Armenians; they told us of some pious persons at Tiflis and that neighbourhood. We have sent them some books that treat on our Christian doctrines. We also find great openness among the Greeks. We do not go to see the Greek Patriarch, as there are some cases of the plague in his palace. We often see in the streets persons attacked with this disease, and it is not unfrequent that we meet the bodies of such as have died with it carried to the grave.

"We were to-day with several strangers—Prussians, Swedes, Spaniards, &c. We directed them to the peaceful Spirit of Christ. We had also another satisfactory meeting at the palace of the British Ambassador; among many others, the various Ambassadors and their wives were present. Sir Robert Liston and wife have acted towards us the part of dear friends, and greatly facilitated our religious services, when opportunity for such has presented."

Having taken their departure from the Crescent City, S. G. goes on to say:—

"Dardanelles, 25th of Seventh Month. Feeling ourselves at liberty to leave Constantinople, we took our passage for Smyrna, in the British brig *Whiting.*

"26th. Smyrna. We came down here with great rapidity, the current being very strong. We had the island of Tenedos on our right, and the spot on which ancient Troy was seated on our left, in Asia Minor. Then, passing by Mytilene, we arrived here this afternoon, where we have taken up our quarters at an inn, kept by a Swiss.

"29th. Our minds are here greatly relieved from the load of oppression and distress under which we were at Constantinople. We meet with a number Greeks who are serious persons, and religiously disposed. We have had some private and more public

religious opportunities among them.   A Dragoman kindly under-
takes to be our interpreter both among the Greeks and such
of the Turks as we visit.   One of these in particular has much
interested us.   He is the Bey Effendi, Director of the Custom-
house.   He sent us an invitation by our Dragoman to visit him.
He is a mild, good-looking man.   When we came to his spacious
apartment, he was sitting after the Turkish fashion in his divan,
on a rich carpet, cross-legged, with several pillows under and
near him.   There were about twenty Turks with him, who
all kept silence.   The Bey had his own Dragoman in attendance,
so ours gave way to him.   He first introduced coffee—a sign that
the visitor is welcome ; then sherbet, a cooling pleasant drink—
a further evidence that he is superlatively welcome ; soon after
which a conversation began between the Bey and us.   His
Dragoman interpreted, but it went on very heavily.   Our minds
were strongly attracted towards the Bey, but there was something
which we could not understand ; it was even distressing to our
feelings.   On our withdrawing the Bey took leave of us in a most
kind manner, as if he had a sense of the state of our minds.   He
called our Dragoman near and whispered to him, 'I cannot
confide in these men (the Turks) about me, but very soon I will
send another request to these friends to come here.'   We felt
at first much disappointed on finding the Bey surrounded by
many more Turks than there were on the preceding day ; but the
Bey now told us through our own Dragoman, 'You may now
speak freely ; *all* these are my friends, in whom I have all
confidence.'   He evinced great liberality of sentiment ; said that
he lamented the benighted state of his nation ; inquired into the
nature of our religious principles, and both he and the other
Turks appeared much pleased with our answers.   He said that if
all men were attentive and obedient to the Spirit of God in their
hearts, peace, harmony, and happiness would prevail over the
whole world ; for all the woe and misery that attend man in
this life are the consequence of his departure from this blessed
and Divine principle.   He made no objection to the testimony we
bore to that redemption from sin that comes by the Lord Jesus
Christ, and to the nature of that kingdom of blessedness and
glory which He has prepared for those, who, believing in Him,
love and obey Him.   Being told that we proposed to go from

Smyrna to Scio, he called for his secretary to write some lines to recommend us to the Turkish Governor there, his particular friend, and son of the Captain Pasha at Constantinople. The secretary wrote on his knees, with a reed. Instead of signing it, the Bey, after their manner, sealed it with his signet, which he carries at his wrist.

" We had several religious opportunities with the Armenians and others; also with many of the Europeans of several nations. We also visited the Greek and Armenian hospitals, for some of whose inmates we felt very tenderly. We had much satisfaction in a visit to a school for about three hundred Greek children.

" 31st. Paid another satisfactory visit to the Bey Effendi; we gave him ' Penn's Maxims,' ' Rise and Progress,' ' No Cross, no Crown,' &c. He desired Regio, our Dragoman, to come and read these to him.

" By the advice of our friends here, we have procured a person to act as interpreter for us, and to provide for us in our future journeyings; without such an attendant, they say we could not get along; for here, as in Russia and particularly among the Tartars, we have to buy our food and cook it ourselves. Sobiesky, our Pole, had been very serviceable to us in these respects. The person we have engaged here is well recommended; he is a Greek, and speaks the Turkish, Italian, and French languages."

Having made these arrangements they left Smyrna, and went on board the boat for Scio, at half-past ten at night.

———

Nearly a month was now occupied by a visit to Scio and Athens, and some of the intermediate islands. Of this, and the perilous incidents connected with it, Stephen Grellet gives graphic details in his journal, from which we make a few extracts :—

" We left Smyrna on the 31st of the Seventh Month, 1819. The boat on which we embarked is of the shape of a canoe, with two men to row it. As it was fine weather it was expected that we should reach Scio in about twenty-four hours; a small

quantity of provision was therefore thought sufficient; we went
on very nicely for a few hours when the wind began to blow
heavily, and the waves washed over us, to our no small danger;
each of us having a large camlet cloak, we spread them over us
and the boat, making a kind of deck; at the same time we were
busy bailing out the water that washed in with every wave; our
rowers meanwhile made great efforts to reach an uninhabited
barren spot, called English Island. We did not discover on it a
single shrub or anything green; perhaps there might have been
some grass before the great heat of summer, but now everything
is parched by the scorching sun. We were thankful in being
able to make a safe landing, for, very soon after we had done so,
the wind increased furiously, and had we been still at sea, we
could hardly have escaped a watery grave. The day after our
coming to this island, two boats with Turks in them also came to
it, landing at the same place we had done. My dear companion
and the rest of the company had taken a walk to seek for water,
and I was left alone in the tent. Some of the Turks came and
sat down at the entrance of it, having with them fire-arms, their
large swords and poignards; they began to fire their guns and
pistols at blank marks, and by their signs urged me to show my
fire-arms; they were beginning to be rude, when my company,
attracted by their firing, returned; they at first thought I had
been murdered; the Turks then retired to their boats, where they
continued during the night—which we passed in some anxiety,
watching their movements; but to our relief, towards morning,
they rowed away to another part of the island. Our stock of provisions being very small, we had to limit ourselves to a scanty
allowance; our greatest difficulty was the want of water; we in
vain sought for some; neither could we discover any fish near
the island, nor birds on it.

"Our minds are preserved in calmness, stayed on the Lord; we
have the confidence that He can open the way for our release from
this state of danger and suffering. In his will we feel resigned;
with reverent gratitude we can also say, that if our mouth is
dried for want of water, our minds are refreshed by his Divine
presence; for truly we feel as David said, 'All my springs
are in thee, O Lord.' Our bathing often in the sea is refreshing.

" Scio, 4th.   The wind abated last night so as to encourage us
to put to sea again early this morning.   It was hard and dangerous work, till we had succeeded in doubling the Cape, and were
well drenched by the waves.   We reached this island early this
afternoon, with hearts prepared to ascribe thanksgiving and praise
to the Lord, who has sustained us under hunger and thirst, and
delivered us from imminent danger.   Blessed for ever and ever
be his holy name!   Amen and amen!

" 5th.   Accompanied by the British Consul, who is an Italian,
we went to see the Turkish Governor, and gave him the letter we
had from Ali Bey.   He received us with affability, and kindly
offered to assist us in whatever way he can, whilst we continue
on this island.   We find here a Greek Neophyte, named Bambass,
a very interesting, sensible, and pious man of Christian liberality.
He takes great interest in the education of the children of his
nation, particularly of the girls, who have been so neglected
in this particular, that there are but few women, even among
the wives of wealthy Greeks, who can read.   Many of the men
have received a good education in several parts of Europe.   Bambass is at the head of the schools here.   With much labour he
has compiled a book of ethics from the ancient Greek philosophers.
His extracts contain the best sentiments out of their works.   He
has a printing-press, and he intends this work for the use of
schools.   It has brought us under much concern that the minds
of the youth should be thus early directed to heathen writers,
instead of having instilled into them the pure principles of
Christianity.   Where can we find any so pure, and so excellent
as in the Holy Scriptures?

" 8th.   Feeling deeply the vital importance that an education
given to young people should be grounded on Christian principles,
we have prepared in the Greek language the same Scripture
Lessons we had compiled in Russia.   We have spent nearly the
whole of these last few nights in completing them.   We have
presented them to Bambass, telling him also of our first inducement for preparing them in Russia.   He examined them with
much attention, then said, ' This is the very thing that is wanted
—surely Divine Providence has sent you here.'   Then, in the
most noble manner, he concluded to lay aside his own work, compiled with so much labour, and immediately to print the Lessons

instead. We have visited several Greeks, who reside in the country. Some of them are men of religious feelings.

"This is a beautiful island. By means of irrigation they render it literally a watered garden, and a great variety of excellent fruits, vegetables, &c., grow luxuriantly.

"We went, this afternoon, four miles out of town on mules, to visit some of the schools of Bambass. Here we met with several of the chief Greeks of the island, with one of whom we and some of the company took a late dinner. The way opened for a religious opportunity with them. The more we are with Bambass, the greater esteem we have for him. He has at heart the best welfare of the people.

"In the afternoon we went to the country seat of Peole Mavrocordati, a very beautiful place; it was a treat to pass the night in a clean and cool lodging, and to sleep on a bed, which we have very seldom done since we left Petersburg; yet even here, as the man was arranging the bed-clothes, a scorpion, near the pillow, stung him so severely that his hand swelled considerably up to the arm, attended with much pain; dressed with some alkali, it was, however, nearly well by morning. Professor Bambass joined us at this house; we had a satisfactory religious meeting with them; the purity and simplicity of the Christian religion, as set forth in the Gospel by the Apostles, was unfolded to them, and contrasted with the many ceremonies, Jewish and idolatrous practices, that have been devised and introduced into the nominal Church by Christian professors under various names. Bambass said, after the meeting concluded, 'I fully unite with the testimony borne this evening among us; I am in the monastic order; I was introduced into it when very young, before my judgment was formed, or I was even of an age to form one. Monks have done much harm to the Church, and they bear some of the strong marks the Apostles gave of the apostacy.'

"13th. Apprehending that the time of our departure from Scio is near, we have hired a boat of about five tons, to take us to several other islands, and thence to the Morea. This evening we went out into the country to John Rodocanaki's, the primate, to have one more meeting with the people in his neighbourhood. Bambass was there. The banker of the Sultan also, and several of the Ephori. We were brought under very solemn feelings together, and the Lord's power was manifested over us."

Having completed their services in Scio, they crossed the
Archipelago to Athens. S. G. remarks :—

" 14th. We took our departure from Scio, accompanied by our
Greek interpreter, with peaceful minds and grateful hearts, for
the Lord's help extended to us on this island, where we leave
many who have been much endeared to us, in the love of the
Gospel of Christ, our Redeemer. We proceeded only ten miles on
our way, for our boat is a dull sailer, unless the wind is very fair.
Our two men and a boy, who manage her, have not much energy.

" 15th. Having passed last night in our boat, the starry
heavens for our canopy, we proceeded on our voyage, but had
come fifteen miles only when our captain cast anchor again. This
is a very rocky coast. We went on shore and found a beautiful
grotto, where, sheltered from the sun, we two sat down together
in this solitary retreat, and held our little meeting. The Lord
contrited our spirits by his good presence ; truly He draws near
to two only, who are met in his name. Though solitary, we feel
at seasons as if we were encircled by many of our beloved friends
in England and America, and some of those precious ones whom
we have visited in several places. We unite with them in our
spirits in proclaiming the love, mercy, goodness and power of a
gracious God and Redeemer.

" 17th. We were intending for Karysto ; but a strong contrary
wind brought us to the island of Andro. We visited their
village, and had a religious opportunity with the people and their
priest. We left with them several New Testaments in Greek.

" 19th. Came to Tino this afternoon. We had proceeded only
a few hours towards that island, when we met a vessel, the crew
of which told us, that last night they were chased by pirates, in
two large row-boats, full of men. They had fired several times
at them, but their vessel sailing well had enabled them to escape.
This was unpleasant information ; but as it was now noon, we
hoped to escape them. As we were going between the two islands,
Andro and Tino, we discovered at a distance a row-boat, which
we thought might be a fisherman, and we kept on our course ;
but the wind dying away we saw two other boats join it and come
towards us. Our captain soon knew them to be pirates of the
worst kind ; who destroy lives, sink the vessel, and carry away

only the plunder. We were very near an inlet on Tino, but there was no wind, and the boat too clumsy to be acted upon by our oars. Meanwhile the pirates had come very near us. It did not appear that we could escape their merciless hands ; when He who commandeth the wind and the sea, and they obey Him, caused the wind to blow from the very direction, which took our boat, fast as the flight of a bird, right into the inlet of the island— where the pirates dared not venture. Had not the Lord thus in his mercy interposed, a few minutes more would probably have ended our mortal lives. Surely we have cause to bless and to magnify his adorable name ! Our Greeks appeared to be sensible of the wonderful escape.

"We visited the inhabitants in their little town ; had some religious service among them, and distributed some New Testaments and tracts. We left them early this morning ; we were nearly out of sight when we saw a boat coming from the island towards us ; they were men who were absent from the town last night ; on their return, seeing the New Testaments and tracts, they were desirous that we should give some to them also, which we did."

With some difficulty and danger they landed at Zea, where they passed the night. S. G. says :—

"Leaving that island, we doubled Cape Colonna ; at the point of which stand many large columns, monuments of Grecian antiquity. The evening of the 23rd the wind so increased that our captain sought for shelter in a bay ; we could not find any inhabitants, though we ascended a high hill to look out for them ; we passed the night again in the boat. The scorpions on shore are so numerous, a small red ant, whose bite is like fire, so abundant, and the danger from robbers so great, that we are told it is safer to be in our boat, at some distance from the land.

"Athens, 24th of Eighth Month. Early this afternoon we landed on the Piræus. We procured asses to carry us to Athens ; two wooden slabs, on which we spread our overcoats, were our saddles ; loops at the end of a rope our stirrups ; another rope served for bridle : thus we made our entrance into that ancient city. It was a two hours' ride ; the road passes through ruins of old buildings, which extend from the Piræus to Mars Hill, and far beyond; the ground to a great distance is covered with broken pieces of earthen vessels, and the remains of large columns are prostrated here and there; some are still standing round about or supporting their ancient temples.

"27th. A Capuchin friar has called several times at our lodgings to see us, and we were told manifested great disappointment at not meeting with us; he left a message pressingly requesting that we would call upon him; a similar message was sent us also by Gropius, the Austrian Consul. I was at first unwilling to go, not expecting to meet in him anything calculated to minister comfort to my soul's distress; but I felt it right, however reluctantly, to call upon him; he resides at a place called the Lantern of Diogenes; on seeing him at a distance, in the rough garb of the true Capuchin, with a long beard, I was the more prepossessed against him, but I had hardly exchanged a word with him when my feelings were totally changed; I saw in him the humble Christian, the spiritually-minded man; I felt I could salute him as the disciple of the Lord Jesus Christ; his name is Paul. We had much freedom in religious and edifying conversation; he is very industrious in distributing the Holy Scriptures among the people generally, and he has given or sold many copies of the New Testament to the Turks, who come privately to him to obtain it; some of them have told him that they read it with great delight, for they are convinced that the doctrine it contains has come from heaven. He came to our lodgings in the evening to spend a couple of hours, when we waited together on the Lord, and felt the refreshings from his presence. He told us that he had disposed of all his New Testaments, and could not supply the present demand. We placed several in his hands for this purpose; also religious tracts in several languages, which he is delighted to have.

"I heard of a converted Jew, who was travelling in Arabia, and had a number of New Testaments in that language, which he distributed on his journey; he was also in the practice of frequently reading it to the people in the market-places. On one of these occasions he was sent for by the Pasha, who, in a rough manner, inquired of him, 'What is this that I hear of you? It is said that you read in a book that declaims against Mahomet and our holy religion, and which is calculated to cause the people to revolt against the Sultan,' &c. The Jew replied, 'You have been greatly misinformed; for the book I read in has not the name of Mahomet in it; it was even written before Mahomet was born; and, so far is the doctrine it contains from exciting the people to revolt, that if they were obedient to it, the Grand Sultan could not have a more peaceable and upright people in all his dominions. To convince yourself of it, please to accept this copy of it,' on which he presented him with a New Testament, in Arabic, very nicely bound. The Pasha took it, examined it, and said, 'It is a very pretty book.' Books in those parts are rare. A few days after, the Jew had occasion to go to the palace of the Pasha; when at the door, he heard the Pasha reading the Testament to many of his people who stood about him; he was then reading some of the miracles recorded by the Evangelists, and now and then made his own remarks to his attendants. Observing the Jew at the door, he called out to him, 'Come in, come in; I am reading out of your book to my people; Christ was indeed a great one; I also observe that all his miracles were made publicly among the people, whereas all those of Mahomet were in private.'

"We found a few serious persons among the Greeks, with whom, as well as in the families of several of the Consuls, we had some religious service."

Before leaving Athens, Stephen Grellet was again brought into much thoughtfulness on account of the time drawing near, when his dear friend William Allen anticipated he might be released from his present religious engagement, and feel at liberty to return home. He thus alludes to it in his last record at Athens :—

"My beloved companion has it under his serious consideration to leave me, after we have visited some of the Ionian Isles, and to return to England. I deeply feel this prospect; especially as I have a weighty service before me; particularly in Italy. To thy guidance, O Lord! and thy Almighty protection, I submit myself. Thou hast hitherto led about thy servant, and instructed and preserved him in the way that thou hast sent him; in the continuance of thy goodness, mercy, and saving strength, O! be thou pleased

to increase my confidence! Thou knowest how weak, and how
poor I am, and what proneness also there is in me to be of a doubtful spirit !

"My mind is frequently brought," he continues, "under deep
feelings for Italy, Rome, &c. It is now upon me by night and by
day. The time appears to have nearly come for me to go there.
Heavy are my Gospel bonds."

CHAPTER XXII.

Third Visit to Europe.

CORINTH—PATRAS—ZANTE—CORFU—BARLETTA—NAPLES.

They now "departed from Athens and came to Corinth." This place so closely connected with the life and labours of the Great Apostle of the Gentiles, and the early progress of Christianity, they found almost crushed under the influence of Mahometan oppression. The city where Paul was once so much "pressed in spirit, and testified that Jesus was Christ;" where he commenced his Christian correspondence with the primitive Churches—from which, or to which, he wrote some of his most important Epistles—and which has so many interesting claims upon the attention of the Christian student,* did not afford much scope for their Gospel labours. They soon left it, and passed on to Patras. Thence they sailed to Zante, among the Ionian Isles. Here they were detained by the serious illness of William Allen. After his partial recovery they proceeded to Corfu, where, having "partaken together of the consolations of the Gospel," their *joint* labours came to a close. With deepened feelings of Christian fellowship they took leave of each other. William Allen went to Malta on his homeward course ; and Stephen Grellet embarked for Italy. Pursuing his narrative, he says :—

"Eighth Month 28th. We left Athens early this morning on horseback. The roads were hilly and stony, and the sun very hot. The country is beautiful, and some of the views are grand. We came about twelve miles to a village which was formerly a considerable town, called Lefsina. From the many ruins scattered

---

* See the "Life and Epistles of St. Paul," by Conybeare and Howson.

about, we judge that it had once large and stately buildings. The
marble columns that sustained some edifices are beautifully carved
and fluted. Many of them are more than three feet in diameter.
The miserable house at which we stopped, and in which we were
glad to have a shelter from the scorching sun, has an earthen
floor. Our horses were admitted as well as ourselves ; but on the
place which we occupied there were some mats to sit upon. I felt
so weary and spent by the heat of the sun, that I would gladly
have laid down to take some rest ; but we had hardly come in,
when about twenty of the villagers came to gaze at us. More of
them followed soon after, and their priest among them. I felt the
love of Christ towards them. I wished to communicate something
to them, but our interpreter had gone into the village to buy some
provisions. Another way, however, seemed to open for conveying
my religious impressions. I opened the Greek Testament on those
parts which contained what I wished to bring before them. These
passages I got the priest to read to them. So forcible is the plain
truth, in the simple language of Scripture, that, on hearing it read,
several of these people were much affected, and broken into tears ;
so that when our interpreter returned, their hearts were prepared
to receive what we had further to impart. We found that they
had never heard the Scriptures read. The priest himself had not
a copy of them. He entreated us to give him one, saying he
would keep it very carefully locked up in the church. We told
him, before all the people, that we would give them a few copies,
on condition that they would not keep them locked up ; but that
frequently during the week, and especially on First-days, they
would meet together, and that the priest, or such of them as are
able, would read them audibly to all the others. They promised
they would do so, and parted from us in great tenderness. Rode
fifteen miles to Megara ; distributed New Testaments and tracts,
and passed the night on the house-top, as is usual here.

"Next morning we rode twenty miles to a large shady tree, near
which there is water—two very desirable objects under such a sun ;
we had just come down a steep, rocky mountain. Here we made
our meal on a piece of bread, and drank some of the water ; it so
refreshed us, that we thought the best served table could not have
proved a better treat to us.

"The Lord, under the shadow of whose wings we have trusted

is mercifully pleased to be our shield and deliverer, day after day; blessed and holy is his name! We reached Corinth at night, and took up our quarters at an inn kept by an Italian.

"30th. We spent some very interesting hours with the Primate of the Greeks in these parts; he is in a feeble state of health, and is a thoughtful serious man; he feels deeply for the degraded and oppressed state in which the people of his nation are kept by the Turkish authorities, the iron yoke being heavier on them here than in any parts where we have been.

" Finding no object to detain us here, we hired a fishing boat to take us, by the Gulf of Lepanto, to Patras. We left Corinth in the evening, and greatly enjoyed the air, the night, and the fine views on this beautiful gulf, the sea being very calm.

"The next day the wind blew hard, and so contrary, that our boatman was obliged to seek for a place of shelter, by going back some distance; here we passed a second night in our small boat which did not protect us from the rain, accompanied by thunder and lightning. The wind having abated in the morning, we moved on again, by rowing for some hours; but at last the sea got so high that we could not safely proceed further; we therefore turned back towards a village, where we landed. We were also in want of provisions; the bread we had taken with us was wet by the waves and rain. In the village we met a number of the Albanian soldiers; we had some religious service with them and the Greeks, and gave them some tracts and copies of the New Testament; they had not seen the latter before, and they promised to collect together and read it, especially on First-days. We passed the night again in our boat, though it is too small for any of us to attempt to lie down. Next morning, the wind continuing high and stormy, we endeavoured to hire mules to take us by land the remainder of the journey to Patras."

Through much difficulty and fatigue they reached that place on the 3rd of Ninth Month. They found the people on the road in a state of great ignorance, and "a truly affecting degree of insensibility; many of the monks not appearing to understand that they had a soul to save, or even that there is a God."

They left Patras the next day, and, after a good passage,

arrived at Zante. There they had to perform quarantine, on account of the plague which prevailed in Turkey and Greece.

"Zante, 5th of Ninth Month. Through the kindness of Colonel Ross and Dr. Thomas, quarters are assigned us in an old monastery, instead of the Lazaretto, which is crowded. Here we have the privilege of a garden to walk in.

"10th. I enjoy these days of retirement, though clothed with great poverty. The Lord is also graciously pleased to settle my mind in much calmness and resignation in the prospect of being left by my beloved companion and co-worker. To the Lord's guidance I must resign him. Now, instead of repining at the prospect of a separation, my soul blesses the Lord for favours received, and is permitted also to hope for more. Through the favour of Colonel Ross, the time of our quarantine is shortened.

"13th. Accompanied by Doctor Thomas, we rode some distance in the island to visit the inhabitants of some of their villages, among whom we had several religious opportunities; in every place they gratefully received the Greek Testaments and tracts we handed to them.

"14th. We had this morning a visit from Prince Cornuto, with whom we had been before. He is a serious, aged man. He went with us to a meeting held at the Protopapa's, which was largely attended by the Greeks and English. Many of the clergy, and military and civil officers were also present. There appeared to be an open door with them to receive what, in the love of Christ, we felt it our place to proclaim to them.

"16th. I spend many hours in retirement, pouring forth my heart with tears before the Lord. My poverty is very great. I am humbled to the dust. No past favour, nor experience of the Lord's power and mercy can, even by a lively remembrance of it, minister to the soul's present wants; its supplies must flow fresh from the Divine fountain. In this state of deep abasement, ability is given to enter the house of prayer, and with supplication to make our wants known to Him who alone can minister to us.

"18th. Yesterday morning the Protopapa, with six of his clergy, came to see us. He was serious. He gives a deplorable account of the ignorance and morals of many of the monks.

"We had a precious religious season at the Governor's house,

and another at Doctor Thomas's, with his family and others. This
evening dear Allen and I had a sweet refreshing season in the
Lord's presence; favoured to resign one another to his will; W. A.
to return home, and I to proceed, single-handed, in the further
service my blessed Master has for me in other nations, not only to
go to Rome, but to die there also, should He order that my life be
like a seal to the Gospel service required of me there."

For some days William Allen had occasionally suffered from
headache. Soon after the preceding record he was obliged to
"give up entirely to nursing," and became very seriously ill.
S. G. says :—

"19th. My beloved companion has a high fever. I also receive
heavy tidings from some of my relatives in France; and of my
beloved wife in America, who was sick. Thus are the troubles of
my heart enlarged; in the Lord alone is my refuge; He can support under every tribulation, and sanctify them all."

The fever of which S. G. speaks ran its course; and for
many days the life of his beloved companion was despaired
of; but through the loving-kindness of the Lord he was
spared; and on the 11th of Eighth Month S. G. writes :—

"I had a letter this day from America; my beloved wife's health
is better; dear W. A. also. My soul blesses the Lord for these
favours.

"12th. A small vessel came in last night from Corfu, and is to
go back this evening; dear Allen has thought that if there was a
vessel here to take him there, the sea air would do him good, and
might accelerate his recovery; his physicians think it would be of
use to him, and I also feel ready to go hence; I have therefore
industriously prepared everything for our departure this evening.

"13th. Cephalonia. I had wished to come to this island, but
did not see how it could be effected in the feeble state of my dear
companion; at four p.m. yesterday he was carried on board the
cutter *Diana;* the weather was fine and serene; after we put out
to sea he felt much refreshed; it acted on his feeble frame as it
did on me when I left the island of Hayti. But our fair prospect
soon changed, a violent storm arose, accompanied with thunder

and lightning, torrents of rain; the sea broke in over us, and dashed into the cabin, so that dear William was completely drenched. The captain succeeded in getting into a harbour on this island; but even here the vessel tossed greatly. It would not have been prudent to remove dear W. A. from the vessel, as the village stands at a distance on a high hill. I went there and had a religious opportunity with the inhabitants; they appear generally to be in profound ignorance, much unacquainted with things pertaining to salvation; a few of them, however, gave some signs of tenderness, whilst I reasoned with them of righteousness, temperance, and judgment to come.

"Corfu, 17th. We left Cephalonia on the 15th; but contrary winds and a high sea prevented us from progressing, except slowly; I was very sea-sick: neither I nor our Greek attendant were able to minister to dear W. A.; but he, amidst these difficulties, continued to gain strength, so that on our arrival he seems like a new man; and here, to our great comfort, we met with Doctor Skey, an old acquaintance of William Allen's. On hearing of our arrival, he came immediately to meet us on board the vessel, and in the most hospitable manner has taken us to his house, where dear William has many of the comfortable accommodations of an English home; he felt so refreshed every way after getting here, that, to our great surprise, he sat with us at the dinner-table; I could hardly believe my own eyes.

"18th. Last night we had a storm, attended with an earthquake; the rain fell as if the flood-gates of the sky had been opened; truly thankful we were not to be on the unstable element. My dear Allen continues to improve, and has come to the peaceful conclusion to go from here to Malta; my own way opens with brightness to go to Barletta.

"19th. Sir Thomas Maitland, Governor of the Ionian Isles, arrived here last night; we had a letter for him from the British Ambassador, at Constantinople, which it was proper I should deliver to him early. The General had received letters from England, by which we were both recommended to his kind attention; he knows dear William by character.

"Understanding that I proposed to go to Naples, he said, 'Why then will you go by Barletta, when from thence you will have a rough and dangerous journey to Naples? my frigate has

nothing to do ; it will be ready at any hour you please, to carry
you to Malta, where you will have a very short quarantine to
perform ; whereas you will have a long one at Barletta.' I
excused myself from accepting his kind offer by saying that I
might meet with some detention in Malta, if there was no vessel
ready to go to Naples. 'You need have no fear on that account,'
he answered, 'for I will send orders, and one of my ships shall
be ready to take you at any time.' Then I told him plainly on
what ground I could not go by a ship of war ; that I was on an
errand of peace ; that besides, I wished to visit some parts of
Italy between Barletta and Naples. 'Well,' said he, 'as you may
meet with some difficulties among those bigotted Papists at
Naples and at Rome, I will have letters ready for our Ambassadors there, also for the Chevalier de Medici, Prime Minister of
the King of Naples, and also for the Cardinal Consalvi, Prime
Minister of the Pope ; he is my particular friend, and I shall
have him apprised of your coming, before your arrival there.' I
stated to the General the deplorable ignorance of the mass of the
people in these islands, and the necessity of endeavouring to
raise them from their degraded condition by establishing schools,
where the children might be educated in the principles of morality
virtue, and religion. The General appears disposed to take steps
towards this, and to have qualified and pious teachers from
England for the purpose.

"20th. At sea, on the Adriatic. This morning, previous to
our separation, dear Allen and I had a very solemn and precious
season before the Lord ; we felt the bond of Gospel love uniting
us closely, and perhaps more powerfully felt than at any time
before ; but believing that our separation is in the counsel of Him
who, in his love and mercy, had banded us together, we resigned
one another to His will, and we commit ourselves to His guidance
and protection. I leave him peacefully, under the care of Doctor
Skey, a very kind friend to him."

———

Stephen Grellet has now arrived at a peculiarly interesting,
if not a critical period of his mission. In company with a

beloved brother and fellow-labourer in the Gospel of Christ, he had visited the Lutheran land of Gustavus Adolphus—he had traversed the regions of the Greek Church, in the dominions of the *Christian* Alexander—he had been in the Crescent City, and had seen something of Mahometan rule —he had mingled with the discordant elements of the motley group of believers and unbelievers, in some of the islands of the Archipelago, and in the Ionian Sea, and at Athens and Corinth. He had left his beloved companion at Corfu, and now, a solitary pilgrim, "alone, and yet not alone," he had set his face towards the land of Popes and Cardinals. Himself, at one time, a child of Rome, then an infidel, now a Christian believer, and a minister of Christ in the religious Society of Friends—a Protestant of Protestants—he was about to enter the precincts of the city of Leo and Hildebrand. It required a very close and humble walk with God, a very chaste adherence to the cause of Christ, a very prayerful attention to the leadings of the Holy Spirit, and a very firm reliance upon "the word of the Truth of the Gospel," based upon the inspired records of the Bible, to come out unscathed from the ordeal that awaited him; meekly bold, he had to "speak the truth in love," on all occasions and to all, without pusillanimously renouncing the simplicity and integrity of his own character, determined to know nothing save Jesus Christ and Him crucified—seeking nothing, pleading for nothing save the Truth, as it is in Him. The sequel will show how he sustained the trial, and stood faithful to his God and Saviour.

On his arrival at Barletta he had to perform quarantine, before he was allowed to go to an inn, and mingle with the inhabitants.

"Barletta, 25th of Tenth Month, 1819. The part of Italy that we have sailed by is beautiful, very fertile and populous. The towns are numerous, and many fine country seats are seen on the sea-shore between them. The chief commerce is in wheat.

" An English merchant, who arrived here when I did, is placed in the same apartments with me, in the Lazaretto, though in a separate chamber. It is by the kind attention of General Maitland, who wrote, it appears, on purpose, that they have given me these separate rooms ; a very great accommodation ; for in the other parts of the Lazaretto they are much crowded—men, women, and children of various colours and nations ; many of them are poor Greeks who come to seek refuge in Italy.

" 26th. My dress has already attracted the curiosity of some of the inhabitants ; six of the principal men in the town have come to see me this afternoon ; they are allowed to do so, provided they neither touch me nor anything belonging to me ; or they would become subjected to the same quarantine that I have to perform.

" 1st of Eleventh ' Month. Ten persons came together to see me ; two are Romish priests, but they appear to have liberal minds ; I had a religious opportunity with that company, directing them not to the knowledge only of the Truth, but to a consistent walking in that religion which is pure and undefiled.

" 7th. Almost every day some persons come to see me. This afternoon about thirty of the principal men of this town came in ; also seven priests with them ; some of them had been present at religious opportunities on preceding occasions ; now all sat together in silence, and I preached to them the Lord Jesus Christ, the Head of the Church, and only Saviour of men ; none of the priests opposed.

" 8th. I was liberated from the Lazaretto this morning ; also Taylor, my companion in confinement. Before I left it, I had a short religious interview with the Greeks ; who have fled for their lives ; I could not well have access to them before ; I feel much for them ; many were sitting cross-legged on the floor, in a very dejected state ; some were serious and tender. Soon after I came to the inn, several of the most serious persons who visited me in the Lazaretto, came to see me ; one priest among them ; he is much pleased with the ' Importance of Religion,' in Italian, that I gave him. I visited an institution for orphan girls.

" I had been so long detained in the Lazaretto that I felt pressed in my mind to proceed as early as I could for Naples : Taylor intending also for that place, we concluded to hire a carriage for the purpose. He is a serious young man, well acquainted with many of our friends at Manchester. It is rather desirable to have a person with me who speaks Italian.

"11th. We were favoured this day also not to meet with robbers. Some of the people where we stopped to refresh our horses seemed to marvel how we had escaped them, but I knew to whom I am indebted ; the Lord is the Almighty protector of those hat put their trust in Him, blessed for ever and ever be his holy name! When we drew towards Naples, in the evening, we passed near Vesuvius ; columns of smoke issued from it, and we travelled a long distance over solid rocks of lava, that had flowed down during former eruptions of this volcano. We were stopped five times by custom-house officers, to have our baggage examined, so that it was late when we reached the Golden Eagle Inn at Naples.

"Naples, 13th. Went to the police to present my passports. They were much offended at my hat ; neither could they for some time understand the reasons I gave them for keeping it on. Finally they asked what I should do if I met what they call ' Le Saint Sacrament' in the streets ; when carriages stop and every-body uncovers himself, whatever be the state of the weather ; many even falling down on their knees. I explained to them why I could not even then uncover my head, as a mark of venera-tion or religious worship to this, or to any thing of the kind. ' Then,' said they, ' you must abide by the consequences.'

" Sir William A'Court, British Ambassador here, receives me kindly. This is very particularly the case with Henry Lushing-ton, who with his wife, appear to be persons of piety.

" 14th. Angelo Nobite came to see me this morning. He greatly deplores the very low state of religion in this place ; superstition, he says, abounds, also vice and immorality : from what I see and hear, I can readily believe him. Bibles are prohibited to be printed or imported. Some weeks since four hundred Bibles were brought in. They were seized, and the Bishop, numerously attended by his clergy, had them burnt publicly in an open square. The priests say, that to allow the people to have the Scriptures in their possession, would endanger the safety of their Church. They also carefully try to prevent the introduc-tion of religious books or tracts ; and yet, though my baggage was several times inspected, my books were hardly noticed.

"15th. Had a refreshing religious opportunity at Henry Lushington's, with his family. They have ten nice, well-behaved children. He accompanied me to Capo-de-monte, to see L'Abbé Campbell, a liberal-minded man. He has established a school for poor children, where he introduces the system of mutual instruction. I met at Henry Valentine's a pious young nobleman, his name is Don L. Bonaprianola.

"In the evening, accompanied by Bonaprianola, I visited the Prince Cardito. Some other noblemen were present. The Prince is a serious man. He occupies the important station of Minister of Public Instruction in the kingdom. He appears to feel the importance of the subject, and wishes that such an education might be extended to the people at large, as would tend to spread amongst them sound principles of morality and virtue. He has very lately presented to the King a memorial on the subject. The Prince made various inquiries on this important point.

"20th. By appointment of the Prime Minister, the Chevalier de Medici, to whom I had sent the letter given me by General Maitland, I went to his hotel; I found in the ante-chamber a great number of persons of all ranks, waiting to have an audience with him; they surveyed me closely, whispering to one another what kind of being I might be, thus to appear with my hat on. I was not left long among them; for it appears that the Chevalier had given orders to his attendants to admit me into his private cabinet as soon as I came; he made me sit by him, and proceeded to inquire into the nature of the engagements I had had in the different nations where I had travelled; then he was very particular in his inquiries into various of our Christian principles and practices. The reading of my certificates, the short account I gave of the order maintained in our Society, as exhibited in our discipline, the manner in which our meetings, both for worship and discipline, are held, &c. &c., pleased him much. I proposed to send him some of our books treating on these subjects, which, he said, it would be agreeable to him to have. He offered to give me orders for admittance to all their prisons, or any other place I might wish to visit, requesting only that I would impart to him what I might see, to which he could possibly apply some remedy. I made several attempts to withdraw, knowing that many persons were in waiting; but he was not ready to let me go, till we had been above an hour together, and then he accompanied through the ante-chamber, where so many were waiting, to the further door; they gazed at me, whilst they bowed very low to the Chevalier, as we passed on.

"In the afternoon I was with the Abbé Mastroti; several noblemen were present, also the young prince whom I saw yesterday. I felt for a while much dejected; a heavy weight was upon my mind, and I did not see how I could throw it off before such a company, who appeared to be of the great and wise of this world; but I thought that if I truly wished to be myself one of the wise in the Divine sight, I must first become a fool, yea, be willing to be accounted so by others. I proclaimed to them the day of the Lord, which shall burn as an oven, &c. &c.; I entreated them to receive Him in the way of his coming, and be of those whose sins go before-hand to judgment, and not of those whose sins follow after; not to trust in the doctrine of a purgatory, but rather deeply to consider the description given by our Lord Jesus Christ himself of what follows after death, as set forth in the parable of Dives and Lazarus; the rich man, not in purgatory—but in hell—lifted up his eyes and saw Lazarus in Abraham's bosom, &c. &c. The Lord's truth was exalted among them.

"In the evening I went to the Prince Cardito's. I feel deeply with him, in his desire for the moral and virtuous education of the youth. I placed in his hands a copy of the 'Scripture Lessons,' which dear Allen and I prepared in Russia. I found with the Prince eight other noblemen, who also manifested great interest in the subject. On returning to my lodgings I found a letter from the Chevalier de Medici, inclosing orders for my admittance to the various prisons, &c.

"21st. Accompanied by Bonaprianola, I began the very painful work of visiting the receptacles of vice and crime. I went to-day through the two prisons for women, a large one for men, and a hospital for their sick. This service took me from nine a.m. till four p.m. But my bodily fatigue is small compared to the anguish of mind I have endured. I do not remember that, in any day of my life, I have been with so many fellow-beings so totally depraved and hardened. Cages of very unclean birds indeed,

I have been in. Many of the inmates of both sexes, and even children, have committed atrocious crimes. I saw fifteen in one cell who are condemned to death. Their crimes are of the deepest dye, and they do not show the least sense of their situation. My attempt to represent to them the awful doom that awaits them shortly, unless by sincere repentance they seek forgiveness through Him who is the only Saviour of sinners, appeared to have no more effect than the dropping of water on the flinty rock. Some boys who are there, at the early age of eleven years, have perpetrated *several* murders. I endeavoured to turn the inmates of these prisons 'from darkness to light, and from sin and Satan to God;' but I do not know that a single individual, out of several thousands I have been with this day, has given the least sign of sorrow for his evil deeds.

"22nd. To-day I visited the foundling hospital, which is a very large establishment. The mortality among the children admitted here is not as great as in similar places in Russia. About eighty nuns have the principal charge of it. In one part there are about four hundred girls, most of whom have attained the age of young women. It is a kind of convent. As I was going through a long corridor, accompanied by several of the nuns and priests attached to this extensive institution, we passed the door of their chapel, which was open. I saw the girls, with several nuns, on their knees before a large Madonna, or representation of the Virgin Mary, very richly and finely dressed. Wax candles were burning before it. They were singing to the image, but at the same time their faces were towards us, laughing. My soul was sorrowful on beholding them, and their superstition and idolatry. The chief of the priests who were with me asked if I did not wish to go into the church to see the girls at their devotions. I told him I should like to do so if it were proper. I felt a strong inclination to go in, but, as from religious principle I do not uncover my head in any place as if it was holy ground, I was unwilling to give offence to any one by going in. The nuns said, nobody here would be offended at it. The priests also said, 'We have on our heads our cassocks; your hat is to you no more than these are to us, especially as it is from religious principle that you act.' Then I told them I would go in, on condition, that, if I apprehended it was required of me by the Lord to communicate anything to the young women thus assembled, he, the chief priest, who spoke good French, would interpret for me. He very readily agreed to do so. We all went in. Besides the girls, most of the nuns were in the church, about their great Madonna. When they had concluded singing their hymn, I told them how greatly my heart had been pained, as I passed by, on seeing the lightness of their conduct whilst engaged in what they call a devotional act; that, I could not however be surprised at, if they truly looked on that image before them as what it really is—nothing but a piece of wood, carved by man's device, which can neither hear nor see; neither do good nor evil to any; our devotion, I said, is to be to Him who sees the secret of our hearts, hears not our words only, but knows our every thought; from Him we have everything to fear if we do not serve, obey, and honour Him; and the richest blessings to hope for, if we love, fear, and serve Him: the worship acceptable to Him is to be performed in spirit and in truth, from the very heart; this is the temple in which He is to be found, and in which He reveals Himself. Here, at noon-day, they have lighted tapers, which cannot enable them to discover the sinfulness of the heart; but the light of Christ, which enlighteneth every man that cometh into the world, and by which everything against which he has a controversy is made manifest, showeth us our sins; that we may look upon Him whom, by our sins, we have pierced. Then I proceeded to proclaim to them the Lord Jesus Christ as the only Saviour of sinners: the only hope of salvation; the way, the truth, and the life, without whom no man can come to God the Father; all that pretend to enter by any other way than by Him, the door, are accounted thieves and robbers. The priest interpreted faithfully into Italian, of which I could judge. The nuns and the other priests said several times, 'This is the truth,' or, 'It is so.' The countenances of the girls had much altered; they hung down their heads, and tears flowed from some of their eyes. Thus did my blessed Master enable his poor servant, in a Popish church, assisted by priests, to bear testimony to his blessed truth, and against the superstitious worship that those poor girls were offering to a carved piece of wood. After we came out some more of the nuns collected about us, and, in answering some of their questions, I further unfolded to them what acceptable worship to God consists in, and also what is the only hope of salvation. No man can save his brother, or give to God a ransom for his soul; that, therefore, it is great presumption for any to attempt to take upon themselves to pronounce absolution from sin on a sinner. I sometimes marvel that they do not lay their hands upon me; but, on the contrary, they parted from me in tenderness, and with expressions of their satisfaction with my visit. Surely this is the Lord's doing; blessed and reverend is his name!"

S. G. was much affected with his visit to the prison of the galley-slaves, which he found in a sad state, but he had comfort in being able to preach the Gospel to them.

"Some of these poor people," he says, "seemed as if they could not believe their own ears, when I imparted to them the encouragements which the Gospel holds out to penitent sinners; that although their sins were as scarlet, yet the Lord, in his love and mercy, could make them as snow or wool.

"I met at the Count Stackelberg's, the Russian Minister and several Prussian and Russian noblemen; some of these I had been with in Russia; the Lord made way once more to proclaim among them the unsearchable riches of his love through Jesus Christ, and to entreat them not to be hearers only of the glad tidings of the Gospel, but so to believe, as to obey.

"23rd. I was a third time with the Chevalier de Medici. I had sent him a statement of some of my observations, particularly among the insane, and in some of the prisons; and I have now laid before him the situation of the galley-slaves. He took such an interest in what I stated in my former report, and his feelings were so touched, that attention was immediately given to it; and now he appears disposed, with equal promptitude, to have a complete change made in these prisons, and at once to have the boys removed. Should my deep sufferings in these visits have no other effect than to mitigate the bodily tortures under which some of my fellow-beings have suffered for years, I am richly repaid.

"I hope also that some of the poor prisoners will find consolation in the Lord Jesus, whose mercies have been proclaimed to them. Bonaprianola, Prince Cardito, and a number of others, appear so to feel for that class of men as to be willing to visit the prisoners henceforth, and to impart to them moral and religious instruction. I particularly recommended to them the juvenile offenders. I had a precious meeting with these benevolent persons, together with a large company of those whom I had met previously; it was a solemn parting meeting.

"I feel now as if I must hasten to Rome; various objects, under other circumstances, might claim a few days of my time. Vesuvius displays a grand sight; in the day, thick columns of smoke rise up to a considerable height; at night, they are blazing pillars; at a short distance from here are excavations made into the streets of Herculaneum and Pompeii, long buried under beds of lava, on which vineyards are now planted; I should be greatly interested in visiting them, but they are not the objects for which my great aud blessed Master has sent me to these nations. With single-ness of heart I must prosecute the business to which He has called me. My bonds for Rome also feel so heavy, that I could not have any pleasure in those things.

"This afternoon the Chevalier de Medici, in a kind and polite note, incloses me an order, to enable me to pass through and out of the kingdom without the detention of having my luggage examined; he also sends me a letter for the Cardinal Consalvi at Rome, who is his particular friend. How great is the Lord's goodness in thus opening a door for me, his poor servant, from place to place! He it is who has the key. If He opens, who can shut? But when He shuts, none can open. Medici, in his note, states that measures are already taken to ameliorate the condition of the Gallerians, agreeably to the representations that I made."

Stephen Grellet was now ready to depart. Six years ago, it will be remembered, during his great conflict at Genoa, he had received an intimation that "to Naples and Rome he should go," but "the time is not yet." Then "the trumpet of retreat gave a clear and certain sound." In the simplicity of faith he obeyed it, and found safety and peace. Now to Naples he *had* been, and Rome was open before him. He followed no uncertain guide.

CHAPTER XXIII.

Third Visit to Europe.

ROME.

Pius VII. was in the last years of his Pontificate. He had lived in eventful times. Raised to the Papal chair in the early days of the French revolutionary wars, he had crowned Napoleon at Paris, in 1804; but was, nevertheless, seized by him in 1809, and kept a prisoner at Fontainebleau, until, almost entirely by the intervention of Non-Catholic powers, he regained possession of his States in 1814. He had nearly reached the advanced age of eighty, when Stephen Grellet visited Rome, and was admitted to a personal interview with him.

During the fortnight which S. G. spent in the Papal city, his Christian labours were varied, and almost incessant. Interesting particulars are preserved in his Diary.

"Rome, 25th of Eleventh Month, 1819. I left Naples on the 23rd, in the evening. Travelling two nights and one day, I arrived here early this morning. Through the Lord's merciful preservation, I have again escaped falling into the hands of banditti, which abound on this road, notwithstanding the severity of the laws against them. Every few miles I beheld the horrible sight of human flesh, hanging on posts or gibbets, by the sides of the road, near the places where murders have been committed, giving evidence that they have been many. Some of them appeared to have been quartered only a few days before; but notwithstanding all this, robberies and murders are no less frequent, especially on the Pope's territory. How often, in these my journeyings, do I feel as if my life was offered up; day after day, and night after night, I know not but that I may fall a prey into the hands of unrighteous and wicked men; but very good and gracious is my blessed Lord : how precious is the sense of his Divine presence ! David said, 'Thou art continually with me.' Truly I may say so likewise ; the fear of offending so good and gracious a Master, was, during these nights, or under such circumstances, greater than any apprehension of what may be suffered to befall my outward man.

"On my arrival here, this morning, I found that this is the day on which the Cardinal Consalvi, Prime Minister of the Pope, gives his public audiences, when all who have petitions or wish to have a private interview present themselves. It seemed as if I could do nothing in this great and ancient city till I had been with him. I had been two nights and one day on the road. I was now in the place for which I had deeply felt for years. Truly, like Paul, I do not know what things are to befall me here, only the persuasion arises that sufferings await me. I changed my travelling garments, took some refreshment, and by eight o'clock I was at the Quirinal, the Pope's palace. I did not know how to act, or what to do ; I was alone ; I knew nobody ; but I thought I would take notice of what others did. I first came into a spacious hall near the foot of the stairs that lead up to the Pope's apartments ; here was collected a large company of priests, monks, military, private citizens, strangers from several nations ; many of them had papers, or rolls of paper in their hands, which I considered might be their petitions, &c., so I had my letters from Maitland and Medici ready. We waited nearly an hour, during which I plainly saw that my dress and hat attracted general observation ; whispering, querying who I could be. They all were uncovered. After a while there was a general bustle among the company. They went out into a large corridor, extending from the staircase, and stood in rows on each side, with papers in their hands. I took my station with them in the ranks. As the Cardinal came on, each, as he passed, presented his papers, which were placed in the hands of his attendants. Some tried to kiss his hand, others his feet. As he came towards me, by my dress he probably recognised who I was, so that before I could hand him the letters, he politely asked, 'Are you not Mr. Grellet ?' to which answering in the affirmative, he said, 'Please to call on me at my own palace, to-morrow morning ;' and I gave him the letters I had for him.

"I now wait to see what may be unfolded for me to do here. Great is the travail of my soul, that I may be preserved watchful unto prayer, and enabled, with singleness of heart and faithfulness, to attend to all my Lord's requirings.

"26th. I went this morning to the Cardinal's palace; in the ante-chamber I had some satisfaction in conversing with two young priests, his secretaries; they evince more liberality of mind than is generally found among that class of men; there were many in waiting to have an audience with the Cardinal, but as soon as he found I had come, he came out from his cabinet, called me in, and made me sit down on a sofa by him; from the nature of his inquiries it would appear that General Maitland had given him a particular account of my late travels and religious engagements through Russia, Greece, &c.; but he was particularly desirous to know more of our religious Society, its principles, doctrines, discipline, &c. On some such occasions I find it proper to give the perusal of my certificates. The religious care of our Society towards their ministers, before liberating them for the work of the Gospel, is much commended by the Cardinal. As there were so many persons in waiting in the ante-chamber, I made several attempts to withdraw; but he had more inquiries to make, which detained me altogether about an hour and a half with him; he was not in anywise offended when, in answer to some of his inquiries, I had to expose pretty fully some of the superstitions of the Romish Church, and to make my confession that the Lord Jesus Christ is the only Head of his Church, and the Saviour of men. I also gave him a full statement of the conduct of their missionaries in Greece; the mischief they are doing there, and what seeds of distress and unhappiness in families they are sowing; I represented to him also the very unchristian and unbecoming conduct of those who, in the south of Russia, did hang and then burn the Scriptures; and of the public burning of the Bible at Naples, by the Bishop and his clergy; all of which the Cardinal reprobates, and properly says, 'It militates against religion.' Finally, before we parted, he wished to know in what he could serve me; I told him I should like to visit some of their prisons and public establishments, and that I should be obliged to him if he would procure me admittance to them; he then took me by the hand, and accompanied me, through those waiting in the ante-chamber, to the door into the court. Surely it is the Lord's doing, in the very centre of Popery, even among the heads of it, to make way for one, who holds testimonies so contrary to them, to proclaim the Lord Jesus as the sole Head of the Church, and the Author of eternal salvation to all that believe in Him. Under the concern that I have in visiting the abodes of human misery and woe, I find that, besides feelings of near sympathy for the sufferings of so many of my fellow-men, it is in some of those places that I often meet with benevolent and pious persons; for in places of public concourse these are not to be found.

"In the evening, the Cardinal sent me a letter, inclosing orders for my admittance into the various places that I wish to visit, with his instructions to go first to the Governor, Pacca, who would provide a suitable person to accompany me, and to interpret for me.

"27th. This morning, about nine, I went to the Government house. At first, under the garb of a priest, I could not recognise the Governor; he, seeing my embarrassment, said, 'You must know that here, at Rome, the clerical garb is that of the court.' I am told that their General is a Cardinal; thus those who profess to be ministers of the Prince of Peace are ministers of war, and generals of armies! O the inconsistency! Many persons were with the Governor, all dressed like priests; I could not find out what they were; one of them was Olgiati, President of St. Michael's Castle, for whom I had a letter from the Cardinal Consalvi, which I handed to him. I was myself an object of curiosity to them, for it is a very novel thing for them to see a Quaker; they had much to inquire after, but were all very civil, and my blessed Lord strengthened me to proclaim his holy name, without equivocation, in simplicity and truth. He performs his gracious promise, 'I will make thee as an iron wall, and a brazen pillar before them.' The Governor sent for a young man, one of his secretaries, to accompany me. Whilst I was waiting for him, in another apartment, the Assessor came in, who, on seeing me with my hat on, was much offended, so that, for a while, there was no room to enter into any explanation; he had never heard of the Quakers, nor of their principles; after a while his clerks came in, for it appears I was in his apartment; by degrees his countenance altered, and in the presence of a number of others that came, he entered into

many inquiries respecting our principles, and what constitutes
true Christianity; he was much brought down, and treated me
with great civility. By that time the young man sent for by the
Governor came in; I felt from the first my heart inclined towards
him; he is a serious young man, and his mind is made soft and
chastened by the loss of his wife within a few weeks, who, I am
told, was a beautiful and virtuous young woman; he speaks good
French. He went with me to several prisons for the Gallerians,
and to the secret prison; here they have a complete system of
espionage; the cells are so constructed that they succeed in becoming acquainted with what the prisoners say to one another.
They have very high ceilings, in which there is an opening, which
appears to be intended only for a ventilator, but here a man is
stationed who can hear nearly every word spoken in the cell.
They place in the same cell such as have been connected together
in crimes, that they may be encouraged to converse with each
other. The person whose business it is to hearken to what the
prisoners say, is particularly attentive to be at his station before
the prisoners are taken out to be interrogated, and on their return
also; on which occasions they are often heard to agree on what
they shall say, and to talk on what occurred during the interroga-
tion, and thus they commit themselves. But the listener may
often hear indistinctly and, by misrepresentation, though without
evil intention, cause these men to be condemned on the plea that
they have avowed their guilt. By their laws no man is condemned
unless he confesses himself guilty, and by this plan they think
they obtain such an acknowledgment; some years past a confession was extorted by the cruelty of torture. I saw some prisoners
confined there on account of religion, but could not understand
for what particulars; my kind attendant is, however, very ready
in interpreting for me whenever I request him, and during some
communications I made through him in several cells, some of the
prisoners were tender.

"28th. I visited two large hospitals called St. Spirito and St.
Charles; and a large poor-house, where, besides aged people, there
are four hundred boys and five hundred girls. I had several religious opportunities, in some of which sensibility was apparent. I
was also in a prison where about one hundred and twenty brigands
are confined. They, and their wives and children, were routed out

of their habitations, and are intended to be settled in distant places. Some of them may be innocent. The tenderness manifested during the religious opportunity I had with them may perhaps induce me to entertain such a sentiment.

" This has been another day of very close engagement and mental suffering. I visited a prison, said to be a place of correction for boys ; very imposing was the sight on my first entering, accompanied by several priests belonging to this establishment, and others connected with it, as they were giving a glowing description of the great reform that they were instrumental in effecting. The apartment I was in is about two hundred feet in length, and forty in height. On both sides of this room were small chambers ; opposite to each door was a boy, cleanly dressed, with a spinning wheel ; all seemed industrious, and profound silence prevailed among them. It seemed to be a pleasing sight ; but, casting my eyes downward, I observed that every boy had a chain at his ankle, allowing him to go only from his cell to his wheel ! Then I beheld several inclined blocks, with stocks to confine hands and feet, and knotted cords and whips, near them. Inquiring the meaning of all this : ' O,' said the priests, ' these are the places where they receive their correction morning and evening, on their bare backs.' ' Is this,' I queried, ' the method whereby you bring about such great reform among these boys ? You may indeed excite the angry passions in them, by such doings, but you will never change their evil heart.' In another part I was with women and girls, towards whom similar treatment is used, to reform them from their vicious habits. My endeavours to plead with these priests, and to set before them the ways that a Christian spirit would dictate, and which, through the Lord's blessing, might prove efficacious to the recovery of these young persons, have, I fear, had very little place with them.

" 29th. I had a suffering night, my mind was under great distress ; I feel at times as if I was among lions and serpents, and as if I was treading over scorpions, and yet, amidst these feelings, it is laid upon me to try to visit the Inquisition ; thus to go into the lion's den.

" This afternoon I visited the foundling hospital, and large schools for boys. In the first I met many of the nuns ; some appeared to have ears to hear, and hearts to feel. I had also an interesting season with a large number of the foundlings, grown up to young women's estate. Some of the priests interpreted for me to them, to the nuns, and to the boys. Priests are often the instruments that the Lord provides for me, to convey to others the things pertaining to his glorious kingdom, and the nature of that religion, pure and undefiled, so contrary to those pollutions that men's devices have introduced into the Church of Christ, and into his worship. This evening I am told that there is a great outcry raised by some of the Cardinals and others, at the liberty granted me to pry into their secret things. Some also say, that my appearing, as I have done, with my head covered before a Cardinal, is a thing never before known. I see no other way for me, but, in simplicity and singleness, to go on in the way that my blessed Master directs me. To Him I leave all the result. My liberty, and even my life, is in his hand. I miss very much the company of my beloved friend William Allen. He was such a faithful fellow-helper, under preceding deep conflicts; but now I am left a poor solitary one; and yet not alone, for I am very sensible that the Lord fulfils his very gracious promise to his poor servant, 'Verily, my presence shall go with thee.'

"30th. I went this morning to the Quirinal, and spent some time with Consalvi; he wishes me to send him an account of my observations, in the visits I make to their prisons, &c. &c. I told him of my wish to visit the Inquisition; he said he could not himself grant such a permission, but he would endeavour to obtain it from Father Miranda, who is the head of the inquisitors. I had a private satisfactory time with the Abbé Capacini, Secretary of the Cardinal; he is a feeling, liberally-minded young man. My visits this day to some hospitals and poor-houses have administered more consolation than on preceding days; I found much religious sensibility with several, also among some monks and nuns. I preached to them the Lord Jesus Christ the only hope of salvation, and described to them what the Christian cross is, and where it is to be borne. One of these hospitals for men only, is attended altogether by monks; I thought some of them evinced genuine piety; their great kindness in waiting on the sick is striking. The dear young man, my faithful attendant, is very useful in interpreting when he has not to give way to the priests; but even then he is a witness that they perform their task with faithfulness.

" 1st of Twelfth Month.   I visited this day a large college,
formerly kept by the Jesuits, now banished from here ; there are
about six hundred students in it. There I was among many priests
also ; when I began to speak some of the young men were somewhat rude ; but very soon, silence and seriousness spread over
them.   The Lord helped me to proclaim the everlasting truth
among them.   Then I went to another school for four hundred
boys, where their teacher, a very feeling man, a priest, acted as
my interpreter.   My next visit was to a nunnery, which has a
school for girls, where the Lord was also near, in enabling me to
proclaim his holy name ; the Superior of the nuns has a pious
mind.   It is marvellous that, though these religious services bring
me into contact with so many priests, monks and nuns, when they
hear doctrines so new to them, which also strike at the root of
Popery, no one has yet made an objection ; but, on my taking
leave of them, they treat me with kindness ; some even say that
they are persuaded that it is the love of Christ that constrains me
to visit them.   I had a satisfactory visit from a young priest, a
Prince of Rome and Austria, his name is Charles Odescalchi ; his
uncle is Nuncio in Spain.   I thought, on seeing this young man,
that there was something lovely in him ; his mind was brought
into great tenderness ; I can but have good hope of him.   Three
pious persons came in also to see me ; two of them are of the
monks that I was with yesterday ; one is a young man.   I had a
full opportunity with them ; I directed them to Christ, and to his
Spirit.   The young monk was broken into tears.   In many of
these opportunities I have to set before them in what true religion
consists, and that it is not by works of righteousness that we may
perform that we can be saved, but by faith only in the free grace
of God, through our Lord Jesus Christ, who is the only Saviour
of men.

" 2nd.   I was occupied very late last night in preparing the
documents that Cardinal Consâlvi wishes to have, relative to my
visits to their public establishments.   I apprehend it my duty to
expose the various abuses that I have observed, and in several
instances, misapplication of money designed for acts of benevolence ; I represent also the sufferings of many of the prisoners in
small, dark, crowded rooms, and the heavy chains on them,
which are not removed from some of them till after death ; I

saw some greatly reduced by long illness, who nevertheless, wore their heavy chains. I met this day, at the Russian Ambassador's, some persons whom I visited in Russia ; we had a season of edification together ; I had another with the Prussian Consul, who came to see me ; he and some others appear to enter into sympathy with me in my religious movements in this city. This evening I had a letter from L'Abbé Capacini, inclosing a letter from the Cardinal for Miranda, the inquisitor : the Cardinal also wishes to see me in the morning.

" 3rd. I went to the Quirinal this morning ; the Cardinal wished to make some arrangement for me to visit the Pope ; I had given him some hints of my apprehension that I should not be acquitted in the Divine sight, without attempting such a visit, if it could be granted. The Cardinal wished to know if I would not be satisfied by being introduced to the Pope, at Court. I told him that I was no courtier, nor desired to visit such places, but that my wish was to be with the Pope privately ; yet I should be much pleased if he, the Cardinal, would accompany me, and be the interpreter for me. He, having told me that though the Pope understands French well, yet he was unwilling to speak it in public, said, that in his capacity of Prime Minister, it would not do for him to go in with me, as the other Cardinals might take offence at it. Then I requested that, if the Pope admitted me, he would endeavour to make choice of such a person to be present, as he could confide in to make a faithful report of what should then transpire. This appeared the more necessary, as the jealousy of several of the Cardinals against me is greatly excited. I did not know what, under such circumstances, would befall me in the Inquisition ; but I committed myself to the Lord, and accompanied by my interpreter, went to the convent of the Dominicans, to Father Miranda, who is a monk of the order, and the chief inquisitor. I gave him the letter of the Cardinal ; he could not read it, his eyes having been lately operated upon for cataract ; he requested my young attendant to read it to him. It was a request from the Cardinal to him, to give me every information I might wish respecting the manner in which the Inquisition was conducted in former years, and is now managed, and likewise to show me every part of it. Miranda said he had not been able to go out since the operation on his eyes had been performed, but that he would send for the Secretary and keeper of the archives, who was better able than himself to give me every information; and thereupon a messenger was despatched for him; till he came, I improved the opportunity to inquire of Miranda how the Inquisition is now conducted; when the Secretary came in, he had the letter of the Cardinal read aloud to him. He was then told to give me every information, and to show me everything in it. On our way I made the same inquiries of him that I had put to Miranda, to which he gave similar answers. The accounts given me by several persons in Rome of the Inquisition, were very contradictory. Some represented it as being in full force, only conducted with more secrecy; but these stated that it had been totally abolished for some years; that when any foreigners at Rome, or in Italy, advance sentiments considered heretical or scandalous to their religion, they come under the cognizance of the civil officers, and are mostly banished from the country; but that when this is the case with citizens of Rome, or subjects of the Pope, they are sent to certain convents, where their most severe punishment is to be kept in solitude on low diet, whilst efforts are being made to reclaim them. The Inquisition stands very near the church of St. Peter. The entrance is in a spacious yard, in which nothing is in view but extensive and sumptuous buildings, containing their very large library, paintings, &c. On the left hand is a door, hardly to be noticed, which opens, through a very thick wall, into an open place, round which are buildings of three stories, with many cells; the doors of all these open into passages fronting the yard. These cells, or small prisons, are very strongly built; the walls are of great thickness, all arched over. Some were appropriated to men, others to women. There was no possibility for any of the inmates to see or communicate with each other. The prison where Molinos was confined was particularly pointed out. I visited also the prisons, or cellars underground, and was in the place where the Inquisitor sat, and where tortures were inflicted on the poor sufferer; but everything bore marks that, for many years, these abodes of misery had not been at all frequented. As we went on, I heard the Secretary say something to my interpreter about the *Secret Library*. I therefore asked him to take me there. He took me to the large *Public Library*. I told him this was not what I wished to see, but the

Secret one; he hesitated, stating that it was a secret place, where
there could be no admittance ; that the priests themselves were
not allowed to enter there. I told him that the orders that had
been read to him were to show me everything ; that if he declined
to show me this, I might also conclude that he kept other places
concealed from me ; that therefore I could not contradict the
reports I had heard, even in Rome, that the Inquisition was
secretly conducted with the ancient rigour. On which he brought
me into the *Secret Library.* It is a spacious place, shelved round
up to the ceiling, and contains books, manuscripts, and papers,
condemned by the Inquisitors after they have read them. In
the fore part of each book the objections to it are stated in
general terms ; or a particular page, and even a line is referred
to, dated and signed by the Inquisitor, so that I could at once
know the nature of the objection to any book on which I laid
my hands. The greater number of manuscripts appear to have
been written in Ireland. Some of them contain very interesting matter, and evince that the writers were, in many particulars, learned in the school of Christ. I could have spent
days in that place. There are writings in all the various modern
and ancient languages, European, Asiatic, Arabic, Grecian, &c. &c.,
all arranged separately, in order. I carefully looked for Friends'
books, but found none ; there are many Bibles in the several
languages ; whole editions of some thousand volumes of the
writings of Molinos. After spending a long time in this place
of much interest, the Secretary said, ' You must now come and
see my own habitation.' I thought he meant the chamber that he
occupies ; but he brought me to spacious apartments where
the archives of the Inquisition are kept, and where is the *Secre-
tairerie.* Here are the records of the Inquisition for many
centuries, to the present time. I looked in some of their books
from the fifteenth century. They are kept as the books of a
merchant's journal and ledger, so that looking in the ledger
for any name, and turning thence to the various entries in the
journal, a full statement is found, from the entrance of the poor
sufferer into the Inquisition to the time of his release or death,
and in what way it took place, by fire or other tortures, or
by natural death. The kind of tortures he underwent at each
examination is described, and also what confessions were extorted

from him. All these books are alphabetically arranged. By examining those of late date to the present day, I find that the statement given me by Father Miranda of the manner in which the Inquisition is now conducted, is entirely correct. I could have spent days in this place also; but the examination of some of the books of several centuries, gave a pretty full view of the whole subject. This is an examination that probably very few have made, or are allowed to make. Here also I saw many of the bulls of the Popes, relating to the conduct of the Inquisition.

"4th. I spent my time in writing, except that several piously minded persons and religious inquirers called upon me; some appear awakened to see the emptiness of their confidence in priests and outward observances; 'What shall we do to be saved?' is their inquiry.

"5th. I had interesting and solemn meeting with several persons of the above description. Accompanied by the Prince Charles Odescalchi, I visited a large establishment placed under his charge; it is a night retreat for every one who chooses to come in the evening; no question is asked who the individual is, where he comes from, nor if he was there before. There are separate buildings for the accommodation of men and women; in each place are spacious baths; provision is also made for those who have cutaneous diseases to be fumigated. They all repair to a place of worship, where the Prince addresses them on subjects calculated to impress sentiments of morality and virtue. Those present, he says, are generally well known to be immoral and vicious characters; preaching to them was not customary, till lately introduced by the Prince, who appears to feel deeply for this poor and wretched class of the community. They all come afterwards to the refectory, where supper is given them, and beds are provided for all. In the morning they have water to wash, and their breakfast before they disperse. Many of them return again in the evening, especially when the weather is stormy, or they have not been successful in begging to obtain sufficient to eat. Sometimes this establishment has four thousand inmates during the night. It was a well-meant institution, but the good intention has been much perverted; yet the pious labours of the young Prince may prove a blessing to some.

"6th.   By appointment* of the Cardinal Consalvi, I went to
the palace of the Quirinal this morning.   The ante-chamber and
parlour were crowded with people and priests ; in the latter were
several Bishops, among whom I remained a short time.   I kept
my mind retired to the Lord ; for in Him alone is my help

---

* It may be interesting to some readers to see copies of some of the
notes addressed to S. G. on different occasions like the present, by the
Cardinal's Secretary.

"MONSIEUR,

          "Recevez ces trois billets avec lesquels vous pourrez
observer tous les hopitaux, toutes les prisons, et le Conservatoire des
enfans abandonnés et des vieillards.   Je vous conseille de vous addresser
avant tout au Gouverneur de Rome, Mgr. Pacca, qui chargera quelque
personne ensuite pour vous accompagner aux prisons, et profiter de vos
lumières pour le bien de l'humanité.   Je viens de parler à Mgr. le
Gouverneur et de lui avoir dit combien vous êtes respectable.   Je vous
prie d'agréer les assurances de ma parfaite estime ainsi que de mon
attachement,

                                        "Votre ami,
" De la Secrétairerie d'Etat,   "FRANCOIS CAPACINI.
     26, Novembre, 1819."

"MONSIEUR,

          "Voici une lettre de son Eminence pour voir la maison
de l'Inquisition.   Vous pourrez envoyer à la Minerva la personne qui
vous accompagne pour présenter cette lettre au Père Miranda qui est le
Supérieur de cette Maison.   J'ai parlé avec lui afin qu'il donne les
ordres pour vous faire voir tout, et pour que vous soyez accompagné de
personnes qui puissent répondre à toutes les questions que vous leur
ferez.   La Maison de l'Inquisition est prés de l'Eglise de St. Pierre.
Le Père Miranda vous donnera l'addresse convenable.

"Mes occupations continuelles ne me permettent pas de venir chez
vous, mais si vous avez quelque moment de loisir pour vous rendre à la
Secrétairerie d'Etat je serai bien content de vous communiquer quelque
chose que j'ai à vous dire.

"Je vous remets votre écrit sur l'importance de la Religion.   Je l'ai
lu avec attention et je me propose de vous en parler quand j'aurai
le bonheur de vous voir.

"En attendant je reste, avec le plus sincère sentiment d'estime et
d'amitié,

                                        "Votre ami,
     " Au Quirinal,   "FRANCOIS CAPACINI.
" Ce 2 Décembre, 1819."

"MON AMI,

          "Je vous préviens que son Eminence vous recevra avec
plaisir demain matin entre les dix heures et le midi, dans le temps qui
vous sera plus commode.

and my strength. The Cardinal at last had me invited to his
private cabinet. I had a full opportunity with him, to the relief
of my mind in various respects. He told me that he had read
my reports respecting the different institutions, prisons, &c. I had
visited ; that the subjects I had noticed as needing help, relief to
the afflicted, &c. were put in a way to be speedily attended to.
He has shown the whole to the Pope, and has had my observations
on the various institutions copied separately, so as to be sent to
those who have the particular management of each ; and he hopes
that thereby greater care may be had to the right application of
the funds that belong to the respective places. I told him that I
had lately heard that the Bishop in Bavaria had hanged and
burned the New Testament, printed at Munich, by Gossner, after
the example of the Bishop of Naples ; and how greatly this militates against Christianity. He said, that for his part he should not
object to every individual having a copy of the Scriptures in his
own hands, only he should wish that care might be rightly
extended to prevent the spurious translations from being circulated, as has lately been done by the Socinians in Geneva and
some other places ; the Bishop Martini, of Florence, has lately
published a Bible which is sanctioned by the Pope, which he
should like to see widely spread. He said also, that the Pope
would be pleased to see me ; that owing to various engagements,
he could not fix a time till now, but that to-morrow evening
he would admit me.   ﹅

"7th. I was to-day with the Governor Pacca, and several
others. He is well disposed to relieve the prisoners from some of
the sufferings which I have represented to him. This evening
I went to the Quirinal as appointed yesterday by Consalvi. I
expected to find L'Abbé Capacini in waiting for me, to take me to
the Pope ; but no one was there who knew anything about my
coming. There is something in this I cannot understand.

" Vous pourrez parler avec son Eminence pour concerter l'heure dans
laquelle vous pourrez vous rendre chez sa Sainteté.

" Je me propose de lire cette nuit l'écrit que vous avez envoyé à son
Eminence et profiter de vos lumières.

" Je suis, avec les sentiments les plus sincères de respect et d'amitié,
" Votre ami,

" Ce 5 Décembre, 1819."   " François Capacini."

"8th. Went early this morning to the palace of the Quirinal.
I was a short time only with Consalvi, who was much engaged.
He says the Pope was disappointed last evening, for he expected
me.   From Capacini, however, I find that monks, priests, and
even Cardinals, are some of them under great excitement and
irritation, highly offended at my having profaned their holy
places, by inspecting their secret things in the Inquisition ; and
the countenance that Consalvi has given me since my coming to
Rome displeases them also.   Some of them, I believe, are particularly sore, because I have exposed their misapplication of the
money, intended, in several institutions, for acts of benevolence,
and which they apply to their private use.   I had hoped to be
able to depart to-morrow for Florence, and accordingly engaged
and paid my passage by the *Courrier*, to-morrow noon, but now a
place of confinement may be my portion.   The Lord's will be
done, so that in bonds or sufferings, even in death, his name be
glorified.

"9th. This morning I had a message from Cardinal Consalvi
to call upon him, before he went up to the Pope, which is at seven
a.m. I went accordingly. He well knows the dissatisfaction of
some of the Cardinals and others towards him, but says it may do
good eventually; that, for his part, he is fully disposed to serve
me in what he can here ; or after my departure, whenever he can
do it. He further said, that it is very proper I should be with
the Pope before I leave Rome ; and requested me to wait for his
return from his apartment, when he might tell me what time the
Pope will receive me. I had, whilst in waiting, an interesting
time with Capacini and other secretaries, &c. Their inquiries led
me particularly to speak of the influences of the Divine Spirit, a
gift freely dispensed of God, which man's wisdom, learning or
power cannot obtain for himself ; much less can he dispense it to
others ; by it only the deep things of God can be known; by it
acceptable worship is performed ; qualification for the ministry of
the Gospel is received ; the Apostles were, by this, rendered able
ministers of the New Testament—not of the letter, but of the
spirit. This led me to state that the Popes, Cardinals, Bishops,
&c., in their ordination of ministers or priests, cannot confer upon
them spiritual gifts, neither have they themselves any in virtue
of their stations ; but Christ Jesus, the Head of the Church, is

the giver of spiritual gifts, and with his divine anointing He gives power ; He alone can forgive sin ; He only is the Saviour of men. They were all very serious whilst these and other subjects of vital importance were treated upon ; that of the mass, confession, absolution, indulgences, &c., were also adverted to. The Cardinal came down, and said the Pope would see me at twelve o'clock. He knew that the *Courrier* by which I had taken my seat for Florence, was to start at one o'clock ; but, said he, 'Take no thought about that ; the *Courrier* shall not go till you are ready ;' he also said that Capacini would be here in time to wait on me up stairs, and that he had provided one of his friends, approved by the Pope, who would, if necessary, serve as interpreter, and moreover be a witness to correct any misrepresentations that envious spirits might attempt to make. I returned to the palace at the time designated ; L'Abbé Capacini was waiting for me ; we went up stairs, through several apartments, in which were the military body-guard ; for the Popes are, as kings of Rome, both earthly princes and heads of the Church. Thence we entered into the private apartments ; the hangings about the windows, coverings of the chairs, &c., were all of brown worsted, or silk of the same colour, all very plain. In a large parlour were several priests ; among these, the one provided by Consalvi to go in with me to the Pope. One, dressed like a Cardinal, but who is the Pope's valet de chambre, opened the door of his cabinet, and said in Italian, 'The Quaker has come ;' when the Pope said, 'Let him come in ;' on which the priest, who was to act as interpreter, led me in, no one else being present ; as I was entering the door, some one behind me gently, but quickly, took off my hat, and before I could look for it, the door was quietly closed upon us three. The Pope is an old man ; very thin ; of a mild, serious countenance. The whole of his apartment is very plain. He was sitting before a table ; his dress was a long robe of fine, white worsted, and a small cap of the same (the Cardinals have it red) ; he had a few papers and books before him ; he rose from his seat when I came in, but as he is but feeble, he soon sat down again. He had read my reports to the Cardinal respecting many of the visits I had made in Rome, to prisons, &c. ; he entered feelingly on some of these subjects, and intends to see that the treatment of prisoners and of the poor boys in the house of correction, and various other subjects that I

have mentioned, should be attended to, so that Christian tenderness and care be exercised ; means, as he said, more likely to
succeed to promote reform among them than harsh treatment.
He reprobates the conduct of their missionaries in Greece ; also
the burning of the Holy Scriptures by the priests and bishops in
several places ; he acknowledges, like Consalvi, that it militates
much against the promotion of true Christianity, and is more
likely further to darken the minds of the mass of the people, than
to enlighten them.   On the subject of the Inquisition, he said, he
was pleased I had seen for myself what great changes had been
brought about in Rome, in this respect ; that it was a long time
before he could have it effected ; that he has made many efforts
to have similar alterations introduced into Spain and Portugal ;
had succeeded in part to have the Inquisition in those nations
conducted with less rigour, but was far from having yet obtained
his wishes.   'Men,' he said, 'think that a Pope has plenitude of
power in his hands, but they are much mistaken ; my hands are
greatly tied in many things ;' he, however, expressed his hope that
the time was not far distant when Inquisitions everywhere will be
totally done away.   He assented to the sentiment, that God alone
has a right to control the conscience of man, and that the weapons
of a Christian should not be carnal but spiritual.   The fruits of
the Spirit being described, he said that to produce such and for
the same end, should spiritual weapons be used.   I represented to
him what I had beheld in many places in Europe and the West
Indies, of the depravity and vices of many priests and monks ;
what a reproach they are to Christianity, and what corruption
they are the means of spreading over the mass of the people.   I
then stated what is the sacred office of a minister of the Lord Jesus
Christ, a priest of God ; what the qualifications for that office should
be, and who alone can bestow them.   As I was speaking on these
and other subjects connected therewith, the Pope said several times,
on looking at the priest present, 'These things are true ;' and the
priest's answer was, 'They are so.'   Other subjects were treated
upon ; as, the kingdom of God, the Government of Christ in his
Church, to whom alone the rule and dominion belong ; that He
is the only door, the only Saviour, and that those who attempt to
enter in by any other door but Him, are accounted as thieves and
robbers.   Finally, as I felt the love of Christ flowing in my heart

towards him, I particularly addressed him ; I alluded to the various sufferings he underwent from the hands of Napoleon ; the deliverance granted him from the Lord ; and queried whether his days were not lengthened out to enable him to glorify God, and exalt the name of the Lord our Redeemer, Jesus Christ, as the only Head of the Church, the only Saviour, to whom alone every knee is to bow, and every tongue is to confess ; that such a confession from him, in his old age, would do more towards the advancement of Christ's kingdom and the promotion of his glory, than the authority of all the Popes, his predecessors, was ever able to do ; moreover, that thereby his sun, now near setting, would go down with brightness, and his portion in eternity would be with the sanctified ones, in the joys of his salvation. The Pope, whilst I thus addressed him, kept his head inclined and appeared tender ; then rising from his seat, in a kind and respectful manner he expressed a desire that ' the Lord would bless and protect me wherever I go,' on which I left him.

" On returning to the other apartment, my hat was given me, and excuses were made for having taken it away ; stating that, as this is done when our Friends appear before the King in England, they thought they could not do otherwise on the present occasion. They also said, ' The Pope must have been much pleased with your visit, for we have never known him give half so much time to anybody in a private audience, nor conversing with them as he has done with you.' My soul magnifies the Lord, my strength and my help. The work is His, and the glory also ! May He bless the work of his own hands !

" The priest who was with me before the Pope was very tender, and has now taken leave of me in great affection. Consalvi met me as I came down from the Pope's apartment. He renewed the expression of his desire to serve me whenever he can ; and, in Christian love, we took a solemn farewell of one another.

" I came to my inn to prepare for my journey ; it was a considerable time after the hour at which the *Courrier* usually sets off ; but when I came to the post-house, I met one of the attendants of the Cardinal, who told me that the *Courrier* had orders to wait for me ; that, therefore, I need not hurry myself. I was, however, ready to go."

So Stephen Grellet concludes the account of his visit to

Rome. By the grace of God, he had been enabled to accomplish all that he believed to be required of him. Without
any direct attack upon the system and the exhibitions of
Popery, and ready as he had been to appreciate and cherish
the good in all, his repeated visits at the Quirinal and other
public places had, nevertheless, attracted the jealous attention of the less liberal Cardinals and inferior officials. A
much longer tarriance near the Vatican might have called
forth the spirit of opposition if not of persecution, and
been the means of interrupting his progress. As it was,—
the singleness and purity of his purpose, the disinterested
devotedness and the Christian integrity in the discharge of
apprehended duty, which had marked his course, and his
faithfulness and zeal in simply pleading the cause of Christ,
had made a deep impression upon many. The practical illustration of the spirituality and freedom of the Gospel dispensation and the simple character and polity of unadulterated
Christianity, which his example and teaching had held forth,
could not be lost;—beautifully reflected as it had been, upon
the dark cloud which scarcely concealed the "mystery of
iniquity" with which he was surrounded, it could not escape
the observation of the more serious and considerate. The
poorest of the poor, and the wretched criminal in his miserable cell, had felt its force; princes and nobles, priests and
ecclesiastical dignitaries of the highest order, had recognised
its influence. He had "done what he could," and, with a
thankful heart, he was now permitted peacefully to retire to
other scenes of labour.

CHAPTER XXIV.

Third Visit to Europe.

FLORENCE—LEGHORN—VENICE—VERONA—MUNICH—AUGSBURG —STUTGARD.

TRAVELLING day and night he reached Florence early in the morning of the 11th of Twelfth Month, 1819, and resumes his journal :—

" After the conflicts of mind, and bodily fatigue I had in Rome, travelling alone in the open air was refreshing to me every way ; besides the grateful sense that I have been enabled by my good Master, to throw off a great load of religious concern, which I had borne for years. Marvellous indeed are the ways of the Lord in making it possible for me to do so—first through General Maitland ; then by so inclining the heart of Consalvi and others towards me ; and also in delivering me from the hands of those envious and persecuting men at Rome. Surely it is the Lord's doing ! All praise and glory belong to Him.

"After breakfast I went to the Prime Minister of the Grand Duke of Tuscany, Count Fesson Brodrion, for whom I had a letter from the Prince Cardito at Naples. I find him, as described to me by the Prince, a man possessed of kind and benevolent feelings, enriched by piety. He encourages me to visit some of their public institutions and prisons, to all of which he gives me free access. The Chevalier Coassini, under whose special charge many of these are, was present, and the Count desired him to give me every aid I may need in those visits, should I undertake them. In the afternoon I called on several persons of whom I had heard as being serious characters. I find some of them are such. I also went to see a family in affliction, and was enabled to sympathise with them and to draw their attention to Him who is the sure refuge in time of trouble.

"12th. Feeling, during the night, fresh concern for the poor sufferers in prisons and poor-houses, I apprehended it was my duty to enter into sympathy with them, at least by visiting some of them. As a man, I recoil from visits of this sort; in such places I have endured great suffering; but my proper business is simply to follow my dear Lord as by his good Spirit He directs my steps."

A few days after he adds :—

"I have been at two hospitals, the asylum for the insane, the foundlings' orphans' house, a large poor-house, and some schools, having religious opportunities in most of these places. In several of them, I was with the nuns who devote themselves to minister to the sick and the afflicted. Among these I meet here also persons of conscientious and pious minds. In the poor-house I was enlarged in directing the inmates to Christ, and to his Spirit. Some of them appeared to have hearts to feel the value of pure religion, and to have tasted of its consolations. The prisons here are very different from those in Naples and Rome. The prisoners are treated with much greater humanity. They do not show themselves so hardened in crime. In the meetings I had with them, brokenness of heart prevailed in many, and but few juvenile offenders are to be seen. The President of Police tells me that, during the five years that he has been in office, in a population of one million and three hundred thousand persons, only *five* have been put to death; that is, one person a year. Crimes have considerably lessened throughout Tuscany; murder is seldom heard of in these parts.

"The Prince Carini has been several times with me. We have visited several families piously disposed, and I had a meeting with some of these collected for the purpose of worship. I have also distributed some religious books, in French and Italian."

Suspending his labours in Florence for a few days, he passed over to Leghorn. Here he pursued the same self-denying services as at other places; visiting prisons, hospitals, &c., and having intercourse with various individuals. His narrative proceeds :—

"19th. On my way back to Florence I stopped at Pisa, where I met but little to claim my attention. I was to-day with the Marquis of Pucci, the Counts Tartini and Puccini; the former is President of the Government; he paid great attention to my statement of the condition of the prisoners in several prisons, and manifested great interest in my plea on behalf of those who appear to be in a penitent state; he assured me that this very day measures should be taken for the relief of the poor sufferers.

"To my comfort I find, this evening, that prompt attention is paid to it, not only in this place, but that orders to the same effect are sent to Leghorn and other parts of this Government; and that both here and elsewhere measures are taken for a better provision for the poor, who are much neglected in some places.

"21st. These two days I have had several religious opportunities in families of pious persons; in one instance, a number of them congregated together for the purpose; it was a season when their spiritual strength was renewed, and their faith in the Lord Jesus Christ was confirmed. The Counts Bardi, Tartini, and Puccini, are much concerned for the education of the children of the poor, and they have established schools for them, which I visited. I have encouraged them to extend to the young people a virtuous and religious education, founded on the pure principles of Christianity. I have given them the 'Scripture Lessons' prepared in Russia, which they proposed to introduce into those schools, and they have accordingly put them in train to be printed in Italian."

Having concluded his services in the Tuscan capital, he proceeded by way of Bologna and Ferrara to Venice.

"Venice, 25th. Soon after my arrival here this morning, I was in company with the Chevalier Naranzi, who is the Russian Consul; he is a feeling and pious man, and through him I am brought to an acquaintance with several others of a similar character. I am told that by German papers, printed at Augsburg, they have here the information of the nature of many of my religious engagements at Rome, and of my visit to the Inquisition and to the Pope; allusion is made to some of the principles I maintain as a member of the religious Society of Friends, and

a minister of the Gospel among them; in this capacity, the
papers state, I now travel in these nations.

"26th. I had hoped that I might not be long detained in
this ancient city, but a field for religious service opens before me,
and I dare not flinch from whatever He, in whose service I am, sees
meet to require. I felt a strong attraction towards the prisons, &c.,
but did not know how to get admittance to them. Whilst I was
with Naranzi, a Venetian nobleman, Prefect of one of the departments, in a respectful manner made various inquiries into our
Christian principles; such as salvation by the Lord Jesus Christ,
divine worship, &c., when Baron Mulazzani came in, and manifested great interest in the important subjects we were treating
of, and also in the nature of many of my engagements, in visiting
prisons, poor-houses, &c. He was formerly the Minister of Police
in this place. He kindly offered to accompany me to such of their
prisons, &c. as I might wish to visit: he is also an excellent
interpreter. The first place I went to was the palace, where the
Doges formerly had their residence. It is in a very poor condition:
the prisoners are crowded, and have heavy irons; yet they might
be said to be in a comfortable state compared to what they were
twenty years ago, or less. I was with the Count Gardanis, President
of the Criminal Tribunal, who appears to be a man of sensibility,
and I hope he will succeed in ameliorating the present condition
of these poor prisoners.

"30th. It appears that I do not escape here, any more than in
Rome, the jealousy of some who are disposed to do me mischief,
if they could. They have, as I am told, written to Vienna, to give
the Emperor their own representation of me. I tread indeed among
scorpions, but the Lord can deliver me out of all evil. I see no
better way for me than to go straight forward in the path and
line of service into which my blessed Lord directs me; the consequences I resign entirely to Him, as I have done also my life
and my all. I visited a hospital and the asylum for the insane;
both these are under the care of the monks called '*Buoni
Fratelli:*' they take care also of such as, by accident or otherwise,
are wounded or hurt in the street. I had a precious time with
these monks, who are devoted to acts of benevolence and charity."

In the afternoon "a solemn parting meeting with many of
the pious or serious persons of the city," closed his reli-

gious labours in Venice, and he left the same evening for
Verona.

From Verona he proceeded by way of Ala, Trent, Brixen,
Innspruck, &c. through the Tyrolese Alps, to Munich. On
the whole of this journey, he did not feel it to be his religious
duty to make any stay in the places through which he
passed. He "felt deeply" for the inhabitants, but "prayer
seemed to be the only service required." The Tyrol much
interested him; "I doubt not," he remarks, "that among
these high mountains and deep valleys, the Lord has a seed,
precious in his sight, which He waters by his own Spirit."

———

Stephen Grellet was again in Bavaria; but many changes
had taken place since his last visit. The sacred rights
of conscience had been little regarded; religious liberty had
been deplorably violated; both King and people had quailed
under Papal oppression; bigotry and persecution had, in
several instances, been but too successful in driving away
the pastors, and in scattering the flocks. Dear as was
the cause of Christ and his Church to him, and earnestly as
his heart yearned towards the humble followers of the Lamb
under every name, his Christian sympathy and concern
could not fail to be re-kindled. On his arrival at Munich, on
the morning of the 7th of First Month, 1820, he writes :—

"It is six years since I was at this place before, and I find that
I must stand resigned to resume the heavy bonds that I had then
upon me.

"8th. I was this morning with the Baron Badder; he informs
me that through the influence of the Popish clergy, much persecution has prevailed, so that several of those pious Roman Catholic
priests I was acquainted with, have been scattered, and have gone
to other nations; Boos* to the Rhine, Gossner to Flanders, and

---

* Martin Boos never actually left the Roman Catholic Church. He
was one of those who thought that his usefulness would be lessened by

Lindel to Russia ; it is said that many thousand persons gathered together at the time of the departure of the latter, to take leave of him ; he then preached his farewell sermon to the multitude ; the soldiers who had him in custody to escort him out of the kingdom, were, like the rest, broken into tears, and joined in the public lamentation, that such a good man should be sent away from them. Sailer, of Landshut, has refused to be made a Bishop ; many obstacles are placed in the way of his great usefulness, in spreading light and religious knowledge among the people. These persecutions have tended, however, greatly to increase the number of serious inquirers ; many are eager to have a copy of the New Testament, printed by Gossner. I have met here with Baron von Ruosch and his pious wife on a visit to their daughter ; they give me the cheering information that the Princess Oettingen, and her sister-in-law, the Princess Jeanette, maintain their love to the dear Redeemer ; with these and others, many of whom I had known heretofore, I had a refreshing meeting in the evening ; the Lord's presence was with us.

" 9th. I have been with the Crown Prince ; I spoke freely with him respecting the persecution that has driven so many pious persons out of the kingdom : for, besides those who formerly stood among them as priests in the Church of Rome, and who, from conscientious principles, have adjured the errors they saw themselves in, and have on that account been banished, a considerable number of other persons have also left the kingdom ; many have gone to Russia, others to America. The Prince deplores it, and acknowledges freely that full liberty of conscience ought to be allowed ; that any attempt against it is an infringement of the prerogative of God ; he regrets much that Gossner has been sent away, and says he loved him, and was a subscriber to his New Testament.

" 10th. I visited their prisons, hospitals, &c. They are in a better state than most I have visited of late.

" I feel great oppression on my spirit on account of the persecution excited by the Popish clergy, to which the King has

such a step. But being banished from his parish at Gallneukirchen, he retired to Dusseldorf, and through the kindness of the King of Prussia, afterwards obtained the appointment of Pastor of the parish of Sayn, near Coblentz on the Rhine, where he died in 1825.

given countenance by banishing so many of his best subjects. I cannot feel peaceful without endeavouring to plead with him on that account, and to show him how such doings militate against him, and how contrary they are to the law of righteousness and truth ; that religion which is pure and undefiled before God the Father cannot induce any to persecute others on account of their religious testimonies to the Truth as it is in Jesus Christ, the Son of God and Saviour of men."

At Munich, S. Grellet met with many pious individuals whom he had seen when there before, and had times of edification with large companies ; some of these were of a mixed character as to rank in life—poor and rich meeting together ; but "very generally composed of those who love the Lord Jesus." As to one of these seasons, however, he remarks :—

"This evening I met at the Baron Ruosch's about fifteen persons of high rank. I had seen but few of them before. It was a close searching season. They were told that pretensions to religion without witnessing the substance of it, could not profit any one, neither could the performance of any ever so plausible ceremonies ; it is at the heart that the Lord looks. 'It is not every one that says Lord, Lord, that shall enter the kingdom of heaven, but he that doeth the will of my Father,' &c. It is not said, he that obeys the Pope, or priests, or the decrees of the Council, &c. I urged them to hearken to and obey the Divine Teacher, who speaketh to the heart.

"I was with Reigersberg, who is the Minister of Justice. He appears disposed to make some alterations that I suggested in their treatment of the prisoners, calculated to promote a moral reform among them. He deplores the ascendancy gained by the clergy, and the persecution that has been the consequence of it. He encourages me to lay this my concern before the King.

"14th. I had several precious seasons in the families of the Lord's visited ones, both of the rich and poor in this world ;— truly God does not accept the persons of men, but all they that fear Him and work righteousness, poor or rich, are accepted with Him. Last evening I was at the Baron Leschenfield's, Minister of Finance. Several persons of both sexes were collected on the occasion. Among others, the Prince Oettingen Wallenstein, a serious youth. The Lord gave us a good time together, so that tenderness of spirit was evinced by several.

"This afternoon the serious people in this place came very generally to a meeting I had appointed for them. The consolations of the Gospel through the Spirit were poured forth upon us ; the word of encouragement and instruction in the way of righteousness flowed sweetly towards them ; there was great contrition of spirit over the meeting. As I left it a messenger from the Minister of Finance came to request me to call upon him. I thought he might have something particular to communicate to me ; but I was greatly surprised, on entering his spacious apartment, to find it filled with a large company. Some of them I had met last evening, but many I had not seen before. This was an opportunity given me, very unexpectedly, to proclaim the glorious Gospel. We were soon brought into silence. A weighty exercise came upon me. I was indeed among one class of men only, as respects their station in this world, but not so as to their inward condition. The greatest part of them were Roman Catholics. The Lord enabled me to divide his word aright unto them, and to exalt Christ our Lord as the Head Supreme of the Church, and the only Saviour. Among those present were the young Prince Oettingen and General Reiss. It was late at night when I returned to my lodgings, where I found a letter from the Crown Prince, stating that the King, his father, wished to see me next morning.

"15th. I went to the Palace. I soon saw that my prayers had been heard ; the heart of the King was opened towards me. I had proceeded but a little way in pleading the cause of his persecuted subjects, on account of their conscientious scruples against the principles and doctrines of the Church of Rome, when the King said, he increasingly felt how delicate, tender and important that subject was ; I encouraged him to take the precepts of Christ for his rule in the government of his kingdom, and to seek for, and act himself under the influence of his Spirit. I made particular allusion to perilous times in which he had lived, and the deliverance granted him of the Lord. I pressed earnestly upon him the necessity, now especially in his advanced life, to spend his remaining days in the fear of God, and in acts of piety, virtue, mercy and justice, desiring that he may himself obtain mercy and favour of God, and have a well-grounded hope, that when he has to lay down his earthly crown, he may be prepared to have it exchanged for one everlastingly glorious. The King was tender. He took me in his arms with affection, and craved that the Lord may grant my heart's desire for him, and bless me wherever I go.

" After this I was with the Crown Prince. I encouraged him to adhere closely to Christ ; to follow the light by which things reprovable in the sight of God are made manifest—for the commission of which the Spirit of Truth condemns us. I told him that it is by the Divine Spirit that power is given us to do, or to cease from doing, what we cannot in our own will and strength. I left him in a tender state of mind. I then went a third time to the Minister of Finance, and had a solemn parting opportunity with him and his family. I hope that the King and his ministers, and the Crown Prince also, are strengthened to resist being any longer made the tools of the Nuncio of the Pope, their Bishops, &c., in the oppression of the pious people here.

" This evening a large number met me once more at my lodgings. Among them was again the young Prince Oettingen. The Lord's power was sweetly felt to be over us. It was a time when solemn resolutions were formed. May they keep their covenants unbroken. I have several messages from persons at court, who wish me to visit them ; but I believe my work here, for the present, has come to an end. I commend them to God, and the word of his grace, which is very near them. He can do the work for them. All that the Lord's servants can do, is to direct men to Christ. He alone is the Deliverer and Saviour.

" Augsburg, 16th of First Month, 1820. This morning early, previous to my departure from Munich, several serious persons came to see me, for the last time, perhaps, and brought me a certificate signed very generally by the pious people I have visited, in which they express their warm feelings of gratitude to the Lord for the favour conferred upon them in his love and mercy, together with their prayers that He may protect and bless me during the residue of my days.

" At about half way to this place I met, at the station where I changed post-horses, with one of the pious persons who attended a meeting at Munich. I had a satisfactory religious opportunity in his family; he accompanied me to this place, and though it was six p.m. when we arrived, he went immediately to his religious acquaintances, and by seven o'clock had about sixty of them collected together, with whom I had a meeting. The Lord made himself known among us by the breaking of bread (spiritually); it was a season when some present were more perfectly taught the way of the Lord. It was in this neighbourhood that Lindel resided, and where he has left a spiritually-minded people; the Popish priest, who now occupies his place, uses every endeavour he can to destroy the good that Lindel had been instrumental in promoting."

From Bavaria he passed over into the dominions of the King of Wurtemberg.

"Stutgard, 18th. I left Augsburg at six last evening, and, travelling all night, came here in twenty-four hours.

"19th. I called this afternoon on several of those pious persons with whom I mingled in the fellowship of Christ six years since, and whom I left gathered in good measure under the teachings of his Spirit. I am encouraged in the hope that some of them have kept near the anointing, and made advances in the Divine life; I had now seasons of refreshment before the Lord in the families of Enslingman, Herring, Flatt, the Countess Seckendorf, and others. I have also been with the Prince Kodalesky, the Russian Ambassador here.

"20th. Accompanied by Herring, as my interpreter, I visited three hospitals and the house of correction, and had some religious opportunities in these places. In the afternoon I had a meeting at Herring's, and another in the evening at Enslingman's: they were both solemn ones.

"21st. I was at several schools for both sexes; three of these, for the children of the poor, were founded by the late much lamented Queen; her watchful care over them extended very particularly to their religious, as well as moral education; this is likewise the case in the asylum for orphans. In all these places, as well as in the public schools, the Scriptures are read daily. The King takes care that all the institutions, formed by the late Queen, are kept in the same order in which they were during her life. Several pious females of the court devote portions of their time to daily visiting these places. It was late in the evening when I finished these services. On coming out of a prison I was met by the Prince Kodalesky, who had been in search of me at several places, to let me know that the King wished to see me this evening; being then not far from the Palace, I went there immediately, though I had not taken any refreshment since breakfast, and I felt much spent by the close engagements of the day. The King was alone, waiting for me; he knew that I was in Russia last winter, and with his Queen's mother and her brother, the Emperor Alexander, a few days after they received the mournful tidings of her decease; he continues to feel deeply his great bereavement; he held me by the hands, whilst large tears rolled down his cheeks. The best proof, said he, that he could give, how much he honoured his late Queen, and how dear she was to him, was to endeavour to imitate her in her piety and virtue, and also to keep up all her establishments of benevolence, on the same footing that she had placed them. He also reverently spoke of the comfort the Lord extends to him, in the assurance that, through his mercy, his dear departed one has made a blessed exchange in passing from time to eternity, so that his great loss is her unspeakable gain. His mind was open to receive what I had to impart of the consolations of the Gospel of Christ, and of the good hope that the Christian believer has, when he shall have fulfilled the days of his earthly probation. I endeavoured to encourage him so to live and act as to honour the Lord during the residue of his life, and to promote, by his example and precepts, the advancement of the kingdom of Christ, which stands in righteousness, peace and joy in the Holy Ghost; that, whatever other kings may do, he may resolve to seek peace and pursue it; to be very tender of the consciences of all his subjects, and to rule over them in the fear and love of God. He was very tender, and fully acknowledged the truth of what I said to him. Before I left him, the King asked if I should not like to see his dear motherless children. I told him that their grandmother, the Empress-Dowager, had requested me to do so. Then he appointed the time of my coming again to the Palace, at seven to-morrow evening.

" 22nd. I visited an institute for girls, mostly of the nobility,

called 'Catherine.' It was founded six months only before the
death of the Queen. It contains about two hundred and seventy
pupils, not all boarders. I had an interesting meeting. Much
religious sensibility was evinced by the dear girls.

" In the evening I went to the Palace at the appointed hour.
I found the King again alone. We conversed for about half an
hour on religious subjects, particularly on such as pertain to that
salvation which is by the Lord Jesus Christ ; also on the religious
and moral education of the youth in general. The King concludes
to send some young men and women to London, to become
qualified to introduce here schools on the plan of mutual instruction, and to have the 'Scripture Lessons' used in them : having
them printed in German. He again fully expressed his views
respecting liberty of conscience, and has lately acted accordingly.
A body of persons had separated on religious grounds, from
the Lutheran Church, and built a meeting-house at Kornthal.
William Hoffman, a member of the Legislative body, is one of the
principal men in the separation. The clergy in a body waited
upon the King to request him to dismiss William Hoffman from
his public office, thereby to manifest his disapprobation of his
conduct. He told them that he could not do any such thing—that
he should not interfere with any of his subjects on account of their
religious or conscientious views. I told the King that I had
heard of those persons ; that some spoke much in their favour,
others against them ; and that I had it under consideration to go
and see them the next day. The King encouraged me to go, and
to judge for myself. He then asked me to accompany him upstairs to the nursery. We passed through a long range of apartments, all richly furnished. I could not refrain from saying,
' How many unnecessary wants we make to ourselves.' We came
at last to the children's apartments—the two little Princesses by
his late Queen, and her two sons by the Duke of Oldenburg.
Mary, the eldest of the Princesses, is only three years old, and yet
speaks good English, French and German. Her sister is only
eighteen months old. The King, on presenting them to me, was
bathed in tears. On our return from the nursery, he took me
through the apartments that the Queen used to occupy. I felt the
love of the blessed Redeemer towards him ; and endeavoured to
encourage him in a faithful adherence to the dictates of the Divine

Spirit, and day by day to wait upon the Lord, that he may receive renewed strength to perform the vows that he had made in the days of his distress. He would follow me to the outer door of the Palace, and, on parting, desired to continue to have a place in my remembrance and prayers, and that if at any time he could serve me, I would let him know. This is a time of gracious visitation to his soul. May the Lord prosper his work with him!

" I am greatly bowed down before the Lord whilst contemplating his power, love, and mercy. I behold the efficacy of it in poor-houses and in palaces, among all classes of men of every nation or religious denomination. The works of the Lord in every part of his dominion proclaim his gracious and powerful name.

" 23rd. First-day. Accompanied by Herring, Enslingman, and a few others, we left Stutgard, early in the morning, for Korn-thal, where notice had been sent of my wish to have a meeting with the Dissenters that reside thereabouts. They have built a good meeting-house; it may comfortably accommodate one thousand two hundred persons; but so many came from the villages round that the house being very crowded contained many more. I found there a tender people; they have become dissatisfied with formal religion and outward observances; their souls long for eternal substance, and no longer for shadows only; we were gathered together into solemn silence before the Lord; truly precious was the cheering hope that the desires of this large company were unto the Lord as their only hope and Saviour. I invited them to come to Him with full purpose of heart, to receive Him as their bishop and shepherd; I unfolded to them the nature and effects of Christ's baptism, whereby also the qualification is received to participate in his supper. The baptising power of the Lord was felt to be over us; the Bread of Life and the cup of his salvation were very graciously offered to us, and the language was revived, ' Eat, O friends, drink, yea drink abundantly, O beloved !'

" I had a satisfactory opportunity with William Hoffman, who is made a valuable instrument of good to that people. We returned to Stutgard in time to attend a meeting appointed there for that evening. It was attended by the people at large; many

of the nobility and several clergymen were present. The Lord
enabled his very poor servant—for truly so I felt myself to be
amidst that large company—to minister to their various conditions.

"24th. This morning I met with a few of those here who
appear to have made the greatest progress, through the obedience
of faith, in the blessed Truth ; we had a contriting season together.
I encouraged them regularly to meet to wait upon the Lord, so as
to renew their strength, to walk in the way of his counsel, and to
worship Him in spirit and in truth. Our parting from one another
was under much solemnity and Christian affection. They are
among those whom I can recognise as a portion of that flock of
the Lord Jesus who know his voice ;—may they also follow Him
wherever He leads !"

CHAPTER XXV.

Third Visit to Europe.

SWITZERLAND — SOUTH OF FRANCE — CONCLUDING SERVICES IN
ENGLAND AND IRELAND.

It was a matter of great interest to Stephen Grellet to
re-visit the scenes of his past labours in the Swiss Cantons.
On the 26th of First Month, 1820, he reached St. Gallen,
and writes :—

"I left Stutgard in the evening of the 24th, travelled two
nights and one day, and arrived here this morning, so little
fatigued that, without taking any rest, I proceeded at once with
the service of love to which my dear Master calls me, in the
prosecution of which my soul is often refreshed in his presence.
Many of those whom I met with in a preceding visit are now
gathered into the heavenly sheepfold ; through the tender mercies
of God, others have entered their ranks in the Church militant :
from children they are now become strong men and women—
burden-bearers in the Church. There is also a precious little
company still living of those to whom I had been heretofore
united in Christian fellowship ; they appear to have kept their
integrity in the Truth. I visited their Orphan Asylum, where
again I have had a contriting religious season with the dear children and their pious care-takers. In the evening I had a public
meeting, which was particularly attended by the pious part of the
inhabitants. The Lord caused the stream of Gospel-love to flow
towards them, and the consolations of the Spirit to distil upon
them. Tribulations have been indeed abundant with many since
we saw one another, but the consolations that are by Christ have
abounded much more. Truly some of these dear people can
testify that their afflictions have been largely blessed.

"I left St. Gallen before daylight the next morning, and in the
afternoon arrived at Winterthür. I visited several serious families, and had some religious service with them.

"Zurich, 28th. I set off again before daylight this morning, and arrived early at this place.

"30th. I was in several families with whom I had religious opportunities. I had also two meetings : one at the venerable, aged Antistes Hess's, at the close of which he bore testimony to the efficacy of that grace and truth that come by Jesus Christ, asserting also his full belief in the sensible influences of the Divine Spirit. 'It is a quickening Spirit,' said he, 'without it, man cannot live the life of Christ ; nay, he is none of his.' The other meeting, this evening, was at pastor Gessner's, where the several branches of his family, and of the Lavaters were also present. A solemn silence prevailed over us all, in which the Lord himself, through his Spirit, ministered to us. We partook together of the one bread, and drank out of the one cup, witnessing the truth that there is but one Lord, one faith, and one baptism. Our souls were refreshed and comforted together."

S. G. left Zurich on the 31st, and went by Berne, Yverdun and Lausanne, to Geneva, where he writes :—

"Geneva, 5th. I was on the road some hours before daylight this morning. On arriving here I was greatly comforted by meeting with my beloved friend, William Allen ; he could not obtain a passage from Malta for France, which induced him to come by land from Italy on his way to Paris and London ; he has recovered his health very nicely. It is cause of much gratitude that we thus meet again ; for a while it appeared very doubtful that his valuable life would be continued, he was brought so very low. Now we are permitted to enjoy very sweetly the preciousness of fellowship in our Lord and Redeemer Jesus Christ ; we had a refreshing and consoling time together in prostration of soul before Him.

"6th. We visited together several pious persons. In the evening we went to pastor Moulinier's, where we had appointed a meeting. We have felt very tenderly for him, and pastor Demalleyer. They have to endure much from several of the clergy in this place.

"We had a satisfactory meeting with the company convened at Moulinier's. It was precious to feel that each one was engaged to endeavour to draw for himself out of the well of the Lord's consolations. A spring of living ministry did also flow towards them. I translated into French what my beloved friend William Allen felt it his religious duty to communicate.

"7th. We met with a very interesting little company at the widow Pillart's : we seemed to be all brought into the oneness of the Spirit in the Lord Jesus. There are several gathered religious bodies or churches that acknowledge Christ for their Head ; great difference however exists among them ; but in all some are to be found who are in the unity of the Spirit in the oneness of the faith, baptised with the same baptism, and partaking together at the same table of the same bread, ministered to them by their one Lord and blessed Redeemer. My soul often blesses Him in that He has given me to mingle with many of this description, and to feel with them the quickenings of his Divine life ; I have found some in every nation and among various denominations.

"10th. During these past days we visited their prisons and schools ; also several pious and afflicted ones in their families ; we had several religious meetings ; one particularly well attended was held at pastor Demalleyer's.*

---

* Amongst the many seals to his ministry which S. G. left behind, it may be interesting to preserve the following :—

In the autumn of 1853, Eli and Sybil Jones, ministers from America, accompanied by Mary J. Lecky and Christine R. Alsop, visited the widow and daughter of pastor Demalleyer, then staying at Clarens, near Vevay, in Switzerland. They were both present at the meeting so briefly noticed above, and gave them this account in connection with it.

A considerable number of serious persons had met at pastor Demalleyer's. After some instructive conversation, a time of silence ensued. The whole company seemed impressed with the solemnity of it. It was some time before anything was said. Stephen Grellet then addressed the company in a very edifying manner. Whilst he was speaking, a gentleman, who was but slightly known to the family, and had never before attended the little meetings occasionally held at their house, entered the room and took his seat by the door, without interrupting the stillness ; and, it was thought, unobserved by the speaker. For a while there was no change in the tenor of his discourse, but towards the conclusion he was led to address himself, with increased solemnity, to an individual whom he described as being in the greatest danger of committing suicide. After a solemn warning against the fearful sin and its awful consequences, the forgiving mercy of God, the bountiful provisions and the entreaties and promises of the Gospel of Christ, and the all-sufficiency of the help of the Holy Spirit, even for the most destitute and sinful, were dwelt upon in such a manner that all present were

"My soul greatly mourns over many dark spirits here ; Antichrist seems to triumph. The majority of the clergy, the Doctors of Divinity, so called, have prevailed : they have decided that the doctrine of the Divinity of our Lord Jesus, and salvation through faith in his name, shall no longer be preached among them ; only their Socinian tenets are to be promulgated. There are those, however, who cannot be restricted by such a law ; they feel it to be their religious duty to preach the Lord Jesus—delivered for our sins, risen again for our justification—and to resign themselves to the Lord, whatever be the consequence. We felt very tenderly for them, and we believed that we had a service in this place, by endeavouring to encourage them to faithfulness in keeping the faith that was once delivered to the saints.*

---

deeply affected, wondering at the same time why they should be thus addressed. But, from that time, it was remarked that the gentleman, who had unexpectedly come into the room whilst S. G. was speaking, became more serious, and frequently attended the evening services which continued to be held by the little company of pious persons with whom he had mingled. It was not, however, till many years after, that the gentleman in question informed pastor Demalleyer, that on the evening of the meeting, he had left his own house, under the pressure of great trials, with the full determination to throw himself into the lake. On his way to it, an involuntary impulse caused him to take a less direct course, which brought him to the house of the pastor. He entered it, he scarcely knew why, and, through the Divine blessing, it proved the means of his deliverance.

* The truth as it is in Jesus is indestructible ; and it is well known that brighter days have since dawned upon Geneva, and many other parts of the continent of Europe. At the very time that Stephen Grellet was penning the above remarks in the city of Calvin, many pious young men, both in Switzerland and in Germany, were undergoing, often unknown to each other, a fearful conflict, in throwing off the fetters of unbelief, and seeking to attain to "the joy of faith and the peace of believing." Not a few of these are now preaching the faith which once they sought to destroy. Of this number is J. H. Merle D'Aubigné, the well-known historian of the Reformation.

He studied at the academy of Geneva, and, after having remained in the cheerless principles of Unitarianism till near the conclusion of his course there, a prayerful study of the Holy Scriptures was made the means, under the Spirit's influence, of bringing him to believe in the Divinity of the Saviour. Convinced of sin, the power of which he had felt in his own heart, and obtaining the blessing of forgiveness through faith in the atonement, he had experienced the joys of the new birth ; but, though "willing to take up the cross of Christ, he was yet weak and preferred regarding it as wisdom rather than foolishness." It was

"Now apprehending that the time had arrived for dear Allen and me to be once more separated for a short time—he to return to London—I to proceed to my Master's service in France—we have taken a solemn farewell of one another."

---

at this time (1817) that he first visited Germany, with the design of studying Theology for a longer period, before entering upon the active duties of the ministry of the Gospel.

"Every Theological journal I read," he says, "every book I looked into, almost every one, both ministers and laymen, whom I met, were affected with Rationalism, so that the poison of infidelity was presented to me on all sides.

"I then entered upon a fearful spiritual struggle, defending with my whole strength my still feeble faith, yet sometimes falling under the blows of the enemy. I was inwardly consumed. There was not a moment in which I was not ready to lay down my life for the faith I professed; and never did I ascend the pulpit without being able to proclaim, with fulness of faith, salvation by Jesus. But scarcely had I left it when the enemy assailed me anew, and inspired my mind with agonising doubts. I passed whole nights without sleep, crying to God from the bottom of my heart, or endeavouring by arguments and syllogisms without end, to repel the attacks of the adversary. Such were my combats during those weary watchings, that I almost wonder how I did not sink under them.

"It happened at this time (1819) that a friend of mine, F. Monod, settled in Paris, was on the point of visiting Copenhagen, where his mother's family resided. Another friend of ours, Charles Rieu, was the pastor of Fredericia, in Jutland. We were all three Genevese; we had studied together at Geneva, and had come at the same time to the knowledge of the Truth, although Rieu had outstripped us in all respects, especially in the simplicity of his faith and devotedness to the Lord. We agreed to travel together to Copenhagen, and to meet at Kiel, the capital of Holstein. Kiel is a German university, and at that time was the residence of Kleuker, one of the oldest champions of German divinity, who had been for forty years defending Christian Revelation against the attacks of infidel theologians, in apologetic works of some celebrity. There were many passages of Scripture which stopped me, and I proposed visiting Kleuker, and asking him to explain them, hoping by this visit to be delivered from my agonising doubts.

"Accordingly I waited on Kleuker, and requested that learned and experienced Christian to elucidate, for my satisfaction, many passages whence some of his countrymen in their writings had drawn proofs against the inspiration of Scripture and the divine origin of Christianity. The old Doctor would not enter into any detailed solution of these difficulties. 'Were I to succeed in ridding you of them,' he said to me, 'others would soon arise. There is a shorter, deeper, more complete way of annihilating them. Let Christ be really to you the Son of God, the Saviour, the Author of Eternal Life. Only be firmly settled in his

Having completed his religious engagement in Switzerland, Stephen Grellet felt once more drawn towards the little company who profess with Friends in the South of France. He left Geneva early in the morning of the 11th of Second

---

grace, and then these difficulties of detail will never stop you; the light which proceeds from Christ will disperse all your darkness.'

"The old Divine had shown me the way; I saw it was the right one; but to follow it was a hard task. God, who had revealed to me the glory of his well-beloved Son, did not forsake me; but He used other agency to bring me to the mark which had been pointed out.

"As steamboats were not at that time very regular, we had to wait some days for the one in which my friends and I intended to proceed to Copenhagen. We were staying at an hotel, and used to spend part of our time in reading the Scriptures together. Rieu was an ear of corn which the Lord had early brought to full maturity, and which was soon after carried to the everlasting garner. Two years after I wept over his grave, amidst his desolate flock. We all three communicated to each other our thoughts, but it was Rieu who most abundantly brought out the hidden riches of the Book of God. We were studying the Epistle to the Ephesians, and had got to the end of the third chapter, when we read the two last verses, 'Now unto Him who is able to do *exceeding abundantly* above all that we ask or think, according to the power that worketh in us, unto Him be glory,' &c. This expression fell upon my soul as a mighty revelation from God. 'He can do by His power,' I said to myself, 'above all that we *ask*, above all even that we *think*, nay *exceeding abundantly* above all !' A full trust in Christ for the work to be done within my poor heart now filled my soul. We all three knelt down, and although I had never fully confided to my friends my inward struggles (for I dared not make them known to any but God alone), the prayer of Rieu, filled with admirable faith, was such as he would have uttered had he known all my wants. When I arose in that inn room at Kiel, I felt as if my 'wings were renewed as the wings of eagles.' From that time forward I comprehended that my own syllogisms and efforts were of no avail, that Christ was able to do all by his 'power that worketh in me:' and the habitual attitude of my soul was to lie at the foot of the cross, crying to Him, 'Here am I, bound hand and foot, unable to move, unable to do the least thing to get away from the enemy who oppresses me. Do all thyself. I know that thou wilt do it, thou wilt even do *exceeding abundantly* above all that I ask.' I was not disappointed. All my doubts were soon dispelled, and not only was I delivered from that inward anguish which in the end would have destroyed me, had not God been faithful, but the Lord 'extended me peace like a river.' Then I could 'comprehend with all saints what is the breadth and length, and depth and height; and know the love of Christ which passeth knowledge.' Then I was able to say, 'Return unto thy rest, O my soul; for the Lord hath dealt bountifully with thee.'

"If I relate these things, it is not as my own history—not the history

Month, 1820.   Passing by Chambery, Grenoble, &c., he
writes :—

"Congenies, Second Month 17th.   On the 15th instant, for the
third time, I came among the little flock here.   I continue to feel
much for them.

"21st.   I had several meetings among this little flock, and also
attended their meeting for discipline, to which came Friends from
divers other places.   They were seasons in which a visitation of
the Lord's love was very graciously renewed towards them ; even
the dear children were much contrited under the sense of his
power extended over us.   I have had, besides, several large public
meetings, to some of which the people from neighbouring towns
and villages came.   The Lord's power was eminently felt to be
over all.   Some of their clergy present said, 'The truth as it
is in Jesus has been proclaimed.'   Between meetings I proceeded
diligently in visiting the families of those who profess with us,
which service of love has been owned of the Lord.   I went through
deep baptism during that engagement, and there was, in some
places, close searching of heart.

"Codognan, Second Month 22nd.   My dear friend Louis
Majolier, accompanied me here this morning.   I visited the few
in profession with us in their families."

After visiting a few more places where he held some meetings, S. G. took his leave of his friends in Languedoc and
passed on to Montpellier.

"24th.   This morning early, accompanied still by Louis Majolier, I came to Lunel, where, after tarrying a short time, we
separated in brotherly and Christian love, he to return home, and
I to proceed alone.

---

of myself alone—but of many pious young men, who in Germany, and
even elsewhere, have been assailed by the raging waves of Rationalism.
Many, alas! have made shipwreck of their faith, and some have even
violently put an end to their lives.   On this account I shall always remember the words of Scripture, 'Thou hast set my feet in a large room.'
' He that glorieth, let him glory in the Lord.'—See D'Aubigné's *Germany,
England, and Scotland*.   New York edition, 1848.

"I arrived at Montpellier early in the afternoon. My old friends, D'Encontre and others, were very prompt in giving notice of a meeting in this place; it was held at D'Encontre's, and pretty well attended; we were refreshed and encouraged together, to hold fast in the way of the Lord, though some of us may find it a path strewed with many tribulations."

From Montpellier S. G. proceeded by Milhau, Rodez, Montauban, &c., to Brives, when he once more saw his aged mother, and he writes :—

"Brives, Third Month 3rd. I am greatly comforted in my beloved aged mother, now above eighty years old. Her mind is clear, and she is green in the Divine life. The Lord Jesus is truly precious to her. I have had some tendering seasons with her, and my other near relatives. Some of them now see beyond the priests, and their prescribed forms and ceremonies in religion.

"6th. I had some satisfactory meetings with the persons I visited when here before, and especially with the dear nuns.

"Limoges, 8th. I arrived here yesterday morning. My parting with my beloved mother was truly solemn. It may probably be a final separation here on earth. On bended knees, my soul was very reverently prostrated before the Lord, and I was engaged in putting up my supplications unto Him for her, when, bathed with tears, she also kneeled down by me.

"My distress for this nation, the land of my nativity, is also great. I see blackness hanging over them. The Lord will overturn, till He comes and reigns, whose only right it is. Since coming here, I have had several religious opportunities in the families of such as I mingled with heretofore in religious fellowship, and some meetings of a more public nature. I was also with several of the nuns; two of whom are my cousins, who retain their religious tenderness.

"Paris, 14th. I entered this great city with a heavy heart. Darkness and impiety prevail to a lamentable extent. But the Lord has a remnant even here, both the Roman Catholics and Protestants, who are as a little salt among them.

"16th. I have been with the Duke de Richelieu, Prime Minister of the King, who was some years Governor in the

Crimea ; he felt much interest in the account I gave him of my
visit to the Mennonites, the Spiritual Christians, and the German
colonists. He appears borne down under the weight of the spirit
of faction that prevails in this nation, and would greatly prize a
retreat among those pious persons in the South of Russia. I
endeavoured to strengthen his hands to walk closely and faithfully under the guidance of the Lord's Spirit, whereby he would
be enabled to repress the evil, and strengthen those in whom
there is some good. There are such here who long that peace in
the nation may be maintained ; but there are many others who
only wait for an opportunity to lift up the standard of war. I
was also with the General Pozzo di Borgo, Ambassador from
Russia to France, for whom I had letters ; and through whom I
have sent some that I have written to the Emperor Alexander,
and to the Prince Galitzin ; also to my beloved friend, Daniel
Wheeler. I had some satisfactory seasons with several companies of serious persons ; some were Papists, others were Protestants ; a number of Roman Catholics came to my lodgings to
unbosom their soul's distress ; they feel the critical state of the
nation, and they dread the consequence of the ascendancy that
the Jesuits begin again to have ; they have become convinced
that the religion of Jesus Christ does not consist of outward
forms and ceremonies, but in the love and fear of God so dwelling in our hearts as to render us obedient to his Divine law,
even the law of the Spirit of life in Christ Jesus, which setteth free
from the law of sin and death ; they see that none of the priests'
masses said for them, their indulgences or absolutions, can avail."

On the 23rd S. G. arrived in England, and he says :—

" My soul was so bowed before the Lord, who has in such a
gracious manner, led me about, and instructed and preserved me,
that I was constrained, on bended knees, to offer up to Him the
tribute of thanksgiving and praise."

———

After an absence of a little more than a year and a half,
Stephen Grellet found himself once more among his English

.   x

friends. He remained about two weeks in the neighbourhood of London, attending the meetings as they came in course, and then went to Bristol, at which place he writes :—

" I had several meetings among Friends and others ; one was in the Moravian establishment. The female, who is at the head of the sisters, gave me such a welcome as I could not at first understand, not recollecting to have seen her before ; but I found that she had been at the head of the Moravian establishment in Dublin, when I visited it some time since. In the course of my religious communication there I particularly addressed a young woman, warning her against yielding to the strong temptation which was assailing her ; for if she did, anguish and misery would be the result ; but if she sought the Lord for help to resist it, He would be her saving strength, and would greatly bless her succeeding days. I knew nothing concerning the young woman, but I could not help thinking my address to her a singular one. Now, I am informed that a young nobleman had found means of obtaining access to her ; and under fair pretences of strong affection and promise to marry her, he had nearly persuaded her to elope with him. This had come to the knowledge of my informant a very short time before I was there. As soon as I went away the young woman came to her, bitterly reproaching her for telling me the circumstances, but she satisfied her fully that she had not been with me, except in the presence of them all, and that nobody could have told me about it, since no other person was in the secret ; she must, therefore, consider it as a particular interposition of the Lord to induce her to flee from temptation, and to escape the ruin that threatened her. The young woman resolved, by the Lord's help, to do so ; she was enabled to resist, and soon after heard that he who had made such fair promises to her was a profligate person.

" I met in Bristol with my beloved friend, William Forster, who had come there to embark for the United States, on a religious visit. The prospect of such a voyage was trying indeed under his bodily sufferings ; a cow had run upon him and wounded him severely with her horns, on his knee, so that he cannot stand. He hopes to recover during the passage. I felt very tenderly for him and his beloved wife at parting from one another under such circumstances. They both were greatly supported, leaning on the Lord's arm, resigned to his Divine will, to be separated for the service of the Gospel."

From Bristol S. Grellet proceeded to Dublin, to attend the Yearly Meeting there; in this visit he was accompanied by his long proved friend, William Allen and his daughter; whilst there he writes :—

" We came to Dublin a week before the Yearly Meeting, during which time we had meetings in the prisons, and in some poor-houses, and visited also some of the sick and afflicted. The Yearly Meeting was a time of deep exercise to us. There is yet much cause for this ; nevertheless, there is great occasion also for gratitude to the Author of all our mercies. The prospect among the dear young people is much brighter. Many of them who were before estranged from the Truth, evince now that they are under the baptising power of it, and that the yoke of Christ is upon them. Dear Allen joined me in some public meetings I had in that city. Many of the Roman Catholics came to one of these. Our services were very harmonious, being together of one mind, of one accord, baptised by the one Spirit, for the one work of the dear Master."

Returning to England, he attended the Yearly Meeting in London. On the eve of retiring from the field of his European labours, it was a time of peculiar interest, both to himself and his friends, and in reference to it, he makes the following record :—

" We left Ireland in much peace ; had at Worcester a solemn meeting with Friends, and another with the inhabitants. Then came pretty directly to London, to be at the Yearly Meeting.

" Having now in prospect soon to be liberated from the extensive field of Gospel labours in these European nations, in which I have been diligently engaged for nearly two years, I spread before my friends of the Meeting for Ministers and Elders, my prospect of soon returning to America ; they gave me their testimonials of Christian unity with my various labours and deep exercises whilst among them, and on the European continent. Our parting from one another at the close of the Yearly Meeting, was under strong and warm feelings of Christian love and fellowship."

He now went down, on a farewell visit to his friends in the North of England, on his way to Liverpool, to embark for America. At the latter place, he writes :—

"First-day, 26th. I was largely engaged to-day, in two crowded meetings, in proclaiming the greatness of the love of God towards poor, fallen and sinful man : ' God so loved the world that He gave his only begotten Son, that whosoever believeth in Him should not perish, but have everlasting life ; for God sent not his Son into the world to condemn the world, but that the world through Him might be saved.' These are subjects that could engross the mind with awful reverence and prostration for ages. The angels themselves desire to look into these things. They were solemn, good meetings.

"27th. Went to see a ship bound for New York, the *James Monroe*, Captain Rogers ; the same who commanded the vessel in which I went to the island of Hayti. I sat down quietly in the cabin, my mind turned to the Lord that He would direct me in the right way, and show me if this is indeed the time for me to return to America, and if his presence will go with me in that ship. I felt sweet peace there ; it seemed to me like a little sanctuary, and now, on the eve of my return home, the gracious promise made at the time of my departure from America was sweetly revived, ' Verily my presence shall go with thee, and I will give thee rest.' Good is the word of the Lord, says my soul, worshipping before Him ! I have engaged my passage on that vessel.

"29th. I was at meeting this day, which was a solemn parting season with my friends ; the Lord broke bread for our soul's nourishment, and blessed it.

"30th. Several friends from London and other places have kindly come to bid me once more farewell before I embark ; among these are Luke Howard, G. Stacey, &c. I am pleased that my dear William Allen could not come ; for these repeated part-

ings are hard to bear. I had this afternoon a most solemn season with a considerable number of friends that came to see me ;
it was an awful solemnity ; I saw evidently, and felt how the
powers of darkness are combining together in the world to try to
obtain the mastery ; to crush and to destroy that which is good :
so that though now the outward sword between nation and nation
is sheathed, yet, the prince of darkness, that ruleth among the
children of disobedience, seems to have great power. My soul felt
deeply, and, like the prophet, when he saw what distress Hazael
would bring upon Israel, I wept bitterly. But our blessed Lord
condescended also to show me, that in his time, by the brightness
of his arising, He would destroy that spirit ; but many may first
be destroyed by it, and houses great and fair be left without
inhabitant."

Thus closed his third embassy to Europe—his second visit
to Great Britain and Ireland.

CHAPTER XXVI.

STEPHEN GRELLET embarked at Liverpool in the *James Monroe*, Captain Rogers. Though sometimes becalmed—surrounded by thick fogs—and exposed to "heavy squalls and stormy winds"—his homeward voyage did not occupy much more than five weeks. He landed safely at New York on the 7th of Eighth Month, 1820.

"New York, 8th of Eighth Month, 1820. I landed here last evening, and met my beloved wife and daughter, who came two days since from Burlington, to await my arrival; and they did not wait long. Our hearts overflowed with gratitude at our being permitted to meet again, after an absence of two years and two months, during which I have travelled about twenty-two thousand miles. Silent and reverent prostration of soul before the Lord was our only language to one another, for some time; then, on bended knees, and with a bowed spirit, thanksgiving, adoration, and praise were offered to the Lord."

A few months after his return an interesting little glimpse of his inner life, and the endearments of home, is afforded in two extracts from letters.

TO GEORGE STACEY.

"New York, Twelfth Month 8th, 1820.

"My dwelling, since my return, is in very low places. My health has also suffered many interruptions. I must expect now to feel the consequences of my late great exertions. There are, however, seasons when I am favoured with a little capacity to appreciate my favours, and to number them. My R. G. and myself are comfortably settled for the present, and, with thankful hearts, enjoy our chimney corners, our little charge enlivening the scene."

TO THE SAME.

"New York, Second Month 28th, 1821.

" My health is but feeble. My exercises, which for years have been chiefly directed towards the people at large, are now pretty much concentrated on behalf of our poor Society, and some of them are of such a nature that prayer and silent travail appear the only way to get relief under them.

" Our dear William Forster is diligent in his Master's service. Perhaps I may see him at Philadelphia Yearly Meeting, where I have some prospect of going, should my health permit. My R. G. and myself are often bowed in much gratitude under a sense of our many favours, and we esteem it a great one to pass now so much time together."

A longer tarriance at home and the renewal of more frequent intercourse with his friends, did not remove his fears. His love for Christ did not allow him to remain a silent observer of what was passing around him.

" 1821. Third Month 1st. The spirit of infidelity is gradually progressing, and the eyes of many seem to be so darkened that they cannot see, nor does their heart understand; very close labour I have had with many of them, privately and publicly, under the sensible feeling of Divine Love ; but I seem to them as Lot was to his sons-in-law when he entreated them to flee from the destruction that was impending. During my journeyings in foreign lands, these years past, perils often threatened me by sea and by land, and among robbers ; but now wounds are inflicted in the house of my friends, among those with whom I had felt, heretofore, the fellowship of the Spirit of Christ, uniting us together in the bond of peace."

In the Fourth Month he attended the Yearly Meeting in

Philadelphia, and returned home in time to be at his own in New York. After that, accompanied by his wife, he went to the Yearly Meeting for New England, and visited many of the meetings belonging to it.

He was now permitted to remain at home for a while. The ensuing winter and spring were mostly spent in the bosom of his own family. The "care of the churches," nevertheless, still rested heavily upon him, and soon after the conclusion of his own Yearly Meeting, in the Fifth Month of 1822, he again entered upon an extensive religious visit to Friends, and others, in some parts of the United States, and Canada. Of these various engagements he gives the following summary :—

"Accompanied by my dear friend, John Hancock, who was my very kind attendant during my religious visit to the island of Hayti, I visited very generally all the meetings of Friends in the States of New York and Vermont, and also in Canada ; and had many meetings among the people at large, where there are no meetings of Friends. The concern that lay with great weight upon me, was that Friends generally, and the dear young people in particular, might be deeply rooted and established in the saving knowledge of God and our Lord Jesus Christ ; for 'to know Him, the true God and Jesus Christ, whom He hath sent, is life eternal.' My commission day by day, and from place to place, was renewed ; to preach Christ and Him crucified, unto the Jews a stumbling-block, and unto the Greeks foolishness ; but to them that believe, the power of God and the wisdom of God ; who also is made to them of God, wisdom and righteousness, sanctification and redemption. He was delivered for our offences, and was raised again for our justification ; and ever liveth to make intercession for them that came unto God by Him. I directed them to Him who is the Lamb of God that taketh away the sin of the world ; and the Author of eternal salvation unto all that obey Him. I rehearsed the words of the Apostle Peter : 'Be it known unto you all, and to all the people of Israel, that by the name of Jesus Christ of Nazareth, whom ye crucified, whom God raised from the dead, even by Him doth this man stand here before you whole. This is the stone which was set at nought of you builders, which is become the head of the corner, neither is there salvation in any other : for there is none other name under heaven given among men, whereby we must be saved.' Most affectionately did I entreat them, many a time, not to give way, in any wise, to those who would seduce them from the hope of that salvation which cometh by the Lord Jesus Christ alone ; it is He who gave himself for our sins, that He might deliver us from this present evil world, according to the will of God and our Father. I had the consolation, at times, to be with those whose faith in the Gospel appeared to be confirmed ; but I bitterly lamented over many who have drunk deeply of the spirit of infidelity, so as to deny the Lord that bought them.

"I found great changes in the face of the country in Canada since my previous visit there. What was then a wilderness, has now become a fruitful field. Friends have considerably increased, and many Meetings have been established.

"Their Half Year's Meeting, held at this time at Yonge Street, was very crowded. The people come from considerable distances to attend the meetings for worship. The Lord owned them by his Divine presence, as He also did those more select, held for Friends only."

Here Stephen Grellet was in the neighbourhood of David Wilson, who had at that time obtained considerable notoriety, and notwithstanding the palpable absurdity of his irreligious and antichristian opinions, and the dishonest and immoral tendencies of his fanatical schemes, succeeded in " drawing away disciples after him." After remarking upon the danger of assuming high notions of spirituality, *apart from* a practical belief in the great facts and fundamental truths of Christianity, made known in the New Testament, S. G. goes on to say:—

"These people surely evince that the description given in the Scriptures of the depravity of the human heart is not painted in too high colours, ' The heart of man is deceitful above all things and desperately wicked.'

"I went up some distance beyond Norwich, having meetings

among Friends and the people at large, and returned into the
State of New York by way of Buffalo; thence visited several
tribes of Indians, among whom I met some serious persons; particularly of the Seneca Tribe. I have been comforted at seasons
among that people, under the apprehension that the language of
the Apostle Peter is applicable to some of them at least. 'Of a
truth I perceive that God is no respecter of persons, but in every
nation, he that feareth Him and worketh righteousness is accepted
with Him.'

"We then proceeded to Long Island, where I attended all the
meetings; but here my soul's distress exceeded all I had known
during the preceding months, though my baptisms had been deep.
I found that the greatest part of the members of our Society, and
many of the Ministers and Elders, are carried away by the principles which Elias Hicks has so assiduously promulgated among
them; he now speaks out boldly, disguising his sentiments no
longer; he seeks to invalidate the Holy Scriptures, and sets up
man's reason as his only guide, openly denying the Divinity of
Christ. I have had many opportunities with him, in which I
have most tenderly pleaded with him; but all has been in vain.
When I saw him last winter, I found that there was no more
room to plead with him.

"At all these meetings I felt myself imperatively called upon
to preach the Lord Jesus Christ as the only Saviour; to expose
the awfulness of the sin of unbelief, and the fearful condition of
those 'who have trodden under foot the Son of God, and counted
the blood of the covenant, wherewith we were sanctified, an unholy thing, and done despite unto the Spirit of Grace.' I laboured
the more earnestly, both in meetings and in several of their families, because I believed this would be the last opportunity I might
have to plead with many of them in this way.

"I felt very tenderly and affectionately for a small company
among them, to whom the Lord Jesus is very precious; whose
portion is among the mourners in Zion, and the heavy-hearted
in Jerusalem. To them the word of Divine consolation went
forth repeatedly.

"I returned home in the Twelfth Month, having travelled in
that journey about five thousand miles, and that under great
pressure of mind, from place to place; and now, since my return,

I sit solitary at home, like mournful Jeremiah, taking up many of his lamentations as applicable to my own people. The great day of the Lord is near—it is near! O Lord! be thou a strong refuge to those who trust in thee, and who cannot deny thee, whatever their sufferings may be!"

For nearly twenty-four years Stephen Grellet had been a member of New York Yearly Meeting. Though, during that time, his religious services in America and Europe had rendered his absence both frequent and long, the city of New York had, for the most part, been his settled place of residence. He now felt it right to leave it, and in the Third Month, 1823, he removed with his wife and only daughter to Burlington, New Jersey. He thus became, and continued to the end of life, a member of Philadelphia Yearly Meeting. To this important movement he refers in his memoranda.

"First Month 26th, 1823. The time appears to have come for my removal with my family to Burlington, New Jersey, agreeably to the prospect I had before my return home from my last European journey, and I am taking some preparatory steps towards it. I have been very anxious to do right, and have sought of the Lord that He would direct my path."

Stephen Grellet was not long permitted to remain with his beloved family in their new place of abode. His mind had often been attracted, in the love of the Gospel, towards some of the Southern and Western States. After again attending his own Yearly Meeting at Philadelphia, in 1824, he entered upon this extensive service, which occupied nearly a year.

"Third Month 6th, 1824. A prospect of religious service that I had before me some years past, so far as New Orleans, came again with weight upon me, during the last year, and having apprehended that the time had now come to engage in it, I committed myself to my dear Lord's guidance, whose I am, and to

whose service, myself, my small substance and my all are offered
up. Truly, we have here no continuing city : my beloved wife
and I are very sensible of it ; ever since our marriage we have
found it to be so ; but the Lord is very good to us ; in blessing
He blesses us, and multiplies his consolations to us ; all this is of
his free and unmerited mercy, for we are nothing but unprofitable
servants. I have no works of righteousness, nor of faithfulness to
trust in ; my hope of salvation and acceptance before God is
through the mercy and love of my dear Redeemer. I have put
my small affairs in order, and obtained certificates of the unity of
Friends, both of the Monthly and Quarterly Meetings, with my
proposed religious engagement."

In this journey S. G. was often much distressed by witnessing the prevalence of the spirit of infidelity before alluded
to, and deeply did he mourn over many whom he had known
under different circumstances, who were now "denying the
Lord that bought them ;" his sympathies, in this southern
journey, were also called forth on behalf of the poor slaves ;
and he often enlarges with much feeling on the evils of the
cruel and iniquitous system with which he was now brought
into contact. He embraced every opportunity of pleading
the cause of the oppressed with their owners, having large
meetings with the slaves and also with their masters. We
can give only a few extracts from the journal :—

"I had at Fredericksburg a very large meeting in the Presbyterian meeting-house. The prospect of having a meeting at that
place, where I have repeatedly seen the poor slaves treated with
great cruelty, felt awful to me. But the dear Master helped his
poor servant to do the work required. I was enlarged in setting
forth the love of Him who has loved us whilst sinners, and has
commanded us to love one another as He has loved us. His love
is to all men, He has died for all, and we must love all, and do to
others as we would they should do to us. Were this the case,
could men oppress one another? could they wage war against
one another? could they hold their fellow-men, of any colour or
nation, in a state of bondage? The Lord's power came over the

meeting in such a manner as to bring conviction to the minds of the people, and seriousness prevailed over all. But, alas! it may prove to many as only the passing of the morning cloud.

"On the way to Richmond, stopping on the road to feed our horses, we saw a large concourse of slaves in an orchard. They were holding a meeting, previous to the burial of an aged fellow-negro. Such a meeting was allowed them on the occasion, and a magistrate was with them to see that order was maintained. There was no need, however, of his interference, for they were very quiet and serious. One of their number was preaching to them. He was earnest and fluent in his communication, and the matter was good and appropriate. It was pleasant to me to stand a while among them, listening to what was said. I doubt not that many of them were offering unto the Lord acceptable worship.

"I had meetings through that part of Virginia as far as Suffolk. These meetings were numerously attended by slave-holders. I cannot describe the weight of distress brought on my mind on these occasions; for the yoke of slavery has become heavy here; their treatment and the oppressive laws against the free people of colour, are not less so. It is very evident that their Colonisation Society, under fair, specious appearances, has for its object to drive the free negroes away from the country; so that slaves, by not seeing any of their colour in the enjoyment of liberty, may the better submit to their state of bondage. They have so increased the penalties on the free blacks, that if any one of these is charged with having stolen to the value of *one dollar and fifty cents*, he is sold as a slave, and transported out of the country. Those that have been set free of late, must leave the state within one year, or else they are liable to be sold again as slaves. Free people of colour are liable to be taken up as suspected slaves, and confined in prison till they can give proof that they are free; but, being shut up, they have not an opportunity to obtain this proof; or, should they obtain it, if they cannot pay the expenses incurred by their imprisonment, they are also sold as slaves. Will not the Lord plead with the people for these things? Will He not arise for the cry of the poor and oppressed descendants of Africa; I feel deeply for them, and not less awfully for their oppressors.

"From Suffolk I went to Norfolk, where I had another large meeting. The Lord's servants can have no other doctrine to

preach than that which He gives them ; and as his word is
yea and amen for ever, so is his doctrine. It cannot change.
' The fast that the Lord hath chosen, is to loose the bands of wickedness ; to undo the heavy burdens ; to let the oppressed go free ;
and to break every yoke,' as He saith by his prophet Isaiah.
O that people would not only hear, but obey the word of the Lord.

"I passed thence into the lower parts of North Carolina,
attended their Quarterly Meeting for those counties, held this
time at Sutton's Creek, which was very satisfactory. The public
meetings were baptising seasons. Great crowds attended them,
and the Lord was pleased to extend his gracious invitation to
return to Him with full purpose of heart. Through those
counties I had several large meetings, some entirely among the
slaveholders, others chiefly among the slaves ; for, although it was
given me to proclaim the Truth, without disguise, to the masters,
their hearts appeared to be open towards me, and they made way
very readily for the meetings I appointed for their slaves. Some
of the masters attended, but generally they said, that they were
persuaded that I would not say anything in their absence that
I would not in their presence. The Lord was very preciously
near in several of these religious opportunities.

"I came to Raleigh, where I had a satisfactory meeting in the
house of the Methodists. There are a few pious persons among
the inhabitants of that place. I went to visit the Governor to
see if some steps could not be taken towards the amelioration of
the condition of the slaves in that state, and to prevent the
arbitrary cruelty exercised by many of their masters. He received
me with kindness and heard what I had to say. The Sheriff and
some other principal officers of the Government were present. On
the broad subject of slavery, he said, it would be a great relief to
him and many others if they could be delivered from such a
burden, under which the masters as well as the slaves are much
to be felt for ; and it was his opinion, that measures, throughout
all the slave states, should be taken to promote their liberation,
similar to those that have been taken by the state of New York.
In answer, however, to what I had said respecting the religious
and moral education, the promotion of the solemn tie of marriage
among the slaves, &c., he remarked, ' As long as slavery continues
as it is, should we cultivate the tender feelings of their minds, we

should only increase their sufferings and misery, for, if the attachment between husband and wife, or parental and filial affection, be promoted, they could not bear it ; their hearts would be rent at the separations which are continually made between individuals thus connected.' Some in the company asserted that the negroes were destitute of tender feelings—that they had no love or gratitude towards their masters. I inquired if, according to their acknowledgment, the masters were endeavouring to destroy the tender feelings and affection between a man and his wife, and all parental and filial love and tenderness, how they could complain that affection and gratitude were withheld from masters, who treated them with such cruelty, as not only to oppress their bodies, but also to degrade and debase their minds below the brutes, who love and cherish their mates and their young. The Governor was very civil, and requested that if I came again to this place, I would come to see him.

" I reached Hillsborough the 20th of Sixth Month, and had a large meeting ; no Friends reside in the place ; I could mingle in spirit with several who love the Lord Jesus. I feel also much relieved from the weight of slavery, which has for many weeks been like a mill-stone upon me. There are but very few slaves in this part of North Carolina. I now attended all the meetings of Friends in these Quarterly Meetings. I felt much interest for the young people, who are numerous; may they yield to the visitations of Divine love extended to them ; the Lord loveth an early sacrifice. In several places some of them have manifested such religious sensibility as to induce me to entertain a good hope respecting them.

" Late in the evening of the 19th of Seventh Month, we came to Stanton ; and the next day I had a satisfactory meeting in the Methodist place of worship. There is only one family of Friends left here. The emigration from this Quarterly Meeting to the Western country has been very general ; they wished to have their residence where slavery does not exist. A few miles before reaching Lynchburgh the same evening, the Lord, in tender mercy, preserved my life from threatening destruction. We came out from the woods to a rough turnpike, at a place where the descent is steep. A herd of cattle, with bells on their necks, came running behind us, which frightened my horse ; a dog at the same time seized him by the hind legs; he furiously ran down the hill, kicking so that his hind feet came very near my head; at last he ran the carriage against a stone with such force as to throw me out; then the carriage passed over me. I had three ribs bent in on the left side, a severe contusion on the head, and the right wrist considerably injured; my back and hip also were hurt. I was assisted into another carriage, and got to the house of my kind and hospitable friend, William Davis, jun., for which I was aiming. I was so well nursed, that very shortly after I was able to ride out three miles to a meeting; by the Lord's refreshing presence, my soul and poor body also, were invigorated.

"Union Town, Eighth Month 8th. Two young friends from Hopewell have kindly accompanied me here, on horseback; they were helpful in getting across the Alleghany Mountains. Some parts of the road have improved since I last travelled over them; but most of the way continues to be very rough; notwithstanding the fatigue of the journey my side is better.

"I attended the meetings of Friends on these mountains, and had some, also, in places where no Friends reside. From place to place I had to proclaim the first principles of Christianity, many having been shaken away from the foundation; the cross of Christ has become an offence to them; they want to devise for themselves a way of salvation more pleasing to their creaturely wisdom and natural understanding; yet there is a remnant in these parts, who are not ashamed to acknowledge a crucified and risen Lord as their only hope of salvation."

From Virginia Stephen Grellet had crossed over into Ohio, and now pursued his labours in the Great Valley of the Mississippi as far as New Orleans.

"New Garden, Ohio, Eighth Month 18th, 1824. I get on under great depression of body and mind; my sorrows are indeed multiplied. I am firmly persuaded, however, that none of the combined powers of anti-christ, the prince of darkness, who was a liar from the beginning, will in any wise affect the blessed Truth; it will stand for ever and ever, and triumph gloriously over all.

" I attended all the meetings in this Quarterly Meeting, and thence I went into Salem Quarter. Some of their meetings in this new country are very large ; many join Friends by *convincement*, as they say ; but very few indeed do I find who, if convinced of the Truth, are converted to it. It is a lamentable fact that many of these so-called *convinced* members are among those who are carried away by the spirit of infidelity, which in this quarter also is greatly spreading. In these meetings I am often reminded of the concern of the Apostle Paul, as he wrote to the Corinthians : ' Moreover, brethren, I declare unto you the Gospel which I preached unto you ; by which also ye are saved, if ye keep in memory what I preached unto you, unless ye have believed in vain. For I delivered unto you *first of all* that which I also received, how that Christ died for our sins, according to the Scriptures, and that He was buried, and that He rose again the third day, according to the Scriptures.'

" The Yearly Meeting for Ohio was numerously attended : several well-concerned Friends belong to it ; they keep a watchful eye over the inroads made in their borders by the adversary, and the anti-christian doctrines that several persons from other Yearly Meetings are now, or have been, promulgating. They have hopeful young people among them, who appear to be bending under the yoke of the dear Redeemer.

" Chillicothe, 24th. From Mount Pleasant to this place I had several meetings where Friends have no settlements, and also among Friends.

" I then proceeded to Richmond, Indiana, taking meetings on the way. That Yearly Meeting was very large ; the immigration from slave states to these parts is great ; it renders them, however, a very mixed company, and it will require time before they can rightly understand one another, and get over their various early prejudices. Their business was conducted harmoniously.

" My dear friend, Benjamin W. Ladd, has come from Smithfield, Ohio, to join me as a companion during the journey I have in prospect, as far as New Orleans. How good is my dear Master in providing me with a helper in such a long, wilderness journey. Truly does my flesh and my heart faint at the prospect of the service, but God is the strength of my heart, and of my feeble frame also. In Him doth my soul trust.

" Cincinnati. Tenth Month 14th. Accompanied now again by Benjamin W. Ladd, I had many meetings on the way to this place, where no Friends reside.

" At Vincennes, an old French town, we had a very interesting and solemn meeting in the Court-house. Many of the French people attended. They generally understood English. Some who did not I addressed in the French language. At the close of the meeting, an aged physician exclaimed in French, in a very serious manner, ' How very consonant is your doctrine to the views I have long entertained of the Christian religion ! My principles agree with yours, and gladly would I become a member of your Society, did any of your Friends reside here.' Accompanied by him we called upon several pious aged persons, Roman Catholics. They were tender spirited. We also were with one of their priests. He at first appeared light and trifling, but towards the last he was sober and civil.

" We crossed the Wabash into the State of Illinois, and traversed several prairies on our way to Vandalia. They have the appearance of a garden of flowers, and the woodlands skirting them add greatly to their beauty. The accommodations on the road were very poor, especially the lodgings. We several times had wild turkeys. They are numerous. Wild honey is abundant. They collect it from the forest trees. At Vandalia I found in the Governor, Edward Cole, an interesting and valuable man. He was a large slaveholder in the Southern States, but he liberated his slaves, and gave them land to settle upon.

" On the 5th of the Eleventh Month we embarked on the steamboat *Superior*, for New Orleans, and sent back our horses and carriage to Indiana, to wait our return.

" We stopped some hours at a town called Herculaneum, where I had a meeting, whilst lead was being put on board our boat ; three-fourths of the inhabitants are French people. Then we came to St. Genevieve, where we stopped a night ; nine-tenths of the inhabitants there are French. I had a meeting among them also. My speaking their own language tended to open their hearts to receive me and my testimony. I felt much for them under their various temptations and privations ; some of their young people manifested religious sensibility and seriousness. I am the first Friend they have seen, yet their deportment in meeting might have led us to conclude they had attended many. Proceeding down the river, we struck on a *snag*, but did not receive much damage ; the water being low we grounded at three different times. It took us some hours of hard work to bring the boat again into deep water.

" Natches, 23rd. We arrived here yesterday, after a long, dangerous, and trying passage, rendered the more so by the dissipation of our company."

S. G. then proceeded to New Orleans, where he arrived on the 5th of Twelfth Month. He had much service among the inhabitants of that place—especially with the French settlers ; he says :—

" I was several times with the mayor, a Frenchman, who treated me with courtesy. Once, when I called on him at his office, he was surrounded by the members of the Council, and some others of the principal men of the city, most of them being French people. It was a novelty for them to see a Quaker, a French one especially. It drew their particular attention. They made various inquiries into our Christian principles and testimonies, which I felt very free to answer, and especially that relating to the keeping of our fellow-men in a state of bondage ; and I stated how great is the injustice of their penal, or Black Code as they term it. The unlawfulness and cruelties of war, connected with this, were also brought under consideration ; when one in the company, an aged Frenchman, said, ' These our practices and our laws are very unjust, for men have no right to make laws that are in opposition to the law of God.' I told them that, according to this sound position, wars, slavery, and all kinds of oppression, were unjust, being contrary to the law of God, which is a law of love and mercy, not of cruelty like theirs. I stated to them that it was love that prompted me to have meetings with their slaves, to endeavour to bring them to the knowledge of our Lord and Saviour Jesus Christ, who could deliver them from the bondage of sin, raise them out of the state of degradation into which they were reduced, and render them meet to be heirs of his kingdom of blessedness and glory. But their law says that if a slave goes to any such meeting, he is liable to be imprisoned, and to receive twenty-five lashes ; and they were the men that put such wicked laws in force.

" On the steam-boat *Indiana*. Twelfth Month 8th. Last evening we had another meeting, chiefly composed of those persons who are piously inclined, or who have been brought under religious convictions since we came among them. It was a solemn and contriting season to many. May the Lord bless the work of his own hands ! I left New Orleans with an aching heart, because of the depravity of the greater part of the inhabitants ; but with near Gospel love and strong solicitude for the little remnant of those who have felt the love of Christ kindled in their hearts. It is now winter, and yet the weather here is as with us in the spring. The roses and other flowers in their gardens are in full bloom. Their orange and lemon trees are full of fruit and blossom. They have green peas and other vegetables. O ! that the light of Truth might so shine upon them, as to induce them to open their hearts to the descendings of the heavenly dew, and enable them to bring forth fruits of righteousness to the Lord's glory !

" 30th. We are very near Louisville ; where we expect to leave this abode of dissipation ; it is like a Sodom. The nearer we draw to the end of this voyage the more intent they are on their gambling and their riotous dissipation. A few of the cabin-passengers, however, join us in the meetings I hold on the upper deck, among whom impressions of a religious nature appear to have been made.

"First Mouth 5th, 1825. We arrived at Louisville on the 30th of last month. In the evening I had a large meeting among the people of that place : we then went to Albany, where another very satisfactory meeting was held to-day, for which favour, and the preservation granted of the Lord during our perilous and suffering passage from New Orleans, our souls have very reverently offered praises and thanksgivings to our gracious Helper. I do not know when I have, during the same number of weeks, endured so many sufferings and privations, and been amidst so many perils : but the Lord to this day has helped us : blessed be his adorable name !"

Crossing the Ohio River he now entered Kentucky. We give a few extracts :—

" In this State I meet with great openness among the people. They come readily to the meetings that I appoint, and hear with all attention the testimony to the Truth I have to proclaim among them. They freely also let their slaves come to meeting.

" First Month 14th, 1825. We came to Nashville, Tennessee, where, this evening, we had a relieving meeting. My mind, in many places, is deeply tried on account of the poor slaves. The visits I pay to slaveholders give me opportunities to plead in private, as well as in public, the cause of that suffering portion of my fellow-beings. How can I but do so, if I proclaim with faithfulness the truth as it is in Jesus ! It is a doctrine that many slaveholders are not accustomed to hear; but the Lord, by his Spirit, raises a witness in their hearts to the truth of it, and they appear also sensible that it is in the love of God, and in love to their own souls, that I act towards them. We can scarcely prevail upon the innkeepers to receive any compensation for their entertainment of ourselves and our horses; but we tell them it is their just due ; and that, as in the free love of Christ we come to visit them, our greatest reward would be to see them turn to the Lord with full purpose of heart."

S. G. and his companion, John Street, had many large and solemn meetings at various plantations, at a Moravian settlement, and also amongst the Cherokee Indians; respecting one of the latter, he says :—

" 24th. We came to another Indian's, John Saundore, who has a large settlement about him. He took particular interest in spreading notice, and preparing a place for a meeting. The Lord's baptising power was felt among us. They are a very interesting people. Great sobriety generally prevails among them. They are strict in preventing the introduction of spirituous liquors. Their law imposes a fine of fifty dollars on every attempt to bring them in, and it is also ordered that vessels in which they are found, shall, with their contents, be destroyed.

" John Saundore told me that when ' the white people landed on our shores towards the sea, they had nothing to eat ; we gave them provisions. They had no cabin, we gave them land to erect some, and to cultivate corn ; we made them sit down on our logs by us ; continuing to increase we gave them more and more room, till now they have crowded us to the further end of the log, and they press upon us so hard, that they will soon have the whole of it for themselves,—and where can we go to spread our blankets ?'

" Augusta, Georgia, Second Month 2nd. Here I find in Dr. Watkin's family some piety; he accompanied me to several serious persons; among others, the mother of the late Caroline E. Smelt, respecting whom an interesting memoir has been published; she made a triumphant end. The Doctor's wife and several young women, her intimate friends, have not lost the religious impressions made upon them, nor the earnest and pious words of Christian counsel that Caroline addressed to them. I had solemn opportunities in some of their families, and with them collectively; also a large public meeting."

At Savannah he writes :—

"The public meeting we had here has been more satisfactory than I feared it would be; I went to it under great depression. The jealousy of some of the inhabitants was excited against my companion, because he is from Ohio; many are in a state of ferment, and lately treated roughly some persons from the Eastern States, who had handed out some pamphlets against slavery. The meeting, however, was largely attended, and very quiet. All human fears were taken away, under a grateful and humbling sense of the Lord's presence and power, so that I flinched not from proclaiming the plain and simple truth. None spoke an unkind word to me, though the circumstance of an alarm of fire in the evening brought some of the inhabitants under anxiety; they dread such occurrences, much fearing lest it should be a signal for the rising of the slaves; on such occasions they repair to their arms. O how many evils slavery entails, both upon the slaves and the owners ! Some of the latter are very sensible of it, and deeply lament the bondage under which they themselves are brought.

" We left Savannah on the 6th of the month, crossed the river, which brought us into South Carolina, and came to the plantation of W. T. Norton, to whom we had a letter of introduction.

" Late in the evening the master of the house came in, with about twelve of the neighbouring planters, all armed; I did not.

understand what I saw nor what I felt. We all sat down to
supper; the master of the house was civil, my distress was not
lessened. After rising from the table, he took me aside and told
me how greatly he was himself tried; for the white population
of the neighbourhood were under arms, and would that night
encircle a swamp where they believed about thirty runaway slaves
had concealed themselves, and they were determined to have them
dead or alive: he could not excuse himself, he said, from going
with his neighbours; but he had resolved, that should he see any
of the negroes he would try to help them to escape; or if seen
by others, so that he could not avoid firing his gun, he would take
care not to point it at any of the slaves; though he himself had
very narrowly escaped being killed by one of these a few weeks
since. He was on the outskirts of his plantation; a negro, probably thinking that he intended to catch him, fired at him, and
slightly wounded his breast. 'But,' said he, 'I pitied him: for
he had a bad master, who had driven him to acts of desperation,
and it is the case with many others.' His own slaves behaved
well, and he was endeavouring to treat them well. 'Slavery,'
he added, 'is a dreadful scourge to the land.' I had a painful
night, and dreaded to hear the result of the expedition. But I
was much relieved from my anxiety when, on his return in the
morning, W. T. Norton told me they had not found a single negro;
they had probably heard of their masters' intention, and retired
to some other hiding-place; he was himself very glad it had
been so."

Of some plantations they visited, S. G. says :—

"We were pleased to see the slaves well clad, and looking so
well. But this is not the case everywhere. The masters of some
told us how greatly they reprobate the treatment of many slaveholders. These bad masters are, they say, held in contempt by
them. So far it is a good step, but may they entirely wash their
hands in innocency from the gain of oppression! When I plead
the cause of the slaves with some of these, who are themselves
kind masters, and direct their consideration to what may become
the condition of the slaves after their death, when the estates
may be divided, and parents and children, husbands and wives,
be sold, and far separated, and perhaps fall into the hands of evil

masters, they appear to feel deeply, and deplore the curse that is
entailed upon them."

At Charleston he remarks :—

"It is cause for deep and heartfelt gratitude, that there are
those whose hearts are prepared to receive, or at least to hear, the
testimony of Truth ; but there is also great darkness in this city,
as is the case in all places where slavery prevails. Vice and immorality abound among the mass of the people."

On his return home S. G. thus closes the account of his
visit to the Southern and Western States :—

"Burlington, 26th of Third Month, 1825. I was favoured to
return to my beloved wife and daughter, for whom the Lord has
very graciously cared, as He has also done for me, his poor
servant. O Lord ! who should not fear thee ! who should not
glorify thy name ! My beloved wife joins me in prostration of
soul in praising and adoring the Lord, our Helper and Saviour.

"I have travelled in this journey about six thousand miles, and
am now favoured, through adorable mercy, with peacefulness of
mind, earnestly desiring that the residue of my days may be
devoted to the service of my dear Saviour."

CHAPTER XXVII.

THE HICKSITE SECESSION.

THE autobiography of Stephen Grellet is now brought to a point at which it would be matter of joy to be able to pause— to pass over in silence, or to obliterate much that occurred in the few succeeding years; not on his own account, but because of the sorrowful events which took place around him in rapid succession, as results of the influence of Elias Hicks and the promulgation of his opinions.

The Christian reader, cordially sympathising with Stephen Grellet in his views of the person, the attributes and the work of the Saviour, the Lord Jesus Christ, must indeed already have found it a thing of painful interest to follow him in the conflicts and exercises which mark some of the previous chapters of this memoir. And that charity which "thinketh no evil—beareth, believeth, hopeth and endureth all things," would gladly sink in oblivion the calamities of those days; but the faithful biographer is not at liberty, in historical truthfulness, to suppress facts that tend to illustrate the Christian standing and character of the subject of his narrative.

Stephen Grellet had come into the Society on the ground of conviction; after a careful examination he had recognised in the religious principles of the Society of Friends the practical carrying out of the Christianity of the New Testament. It was at no small sacrifice that he had made them his own; he had "bought the Truth," and he knew what it had cost him. Deeply feeling, as he did, the absolute need of the enlightening influence and power of the Holy Spirit to a right understanding and a saving application of the truths of the Gospel, had he been asked " a reason for the hope that was in him," he could have unhesitatingly adopted the words of George Fox :* "Jesus, who was the foundation of the holy prophets and apostles, *is our Foundation;* and we believe there is no other foundation to be laid but what is laid, even Christ Jesus; who tasted death for every man, shed his blood for all men, is the propitiation for our sins, and not for ours only, but also for the sins of the whole world: according as John the Baptist testified of Him when he said: ' Behold the Lamb of God, that taketh away the sin of the world.' " With equal readiness he could have said with Robert Barclay :† " We firmly believe it was necessary that Christ should come, that by his death and sufferings He might offer up himself a sacrifice to God for our sins, who his own self bare our sins in his own body on the tree, *so we believe that the remission of sins which any partake of is only in and by virtue of that most satisfactory sacrifice, and no otherwise.* For it is by the obedience of that One, that the free gift is come upon all, to justification." And most cordially could he have united also with the statement of William Penn‡ in reference to this point: " The first part of justification, we do reverently and humbly acknowledge, is only for the sake of the death and sufferings of Christ, nothing we can do, *though by the operation of the Holy Spirit,* being able to cancel old debts, or wipe out old scores. It is the power and efficacy of that propitiatory offering, upon faith and repentance, that justifies us from the sins that are past." As fully did he accord with the same writer, in his open avowal that " it is the power of Christ's Spirit in the heart that purifies" the penitent convert—looking in faith to Jesus, *the Lamb of God that taketh away the sin of the world,*

---

* See his *Epistle to the Governor of Barbadoes*—1671.
† *Apology, Prop.* v. and vi.
‡ *Primitive Christianity Revived.* Chap. viii. § 4.

and freely forgiven in *virtue of the one most satisfactory propitiatory sacrifice*—and strengthens him to "go on unto perfection." Thus, humbly trusting in Christ alone, as the Rock of his salvation, Stephen Grellet pressed towards the mark for the prize, studying to show himself approved unto God, a workman that needeth not to be ashamed, rightly dividing the word of Truth.

It was in no sectarian, but in a truly catholic spirit, that he loved the Christian community of which he had become a member, and, with a godly jealousy, he watched over its interests, and sought to promote its spiritual prosperity. With tender susceptibility, quickened by Christian solicitude, he had marked some of the earliest aberrations of Elias Hicks, and had observed with no small concern his wider departures from the Truth as it is in Jesus. He had clearly foreseen the consequences, and had faithfully forewarned his brethren of their approach. The hidden fire now burst out into an open flame; the breath of popular excitement swiftly carried it to nearly all parts of the Society on the American continent.

Rising out of and above the civil and religious struggles of the seventeenth century, the Christian Society of Friends had existed nearly two hundred years. It was widely spread over North America, and the number of its members on that continent was large. Being to a great extent the descendants of the first emigrants from Great Britain and Ireland, they professed to hold the same religious principles as the "early Friends"—George Fox, and the faithful of his day.

George Fox himself was a man of no ordinary character. Though possessed of but little of the "learning of the school," yet, as a Christian, his spiritual understanding was sound, clear and comprehensive. Christ was its centre, and the Truth, as it flowed from him, its area and circumference. With a mind as humble and child-like in its

willingness to be taught, as it was fearless and unflinching
in its obedience to what it had already learned, he had comprehended the practical bearing of the great Christian
doctrine—*the simple fact*—of the direct influence and perceptible guidance of the Holy Spirit; he saw and appreciated not only its entire accordance with the Holy Scriptures,
but its importance also as an essential part of Gospel
truth. The Old and New Testaments were the canon of
his religious belief. In doctrine he fully recognised the
conclusiveness of their Divine authority; in practice he felt
it to be his bounden duty, under the guidance of the Holy
Spirit, at all hazards, faithfully to carry out in life and conversation all that was required by their teaching; and he
was ever willing that both his principles and his conduct
should be brought to the test of their decision. Mere human
systems were nothing to him in point of authority; ecclesiastical establishments with their Popes and Cardinals,
"Right Reverend Lord Bishops," and the lower grades of
the priesthood, were, in his view, unscriptural institutions,
inconsistent with the spirituality and freedom of the Gospel
dispensation. In willing subjection to the enlightening
operations of the Holy Spirit, he had prayerfully and
diligently "searched the Scriptures," and in humble faith he
had come to Him of whom "they testify." In Him he had
beheld his Saviour and his God, and he could "call no man
master on the earth." Taking a firm footing upon the only
true foundation—Christ Jesus himself—he stood forward as
a *practical* reformer, with a mind of no common grasp; with
one great stride he stepped over centuries, and reached a
point of Christian development, and originated and sustained
a Christian polity, than which nothing could well be more
Scriptural, or more in accordance with the words and spirit
of the Saviour's teaching.

Calmly looking back on the characteristics of early
Quakerism, as it regards the *comprehensiveness* of its

Christian principles, the *completeness* of its standard of
Christian practice, and the *spirit* of its Christian discipline,
and viewing them in connection with the universal Church
of professing Christendom, it appears to be a simple historical
fact, that wherever, in any direction, there has been real progress—any onward movement—it has been towards the position occupied by the early Friends—George Fox and his
associates. It is not needful to particularise; the thoughtful
and intelligent reader will be able, at a glance, to fix his eyes
upon various points of Christian principle and practice, which
illustrate what has been said.

In taking this estimate of the early Friends and their
sphere of usefulness, it would not be serving the cause of
truth to attribute to them a freedom from human infirmity
to which they themselves laid no claim ;* and in justly appreciating their worth, it is well to bear in mind that they
were fallible men of like passions as we are, liable to be
biassed in judgment and influenced in their actions by the
difficult times in which they lived. They did not seek but
rather avoided the use of terms of scholastic theology ; yet,
as Christian men, under a strong sense of their accountability
to God, they did not hesitate plainly and honestly to declare
their religious belief. They did not leave the world in doubt
as to their Christian stand-point ; and a careful and candid
perusal of their writings and biographies will afford incontro-
vertible evidence that they were thoroughly sound in the fundamental doctrines of the Gospel. They had no *new Gospel*
to proclaim. In common with other orthodox professors
of the Christian name they most fully recognised the Divine
inspiration and authority of the Holy Scriptures, and
thoroughly believed in all that is revealed therein concerning
the unity of the Godhead—the Father, Son, and Holy Ghost

---

* It ought not to be forgotten with what chaste attachment to the
Redeemer's cause George Fox exclaimed, respecting himself and his
brethren: " We are nothing : CHRIST IS ALL."

—one God over all, blessed for ever: they unhesitatingly
held the utter depravity of human nature in consequence of
the fall; the pre-existence and incarnation of the Son of God;
the proper, eternal Deity, and the real manhood of the Lord
Jesus Christ; the need and efficacy of his propitiatory sacrifice as an atonement or expiation for the sins of mankind;
his mediatorial intercession and reign; the forgiveness and
reconciliation of the repenting sinner through faith in Him
alone;* the work of the Holy Spirit in the conversion of the
sinner, and in the preservation, guidance, and sanctification
of the believer in Jesus; the immortality of the soul; the
resurrection, and the final judgment of the world by our Lord
Jesus Christ; the eternal blessedness of the righteous, and
the eternal punishment of the wicked.   In reference to these
things, William Penn, in the full maturity of his judgment
and the brightest period of his Christian experience, had
explicitly, declared: "Where we are vulgarly apprehended
to differ *most* we dissent *least*, I mean in *doctrine.*—For,
except it be the *wording* of some of the articles of faith in
school terms, there are very few of those professed by the
'Church of England' to which we do not heartily assent.—
I say then, that where we are supposed to differ most, we
differ least.—It is generally thought that we do not hold the
common doctrines of Christianity, but have introduced new

---

* It is interesting to notice the beautiful harmony between one of the
first *testimonies* and one of the last *exhortations* of George Fox in reference to the Saviour. "The sins of all mankind were upon Him, and
their iniquities and transgressions with which He was wounded, which
He was to bear and to be an offering for, as He was man, but He died
not as He was God; and so, in that He died for all men, and tasted death
for every man, He was an offering for the sins of the whole world."—
Æt. 21. "Christ reigns, and his power is over all; who bruises the
serpent's head, and destroys the devil and his works, and was before he
was.   So all of you live and walk in Christ Jesus: that nothing may be
between you and God, but Christ, in whom ye have salvation—life, rest,
and peace with God."—Æt. 66, and three days only before his death.
Fox's Journal, vol. i. p. 51, and vol. ii. p. 352, *Armistead's Edition*,
Leeds, 1852.

and erroneous ones in lieu thereof: whereas we *plainly* and
entirely believe the truths contained in the creed commonly
called the 'Apostles' Creed,' which is very comprehensive as
well as ancient.—If keeping to the terms of Scripture be a
fault, thanks be to God, *that* only is our *creed*; and with
good reason too : since it is fit that *That* only should con-
clude, and be the *creed of Christians* which the Holy Ghost
could only *propose* and *require* us to believe."*

It is evident that those Christian testimonies by which
the early Friends were more especially distinguished from
their brethren of other denominations,—their views on the
direct influence of the Holy Spirit, on worship, the ministry,
and the " ordinances," on liberty of conscience, war, oaths,
ecclesiastical impositions, and some other points, were all
based on the essential doctrines of the Gospel. Their
whole superstructure plainly and broadly rested upon the
immutable foundation of the revealed truths of the
Bible.†

It would be a great mistake to suppose that the separation
among Friends in America, which arose out of the course
pursued by Elias Hicks and some of his adherents, hinged
upon *non-essentials*. It was what William Penn calls the
common doctrines of Christianity, those essential facts and
truths without which Christianity would be a mere name—a
shell without a kernel—that were the objects of attack, and
were boldly denied. That faith in a crucified and risen Lord
which overcomes the world, the flesh, and the devil, and is
abundantly fruitful in holiness and good works, was sought

---

* *Defence of Gospel Truth.* Works, 3rd Edition, vol. v. pp. 380,
381, and 417.

† In proof of these statements it is sufficient to refer to the *Selection
from George Fox's Epistles*, by Samuel Tuke; Second Edition, London,
1848; *Evans' Exposition*, Philadelphia; *Rules of Discipline, and Ad-
vices of the Yearly Meeting of the Society of Friends in London :* London, 1834; and *Epistles from the Yearly Meeting of Friends, held in
London from* 1681 *to* 1857 *inclusive*, 2 vols.; London, 1858.

to be supplanted by a refined and spurious spiritualism; which under a partial adherence to a scriptural phraseology, totally rejected the true scriptural "*Doctrine of Christ*." Few, perhaps, besides Elias Hicks, and some of the prominent characters among his followers, had any clear perception of the real merits of the controversy, and the vital nature of the points at issue; many young people, as well as others, unwittingly followed their leaders, little suspecting, it may be, the wide departure from "the word of the truth of the Gospel," to which they were in danger of being carried. Without attempting to lay open the depth and significance of some of the causes which led to the deplorable results that followed, it must not be overlooked, that, at the time referred to, a very inadequate provision for the instruction and religious education of the young, and the habitual neglect of the perusal of the Holy Scriptures, had left many in great ignorance of the saving truths of the Gospel, and destitute of a clear understanding of the real nature and grounds of their religious profession. The knowledge of the Christian principles of the Society was, with many, merely traditional; and little calculated to afford them the means of detecting points of divergence. Thus, blind to the danger and almost defenceless, they were ill prepared to meet the subtle fallacies which assailed them, and fell easy victims to the "spirit of error" that prevailed around them. It is thought that about one-third of the Society in America was swept away by that fearful schism.

Stephen Grellet stood unmoved in the midst of the storm. He loved Quakerism because to him it was identical with pure and simple Christianity.

In the Tenth Month, 1826, he makes the following memorandum :—

"I have been most of my time at home since last year, except attending some meetings not far distant. During the summer I visited most of the meetings in this State, New Jersey, in which service I was repeatedly brought under deep and trying exercise ; for principles of infidelity are here also gaining the ascendancy over many minds. At our last Yearly Meeting we had the very sorrowful evidence that there are very few sections, if any, in this Yearly Meeting, where the baneful influence is not felt to a lamentable extent."

The crisis was now at hand. The Society was on the eve of a separation. Many faithful labourers from the various Churches in America, and some from Europe, nobly contended for the "faith once delivered to the saints," and earnestly sought to restore the erring, and to guard the unwary, by "manifestation of the Truth." But the development of what had long been worming itself into the foundation and bulwarks of the Society, produced a state of things which left but little hope that the breach could be healed. At this juncture Stephen Grellet felt it to be required of him, in the love of Christ, to pay a general visit to Friends in the compass of his own Yearly Meeting. On his return home from this engagement, which occupied about five months, he takes the following review of the service :—

"Ninth Month, 1827. I have just returned from a very trying engagement throughout this Yearly Meeting, except this State, New Jersey, which I visited last year. It was a duty that pressed on my mind, and, during the last few months, I felt it in a manner so imperative that I could not understand the nature of the attending impressions. 'Now or never!' seemed to be the language proclaimed in my ear. But now I can 'run and read'; for it was only *then*, indeed, that a service of this kind could be performed. One day later would have prevented my attendance of many of the meetings I visited. It was at many of those Quarterly, Monthly, and other Meetings, that those who have rejected the Lord Jesus Christ as their Saviour and Redeemer, and counted the blood of the covenant, which was shed on Calvary as an atonement for sin, an unholy thing, organised themselves as a separate body from us, and publicly identified themselves with the followers of Elias Hicks.

z

"Since my return, remembering the many sore services during that journey, and the frequently renewed expression of the Lord's love and mercy towards the backsliders, my afflicted soul still weeps bitterly over them. How applicable to them is the Saviour's lamentation over Jerusalem, 'How often would I have gathered thy children, &c., but ye would not. Behold now thy house is left unto thee desolate, and the things that belong to thy peace are hid from thine eyes.' Ah, how awful is the language ! My soul trembles with fearfulness lest this be actually the state of many of these people."

In the year 1829 Stephen Grellet paid a visit in Christian love to the New York Yearly Meeting. He had long resided in their midst; his heart had yearned towards them in Gospel love and sympathy in their trials, and he felt it a privilege to impart to them some of those consolations which the Lord permits to be handed as from faith to faith. He was absent from his home till the end of the year; and after this visit he was permitted to enjoy a time of peaceful repose in the bosom of his little family.

CHAPTER XXVIII.

Fourth Visit to Europe.

VOYAGE TO LIVERPOOL — VARIOUS RELIGIOUS ENGAGEMENTS IN
ENGLAND — HOLLAND — HANOVER — BERLIN — HALLE —
WEIMAR, ETC.

It was now nearly eleven years since Stephen Grellet's return
from his third visit to Europe. Much of that time had been
spent in various religious engagements, both in his own
Christian community and amongst others, in many of the
States of the Union, and in Canada. The last few years of
his life had been peculiarly marked by circumstances and
events which deeply afflicted his soul, in sympathy with a
suffering Church. But none of these things had moved him.
As he had partaken largely of the Gospel, so his consolations
also had often abounded by Christ. Nor did he now count
his life dear unto himself, so that he might *finish* his course
with joy, and the ministry which he had received of the
Lord Jesus to testify the Gospel of the grace of God once
more in distant nations.

His mind had for some time been preparing for a "fourth
missionary journey" in Europe, and in reference to this he
writes :—

" Third Month, 1831. My religious concern to cross once more
the seas and to visit Friends in England, and other nations on
the continent of Europe, in the love of the Gospel of Christ, my
Lord and Saviour, having ripened to clearness, with the evidence
that now is the time for me to make the requisite preparation for
engaging in so solemn and important a work, I have set my small
affairs in order, and obtained certificates of the Christian sympathy
and unity of my friends. My beloved wife on this occasion, as on

all preceding ones, which have not been few since we became united together by the endearing tie of the marriage covenant, freely and with Christian cheerfulness resigns me to the Lord's service. She is uniformly a great encourager to me to act the part of a faithful servant of the best of Masters ; her soul travails with mine in such a manner that she had been deeply sensible of the nature of the service that the Great Master called me to, before I had disclosed to her or to any one else the secret exercises of my heart. We have several times parted, with the apparent prospect of never seeing each other again in this state of mutability, but the Lord, in whose hands is our life, has brought us together again. He may still do so if it be his good pleasure. Into his hands, and to his sovereign will and disposal, we commit ourselves and our beloved daughter—our only child.

"Friends, at our Yearly Meeting in Philadelphia, entered feelingly into sympathy with me under the weighty and extensive prospect of service in several of the nations of Europe, and gave me their certificate, recommending me to the Christian notice of all those among whom the Lord may be pleased to direct my steps."

After the Yearly Meeting Stephen Grellet returned home for a short time ; but the hour of parting soon arrived. On the 2nd of Sixth Month, 1831, he embarked at Philadelphia in the packet-ship *Algonquin*, Captain West, for Liverpool.

"My beloved wife and daughter accompanied me to Philadelphia. My dear child deeply felt the approaching hour of separation ; but she knows that she has an everlasting and almighty Father to lean upon, who will ever be near to support, comfort, care for and bless her. To his Divine keeping and protection I left my beloved wife and her, and came on board."

Stephen Grellet arrived in Liverpool on the 30th of Sixth Month. At Liverpool he held meetings with the Friends and with the other inhabitants. Thence to Birmingham and Coventry, where he was similarly engaged. He then proceeded to Stoke Newington, to the residence of his beloved friend William Allen. Their first interview was attended by such a humbling and grateful sense of the Lord's goodness, that for a length of time no words gave utterance to the feelings of their hearts : and then acknowledgments were made on bended knees to the Lord's goodness.

His secret prayer, that William Allen should accompany him, was answered: not only as to the greater part of his service in England, but also on the European continent.

Space will not allow us to give more than a rapid sketch of these important engagements in England.

In the first place the meetings of Friends in London were visited, with various other services in the metropolis and its vicinity. He then went into the counties of Kent, Surrey, Sussex, &c. At Lindfield he visited William Allen's benevolent institutions—the Industrial Schools—" The Colonies at Home " for the poor, with comfortable dwellings and garden allotments, &c., having very interesting service among the cottagers and in the schools. He then visited all the counties westward as far as Somerset, and returned to London. S. G. says, " We mostly had two meetings a day, and those in the evening were generally of a public character." Some of the Eastern counties were then visited. At Saffron Walden, in the course of his ministry, he felt it his duty to speak on the evils of infidelity, when a young man present was brought under such strong convictions under the Lord's power, that he wept aloud. Jesus, the Saviour, whom he had rejected and denied, was presented to his view, who came not to destroy but to save. After a time the young man became calm. He had been a notorious infidel. In the Midland and Northern counties he had much service among the colliers and miners, whose privations deeply called forth his sympathies.

Near Sheffield he met with a severe accident, which he thus describes :—

" On my way to Sheffield, I was accompanied by a dear friend, who imprudently took off the bridle of my horse as he stood harnessed to the gig ; the horse was so frightened that he darted

forward, threw me down, and both he and the gig passed over me ;
I received considerable injury on the head, shoulder, knee, and
leg.   As I lay prostrate on the dusty road, the bystanders thought
I was killed on the spot, for I could not move ; but my mind was
wrapped up in a grateful sense of the love of God, through Jesus
Christ my Saviour.   I felt indeed the strokes of the horse's feet
and the wheels of the carriage passing over me, and was perfectly
sensible of what might be the consequence ; but the language was
distinctly proclaimed in my soul, ' Thou shalt not die, but live.'
And then Spain was placed again forcibly before me, with the
conviction that the Lord had a service for me there. I was assisted
to a house near, and soon after taken to Sheffield to my dear and
valued friend William Hargreaves, where medical aid was immediately obtained, and every kind attention bestowed. My beloved
friends, Lydia Hargreaves and her brother, nursed me in the
most tender manner."

On the 25th Lydia Hargreaves writes :—

"TO MARY HUSTLER.

" How delightful to be able to tell thee of the improvement in
our beloved friend—though I believe he still suffers considerable
pain.   I unite with thee in fearing that so much writing is not
good for him ; but it is impossible to repress the grateful feelings
of his kind and affectionate heart, which, like the fountain of
love, seems always open, and always new.   Whatever he suffers,
we never hear him complain, for he always makes the best of
everything : and I never saw the Christian character so strikingly
and so beautifully unfolded and exemplified."

The journal continues :—

" I recovered so rapidly that the 30th of the First Month I was
able to be dressed, and to ride to meeting ; I had hoped to have
sat the meeting silently, engaged in pouring forth my soul with
gratitude before God, and worshipping his great and adorable
name.   But He, whom I desire to serve, and who, for the very
purpose that I should serve Him, has again preserved my life,
when on the very brink of destruction, saw meet to introduce me
into deep feeling and exercise with a commission to proclaim the

message given me for that congregation. I did not know that I was able to stand on my feet, but He who is the God of everlasting strength helped his poor servant. It was a very solemn season : deep reverence was the clothing of many minds. I forgot that I had any bodily ailment, and contrary to the apprehension of my friends, who thought that after such exertion I should be quite sick, I came down stairs in the evening, and, amidst a numerous company of Friends, we had a refreshing religious season together, and the stream of the Gospel was permitted to flow among us. My bodily strength felt so much renewed that I saw my way open to proceed on the embassy for which I have been sent to these nations. Great is the Lord, and glorious is his holy name !"

He was now enabled to proceed with his service, and next visited Birmingham and Bristol, and subsequently Devonshire and Cornwall : in these counties the miners were not forgotten. Then returning through Gloucestershire and Oxfordshire he reached London: there his way opened for much religious service, at the time of the awful visitation of cholera, which then took place in some parts of the city and neighbourhood. Stephen Grellet now attended the Yearly Meeting in London, in reference to which he remarks :—

"Sixth Month 2nd. The Yearly Meeting concluded this day. There was a living travail or spirit present. The Lord and his truth were exalted. The Lord alone can frustrate the designs of Satan. I rejoice in the belief that many beloved brothers and sisters are sensible of his devices ; and that watchfulness unto prayer is the position occupied by many of these."

After some further service in Essex, Suffolk, and Norfolk, and large public meetings in those parts, his friend, William Allen, having now made the needful preparations to unite with him, he took his departure for Holland.

Since his landing at Liverpool, Stephen Grellet had now spent a whole year in diligently labouring in the service of the Gospel among his brethren in religious profession, and the community at large in England. He now went forth, for the last time, as an ambassador for Christ to nations of other languages. His "Fourth Missionary Journey" on the continent of Europe was the most extensive one. It embraced parts of Holland, some of the minor States of Germany, the dominions of Prussia, Saxony, Bohemia, Austria and Hungary, Bavaria, Wurtemberg, Switzerland, Piedmont, France and Spain. The difficulties of such an undertaking were obvious, but "eternal wisdom was his guide—his help Omnipotence." He had now grown grey in the service of the Lord; and the richness of his personal experience gave peculiar interest to this labour of love, and brightness to this work of faith. It was like distributing the well ripened fruit of his autumn life. He writes :—

"Seventh Month 4th, 1832. In company with dear Wm. Allen I left London yesterday, by the steamer *Atwood*, and came to Tiengermeten Island in Holland, where, on account of the cholera, a quarantine has to be performed. We are much crowded on the vessel, there being many passengers ; but we are under the necessity of remaining on board as the number of persons on the quarantine ground is such, that all the buildings there are crowded ; they have come from France, England, and other parts.

" We were released from quarantine on the 15th. The preceding evening we had a satisfactory parting opportunity with the Dutch Ambassador and his family. We came the same afternoon to Rotterdam ; the country is very flat ; we crossed dyke after dyke. The land is in a high state of cultivation, and has many fruit trees upon it ; the pastures are luxuriant ; the cattle beautiful, being of the species that appear as if they had a white sheet over their backs ; they give abundance of milk ; the premises about the farms are neat and clean ; their milk vessels of wood are quite white, and their kettles of brass like shining gold.

" We found John S. Mollet, from Amsterdam, who had kindly

come to meet us, and to act as our interpreter. We are much
favoured in this particular, now, as we were on our preceding
visit to the continent ; to the Lord our bountiful provider is the
praise ascribed ! We three sat down together and held our little
meeting ; it was a season of lowness and much poverty, attended
also with a feeling of weight on account of the service that may
be required of us. Our prayers unto the Lord were that He would
direct us in the way He would have us to go, and enable us to
perform whatever He may require. I feel very poor and stripped,
but our sufficiency is of God. It is He who giveth to his servants
both to will and to do of his good pleasure."

From Rotterdam they proceeded to Amsterdam, where
S. G. says :—

"We came to Amsterdam on the 18th, and visited the Infant
School, supported out of the interest of the residue of the money
proceeding from the share of John Warder in the prizes made
during the war by a vessel in which he was concerned.* They

---

* Before his removal from England, the late John Warder, of Philadelphia, had a share in the ship *Nancy*, which, without his knowledge
or approval, was armed by his partner, who was not a member of the
Society of Friends. During the American war, Holland being one of
the Allies of the United States, the *Nancy* aided in the capture of a
Dutch East Indiaman, on her homeward voyage to Amsterdam. From
the nature of the cargo the prize turned out to be a rich one, and John
Warder's share of the proceeds amounted to a considerable sum. To
apply to his own use money so obtained was felt to be inconsistent with
a faithful support of the Christian testimony against all wars and fightings, and restitution of the property an obvious duty. But in the midst
of international hostilities it was no easy matter at once clearly to ascer-
tain the parties justly entitled to it. Under these circumstances John
Warder ultimately placed the amount he had received upon trust for
effecting the restitution, when practicable. Both before and after the
termination of the war, efforts were made to find out the real owners of
the property, and, as far as possible, it was restored to them; but some
could never be traced. Being originally derived from Holland, it was
finally thought most in accordance with strict justice to appropriate the
unclaimed residue to Dutch purposes. The result was the establishment
and support of the Infant School alluded to at Amsterdam. The citizens,
appreciating its value and the character of the origin, called it " Holland's
Welfare :"—the name borne by the captured vessel, and by that name
it is still recognised in their list of Public Schools. A large number of
children have been taught in the Institution. It was the first of the
kind in Holland, and now similar ones are very general in that kingdom.

have now upwards of sixty children in that school. The building
purchased for the purpose is a convenient one, and the matron,
under whose especial care it is placed, appears to act the part of
a Christian mother towards those young children. Our testimony
against war is exalted through this act of justice and benevolence.
Many persons come to visit the establishment.

"We had several meetings in Friends' meeting-house, which is
a convenient one; others were held at the house of J. Muller, a
pious Mennonite, and in some other places. One of these was
attended by many of the principal inhabitants of this city; as
they generally understand French, I spoke in that language. In
the other meetings, J. S. Mollet interpreted for dear Allen and
myself. All these meetings were quiet, and some of them solemn.
There are piously-minded persons in this city, towards whom we
felt strong attractions in the love of Christ; we visited a number
of them in their families to our comfort and edification."

They visited the establishments for the poor at Frederick-
soord and the colonies of Ommerschans, of which S. G.
gives very interesting particulars. Thence proceeding to
Dusseldorf, he observes :—

"We travelled through several fortified places, which are
numerous in Holland; among others we went through Deventer.
Nineteen years ago I had a narrow escape from being shut up in
some of these places by a part of the French army that occupied
those fortresses for some time, after the Allies had entered France.
We tarried a little while at Arnheim, and entered Prussia at
Elten. As we had left Amsterdam previous to any appearance of
the cholera there, we were allowed to enter that kingdom without
performing quarantine on the frontiers.

"At Dusseldorf there are some valuable and benevolent persons.
But since we left Zwolle our spirits have continued day by day
to be greatly depressed; darkness and ignorance prevail to a high
degree among the Roman Catholics where we have travelled. I
felt anxious also on my own account, how far my health would
allow me to prosecute our journey; but since coming to Elberfeld
we have been comforted and cheered various ways; letters from

England and America do not represent the spread of the cholera, and the mortality thereby, such as to warrant the statements that we have seen. Here also we met with a number of those pious individuals with whom I mingled years ago, when they were under severe trials, and when the Lord condescended to cause the consolations of his Gospel to flow among them in such a peculiar manner that the remembrance of it continues to be fresh with many of the people, both of Elberfeld and Barmen."

About two weeks were spent in service among those professing with Friends in Pyrmont and Minden, and on the 13th of Eighth Month they went to Hanover.

Their stay in Hanover and places on their way to Berlin was short; but in the Prussian capital they were detained nine days in the prosecution of the interesting objects of their Christian embassy. They met with many who "worshipped God, and whose hearts the Lord opened that they attended to the things which were spoken" by them.

At this place they visited the Duke of Cambridge; S. G. says :—

"He recognised William Allen, who had been with him in London; he listened with attention to what we had to communicate to him, and manifested great openness towards us. Here, also, we had to plead for full liberty of conscience. The Society for the circulation of religious tracts there has met with many impediments. Every sheet that is printed has to pass under the consorship of the military or civil department. We hope that some of the oppressive restrictions on the press will be removed.

"We came to Berlin early in the morning of the 19th. As we frequently travel during the night we are enabled to save much time on the road. Soon after our arrival I went to see Gossner, one of those Roman Catholic priests convinced of the errors of Popery, whom I met with about nineteen years since at Munich. He, with others, underwent much persecution; being banished from Bavaria, he wandered to various places till he received an invitation to go to Russia; this was done through Prince

Alexander Galitzin, whom I made acquainted, whilst at Petersburg, with the sufferings that Gossner and others had endured on account of their faithfulness in maintaining sound
Christian doctrines. Gossner's labours, after coming to Petersburg, were chiefly among the Germans, who are pretty numerous
in that city ; the Divine unction attended his ministry, and the
Lord's blessing upon it was such that it caused a great sensation
in Petersburg. The religious meetings that he held were attended
by a large number of persons, and such was the change in their
lives and the evidence of real piety apparent in many of them,
that it excited the jealousy of some of the clergy of the Greek
Church : and the more so because some of the Russians forsook
them to attend the meetings held by Gossner. He preached
Christ and the truths of the Gospel, divested of those inventions
that the blind zeal and activity of man have mingled with it, in
the Roman Catholic, the Greek, and other Churches. His great
aim was to bring men to Christ, and to an acquaintance with the
operation of the Holy Spirit on their own minds, and to encourage them watchfully and faithfully to attend to the dictates
thereof, because it is the Spirit that leads into all truth ; it is He
also who reproves or convinces the world of sin, of righteousness
and of judgment, according to the words of the Lord Jesus, ' I
will not leave you comfortless.' ' I will pray the Father and He
shall give you another Comforter, even the Spirit of Truth,' &c.
Gossner's example was in harmony with his precepts ; for he was
frequently engaged in silently waiting on the Lord, seeking for the
guidance of the Divine Spirit, and for his assistance in the
performance of the solemn act of worship ; which, as Christ said,
is to be in spirit and in truth. Persecution here also was finally
stirred up against him, and he was obliged to retire elsewhere.
He came to Berlin ; the King of Prussia, who had heard of his
great piety, gave him a kind welcome. The pastor of the Bohemian
Church had lately died, and this appeared to be the field prepared
for Gossner to enter into the labours of the Gospel. These
Bohemians, or their parents, had been obliged to flee from their
country on account of persecution by the Romish Church. They
now compose here a large Church, which is also attended by
many of the inhabitants, particularly of the pious in high rank,
among whom Gossner has much place.

"We had, for a length of time, very little to communicate to one another by words ; but we were all of us retired in reverent and solemn silence before God, and refreshed together under the precious evidence, that our communion and fellowship is with the Father, and with the Son, Christ our Lord, through the Spirit.

"Dear Allen was not with me this morning ; he needed rest after the past days of close engagements and travelling. Previous to leaving Gossner I appointed a meeting for divine worship, to be held this evening, of which he undertook to spread the information. Those that collected together on the occasion were generally persons of piety. It was a season when refreshings from the Lord's presence were very sweetly extended to us. We felt the baptising power of the Spirit to bring us into the oneness, enabling us reverently to worship the Father, and to drink together into the one Spirit. Among those present were Elsner, the Secretary of the Bible Society here, and Charles La Roche, who is at the head of the department of the mines in this kingdom. One of them interpreted for dear Allen and for me.

"20th. We visited some pious persons ; one was Theodore Julius Gamet ; we were also with the Count and Countess Von der Gröben ; they are acquainted with vital religion. We thought we could salute the Countess as a disciple of the Lord Jesus. It was truly comforting to us and refreshing to our spirits to be with them.

"We next went to Doctor Julius, Inspector of the Prisons. He accompanied us to several families."

Several days were spent in this private Gospel labour; and on the 24th, S. G. says :—

"By appointment we visited this morning the Prince Wittgenstein ; he is the King's Prime Minister ; he received us with kindness and openness. We imparted to him several subjects that have rested with weight on our minds since our coming to Prussia, which we wished to be brought before the King for his consideration ; and which the Prince has a full opportunity of doing, as he is daily with the King. We met there General Boye, who was with us yesterday at the Major-General Rudloff's. From conscientious motives he has retired from a military life ; he finds, he says, that a private character is more consistent with the

Christian course which he desires to pursue. The Saviour said, 'My kingdom is not of this world;' and the weapons of the Lord's servants are not carnal. He now devotes a portion of his time to benevolent objects; he accompanied us in a visit to the prisons and to the hospitals for the prisoners, and was our interpreter. We had also in company a young man of a very tender spirit, who, from religious motives, is much devoted to visiting the prisoners and the afflicted. In one of the prisons we met with about one hundred and fifty Jews, who composed a band of robbers linked together, but scattered over various parts of this kingdom. The prisoners are numerous; this is owing to the very slow process with which the laws are administered, which is a great injury; there are not any public executions: we are told that no life has been taken in this way since 1819, and they have no place abroad to transport their convicts to.

" In the evening we had a religious meeting at the house of Elsner; we felt sweet unity and fellowship of spirit with many that met us there; I translated into French for dear Allen; those present generally understood that language. Elsner is a very useful and devoted man; besides the many thousand religious tracts that he translates, or has printed and puts in a way to be distributed through Germany, he takes journeys himself for the purpose. In this way he distributed about thirty thousand last year.

" 27th. At the suggestion of the Prince Wittgenstein, we went to see Köhler, Minister of the Interior. The Prince said that he might be of service to us in promoting some of our views for the better treatment and accommodation of the prisoners whom we had found very crowded in small apartments, badly ventilated, so that the air is rendered very foul. We also thought that their ration of bread is too small, and the quality of it bad, so that their countenances bespoke their suffering condition. We hope now that relief in these respects will be extended to them, and that by a more speedy administration of justice the number of those so confined will be considerably lessened.

" We spent some time very agreeably with Gossner, who gave us further interesting accounts of his religious labours in Russia. It was his general practice there, as it is here also, when other religious services do not prevent, to have a company of pious persons meet with him at his house in the evening ; they spend together a considerable time in silent waiting on the Lord, thus reducing to practice what he frequently recommends to them in his public communications ; for he believes in the truth of the Scripture assertion, ' They that wait on the Lord shall renew their strength.'

" In the afternoon the Prince Wittgenstein came to see us ; he said that the King was desirous to be with us ; but that he was very unwell, and therefore under the necessity to leave Berlin for his private summer residence ; he gave us also a kind message from the Crown Prince, telling us that he regretted not to be able to see us, being obliged to go immediately to Pomerania ; but that the Royal Princess, his wife, wished to see us to-morrow morning, if we were not otherwise engaged.

" 26th.   We went this morning to the palace, to the Baron von Schilder, Grand Master of the Court. The Baron received us with Christian affection and tenderness.   Instead of a haughty spirit, which we thought we should meet, we found in him lowliness and humility ; even saying that he considered it a favour that the Lord had directed us to him.   Having understood that Prince Wittgenstein had recommended us to see the Minister of Worship, the Baron said he was his wife's father, and that he would introduce us to him.   He then accompanied us to the old palace, where the Crown Prince and the Princess Royal, his wife, reside. We were immediately introduced into the private apartments of the Princess, where she received us, accompanied by one of her attendant ladies only. She is sister of the present King of Bavaria ; and remembers me when, some years since, I visited him and her father, who was then living. She made some apology for desiring to see us, but wished to obtain correct information of our views respecting divine worship, and the manner we conduct that solemn act ; also respecting prayer, the ministry, women's preaching, the influence of the Divine Spirit on the heart of man, &c.   Soon after she began to make inquiries into these interesting subjects, the Crown Prince, her husband, came in ; he said he had succeeded in putting off his journey into Pomerania for a few hours, and availed himself of them to be with us. As he speaks good English, dear William Allen had a full opportunity with him : and I proceeded in French to answer the inquiries of the Princess, which appeared

to proceed from a mind under religious exercise, and seeking after
the Truth.   This desire after the knowledge of the Truth began
in her years since, when I was at Munich with the King, her
father.   She had also heard of the religious meetings I had then,
which were attended by many of the people at Court.   Here,
again, by the Countess Von der Gröben and others she hears
much of the spiritual doctrines held forth by Gossner, and of the
seasons of silent retirement that they have with him.   My mind
was enlarged, in the love of Christ, to give an answer to the several
inquiries of the Princess.   I drew her attention to the teachings
of the Divine Spirit, which is ever near the believer in Christ, to
direct and instruct him, to help us under all our infirmities, and
to comfort us under all our trials.   Her heart was open to receive
the words of encouragement and consolation given me to communicate to her.   Her spirit also was very tender.   The conversation
then became more general with the Prince ; particularly on the
subject of liberty of conscience, and our Christian testimony
against war, consistent with the precepts of Christ, that we should
love one another, even our enemies, as He has loved us.   He
promised us to use his influence to promote this, and he hoped
that the cruelties exercised by military laws against our Friends,
or others, would never be enforced again.   After a time of solemn
silence, feeling my mind constrained by the power of Gospel
love, I imparted to them my soul's concern for them ; that they
may so live in the fear of God, and maintain the faith in our
Lord Jesus Christ, that after witnessing the blessing of preservation from the many snares and temptations attending their high
stations in life, they may, through the redeeming love and mercy
of God in Christ Jesus, become heirs of his everlasting salvation.

" On parting the Prince said that he regretted he could not be
longer with us ; that the King, his father, regretted also that his
bodily indisposition prevented him from seeing us, remembering
the visit that we both had made him when he was in London ;
and that he would not fail to impart to him what we had said,
especially on the subject of liberty of conscience, and the severity
of the military laws, which, though not enforced at present, are
not repealed.   We told the Prince and his Princess that they
must expect to have tribulations, if they were sincere in their

desires to live a godly life in Christ Jesus; for, if they did so indeed, they could not please the world; and if a man will please the world, he is at enmity with God; further, we told them that if they were true in their desires to be found followers of the Lord Jesus Christ, they must not stumble at the cross, but follow Him in the path of self-denial. We parted from them in Christian affection.

" That afternoon we had a meeting with a numerous company, who collected for the purpose at Gossner's. We had requested that the invitation might be especially extended to such as are known for their piety. We sat together a considerable time in solemn silence; truly those that are joined to the Lord are of one spirit; we were engaged, as being baptised together by the One Spirit, in offering to God spiritual worship; and as worship is not performed in silence only, but also by the offering up of every sacrifice and gift of his preparing, whether it be by the ministration of his glorious Gospel, or the offering at his sacred footstool of vocal prayers and intercessions, thanksgivings and praises, the Lord was pleased to call upon dear Allen to proclaim the truth of his Gospel of life and salvation among that interesting congregation; and to give us access to the place of prayer, when, through the Spirit, living praises were offered up to God and to the Lamb. It was truly consoling to behold so much of the oneness of spirit among that company, composed of such as are poor in this world, and of many others of the highest rank in life, but who all witness the truth of Christ's saying, 'One is your master, and all ye are brethren.' There are in this city many pious characters of the nobility, and from them I understand that many similarly minded are to be found throughout this kingdom, especially in that section of the country which extends towards and along the Baltic Sea. What a wonderful change has taken place in this palace and those that frequent it. During the reign of the present King's ancestors, dissipation and infidelity prevailed in a high degree, and received every encouragement; surely this is the Lord's doing. His works loudly proclaim his praise.

" We went to the Baron Altenstein, at Schoenberg, the Minister of Worship. He is now an aged man; he has for many years occupied important stations in the Government, and was during

some years Minister of Finance. We found him as represented
to us, a serious and pious man ; he received us with Christian
kindness and affability. We told him of the sufferings that some of
our Friends had endured at and about Minden under the military
laws, and the threatened execution of these on some at Barmen.
He told us that the subject respecting the military law came not
under his immediate notice ; but that he would use his influence
so as to prevent further proceeding in the case at Barmen ;
' There is no law,' said he, ' as yet, that protects your Friends,'
but he hoped one would be made ; he had always been opposed
to the molestation of men who had religious scruples against
bearing arms.

"29th. We were with Elsner, and made arrangements for
printing five thousand copies of the ' Importance of Religion'
in German, and the same number of the ' Scripture Lessons'
that we prepared in Russia. We find the former very useful for
distribution in this land, and the Scripture Lessons are intended
to be introduced into their public schools. Their Tract Society
concludes to issue double that number."

———

Halle, Weimar, and Leipzic, places of peculiar though very
different interest, next attracted their attention, and they
spent some days in each. On their way from Berlin to the
first, they passed through Wittenburg, the cradle of the
Reformation, and the scene of "Luther's development, and
Luther's work." *

"It was here," says Stephen Grellet, "that he first engaged in
the great work of the Reformation—from hence it spread so widely,
and shook the strongholds of Popery to their very foundation.
Portions of the monastery, which was his abode, are still standing. In front of it they have erected a statue of him, to perpetuate his memory. Much better would this be done, by all
those who commend his Christian labours, endeavouring, under

———

* D'Aubigné's "History of the Reformation."

the influence of the Divine Spirit, to build upon the same foundation that he did ; and to love and exalt the name of the blessed
Redeemer, the Lord Jesus Christ as it was his concern to do—and
in the doing of which he loved not his life unto death, but was
ready to suffer and die, for Jesus' sake."*

"We tarried here a short time, and then pursued our journey
to Halle, in Saxony. We had a trying night. The roads were
rough, and we had crowded, uncomfortable seats. My lame
shoulder gave me great suffering, but our minds were clothed
with such a sense of gratitude to the Lord for the consolations
bestowed upon us in Berlin, and the favour to have been able to
mingle with so many who love the Lord Jesus, and others who,
we believe, are serious inquirers after the truth, that thanksgiving
and praise were our silent engagement most of that night.

"We arrived at Halle about noon, the 28th. The Lord, who
doeth all things well according to his divine purpose, which we
poor short-sighted mortals cannot fathom, was pleased to prepare
another dispensation for his poor servants ; for we soon became
sensible of the darkness that covers the minds of many of the
people in this place—the seat of knowledge, as it is termed by
many, because of its renowned university ; the greatest part of
the professors, men of great learning, are unbelievers in the saving
truths of Christianity ; and teach their pernicious doctrines to the
numerous young men sent to this place, who return to their distant homes with minds poisoned by Socinian principles ; and,
in their human reason, exalted above the simplicity of the Gospel
of Christ. I lament bitterly over them. I have felt as if my
soul was made sorrowful, even unto death. My sorrow is also
increased by letters from America, bringing the affecting tidings
of the spread of the cholera in the United States, particularly in
New York and Philadelphia ; informing me also of the illness of
my beloved wife and daughter ; but surely the Lord is a strong

---

* To some readers it may be interesting to see the original of the last
words of his noble defence at Worms :—

"Es sey denn dass ich mit Zeugnissen der heiligen Schrift oder mit
öffentlichen, klaren und hellen Gründen und Ursachen überwunden und
überwiesen werde, so kann und will ich nicht widerrufen, weil weder
sicher noch gerathen ist, etwas wider Gewissen zu thun—Hier stehe ich ;
ich kann nicht anders; Got helfe mir. Amen!"

and sure refuge in time of trouble. He is the Rock, and there is no unrighteousness in Him. If my soul is sinking under the weight of oppression, let it be, O Lord, to sink only to come through the deeps to thee, my rock and sure foundation. To thee my life, my all has been offered up ; into thy hands, and with resignation to thy sovereign will, the whole of my offering is renewedly made, by thy assisting grace.

"This evening the Lord sent us comfort, blessed be his name ! by a visit from F. Tholuck, who is one of the professors at the university here, but a man of a totally different spirit from the generality of them ; he is a full believer in the dear Redeemer, the Lord Jesus Christ ; in all his offices, according to all the great truths revealed to us by divine inspiration, and contained in the Holy Scriptures. In opposition to his fellow-professors, he teaches these faithfully, in his chair as a prsfessor, and from the pulpit also as a minister of Christ ; and he adorns his doctrine by a consistent life and conversation ; he is well versed in, and teaches the oriental and many ancient languages ; but, so far from assuming anything because of his attainments, meekness and humility are his covering. He is acquainted with Friends' religious principles. He resided at Berlin when our dear friend, Thomas Shillitoe, visited it. Tholuck acted as his interpreter in the meetings he had there, as he understands and speaks English well.

"29th. We visited this morning the spacious Orphan Asylum, founded by Franke, celebrated for his piety and extensive benevolence. Its fruits will extend to many generations. Numerous are those who yearly partake of the benefits of it. This establishment is a little town of itself. They have at present only one hundred orphans boarders on the premises ; but they have in their schools above two thousand pupils, of various ages. We had some religious services among these.

"At eleven a.m. we met with a number of young men who study under Tholuck ; they appear to have received, as into good ground, the seed of piety sown in their hearts, which Tholuck is endeavouring to cultivate ; they meet with persecution here ; they are reviled by the students under the other professors, but these sufferings appear to be blessed to them.

"Tholuck has an arduous path to tread, but the Lord supports him amidst his numerous difficulties ; his enemies, like those of

Daniel formerly, can find no occasion against him, save concerning the law of his God. He has from two to three hundred young men, steady attenders at his lectures at the university. He has the consolation to hope that every year from thirty to forty of these young men go from the university to various parts of Germany, thoroughly established in sound Christian truths; giving evidence also that they love the Lord Jesus Christ in sincerity.

"30th. We left Halle yesterday, and travelling during the night, we came to Saxe-Weimar this afternoon. I had for years felt my mind strongly drawn to this place. The Duke and Duchess were persons of great benevolence and piety; they were much tried at the prevalence of anti-christian principles in these districts, and to a lamentable extent throughout most parts of Saxony. My mind is greatly pressed down under this dark spirit, so much so, that though now here, I have been almost tempted to take my flight; but I am sensible that it is the love of Christ that has brought us here. He may have a service for us, and should it be only silently to suffer for his sake, his will be done.

"31st. We were with Counsellor Peucer, who takes an interest in the spreading of the Scriptures of Truth, and thereby evinces that he is a Christian believer. We were also with Dr. von Froriep, who knew my dear William Allen in England; he is the Physician of the present Grand Duchess; she had heard of our arrival at Weimar, and he came to tell us that she requested that, if our time allowed, we should go and see her at twelve o'clock, at the palace. We accordingly went at the time appointed; she was much affected at meeting with us, for it brought her to feel afresh the great bereavement she has sustained by the decease of her very near and beloved relatives that she knew we had been with —the Empress Dowager of Russia, her mother; the Emperor Alexander, her brother; the Empress Elizabeth, his wife; and the Queen of Wurtemberg, her sister. She was much attached to them; the natural dispositions of her brother and sister were similar to her own; and, besides this, there existed between them a religious fellowship which is stronger than the ties of nature; her son, an only child of about fourteen, was the only one present with us; he is an intelligent and amiable youth. Our interview was of a religious character, and she appears to like to dwell on serious subjects ; she also takes much interest in the promotion of benevolent objects ; besides giving her care and support to the various establishments formed by the late Duchess, mother of the Duke, she has formed others herself. On parting, she took us by the hand in an affectionate manner, requesting that we would visit her again before our departure from Weimar. We had not reached the out door of the palace when Dr. Froriep overtook us to give us an invitation from the Duchess to dine with her the next day ; we excused ourselves, stating that we should prefer, if it was agreeable to her, to pass a little time with her in a more select manner than could be done at dinner. On receiving this information, she sent us an invitation to take tea with her at her more private palace of Belvedere.

"Ninth Month 1st.   Yesterday afternoon and to-day, we visited a number of the public institutions, schools, hospitals, the poor-house, and prisons.

"At about six p.m. we rode to the palace of the Belvedere. It is about two miles and a half from Weimar. The Duchess received us in her drawing-room. For a short time we were by ourselves ; but when tea was brought in, her son and several of her attendants came in, with whom the conversation became general. The Duke, her husband, is absent from home at present. After tea we had a religious opportunity with them, and were afterwards mostly with the Duchess alone. She appears to have been taught in the school of affliction, and has learned also under the teachings of the Lord's Spirit. Thus she has obtained a portion of that knowledge which it is life eternal to possess. Our spirits were contrited together under the sensible evidence that the Lord's presence was with us. He enabled us reverently to bow down together at his sacred footstool. We declined staying to supper ; our object in a private interview was accomplished. We retired about nine o'clock, with peaceful minds. We trust also that the Duchess will be strengthened to exert, with fresh courage, her influence with the Duke, so as to put some check on the endeavours of the Socinians, both by private priestly influence and the pulpit, to disseminate their anti-christian doctrines.

"2nd. We had this day some religious opportunities, in which we preached Christ and Him crucified ; delivered for our offences and

risen again for our justification ; a doctrine which continues to
be a stumbling-block to the Jews and foolishness to the wise.

"3rd. We set off for Leipzic early this morning, and travelled
over very extensive plains highly cultivated, and on which an
immense quantity of grain is raised ; a forest tree is hardly to be
seen, but there are excellent fruit trees ; the public road is planted
with rows of them ; alternately apple, pear, plum, or cherry trees ;
and at suitable distances there are seats for foot-travellers and
fountains of water. Leipzic is a place where great champions of
infidelity have their seats in the university ; but here, as at Halle,
there are a few preserved, who are the Lord's instruments in
counteracting the evil and the poison ; to these our minds were
particularly drawn in Christian tenderness and affection, with
desires that the Lord may enable us to encourage and strengthen
them under their various difficulties and trials. Soon after our
arrival we were with Professor Lindner, who is one of those pious
and decided characters on the side of Christ and his truth ; he
appears to have a right sense of the nature of the religious engagement that has induced us to come to this place, and has
welcomed us with warm Christian affection. Understanding what
class of men we wished to be with, he has undertaken to have
such invited to meet us at his house this afternoon.

"We found there a larger number than we anticipated, among
others were Senator Volkman, for whom we had a letter of introduction, Professor Seyffarth, Recklam, and others of that class ;
also a number of young men, students under these piously-minded
professors. We had a satisfactory and instructive season together,
the Lord giving us to feel his baptising power. He also enabled
dear Allen and myself to impart to them the word of encouragement and tender counsel.

"We visited various of their public establishments, as the
orphans' asylum, poor-house, house of correction, &c. Recklam
was our interpreter.

"On the 6th, in the afternoon, we had a good meeting at
Doctor Hahn's, one of the professors of the university. He is
a man of a strong mind, improved by grace, and brought down
into the valley of humility, by the power of Truth, and the
softening influence of heavenly love. As he has learned in the
school of Christ, it is his endeavour to direct his pupils to Christ,

and to press on them a close attention to the teachings and guidance of his Spirit. In the evening we had another meeting at Professor Lindner's. It was intended chiefly for the young men, students at the university under these pious professors. It was a tendering season,—many of these young men publicly testify that they wish to be Christians, by attending those who preach and exalt the name of a crucified Saviour and risen Lord, and not those professors who set up human reason, and after whom the greater part of the students flock.

THEY now paid an interesting visit to Dresden, where they
arrived the 8th of Ninth Month, 1832. S. G. says:—

"9th. We were this forenoon with Von Lindenau, Prime
Minister of the King of Saxony; we spent about half an hour
with him; he appeared to take a deep interest in subjects of a
serious character."

On the 10th they visited several pious individuals and
schools; one for four hundred children founded by Count
Einsiedel, they found under good Christian management;
and on the 11th they received an invitation from the Prince
Regent, nephew of the King, through the Prime Minister.
Of their interview S. G. writes:—

"We were at once introduced to the apartments of the Prince.
The King, his uncle, has no children, and, as he is now old, the
reins of government devolve on Prince Frederick, who is successor
to the throne after his uncle's decease; his own father, Prince
John, also being an old man. The Prince received us with affability and kindness. He said he knew our disinterested motives
for travelling as we do; for love to God and man prompted us.
'In this love and good will,' he added, 'you embrace men of
every description, of every religious denomination, rich and poor;
you go among the most wretched in prisons and poor-houses, and
come to some of us also in our palaces.' As his heart was open
towards us, we felt ours enlarged towards him, and freely spoke
to him of the things of God, and of that salvation which comes by
Jesus Christ. We told him that sin is the cause of all private

and public misery. A Government can have no stability where these prevail. No power can eradicate them but that of the Lord Jesus Christ, who came into the world to deliver us from our sins. He came to put an end to sin, to finish transgression, and in the room thereof, to bring in everlasting righteousness ; and to as many as receive Him, He gives power to become the sons of God, even to as many as believe on Him. We entreated him to consider the sad effects of unbelief and infidelity, and urged the promulgation of sound Christian doctrines throughout his dominions ; and the repression, in a firm but Christian spirit, of the great latitude taken in some of the universities in the kingdom, where infidelity is openly taught, and the minds of many of the youth receive the deadly poison, which they again disseminate in various parts of the nation. We entreated him also to live and walk in the fear and love of God, through the grace of Jesus Christ, that, by his Christian example, he may encourage his subjects to enrol themselves under the banner of the Prince of Peace. He was attentive and serious. At his own request we also visited the younger brother of the Prince Regent, Prince John, whom we found evidently prepared to receive what in the love and fear of God we might have to say to him ; for he was well aware, as he acknowledged, that we had no personal favours to ask, but that it was his good and that of the people at large that we sought after. We encouraged him to cultivate a state of watchfulness unto prayer, that by close attention to the leadings of the Holy Spirit he may increase in the knowledge of our Lord and Saviour Jesus Christ, and be strengthened to walk in obedience to the will of God. The Prince feels interested in the promotion of temperance, for he sees that the use of intoxicating drink is an inlet to much misery and to the commission of many crimes. We presented him with the reports of the Temperance Society in England, and those on prison discipline and public schools ; with all of which he was much pleased, and not less so with various publications treating on some of our Christian testimonies, of which he desired to have a more perfect knowledge."

On the 12th S. G. writes :—

" The meeting concluded upon yesterday was held this afternoon ; it was well attended by the class of persons we had par-

ticularly desired to see. The Baroness Drechsel, a pious person,
well acquainted with both French and English as well as her
native tongue, the German, kindly undertook to interpret for us.
From the first of our entering the assembly we felt a solemn covering over us, like the over-shadowing of the Lord's presence ; it
reminded me of the language, ' Keep silence before me, O islands,
and let the people renew their strength ; let them come near,
then let them speak ; let us come near together to judgment.'
Those present seemed to feel the force of the words, for all
appeared to be gathered with one accord into solemn silence
before God, in which we continued some time ; when with my
heart filled by the love of the Gospel I stood up ; the Baroness
stood by me, and with great gentleness and modesty, but with striking dignity, she interpreted sentence by sentence, from the French,
what I communicated ; her own mind was very tenderly affected
whilst thus engaged. The great love of God in sending his well-
beloved Son, Jesus Christ, into the world as a Saviour and Redeemer, was proclaimed among them. The meeting continued in
a state of solemn silence after I sat down, when Doctor Leonardi
spoke a few sentences in German which the Baroness interpreted
into French, saying that the Gospel truths that had been declared
were the Christian's sure and only hope, and craving the Lord's
blessing upon the word preached. After that William Allen bore
a solemn and impressive testimony to the power and efficacy of
the Spirit, by whom deliverance from the dominion of sin is obtained and we are made partakers of the grace and truth which
come by Jesus Christ. Towards the conclusion of the meeting,
access was graciously given to the throne of grace, and on bended
knees, prayer, adoration, and praise were offered up to God in the
Saviour's name through the Spirit."

They then left Dresden and proceeded to Herrnhut and
Bertholsdorf, the "mother congregation of the Renewed Church
of the Moravian Brethren." Sprung from a small seed of
bold confessors of Christ, who, tried in the fire of persecution,
remained faithful even unto death, that "beautiful little
church," as Milner calls it, had weathered many a storm.
" It could look back to a cloud of faithful witnesses of Divine
Truth, who, amidst calumny and opposition, in bonds and

imprisonments, under a tropical sun and in boreal climes, far from home and kindred, in the east and west, in the north and south, have erected the standard of the cross, and enlisted thousands to allegiance to Him who died to save a world of perishing sinners." This interesting community still gave evidence of lively zeal for the honour of their Lord, and for the propagation of his Gospel, when Stephen Grellet and his companion visited them. They arrived at Herrnhut early in the morning of the 13th of Ninth Month. Of this establishment, of the pious individuals there at the head, and of their own services amongst them, S. G. gives a very interesting account; of one of the meetings he says :—

"In the evening we had a meeting for divine worship in the Count Donha's house, which was largely attended. The Lord owned us very graciously by his Divine presence. The baptising power of the Spirit of Truth was felt, and tears were shed by several. My soul magnifies the Lord, who has given us the opportunity to meet with these sheep of his pasture, and lambs of his fold, and to unite with them in ascribing glory, honour, majesty and praise to Him the Lord God Omnipotent, and to the Lamb, our crucified Saviour and risen Lord.

"The next morning, previous to our departure, the Count came to see us once more to bid us farewell. Both he and his pious Countess will long live in our memory. Our intercourse and fellowship with them, and many others in this place, have been sweet."

They now passed over into the land of John Huss and Jerome of Prague. It was soon to be observed that they had entered a Roman Catholic country, by the many crosses erected by the roadside; but they had no opportunity of holding up the light of salvation; and after speaking of a little difficulty with some officers about their passports at Rumburg, S. G. observes :—

"After some detention, two young men, travellers from Vienna, came in. They spoke both French and English, as well as Ger-

man, and matters with the public officers were soon adjusted ;
but, by that time, a crowd had collected about us, attracted by
curiosity to see the strangers. They were, however, very civil,
and I felt my mind drawn towards them in the love of God, who
has made of one blood all the nations of the earth, whether they
be Europeans or Americans, white, red, or black ;—Christ Jesus
has died for all, would have them all to be saved from their sins,
and to become joint heirs with Him, of his kingdom of everlasting blessedness and glory. One of the young men from
Vienna interpreted what was said. They bid us farewell, wishing
us a pleasant journey.

"Late in the evening of the 16th we arrived at Prague ; we had
stopped a short time at Jung Bunglau on our way ; superstition
greatly abounds there ; there are, nevertheless, those among them
towards whom our hearts were warmed with Christian love, and
we much regretted that no way opened for more religious intercourse with them. It is a great consolation to me to have the
persuasion that there are those among the various nations and
the various Christian professors, yea, among the Jews and Gentiles, who fear God, and according to the measure of grace that
they have received, work righteousness, who are accepted with
Him, through the one Mediator.

"17th. We went this morning to the Governor's palace ; he
is absent, having gone to Italy ; but the Count Prozka, Vice-
Governor, offered at once to give us every assistance in his power
during our continuance in Bohemia. We obtained from him
some interesting accounts of the state of morals and of the education of the people throughout the country. As we wished to
visit their great prison, the Count sent for one of his secretaries
to accompany us, and to serve us as interpreter. On our way to
the prison we passed through the public square, where the faggots
were formerly kindled, and the flames devoured many pious
Christians, under the hands of the Inquisition of Rome. The flat
stones on which the piles were erected and the victims were
placed, identified the very spot where such cruelties were perpetrated under the mask of religion ; but I was not less deeply
grieved at beholding the stately buildings around the square,
with the many large windows opening upon it, which used to be
crowded with spectators to see the savage proceedings prompted

by blind superstition ; some of these windows still show the conspicuous seats occupied by their great men, both of the clergy and civil officers, during those exhibitions of cruelty.

" We found about six hundred prisoners in the prison. They carry on there a variety of trades. By the sale of the articles made, the income considerably exceeds the expenses. These prisoners generally wear heavy irons, and are kept under severe discipline. We saw in one prison one hundred and fifty women under heavy irons also. It is the first time that I have had such a painful sight.

" In the afternoon we went to the Lutheran pastor's. We found him a man of humility and piety. His community is composed of about three thousand persons. They are kept under great restrictions ; they are not allowed to print anything without special permission, which is obtained with difficulty. From the same causes they have but few Bibles among them. The penalties are very severe on a Protestant clergyman, or any other person attempting to proselyte any Papist to their religious tenets. The minister may preach his doctrine in his own place of worship, but not out of it ; and if a Papist attends the meetings of Protestants, he is liable to be prosecuted. We feel very tenderly for those who live under such restrictions. Sufferings, however, are, we hope, blessed to some of them ; their hearts are kept soft under it, and they appear to have a part in the blessing pronounced upon those who are persecuted and reviled for Christ's sake.

" On my return to the inn I found the waiter in my chamber, attentively engaged in reading in my French Bible. He appeared at first disconcerted, and began to make apologies, but I soon removed his fears. He said he had not seen a Bible for some years ; formerly he had access to one which it was his delight to peruse, but here it would be impossible for him to obtain one, and if he did, he should be obliged to keep it closely concealed from the priests. On conversing with him, we found him to be a person of a pious, seeking mind ; he knows several others under like religious concern with himself ; but they are obliged to keep very silent, otherwise persecution or a prison would soon be their portion. We presented him with a Bible in German, and a few tracts in the same language ; it seemed as if he was receiving a treasure ; which, he said, both he and his friends would greatly

appreciate, and endeavour to keep very private. There are, we
hear, many such pious and hidden ones in Bohemia, well known
unto the Lord though unknown to man."

———

The Austrian empire did not appear to afford much scope
for their Christian labours, and they proceeded at once from
Prague to Vienna. Here they received much kindness from
Prince Paul Esterhazy, and through his means way was
remarkably prepared for a short visit to the borders of Hungary. But, on returning to the Austrian capital, no opportunity for extensive usefulness seemed to be open, and they
soon felt themselves at liberty to leave the dominions of the
Emperor.

Stephen Grellet gives the following account :—

" We left Prague at five o'clock p.m. on the 17th of Ninth
Month. Thirty-seven hours of close travelling brought us to
Vienna.

" 21st. On arriving in this city we had to present ourselves at
the police office with our passports ; close questions were put to
us respecting our objects in coming here ; our answers attracted
their attention and led to the explanation of some of our Christian
testimonies and practices, which appeared things very new to
them ; they treated us civilly, but we were very sensible that a
jealous and suspicious eye was upon us ; we did not flinch from
telling them with Christian candour and clearness what our engagements had been in other parts, and what was our inducement
in coming among them.

" The Baron D'Escheles, and the Baroness his wife, came to
see us. He is the Danish Consul. They are persons of superior
minds. We were also with the Prince Esterhazy, who has been for
many years the Austrian Ambassador in London, and with whom
dear Allen is acquainted. A particular object that we had in
seeing him, was to obtain information respecting Hungary, a
country towards which I had felt my.mind attracted, with no
prospect, however, that I am required to go much into it. The
Prince, besides owning large estates in Austria, has extensive ones

in Hungary. I think we were told that he has about eighty or
ninety thousand persons on his lands there. Many are Roman
Catholics and Protestants, others are of the Tartar or other nomad
tribes. There is much good land in that country, where the vine
is cultivated, and a great deal of grain ; but it has also extensive
uncultivated plains, as in the Crimea, among the Tartars. There
large flocks of cattle and sheep are fed. The revenues of the
Prince, in wool, are very large. He is well disposed towards his
people, and, as far as he can, independently of Austria, he grants
them full liberty of conscience ; consequently the free circulation
of the Holy Scriptures is allowed among them. He is anxious
that schools should be established throughout his estates, where a
moral and virtuous education might be given to the people generally. He encouraged us to go a little way at least into Hungary,
to see for ourselves. This I was willing to do. The Prince told
us that about forty miles up the Danube, he has one estate on
which are some towns and villages settled mostly by Protestants,
and that the whole tract of country between here and there belongs to him or his father. He added that we must expect to find
there a very plain and simple people. We inquired if we should
find places to lodge at. 'Yes,' said he, 'there are some places
where you may have some kind of shelter, and also simple but
wholesome food.' We wanted no more we told him. Then again
he said, ' As you have no vehicle of your own, and will be in a
strange country, make use of my plain travelling carriage, with a
man to accompany you.' All these were unexpected offers to us ;
we took time to consider of it, when, finding that we could not
well proceed there otherwise, we accepted the kind offer, and have
made arrangements to set off to-morrow morning.

"We had engaged to take tea that evening at the Baron
D'Escheles', whose residence is four miles out of the city, and
very near to the palace of the Emperor. We expected to be with
the Baron's family only, but we found ourselves in the midst of a
numerous company, mostly of the nobility, who, it appears, had
been invited on our account. It was an opportunity that we
could not have obtained by efforts of our own, for the police is so
strict, that we could not·appoint any public meetings. We are
well aware also, that we are most strictly watched ; for even the
valet-de-place, who is the servant that attends upon us at the inn,

or who goes out with us to show us the way to the places we visit, is an emissary of the police ; they contrive to place such over every stranger, that all their movements may be closely watched. The whole of the company spoke French ; our communication with one another was therefore without an interpreter, on my part at least ; we were for a while engaged in answering the inquiries made by some who collected about us for the purpose ; but after a time way was made for our having a full opportunity to proclaim before them all the glorious Gospel of Christ, who is the Head of the Church and the only Saviour ; we told them that He alone can save from sin, and if those who wish to try to enter his kingdom by any other way than by Him who is the door, are accounted in the Scriptures but thieves and robbers, how much more are to be accounted as such those who assume the power to open or close that door at their pleasure ! We directed them to Christ who is the way, the truth, and the life, without whom none can come to the Father ; finally we commended them to God and to the word of his grace, which is able to build us up and to give us an inheritance among all them which are sanctified. Great seriousness prevailed over the whole assembly ; the doctrine was new to many of them, but the faithful witness in their own hearts brought home the conviction that it was the Truth as it is in Jesus ; therefore no objection was raised by any one. Our spirits have magnified the Lord ; for his great goodness in thus making a way for us to proclaim his Truth, in a place where we seemed to be hedged in on every side.

The next morning the Prince Esterhazy sent his travelling carriage to us, as agreed upon ; it is a light but very plain vehicle ; we had post-horses put to it ; but we were much surprised when at every station on the road where the horses are changed the Postmaster refused to receive any money ; to this effect orders had been sent from the Prince, to whom or to his father that tract of country as well as the post-horses belong. But we were much more surprised when, arriving at Eisenstadt, where we expected to find a village only, and where the Prince had told us we should find some kind of shelter and plain, simple food, we were driven to the Prince's château, a spacious palace, and his steward, to whom information had been sent of our coming, was waiting for us, and had dinner prepared. At first we thought that surely

there must be some mistake; but the steward, to remove every
such apprehension, showed us the directions he had from the
Prince to' have us accommodated in the palace, and also to facilitate our going to the different villages or places that we might
wish to visit, and to supply us with horses for the purpose out of
his stables.

" The Prince generally spends a few months here every year,
but at present there is nobody in the château, except the steward
and his attendants; there is, however, a regiment on the premises, and the guard is mounted. This palace stands in the
midst of a fertile plain, high hills and mountains are near; the
latter are covered with snow. They are a continuation of the
Alps that runs through the Tyrol. The Danube flows between
the plain and them. The view is most beautiful, and the air is
very pure.

" It was not the country we had come to see, but the people;
to them, therefore, our attention was directed. The mass of the
people here speak another language. The steward kindly provided us with an interpreter who speaks English. The first
villages we visited are settled by Croats. We visited three of
their villages, which contain together upwards of three thousand
inhabitants. We found in some of these people religious sensibility.

"We went to Oedenburg, the first town of any size in
Hungary. One half of the inhabitants are Protestants. We
paid a satisfactory visit to the pastor of their church. He is the
head of one hundred and forty churches of the Lutherans, in the
districts on this side of the Danube. Protestants are numerous
in Hungary. There are about two millions of the Reformed
Church, and one million of Lutherans; the rest are Roman
Catholics and Mahometans. John Kiss, the Lutheran minister
here, tells us that they have many schools among themselves, but
the Austrian Government places great obstacles in the way of
their being supplied with suitable school and religious books,
and with the Scriptures also; but that nearly every person in
their congregations can' read, and that every one also has an
opportunity of hearing the Scriptures read, or of perusing some
of the few copies they possess, which they consider a great privilege. What this clergyman tells us of the state of morals among

the Protestant community in Hungary generally, is very satisfactory ; it appears to exceed that of the Roman Catholics. He
can speak of this with confidence, particularly as regards the
numerous churches under his superintendence, which he visits
once every year ; and he further says, that the Socinian doctrines
are scarcely known among these, and that their church discipline
would not allow them in any of their members. The little intercourse we have had in this place, with a few individuals, is very
satisfactory ; but no way opened for a public meeting."

After visiting these and one or two other villages, Stephen
Grellet writes :—

" We felt ourselves released from going further into Hungary,
and we returned to Eisentadt, to the Prince's palace, where we
remained but a short time, being anxious to return to Vienna.
That palace contains one hundred and six bed-chambers ; but
the steward tells us that on some occasions he has found beds
for above three hundred persons. The chamber that I occupied
fronted the Danube. A little below it is the ancient castle, where
the treasures of the family of the Princes Esterhazy are kept.
Prince Paul, as we saw him at his residence at Vienna, would not
give an idea that he possessed such great wealth. We found him
quite simple in his own person.

" Soon after returning to Vienna, we were with the Prince, to
acknowledge his unexpected and very kind treatment. He took
great interest in the account we gave him of the situation of his
Protestant subjects, and the difficulties under which they are
placed. He thinks that he may succeed in removing the restrictions which prevent their having free access to the Scriptures,
and a supply of suitable books in their families, and for the use
of their schools. We had free communication with him respecting the value of the exercise of liberty of conscience, and how
oppressive it is in a Government to prevent this ; but he knows
that this is a delicate subject to treat upon, in this Empire, where
Popery has so great an ascendancy. Before retiring from him,
we had a solemn religious opportunity, and we left him in a
tender state of mind."

They did not remain long in Vienna ; but they had free

intercourse both with the Lutherans and those of the Reformed Church. They learnt that the religious condition of the Protestants in that city was deplorable, but that there are a few to whom Christ is precious; and who endeavour to adorn their Christian profession by piety and virtue; some of these are especially to be found in the surrounding villages.

"Through the medium of pious characters we have put a number of religious tracts, in the German language, in a way to be extensively spread throughout Hungary as far as Bucharest, and also here in Austria and Bohemia."

On the day before their departure from Vienna, S. G. writes to a friend in England :—

"Last night the prospect having unfolded that we may proceed towards Bavaria, after properly weighing it, we have attended to the needful preparation, and taken our places in the diligence for Munich. Were we to stay weeks here, very probably many things would open to our view; there is indeed a great deal to excite our interest; amidst many baptisms a precious and consoling relief is obtained at the throne of grace, where our merciful High Priest is pleased to sanctify and render acceptable to God the sacrifices that are laid upon the altar of offering.

"We are glad, however, to be able to get away from Vienna; the jealousy of Government and the whole of the police is such, that the way to visit their prisons is much shut up. The pious people among Protestant are under fear of speaking."

CHAPTER XXX.

Fourth Visit to Europe.

BAVARIA—WURTEMBERG—STRASBURG—BAN DE LA ROCHE— SWITZERLAND.

Though favoured to obtain a peaceful release from the Austrian capital, the darkness, superstition, and bigotry which so much prevailed, left a sorrowful impression upon these devoted servants of the Lord Jesus. They could not rejoice when the ways of Zion mourned; they could not but be partakers of the "sufferings of Christ," where the light of the Gospel of "His glory" was so much obscured by unbelief or misbelief, and the spirit of the world. They set off for Bavaria on the 26th of Ninth Month, and, travelling night and day, arrived at Munich on the 29th. S. G. writes:—

"Munich, 29th. Our way was for some distance up the Danube, over a very fertile country. We had the Austrian Alps on our left, covered with perpetual snow; we had beautiful views before us. Many monasteries are to be seen, inhabited by that kind of monks who live luxuriously, whilst the poor cultivators of the land are greatly oppressed—not in their outward circumstances only, but in their consciences also. We felt much for some of these, but no way opened for having any intercourse with them. Near Linz there is one village where the whole population have become convinced that Jesus Christ is the only Saviour and Redeemer; consequently they have turned away from the priests. Some of the Popish priests whom I visited some years since, and who had renounced their errors, resided in these parts; fruits of their pious labours now appear; they have suffered great persecution; others also are now made willing to suffer for Christ's sake.

"Many changes have taken place in Munich since my last visit;

the unsparing messenger of death has removed many of those pious persons with whom I mingled here in religious fellowship, to a better world, I hope.   The then Crown Prince is now King; we cannot see him, as he is absent; I can only by writing impart to him my continued solicitude on his account, that the love of Christ may have free course in his heart, so that he may partake of the blessing of salvation in time and in eternity.

"We were with Frederick Roth, President of the Central Consistory of the Protestants in Bavaria; the account he gives us of the removal from office of all those of their clergy who had embraced or promulgated Socinian doctrines is grateful.   Tholuck, of Halle, was very useful in promoting this; he was at Munich a few years since, on his return from Rome; on one occasion he attended the Protestant place of worship, where their great and learned Unitarian preacher expounded their principles at great length, before a very numerous congregation.   Tholuck was requested to preach that afternoon; he tried to excuse himself, having arrived at Munich that morning early, after travelling some nights; but from a sense of Christian duty he consented.   The congregation in the afternoon was fully as large as in the morning; Tholuck went over the several heads of the subjects that had been treated upon in the morning, and answered them so fully and clearly, that the assembly appeared convinced of the truth that Jesus is the Christ, the Son of God, and the only Saviour.   Their great preacher was so confounded that he has not dared since to lift up his head. The same work of reformation went on throughout the other Proinstant churches in Bavaria.

"Tenth Month 2nd.   Yesterday and to-day we had several private religious opportunities with pious persons on whom we called, or who came to our inn to see us.   Many of these I had known during my former visits here, and they appear to continue in a tender frame of mind.   We had also a meeting with a number of them, who collected for the purpose.   We had likewise a religious opportunity at the British Ambassador's, Lord Erskine, with whose father dear William Allen was well acquainted.   Among the interesting visits made us, was one by the Baron Raflin.   It is about twenty years since I became acquainted with him.   He was then a lovely character.   He appeared in earnest, the love of God constraining him to join himself to the Lord, in a perpetual covenant never to be broken. He tells us that he maintained his integrity for some time after we parted from him; but the tide of worldly prosperity rose high upon him; he was advanced to important stations in the Government; riches also increased; under these changes his heart became lifted up, and in the same proportion as he pursued the ways of the world, he departed from the way and the love of God; but the Lord, in his great mercy and compassion, did not forsake him; He extended over him his fatherly rod; He visited him with heavy affliction, took away his idols, and, by his refining fire kindled in his heart, removed the dross from it, and rendered it soft as in former days. With tears the old man unfolded to me how graciously the Lord has dealt with him. His wife and eldest son are like-minded. They sit down daily together to read the Scriptures; and then in silence and reverence to wait upon God, so as to be enabled to worship Him in spirit and in truth."

S. G. describes many visits of the same character to those whom he had met with when in Munich before, and he was much comforted in finding that many of them had grown in the Christian life. The Prince Oettingen Wallenstein went to see them at their hotel, and of whom he says:—

"We spent about three hours together. His Christian protection of those Roman Catholics who have seen the errors of Popery, shelters them greatly from the persecutions they would, otherwise, be subjected to. Several of their priests and nuns continue to make public confession that the Lord Jesus Christ is their only hope of salvation, and that they consider and acknowledge Him, and not the Pope, as the only Head of the Church. The Prince, understanding that we proposed to visit some of the villages on the Donau-Moos marshes, where many persons have been convinced of their former errors, has not only encouraged us to go there, but has also sent for the Baron Baader, who speaks good English, to accompany us there, and act as our interpreter."

S. G. adds:—

"My spirit is reverently bowed with gratitude before God, in being now permitted to mingle again with a few among the poor, and of those who have their dwellings in palaces, whom He has rescued from the corruptions that are in the world, and whom He enables to approach his sacred presence, with broken hearts and contrite spirits.

"3rd. Accompanied by the Baron Baader, we left Munich early in the morning for Neuburg, and continued in that neighbourhood till the 5th, visiting many of the villages on the Donau-Moos. This was an extensive, barren, swampy tract of land, which has been, of latter years, drained and brought into a state of cultivation ; the land thus recovered is about forty miles in circumference. Some of the villages are settled by Roman Catholics ; others by Protestants ; one or two by the Mennonites. Many of the Roman Catholics have seen the errors of Popery. In the largest village, nearly the whole of the inhabitants have turned away from the Church of Rome ; and what is remarkable, this village, Carlshuld, was the most dissipated ; revelling and drunkenness were prevalent among the people. Lutz, the Romish priest among them, became dissatisfied with many of the anti-christian doctrines and practices of the Church of Rome ; he saw their inconsistency with the Holy Scriptures, which he was induced to peruse with greater attention ; when the truths of the glorious Gospel of Christ became more and more unfolded to his view : with this his love to God and to our Lord and Saviour Jesus Christ increased, and his heart was also enlarged in love and religious concern for his parishioners. These became tenderly affected by the new doctrines now proclaimed to them by their pastor ; and the more so, as his life and conversation adorned what he preached. This, together with the convictions of the Lord's Spirit, the faithful witness, wrought so powerfully on their minds, that a general convincement took place among them, and a reformation also, so that morality and virtue became some of the first fruits ; proclaiming that they had turned from darkness to light, and from the power of sin and Satan to God. This brought persecution upon them ; it fell particularly upon Lutz, their minister ; for a time he maintained his Christian profession with firmness ; but at last, under suffering on the one hand, and flattery and specious promises from the bishops on the other, he turned away from the faith once delivered to the saints, and subscribed again to the errors of Popery ; and now, instead of the fair prospects held out to him, he is immured in a convent ;

but the people of the village maintain their faith and their allegiance to Christ, and they are protected from the Popish clergy by the Prince Oettingen Wallenstein. They have nearly completed a meeting-house, in which we had a meeting for divine worship—the first held in it; it was a solemn and tendering season.

"It was noon when we came to the village of the Mennonites. Those who had been in the fields had just returned home to their dinner; their minister, who had been at the plough, on being told that we wished to see the people collected together, mounted one of his horses and spread the information with such speed, that in a very short time, men, women, and children were assembled; on coming to the grounds that they cultivate, we had been forcibly struck by the neatness and luxuriance of their fields, where hardly a weed could be seen; but on sitting with them, we contemplated with much greater admiration what we saw of their Christian deportment and felt of their spirits; there was before us what seemed to be a field that the Lord has blessed, and which He waters from his holy habitation. The Gospel given us to preach among them had free course in their hearts—men, women, and children were broken into tears, and the Baron Baader, whilst interpreting our communications, was greatly affected. It was a most solemn time.

"We were anxious to obtain correct information of the religious and moral condition of the inhabitants of these colonies, especially of those villages where Popery has been renounced, as well as of the others who are evincing their uneasiness under the Popish yoke. Much pains has been taken to misrepresent these people, and the Romish clergy have tried to persuade the Prince O. W. that they were evil disposed towards the Government, or that they have embraced the impious tenets of the St. Simonians; but we are now prepared to give the Prince a full and pleasing account of the state we find them in, and of the fruits of genuine piety that we behold among them.

"We returned to Neuburg late in the evening, and spent a part of that night in preparing our report to the Prince O. W., to be sent by Baron Baader on his return. We request that the King would extend his protection towards the Mennonites, who have a Christian testimony against oaths and war, so that they may be exempted from every requisition that they feel to be contrary to the law and the testimony of Jesus Christ.

"Early in the morning some of the colonists from several villages came to our inn at Neuburg ; some had come that night twelve, others twenty miles to see us ; they were from home when we visited their villages, they wished to be with us a little, and requested that we would give them some books like those we had distributed among the people ; they told us that on their return to their homes, late in the evening, they found every family collected, listening attentively to what one read to the others out of the tracts we had left them, and that parents and children were in tears. One of them, on returning home in the afternoon, met some boys on the road reading a tract with much attention ; he listened for a while, and felt such a strong desire to have one of the tracts that he offered a large price for one, but the children replied that no money could induce them to part with such good books. We were sorry that we had not a single one left to give to these dear people, but we promised to send them some from Stutgard, where we expect to meet with a fresh supply."

Their interesting labours in Bavaria being now nearly concluded, they proceeded to Stutgard, and G. S. remarks :—

"Soon after our arrival at Stutgard, we were visited by many of those pious and very interesting persons, who have been dear to me these many years ; that evening we had a religious meeting at the house of Herring ; three large rooms that open into each other were crowded ; but, above all, the Lord's glorious presence seemed to fill the house ; many of our hearts were brought under an awful sense of the Divine Majesty, and were reverently prostrated before the Lord.

"We find that the people in several parts of this kingdom are becoming dissatisfied with man-made ministers ; the people wish to hear the Gospel through ministers of the Lord's own appointing, and not from those who preach for hire, or who have received their commissions as ministers of the Gospel from man. I am comforted in hearing that Hoffman, and the congregation gathered by him, about six miles from this city, whom I visited when I was last here, maintain their place in the Truth. Their number has enlarged, and another congregation, on similar Christian grounds, has been formed not far from them.

"Tenth Month 10th. We wished to have been with the King, but found that he had left Stutgard this morning, and the time of his return is uncertain. As dear Allen and myself did not think that we should stand acquitted in the Divine sight without endeavouring to be with the Queen previous to our departure from here, I wrote a few lines to her to request an interview. Immediately on the reception of the note she sent us a message, that she would receive us at twelve o'clock. We went to the palace at the time appointed. The Queen was in her drawing-room with her two young princesses only, the eldest ten, and the other eight years old ; she made us take seats near her on the sofa. Our minds were soon brought under a sense of much solemnity and reverence before the Lord. The heart of the Queen was prepared for our visit ; it was tender when we first came in, so that there was no need to utter many words, for her inward ears were open to hear the language of the Spirit ; she loves the Lord Jesus, and she endeavours to instil into the hearts of her young princesses the knowledge of the Saviour, which her worthy mother, the Duchess of Wurtemberg, had succeeded, by the grace of God, to impart to her and her sisters. She told us that her mother had wished that information might be sent to her as soon as we came to Stutgard, for she desired to see us, but she was from home at present. It has been a comfort to us to hear, from other quarters, that the Queen's mother and her two sisters, the wife of the Grand Duke of Baden, and that of the Crown Prince of Austria, maintain Christian humility and watchfulness. It is rare to find the labours of love in a woman of the rank of the Duchess, thus blessed towards three daughters, occupying such high stations in life."

After describing some other interesting labours at Stutgard, the narrative proceeds :—

" Amidst the close engagements that have pressed on my mind for a length of time past, I have felt deeply the prospect of parting with my beloved friend and co-worker in the Gospel of Christ our Redeemer, William Allen ; he has been looking to this place as that where he will feel himself liberated to return to England.

I feel heavily under it; we have been so closely united, and
harmonised in our prospects and services. I feel it the more as I have
weighty religious engagements before me. Spain in particular is
night and day on my mind; and as the time when I may have to
enter that nation is drawing near, the difficulties of proceeding
there are multiplying greatly.

"O Lord! all things to thee are possible. Thou canst make a
way for thy poor servant, where none now appeareth. My life,
there also, thou canst preserve, if it is thy gracious will! My
dear Allen also thou canst direct to return to me, though now we
are going to part. Thy will, O Lord, in all things be done.
Condescend only graciously to continue to fulfil thy blessed word
of promise, 'I will teach thee and instruct thee in the way
in which thou goest, I will guide thee with mine eye.'

"11th. This morning we received a note from the Minister of
State informing us that the King returned last night, and would
see us at about one o'clock. We went accordingly; he received
us in his private apartment, no other person being present, as
had been the case in my former visits to him. He expressed his
satisfaction at seeing us once more in his dominions, and made us
take seats by him; we continued about two hours and a half
together; liberty of conscience, the religious and moral education
of the youth, the treatment of prisoners so as to endeavour to
obtain their reform, were amongst the subjects treated upon.
The nature of the peaceable kingdom of Christ was also fully set
forth, and the King was entreated to endeavour so to act and to
live as to give evidence to his subjects that he acknowledges the
Lord Jesus Christ for his King and his Lord. He was serious
and very tender under what, in the love of the dear Redeemer,
we imparted to him. Our separation was solemn; he said,
'These hours we have now spent together are among the most
precious of my life;' he desired that after my return to America,
I may continue to have him in remembrance, and put up my
prayers for him unto the Lord.

"As we were on our way from the palace to our inn, we were
overtaken by a young woman, a messenger from the Queen, who
handed us a letter from her, by which she bid us once more a
Christian farewell; she had hoped, she said, to have done it in
person, by being present during our visit to the King, but that

he thought it was best that he should be alone with us; the Queen then alluded to the solemn visit that we had paid her,—a solemnity which she continued to feel,—and concluded by desiring that we might continue to have her in our remembrance and prayers, that she may be supported under every trial, and preserved from every temptation.

"That same evening I parted also from dear William Allen; we both felt keenly on the occasion; but could with assurance of faith resign ourselves and one another to the Lord's disposal and almighty keeping. Dear Allen was to set off for Frankfort a few hours after my departure, on his way home."

Though Stephen Grellet had left William Allen at Stutgard, with the "comforting hope" that they would be united again in the "service of their Lord," he deeply felt the separation from his "beloved brother and nearly attached co-worker in the Gospel." As he pursued his lonely journey towards the Rhine, his heart often turned to him in Christian affection—and, on his arrival at Strasburg the next day, he thus writes:—

"TO WILLIAM ALLEN.

"Soon after we parted, the recollection of our reading in the morning was sweet, particularly the latter part of the chapter (Acts. xx.), the parting of Paul with those who came to him from Ephesus. I reflected, with grateful feelings, on the help that the Lord has granted us, and on the sensible guidance of his Spirit, in directing our steps aright during our various journeyings, and also that he had enabled us to close our *united* engagements as we have done, peacefully. I did not doubt, my dear brother, that thou wouldst carry thy sheaves with thee, and, in the retrospect, feel that peace which the Lord alone giveth. 'Thou wilt ordain peace for us, for thou only hast wrought all our works in us.'"

Stephen Grellet arrived at Strasburg on the 12th of Tenth

Month, and was engaged on that day and the next in paying
visits, as he was wont, in the love of the Gospel, to those who
were prepared to receive him as an Ambassador for Christ;
of one of these visits he says :—

"One of the persons I visited is Krafft, a useful and valuable
man, who occupies an important station, the responsibility of
which he feels deeply ; he is here what Tholuck is at Halle, and
Hahn at Leipzic. Infidelity greatly prevails here, and Krafft
feels it laid upon him to endeavour to counteract it, as through
the grace of God, he is enabled to do. He has great place among
the young people. In the evening I had a religious meeting. It
was held at the house of Gaspard Wegelin. The notice was spread
chiefly among the pious part of the community ; the Lord owned
us very graciously ; my soul is often very sorrowful, but at seasons I am enabled gratefully to rejoice in the Lord, in meeting
with a seed, here and there, which He has planted, and which,
through his assisting grace, and by living faith in Him, brings
forth fruit to his praise. We were comforted and edified
together.

"I left Strasburg before daylight on the 14th, for the Ban de
la Roche, the former residence of Oberlin, that humble but great
man, and useful servant of the Lord, whose works continue to
proclaim his love to God and man. I came thirty-four miles to
Fondai, where resides Le Grand, the particular friend of the late
Oberlin ; he is solicitous that the useful institutions formed by
him should be conducted on the plan he designed. Le Grand has
two sons, who with their wives and families reside on the same
premises with him ; they carry on an extensive manufactory of a
variety of tapes ; it was one of the plans of Oberlin to procure
employment and the means of an honest livelihood to the numerous inhabitants of a poor and stony land. Immediately after my
arrival Le Grand very kindly sent messengers to the several
villages on these mountains, with the information of my intention to have a religious meeting with them that afternoon to be
held in the central village where Oberlin used to reside ; his
house there is at present occupied by his son-in-law, who has
succeeded him as pastor. Accompanied by Le Grand I went
there, and was much pleased on meeting with faithful Louisa, who

was the right hand of Oberlin in promoting the religious, moral, and literary education of the inhabitants of those mountains. She is now aged, but still active ; every week she takes her walks round the villages, visits the schools, the sick and the afflicted, imparts religious instruction to the young people, and performs her labours of love. She has trained several mistresses who are engaged in the schools ; she introduced me to some of these, whom she calls her fourth generation. Oberlin's daughter is a pious woman. Before the hour at which the meeting was appointed, the people were seen running down the rocky mountains and collecting in great numbers ; it reminded me of what I saw several times when on the island of Hayti ; they came from four to eight miles, though the notice was so short. The meeting was held in their place of worship ; the word of instruction, comfort, and encouragement was given me to preach among them ; but I had also a solemn warning to proclaim to some, accompanied with earnest entreaties to turn away from their rash and evil purposes, and after the example of the prodigal son, to return to their Heavenly Father. I was astonished at myself, to have this kind of labour among such a people ; but I was told afterwards that a son of the late worthy Oberlin was in the practice of frequenting unprofitable company ; he had concluded to go that very night to Strasburg to enlist as a soldier ; hearing of the meeting, curiosity brought him there ; the word preached sank deep into his heart ; the Spirit of Truth, the faithful witness, performed his office in him ; his purposes were changed, and he spent the night in retirement and prostration of soul before God ; so that it might be said of him as of Saul, after the Lord had appeared to him in the way, 'Behold he prayeth.'

"16th. I returned in good time to attend a meeting I had appointed to be held last evening at Strasburg, in the house of Krafft. It was another solemn season when, by one Spirit, we were baptised together into the one body, and drank into one Spirit."

At Strasburg S. G. became acquainted with some Jews who had come to the knowledge of the truth as it is in Jesus, of whom he says :—

" Some of them appear to have clear views of spiritual worship ; of the Christian baptism, by the washing of regeneration and the renewing of the Holy Ghost ; and of the real Christian communion, which is a participation of the Bread of Life, Christ Jesus, who is our passover. They seem to understand how all the various services in the outward Temple pointed to that most solemn service now in the temple of the heart, where spiritual sacrifices are to be offered up, acceptable to God, by Jesus Christ, the High Priest of our profession. Their various ablutions for the purifying from outward defilements, they see, point to the sprinkling of the blood of Christ, who has loved us and washed us from our sins in his own blood. I endeavoured to encourage them in coming to God through Christ with full purpose of heart ; being of the true circumcision, who worship God in the Spirit and rejoice in Christ Jesus, having no confidence in the flesh.

" I left Strasburg on the evening of the 17th, and arrived at Basle the next day. Way opened for my having several meetings in that place ; two at the Mission House ; the last was attended by a large number of the pious inhabitants. Two others were held at Miriam Stackelberg's. She is a pious, rich widow, who endeavours to honour the Lord with her substance. She has an infant school for fifty children, and two others for boys and girls.

" 21st. Accompanied by Spittler, and a son of Le Grand, from Foudai, Ban de la Roche, we went ten miles up the Rhine to Beuggen, to visit an interesting establishment for eighty poor orphans of both sexes, and for twenty-four young men who are educated as schoolmasters for institutions in which the pupils support themselves by manual labour of various kinds. Zeller and his wife, who are the superintendents of it, are persons of rare piety ; it is from an apprehension of religious duty that they occupy these stations ; Christian love and kindness are very conspicuously prevailing in their hearts ; by these they govern. The same love seems to flow back from the young people towards them. I had in the forenoon a satisfactory meeting in the establishment, attended also by the people of the country near ; early in the afternoon, I had another meeting with the inmates of the institution much more select. I could but compare this house to that of Obededom, on which the Lord's blessing rested. The wife of Zeller devoted herself in very early life to the Lord, and to this day she appears to be faithful in endeavouring to perform her solemn vow. When about five years old, she was playing on some of the rocky hills of the country; one of their large eagles saw her, and darted down upon her head; a man with a gun, not far distant, watched the motions of the eagle, but did not see the child; he fired, and killed the bird, at the very moment of his darting upon the child's head; great was his surprise, on coming to the spot, to find the dead eagle by the side of the child. The deep wounds made by his talons on her head show what a narrow escape she had from the voracious bird, and from being wounded or killed by the gun. This dear woman considers that her life, thus spared, is to be wholly devoted to the service of God.*

"Zurich, Tenth Month 23rd. I left Basle early this morning, and arrived here this afternoon. I greatly enjoyed the ride. I was alone in the carriage most of the way. Beautiful and grand was the scenery before me; it loudly proclaimed the Lord's power and wondrous works.

"24th. Antistes Gessner, hearing that I had arrived, early came to see me. I went back to his house,—the same which was occupied by the aged Antistes Hess, his predecessor, and where, some years since, I had solemn meetings. The dear old

---

* "The venerable Zeller died on the 18th of May, 1860, in the eighty-first year of his age. After having studied at Jena, his inclination led him to become a tutor, and he soon received an influential appointment in the Canton of Aargau. Here, through intercourse with a Christian man, he learned to love Christ with all his heart, and love to the Lord constrained him to give up his situation. Aided by Christian friends in Basle, in spite of much derision excited by what was deemed his fanatical undertaking, he went to Beuggen, and founded a Christian seminary. His simple faith, his earnest confidence, his fresh, child-like manners, gave to the Institution a healthy, Christian stamp, so that it was visited from the different countries of Europe as a pattern Institution. Nearly two hundred and fifty schoolmasters here received an education during Zeller's forty years' labours, who have shed the Christian spirit with which they were filled at Beuggen over many thousands of poor children. It is related that even Pestalozzi, far away as he stood from true Christianity, on visiting Beuggen was so overpowered by the spirit which there breathed around him, as frequently to exclaim, 'Enormous power! enormous power!' The establishment is now conducted in the same spirit by two sons and a daughter of Zeller."—C. R. A.

man departed this life full of the love of God, and peace and joy
in the Holy Ghost."

He now went forward, visiting his former friends at each
place : to St. Gallen and Berne ; to M. A. Calame's at Locle,
and thence by Yverdun and Lausanne to Geneva.

In many places he was comforted in finding seals to his
Gospel labours on former visits. The following is an instance
noticed at Berne :—

" I was recognised by a person as I passed her in the street ;
she saw me when I was here before, and was at a meeting ; she
says it was the first time.in her life that she had been in a Christian assembly ; she was greatly astonished at my communication,
for it seemed to her as if I was singling her out of the company
and exposing her conduct, even her secret thoughts, before them
all, and yet she knew that I could not have any knowledge
of her, nor could anybody have informed me of what none knew
but herself ; but she has since found that there is One who
knoweth the secret of our hearts ; now she knows and loves God,
and is willing that He should try her, prove her, and show her her
thoughts."

" Locle, 2nd. Locle stands nearly on the top of the Jura, yet
it is in a hollow, and is thereby protected from the bleak winds ;
it is said that there was formerly a large lake in this hollow,
whence this small town derives its name. The land about it is
well cultivated ; many cattle and sheep are fed on it, and excellent butter and cheese are made. Mary Anne Calame, well
known for her great benevolence, resides in this place, together
with Catherine Zimmerling, her intimate friend ; who, during
eighteen years, has shared actively in her works of benevolence
and charity.

" The establishment of M. A. Calame is about a mile and a
half from the town. I went there with her in the afternoon. It
was very touching to me, as we entered on the premises, to see
the young people we met, saluting her with filial respect and
affection, by the name of ' Ma chère mère '—' my dear mother,'
—and she calls them 'my children,'—and she acts truly towards
them the part of a mother ; her time and property are devoted to

them ; but her necessities in the maintenance of so large a family, and the erection of the needful buildings, which she has yearly to enlarge, are such that she has to be dependent on public benevolence ; in this she has never been disappointed, though she has been repeatedly reduced to the last extremity, not having even the ' handful' of meal left in her stores ; but the Lord, the Father of the orphans, in whom is her confidence, has never forsaken her ; many and very interesting are the circumstances under which her great wants have been supplied. In a number of instances she has not known by what human hand help was extended, but she had the conviction that the Lord had done it. The dear woman who knows that there is no limit to Omnipotence, also feels that there is none to her benevolence ; thus she considers not her want of means, but the needs of the poor orphans, whom she cannot refuse to admit to her asylum, whenever they are brought to her. She first introduced me to the youngest children, from two to six years old ;—they were all sitting on low benches, at their various employments ; knitting, sewing, or having their books ; and the very little ones were unravelling pieces of old silk, which, in another part of the house, is carded and spun. Perfect stillness prevailed ; if they had anything to say to a motherly woman who sat facing them, it was in a whisper ; except that when we entered the apartment they all rose, apparently delighted to see Mary Anne. They saluted her, ' Ma chère mère,' and such as were near tried to kiss her hand ; but they soon resumed their seats and occupations. Mary Anne went among them giving them a few sugar-plums. Their mistress strongly attracted my attention. She was herself knitting ; and conveyed instruction to the children with much kindness and affection, on such a variety of subjects, that I could hardly credit that I was among such a class of children, and so young. The greater was my astonishment when I found that this young woman was blind. Some of the teaching was on this wise : ' Children, you have heard of the birth of the Lord Jesus Christ, our Saviour ; can you, Mary, tell me where He was born ? And you, Sarah, do you know what kind of people came there to see Him ?'. Of another she inquired how they knew that He was to be found there ? After a number of questions connected with the Scripture narrative, to which the children answered very correctly,

she said to another, 'Can you tell me some particular circumstance
that occurred at the time of the birth of our Saviour?' Several
of the children said, 'There was then peace on all the earth
and the temple of Janus was shut.' Then again she said, 'And
where was the temple of Janus?' 'At Rome,' was the answer.
She pursued, 'But where is Rome?' &c. &c. Thus the blind
woman, whilst going on with her knitting, conversed with the
children, on the Scriptures, history, geography, &c.; and they
answered her questions without raising their eyes from their work.
I had a meeting with the children and their teachers, and other
members of the household. It was a solemn and tendering season.
In the evening I had a meeting in the town, which was also
attended by M. A. Calame and her family; it was a good meeting, for the Lord was with us."

"Geneva, 8th. I arrived here last evening. This day has been
closely taken up in visiting a number of pious families. My soul
is made glad in the Lord on finding that, though some of them
have been sorely chastened under the rod of affliction, both of an
outward and spiritual nature, they have not been forsaken under
their sore trials. The Lord has been with them. I have sweetly
mingled again with Moulinier, who seems to be fast ripening for a
better habitation, even a heavenly; his colleague, pastor Demalleyer, also; they, together with Galland, maintain with firmness
their Christian ground against the strong body of Socinians here
on the one hand, and the Calvinists on the other. The sisters of
Galland, Mary Ann Vernet, and others, continue in Christian
meekness; they seek their supplies from Christ, the pure and
everlasting spring."

After alluding to many visits to former friends, he concludes:—

"May the Lord himself feed this little flock of his pasture,
guide them by his Spirit, and finally receive them to glory!"

STEPHEN GRELLET had now taken his final leave of Switzerland. His heart had often turned with much Christian love towards the Protestant inhabitants of the valleys of Piedmont, who have so long attracted the notice, and called forth the benevolent exertions of their fellow Christians of other nations: and to that interesting people he now turned his steps.

On leaving Geneva, he took the direct course to Turin, where he arrived, after a perilous journey on account of the deep snow, on the 18th of Eleventh Month. We make the following extracts from his narrative :—

" 20th. Latour, in the valley of Lucerne. Here is the largest congregation of the Waldenses, composed of about two thousand adults; their whole number in eleven towns, villages, and hamlets, scattered in these valleys, is about twenty-two thousand persons : they have about four thousand five hundred children at their several schools ; but most of these schools are held only in winter.

" I went to most of their villages, and visited their schools : at Bobi I was pleased with one for girls ; it is conducted by a pious widow. Most of their pastors also appear to be conscientiously concerned for the spiritual welfare of their flocks. A few years ago some clergymen from Geneva came among these poor, simple-hearted people ; and, under the disguise of Christian kindness, brought in among them Socinian doctrines. It took some root among individuals, and in one of their pastors. By strict attention, and the Lord's blessing especially, they hope that it is now pretty much extirpated. It has, however, rendered them very watchful over the visitors who come among them, that the moral and sound Christian views of a people descended from ancestors who have deeply suffered for the testimony of Jesus may not be corrupted.

"These visits were fatiguing, for I had to perform the journeys mostly on foot; the snow was deep; and the rough paths on the high ground being covered with ice, rendered walking laborious. This was particularly the case in going up the mountain to Angrogne. It is in that valley, and on that mountain, that many battles were fought during the wars of extermination, waged against the Waldenses at the instigation of the Papists, whose armies were accompanied by the inquisitors. Many of those poor, unoffending people, who escaped the edge of the sword, were burned by the Inquisition; their great crime was their religious and conscientious scruples which prevented their bowing down to and worshipping images made of wood, stone, silver, or brass, &c.; and their placing their only hope of salvation in the mercy of God through our Lord and Saviour Jesus Christ, and not in the indulgences sold by the Popish priests, or the absolutions pronounced by them."

At Turin S. G. writes :—

"Turin, 25th. I returned here last evening late. Before my departure from La Tour I visited their hospital. It was founded but lately, and much aided by the Emperor Alexander. The circumstance, which I had heard only in part before, is now related to me by a valuable young man, the son of John Paul Vertu, a banker in this city. My dear friend, William Allen, was at Verona, about ten years since, at the time of the congress of the sovereigns of Europe. Being then with the Emperor Alexander, their conversation turned on the subject of the oppression and persecution exercised at that time against the Waldenses, by the then reigning King and the Popish priests. Allen requested the Emperor to use his influence with the King of Sardinia, in favour of that portion of his subjects; and the Emperor desired him, on his return to England, to visit these Waldenses, and to send him a statement of the circumstances under which he found them. William Allen did so; he found them in a suffering condition. Much distress and poverty prevailed among them; their sick and

aged felt it very heavily. The Russian Consul here at Turin, not
having occasion then to send a messenger to the Emperor, said he
would constitute as such, any one whom Allen would recommend.
This young man, my informant, very kindly offered himself to be
the bearer of these despatches. That he might have immediate
access to the Emperor, Allen gave him a letter to Baron Wylie,
his physician, who also was a particular friend of ours when we
were in Russia. It was late when the young man arrived at
Verona. Wylie had been introduced into the apartments of the
Emperor. On reading the despatches, Alexander was much
affected ; he was left alone. Wylie, as usual, came in to pay his
visit as physician ; he was surprised to see the Emperor leaning
his head on his hand near the table, and in tears. 'What has
happened,' said Wylie, full of emotion, 'that you are under
so much affliction ?' On which Alexander handed him Allen's
letter, and said, 'Read this, and see if I have not reason to
be afflicted !' The very next morning he endowed this hospital
for ever ; made some other benevolent provisions in favour of the
Waldenses, and took immediate measures to try to induce the
King of Sardinia to repeal his severe laws against them. It is in
consequence of his interference that the present King has become
better acquainted with this people, their peaceable spirit, and
their industrious habits ; and that he treats them greater mildness
than was the case under the administration of his predecessors.
Baron Wylie has continued to correspond with my friend William
Allen ; through him we had repeated messages from the Emperor Alexander, whose kind remembrance of us, after we left
Russia, continued to the close of his life ; shortly before his death,
he commissioned Wylie to let us know that his warm Christian
love flowed towards us. Various reports have been circulated
respecting the cause and manner of his death, but the account
sent by the Baron shortly after his decease is one that may
be depended upon, coming from an eminent physician, who for
years had been the constant attendant of the Emperor, and who
was much attached to him ; he says that the fever with which the
Emperor was attacked came upon him whilst he was travelling in
the low, unhealthy parts of the Crimea, near the Black Sea.
During his illness, his mind continued to rest on the Lord Jesus
as his only hope ; his delight was to have the Scriptures read to

him ; he also wished frequently to be left alone ; there is every
reason to believe, for the purpose of prayer and spiritual communion with God.

"Finding that the schools among the Waldenses are very destitute of books, I have made provision for some to be sent to them ;
among others, the *Scripture Lessons* in French, and a quantity of
Bibles and Testaments. Here I had two meetings—one of them
attended by several of those Roman Catholics that I was with on
my former visit ; but I do not find that they have made much
advance in vital religion, the way to the kingdom is too narrow
for them."

Returning from the valleys of Piedmont, Stephen Grellet
went to revisit the scenes of his early college life; to mingle
once more with the little company of those who profess with
Friends in the South of France; and to pay a last farewell
visit to his beloved mother and near connections in the
different places of their abode, on his way to the borders of
Spain.

In continuation of his diary he writes :—

"Lyons, Eleventh Month 30th. I arrived here late last night,
by the way of Susa, Mount Cenis, and Chambery. We travelled
night and day. The drifts and depth of snow on the mountains
rendered our journey perilous. I have been to-day with several
pious persons."

And he adds :—

"My mind is introduced into much seriousness by visiting this
place. Here I received part of my education at the college of the
Oratorians. Here, also, the Lord graciously extended very peculiar visitations of his love to my benighted soul. It was, indeed,
as a light shining in a dark place, to which I have frequently
returned with reverent gratitude and wonder at the gracious condescension."

It is very interesting to find the estimate of Christian

character which Stephen Grellet often formed by the early indications which he saw. All will be struck with the following remarks :—

"Twelfth Month 1st. I was this morning with Monod, son of the worthy man of the same name at Paris. This young man was the pastor of one of the Protestant churches here, but his spiritual views of religion, worship, ministry, &c., have induced him to withdraw from that office ; he holds meetings, however, which are attended by many of the most pious among the Protestants, and also the Roman Catholics. His exemplary life and the purity of the doctrine he preaches, which has for its object to bring men to Christ through the obedience of faith and the teachings of his Divine Spirit, induce many to gather about him. He has been a remarkable instrument in bringing the inhabitants of several villages hereabout to see the errors of Popery so as to desert their priests. When he cannot be with them, they meet together to read the Scriptures. This young man is very zealous and mighty in the Scriptures. He reminds me of what he said of Apollos. What endears him particularly to me is that he appears to have a heart open to become more perfectly instructed in the way of the Lord.

"2nd. I had a satisfactory, small meeting at Doctor Gillibert's, with a few other seeking persons. His wife appears to be a sincere inquirer after the Truth. I had another meeting at Adolphe Monod's, which was attended both by pious Protestants and Roman Catholics, who desire to come to the Shepherd and Bishop of souls, the Lord Jesus Christ."

From Lyons he passed on to Nismes, and, having visited a few persons there, he proceeded at once to mingle, for the last time, with the little company of Friends in those parts.

"Congenies, 6th. I came here last evening, and was very kindly received by my valued friends, Louis Majolier and family ; this is the fourth time, in the course of twenty-eight years, that I make a religious visit to the little flock in these parts, who are called by the name of Friends."

At this place, and in the different villages where Friends reside, S. G. had meetings, and visited Friends in their families.

The last meetings he held was at St. Gilles.   At this place he
writes :—

"St. Gilles, 25th.   I arrived here yesterday afternoon, in time
to visit four families of Friends, and to-day I had two meetings.

"The meeting I had in the forenoon was held in the Friends'
meeting-house. It was attended by those who go under our name,
both here and in the neighbourhood. I have some hope of them,
here also, that they may henceforth walk with greater circumspec-
tion and watchfulness.

"The meeting in the Temple in the afternoon was very large ;
it was a mixed company. I thought there were pious persons
present, to whom the word of comfort and encouragement was
preached ; but there were others with whom I did earnestly plead
of righteousness, temperance, and judgment to come. Whilst I
was proceeding, my own heart being much affected with the awfulness of it, I stated how solemn it was thus to join in company with
those who are met together to worship God, and publicly to acknowledge and bow down in spirit before Christ Jesus, the Saviour of
sinners ; who came into the world for this very purpose, that He
might save us from our sins ; but that possibly whilst some keep
this day as a memorial of the coming in the flesh of the Eternal
Son of God to be unto us a Saviour and Redeemer, they have,
perhaps, concluded on and made preparations to spend this very
evening and night in a riotous and sinful manner. As I was uttering this, a man fell down from his seat on the floor ; there was
some bustle for a short time ; they carried him out, and I continued
to speak, a considerable increase of solemnity appearing over the
meeting. After the conclusion, I heard the people say to one
another, 'He is dead, he is dead.' I was then told that this very
man had made extensive preparation for a sumptuous banquet
that night, when a variety of diversions were to be introduced ;
that, on coming, he had boasted how he would honour the Lord
and sanctify this day, by going to a place of worship first, and then
close it in feasting and revelling. Some persons, hearing him
speak so, had reproved him for it, which he answered by impious
expressions. The people appeared struck with astonishment at
the awfulness of the event. I received a deputation from the
inhabitants in the evening, requesting that I would have another

meeting with them, but I did not feel it my place to do so. To
the Lord and his Spirit I leave and commit them.

"28th. Early this morning several pious persons came to my
inn to bid me farewell in the Lord ; we sat down together, and
were comforted in his presence. He condescended to bless and
break a little bread among us, and to hand us a cup of consolation."

After this parting opportunity Stephen Grellet set off for
Montpellier, and arrived the same evening. Hence, proceeding to Toulouse, he writes : —

"Toulouse, First Month 2nd, 1833. On presenting myself at
the Police office the day before yesterday with my passport, I
found among the chief magistrates present a good deal of seriousness, and a desire to obtain information on Friends' Christian
principles and peaceable testimonies. The subject of war is one
of peculiar inquiry and interest to some of them. Very nearly
connected with this is faith in God, and in our Lord Jesus Christ,
the Prince of Peace. If we believe truly in Him, we must necessarily keep his commandments. This is his commandment, that
we love one another as He has loved us. How can then the
servants of the Lord Jesus Christ fight ? Their weapons are not
carnal, but spiritual ; their sword is that of the Spirit ; their
whole armour is that of Light. Many will assent to these Gospel
truths, but the obedience of faith is lacking in them. In the
evening I had a satisfactory meeting, attended mostly by Protestants, and a few serious Roman Catholics.

" Chabrand, the Protestant minister, long known to me, continues to be a useful man. He is spiritually-minded, and his ministry has the tendency to draw the attention of his hearers to the
influences of the Divine Spirit on their own hearts. The brothers
Courtois, also, continue firm in their love to the Truth, and are
indefatigable in their labours to spread the Scriptures and religious
tracts among the Roman Catholics in many parts of France, and
Spain also. They have many colporteurs employed in that work."

A wintry journey of two nights and one day brought him
once more to Brives, where he writes : —

"5th. I find my beloved mother in a very tender state of mind, green in old age. Her heart seems to be full of love to the dear Saviour. She appears weaned from a dependence on the priests, or outward observances. Her heart is fixed, trusting in the Lord alone. It is rare to meet with any one at her advanced age who retains such bright mental faculties."

S. Grellet again visited many whom he had seen before; he particularly mentions the nuns of the hospital, "who," he says, "received me with Christian affection"—now, the fourth time of his revisiting the scenes of his childhood. Bidding a final farewell to these parts, he now turned his steps towards Spain. His narrative continues:—

"Bordeaux, First Month 24th. I arrived here yesterday; my mind is under such weight of exercise for Spain, that I have no qualification to enter on any religious engagement in this place."

He was, however, cheered the next day, and says:—

"Bayonne, 25th. Here I am on the frontiers of Spain; I received, this day, a letter from my dear friend, William Allen, stating that he feels himself so forcibly brought under the weight of religious concern to join in my Gospel engagements in that nation, that he expected to be able to leave London to-morrow, the 26th, and to join me here. How great is the Lord's goodness! I arrive here surrounded with difficulties and discouragements, and He opens a bright path before me.

"Second Month 3rd. I have met here several serious persons, Protestants and Catholics, some of whom are Spaniards, with whom I have religious opportunities. Some of them are of a seeking mind. One of these is the *Sous Préfet*, a man of a liberal and benevolent spirit. I felt much distressed when I came here, on beholding the multitude of beggars in the streets. They are unwilling to do any work at all, whilst they can obtain a precarious and scanty living by begging. I noticed that benevolent men or women sat at their doors with bags of copper money, and gave to the beggars as they came to them, as long as their bags held out. By this mistaken benevolence in almsgiving, the sys-

tem of begging is encouraged. I thought that this could be
remedied, if the alms given by the citizens were properly administered, by which means a better provision could be made
for the sick and aged. I formed my plan accordingly, and submitted it to the *Sous Préfet*, who was so much pleased with it,
that the chief magistrates in the town were called together ; and
with their approbation, it was concluded to call a meeting of the
benevolent citizens; for nothing can be done availingly without
their co-operation.

" 6th. Dear Allen met me the 3rd instant, in the evening ;
he has been almost constantly on the road since he left London
the 26th of last month. We have met in the fulness of Gospel
love ; we rejoice together in the Lord, and we are also permitted
to hope that through his assistance we may endure, with Christian patience and resignation, whatever suffering may be permitted
to come upon us in Spain. Dear Allen enters cordially into the
plans formed to endeavour to alleviate the misery of many of the
people here, and to put them in a way to support themselves by
their industry and not by begging. The principal citizens met
last evening, also the public authorities; the plan formed was
approved by them ; the mayor and others were appointed a committee to see that it be carried into execution, and, as soon as they
are prepared for it, begging will be prohibited, work given to
those destitute of it, and the wants of the sick and the aged liberally
provided for. This conclusion being now formed is a great relief
to my mind."

CHAPTER XXXII.

Fourth Visit to Europe.

SPAIN—MADRID.

STEPHEN GRELLET now entered upon an entirely new field of labour. In company, once more, with his faithful friend, William Allen, he had crossed over into Spain at a time peculiarly favourable to the accomplishment of his mission.

The attempts of Don Carlos, at the head of a powerful and bigoted party, publicly to assert his claims to the succession against the right of the young Infanta, had been defeated by the King's unexpected recovery from a serious attack of illness, after he had been announced as already dead, and his body had been exposed in one of the halls of the palace. Queen Christina had regained her ascendancy over the mind of her husband; Ferdinand had dismissed Calomarde, and called Zea Bermudez to the ministry; a short calm had succeeded a time of great political excitement, and some good measures had been determined on and were in progress of being carried into execution, when S. G. and W. A. entered the Spanish dominions.

They arrived at Irun, the first town in Spain, on the 11th of Second Month, 1833, but were obliged to perform another quarantine, from which they were released on the 16th and proceeded to Madrid, where they arrived on the 20th of Second Month, 1833.

"22nd. Since our arrival at Madrid we have been in company with a few well-disposed persons, through whom we may expect to become acquainted with others. We were to-day with Cambrone, a Jurisconsult of eminence, and a conscientious man. He is strongly opposed to slavery. He and his particular friend, Solon, another eminent lawyer with whom I became acquainted

at Toulouse, are now preparing works against slavery, both under
this government and that of France.   They have also in view to
publish periodicals to spread light and interest among the people
on this subject.   These two men are not merely philanthropists,
but Christian believers also.

" Through the medium of Sir Henry Addington, the British
Ambassador, we receive information that the Count D'Ofalia, the
Minister of the Interior, has heard of our arrival, and wishes to
see us this evening.

" 23rd. According to appointment we were last evening with
Count D'Ofalia ; he was some years since Ambassador to the
United States, when he obtained a considerable knowledge of the
Christian principles and testimonies of our religious Society.   He
received us with courtesy, and kindly inquired in what he could
serve us in promoting the object of our coming here.   We had
previously felt our minds drawn to visit some of their prisons,
hospitals, &c.

" We next went to Vanness, our American Ambassador here.
I knew a brother of his in America.   His wife is a pious woman ;
before her marriage she resided in New York for a few years, and
knew some of our Friends ; we had a satisfactory opportunity
with her and her family.   It was concluded to hold a meeting for
divine worship at their house next First-day morning.   We next
went to Sir Stratford Canning's, who is Ambassador Extraordinary
here, besides Sir Henry Addington, the regular one.   Allen had
letters for him from London, and it appears that he had received
some others recommending us to him ; both he and his lady are
serious persons ; our intercourse with them was to edification,
and we had with them and their family a refreshing religious
opportunity in the evening.

" 24th.   This morning at eleven o'clock we went, as appointed,
to the Count D'Ofalia's ; he manifested great freedom in conversing with us on subjects of benevolence and piety, on the distribution of the Scriptures, and the state of religion in Spain,
which he acknowledges to be very low ; he told us that he was
yesterday with the King, and spoke of us to him ; he informed
him also of our intention to visit their prisons and other institutions ; the King directed that an order for our admittance to
any place we may wish to visit should be made out in his own

name ; he also requested that we would furnish him with any remarks we may make in these visits. How remarkable that the Lord should thus set an open door before us, in places where, but a very little while ago, anarchy prevailed, streams of blood flowed, and the prisons were crowded with innocent victims."

The 25th, 26th and 27th they were engaged in visiting several prisons, and also the Foundling Hospital, of which S. G. says, " I have not seen any of the sort kept more clean; the mortality is, nevertheless, great ; during the first seven years it amounts to seventy-eight per cent." They also visited a nunnery : in his description of this visit, S. G. says :—

" On entering the chapel, some of the nuns, dipping the finger in a basin containing their ' blessed water,' handed it to us to make the sign of the cross as they did. I succeeded in making them understand, quicker than I expected, our reasons for not conforming to such a practice ; but, when we passed close before the altar, they all knelt down, and those by me urged me to do the same, saying, ' the holy sacrament (*i. e.* the consecrated wafer) is now exposed.' I could then only say, ' By and by I will tell you why we cannot do this.' And though our going in and out of the wards brought us repeatedly through the chapel, they did not ask us again to bow down to the altar, and they finally omitted to do it themselves ; neither did they take notice that we kept our hats on. Our visit to these being accomplished, I said to the nuns, ' Now I will explain to you what are our reasons for not using your *blessed water*, as you call it, or bowing before your altar ;' upon which the Superior brought us to her apartments, where, with most of the nuns, we sat down. They very quickly understood that the sign of the cross, as it is called, cannot be the real cross, or that cross that a man must bear if he will be a disciple of the Lord Jesus Christ. The Superior said, ' My dear father used to speak exactly so.' Then respecting the chapel, the altar, the burning of tapers upon it, the consecrated wafer to which they bowed and worshipped, I opened to them those various subjects according to the Scriptures ; a wide door was also open to preach to them the Lord Jesus Christ ;—the nature

of the offering that He has made of himself once for all, for the
sins of the world ;—that the temple in which He is to be received
by faith, is that of the heart, where He is to be found ever present,
and to be worshipped in spirit and in truth ;—there also it is that
the true light, Christ the Light of life, is to shine with brightness.
Dear Allen spoke excellently on some of these subjects. The
nuns seemed to feel deeply, and several times the Superior said
again, 'My dear father, my pious father, used to speak to us
exactly so.' We parted from them in Christian love, and they
evinced much tenderness."

Several days were now spent in obtaining interviews with
persons of rank, and in visiting the large prisons and other
institutions. S. G. remarks :—

"We stopped at Colonel Downie's, who had come to our
lodgings to see us. We had given him a Bible, which we found
him engaged in reading. He told us, that on coming once into
his chamber, he found one of his Spanish servants reading the
Bible : he was greatly affected, and said, 'Our priests never let
us know the contents of this good book, and no wonder, for it
proclaims all their doings in their churches to be nothing but
idolatry : I would give,' he said, 'all I possess in the world to
obtain such a treasure as this Bible.' We presented him with
one.

"We dined at Count de Teba's, with a pretty large company of
Spaniards of rank. These are trying occasions to me — very
humiliating ; but they are seasons when the Lord gives opportunity to exalt his blessed Truth, and the testimonies thereof.
I dare not flinch from such exposures ; for this very purpose He
has sent me here, to exalt his great name. We had a full opportunity to proclaim the Truth among that assembly, and to direct
them to Christ and to his Spirit.

"7th of Third Month. We were occupied great part of the
last two days in preparing a report to be laid before the King, of
our visits to the prisons and other institutions—the state in which
we find them, the abuses which exist, the causes which lead to
the commission of many crimes, and the remedy which we submit
for consideration. The whole is sent to the care of Count D'Ofalia.

The Count sent us a message this evening, requesting us to call upon him ; he told us that he was with the King last evening, and read to him our report.   The King was anxious to have early attention paid to the improvements suggested, in order to diminish the mass of misery and evil prevailing in the land.   He knew that we were preparing for our departure from Madrid, and proposed very soon to see us.

" 10th.   Early this morning we had a note from D'Ofalia, requesting us to call upon him at eleven a.m., stating that the King would see us at five p.m., at his palace.   D'Ofalia received us with his usual kindness, and said that the King had told him again that he much approved of our remarks in the report, and had ordered that we should be furnished with letters to the Governors of the Provinces where we may travel, and to the public authorities, directing them to treat us with all civility, and to let us have free access to every place that we may wish to visit. These letters, signed by the King himself, were handed to us.   He told us also that orders had been given at the palace to receive us with the quietness and simplicity that he knew we wished ; that the Duke of Aragon, Captain of the King's Guards, would be in readiness to introduce us ; but he advised us, as a matter of civility, to be with the Duke a short time before we went to the King.

" The hour now had nearly arrived for us to repair to a meeting for divine worship that had been appointed at the American Ambassador's : it was attended by many persons.   The Lord very graciously gave us access to his holy presence, and enabled us reverently to worship at his footstool.   The meeting continued a long time in solemn silence, when, on bended knees, prayer and supplication, thanksgiving and praise were offered unto Him.

" We went to the palace about the time appointed ; the Duke of Aragon received us with much civility ; they had even removed the military that almost always stand about the palace.   The Duke brought us up the great staircase ; we first came into the apartment occupied by the King's officers and guards, who at once introduced us into another spacious hall, where the King's immediate attendants were in waiting.   The Chamberlain soon brought us into what appeared to be the court-room ; we saw nobody at first, but very soon two persons came towards us, holding a little girl by the hands between them.   We did not think they were the King and Queen, till I observed her features, which reminded me of a portrait I had seen of her, and I queried, 'Is it the Queen before whom we stand?' 'Yes,' she replied, 'and this is the King, and here is our young Princess,* our eldest, two and a half years old.' We soon explained the reason of our embarrassment, for we did not expect that the King was well enough to be out of his chamber, and feared that his standing would be too great an exertion for him; but they declined sitting down. After some remarks respecting our visits to their public institutions, and answering their inquiries on several subjects relating thereto, in which the Queen took part with interest, I noticed that the young Princess looked at us with great earnestness, which the Queen also observing, I said that it was probably the first time that she had seen two persons like us, stand with their heads covered before the King and Queen. This led to subjects of a religious nature, and an inquiry into some of our Christian testimonies and practices; then, under a sense of the Lord's power and love, I uncovered my head and proclaimed to them, as the Lord through his Spirit gave me the word of reconciliation and of life and salvation through faith in Christ. I felt much for the King under the severe trials that have attended him, and the remarkable manner in which his life was preserved, when in a state of stupor, the prevailing party urged the physician to have a *post-mortem* examination made, though he protested that he was not dead. I alluded to Nebuchadnezzar, and remarked that the King, like him, had been driven out of his kingdom, had endured many afflictions: but now the Lord had restored his kingdom, and instructed him to know that it is by Him that kings reign. The King queried, 'Who is this King Nebuchadnezzar?' The Queen at once explained to him in what part of the Scriptures he would find it. I then expressed my earnest desire that, like him, he may honour the Most High, by breaking off his sins by righteousness, and his iniquities by showing mercy to the poor.

"We also entreated the King to mark the last years of his reign by acts of clemency and piety, and the noble deed of giving to his subjects full liberty of conscience. Both the King and the Queen

---

* The late Queen of Spain, Isabella II.

were serious, and, on parting, gave evidence of kind feelings towards us.

"From the palace we went to dine at Sir Stratford Canning's; several persons came in afterwards with whom we had a time of religious edification."

They left Madrid early in the morning of the 12th of Third Month. On reaching Valencia Stephen Grellet continues his journal :—

"Valencia, Third Month 15th. We arrived here about noon this day. We were favoured to escape falling into the hands of banditti, who are numerous on that road. Only lately they attacked the diligence, which they robbed of a considerable sum of money. As we passed through the towns on our way here, we were much surprised to see the streets full of people looking at us. At the public-houses also where we stopped to take refreshment, many of the better sort of inhabitants came into the room we were in, and manifested a desire to obtain information respecting our Christian principles. We could not understand the meaning of all this; we had never observed such curiosity anywhere else. A Frenchman, who was a fellow-traveller part of our journey, though not in the same division of the carriage, came in a very civil manner to our apartment and requested more information respecting our religious Society. He said that on the road he had endeavoured to give to the people the little information he had, and many now come to him with inquiries that he is not able to answer. We asked him how the people knew anything about us. ' Have you not read the newspapers ?' he replied, and handed us one containing an extract from the *Madrid Gazette*, with a copy of the order sent by the King to the Governors of the Provinces and the public authorities, and people where we may travel, directing that due civilities should be shown to us by all, and that free entrance be allowed us to any place we may wish to visit. It states, also, that we are members of the religious Society of Friends, known by the name of Quakers. Orders are given that no molestation be offered us on any account whatever. It appears that this order was made known in the places we passed through, and excited the curiosity of the people to see us.   Here, also, this order is published in their newspaper.   We are thereby rendered very public characters.   It places us, in some respects, in a trying situation ; but, in others, the Lord's hand may be seen in it, for it furthers the object for which we have come to Spain :—pious and serious persons are attracted to us.   Several of these have been with us this evening.   By this order of the King, also, we may escape being annoyed or molested in the streets, where frequently the priests are met with, accompanied by persons with lighted tapers, carrying the consecrated wafer to a sick or dying man, when the passengers not only take off their hats, but fall down on their knees.   We did not meet with any of the priests on such occasions whilst we were in Madrid ; had we done so in some particular streets, we might have been exposed to much abuse, if not to the loss of our lives.

"16th.   We paid a visit to the Governor General.   It was proper we should early deliver to him the King's letter.   He received us with kindness, and said that he had a private letter from the King to the same import.   We were gratified to find in him a mild, serious man."

Feeling it to be their religious duty to visit the prisons, &c., the Governor kindly found a person to accompany them and serve as interpreter, named Gautier D'Are, a French physician.   Various prisons were now visited.   In one were confined those who were under sentence for terms of from one to ten years.   Many were shut up in dark cells seven feet square : light and air admitted only through a hole about five inches square in the thick wall, and two or three persons in each cell.   Other larger cells were more crowded in proportion.   Most of those immured were loaded with heavy chains ; but more horrible than all were the cells of those condemned to death.

In one poor-house, with six hundred inmates, the allowance of food was found insufficient ; but in another, richly endowed by the canons, with eight hundred inmates, the apartments

were spacious and very clean, with good rations. Their
attendant told them that these young persons were mostly
the children of the canons or priests. A handsome hospital
was then visited; then one for foundlings, where from twenty
to thirty of these wretched infants are admitted every week,
of whom five out of six die the first year. The institution for
the insane is described as the worst place he had ever beheld,
where the poor creatures were enclosed in cells, formed of
iron rails in front and at the side, paved with marble, where
their food was thrown to them as to wild beasts. Afterwards
a place was visited which was said to be for orphans of both
sexes, but it was found that they were the children of priests.
The boys' dress gave them the appearance young monks;
they were altogether under the care of priests trained in the
habits of mendicant friars, and sent daily into the streets
with a small bag about their necks, into which pieces of
money are dropped. "We could not feel excused," says
S. G., "without proclaiming pretty close doctrine to the
priests." The prison for condemned women was clean and
well conducted by a pious matron. They had a satisfactory
religious opportunity with the inmates.

The physician told them that about a year before, he had
been sent for to a nunnery to visit one of the nuns; she appeared to wish to speak to him: he put his ear to her mouth;
unobserved she placed a paper in his hands, and said in a
whisper, "I have no bodily disease, but distress of mind."
The contents of the paper were to entreat him to devise some
means to rescue her from that horrible place. She was a
young woman of fortune from Italy. After her father's death
her brother got possession of the estate, and, through the
agency of some priests, removed her to Spain, and shut her
up in this convent.

They then visited the prisons, the poor-house, and an asylum
for the insane. After a day thus spent, on the 17th S. G.
writes :—

"This has been a wearisome and trying day ; the air we have breathed, the mass of human misery and depravity we have beheld, appeared sometimes to be more than we could bear ; we did not find in any place anything that could administer a drop of consolation to our afflicted spirits, except the thought that our representations to the King may be a means of diminishing this mass of human woe. Curiosity could never induce me to visit such places ; the hope of being an instrument in the Lord's hand to turn some from darkness to light, and from sin and Satan to Christ the Saviour, and that their bodily sufferings also may be alleviated, constrains me.

" 18th. We went to a prison for condemned women. Here we found them quietly and diligently engaged in manual labour of various kinds. It looks like a manufacturing establishment. Both the house and the prisoners are clean. A motherly-looking matron has the oversight of them. She is pious, and by kindness and love she appears to obtain such ascendancy over them, that the most unruly seem changed soon after they enter this prison. Among the inmates of this prison we had a satisfactory religious opportunity. Tenderness of spirit was manifested by many of them."

They received many visits from pious individuals during their stay in Valencia, and became well acquainted with the state of suffering of many of these during the previous state of things. All these details would be read with interest in the larger work.

Their services in this place being concluded, they took the diligence on the evening of the 19th, and pursued their journey along the Mediterranean coast. S. G. writes :—

"We had the coupé to ourselves. It was a great relief to be alone. I was pretty comfortable the fore part of the night, but next morning a violent chill and high fever came on, and I was in a poor condition to travel ; there was, however, no place to stop ; towards evening we came to the Ebro, which is there a pretty broad river ; we crossed it in a sail-boat ; the wind was high and cold, which seemed to pierce me through ; on the other side of the river an open kind of waggon took us four miles to a

miserable inn, to wait for the diligence; there I lay down for a
couple of hours, which refreshed me a little. About nine in the
evening we arrived at Villafranca, where I hoped to have had
more rest; but instead of this, we found many persons collected
at the inn, who, it appears, had heard of our coming; some from
curiosity, others prompted by better motives, wished to see us;
most of them spoke French; they seemed very desirous to improve the opportunity to inquire into our religious principles;
some appeared to have tender scruples, and to be very uneasy
under the yoke of bondage imposed upon them by the Church of
Rome; they could not reconcile the priests' conduct with their
views of what a minister of Jesus Christ ought to be; others
seemed to be spiritually-minded persons; instead of obtaining
rest, my time was closely taken up with these people. It was an
opportunity attended with much seriousness and edification.

"We arrived at Barcelona on the morning of the 22nd, and I
kept in to nurse myself whilst dear Allen went to visit the
Governor and others, and their hospital. In the afternoon several
persons, having heard of our arrival, came in to see me; one is
Don Felix Torres Amat, Bishop of Barcelona. He is a remarkable
character; notwithstanding the many obstacles put in his way, he
has succeeded both in translating and printing the Scriptures from
the Vulgate; it is a large work of seven volumes; he has presented
me with a copy of it. He was under the necessity thus to make a
large work, to obviate some strong objections against issuing it;
it is printed with both the Latin and Spanish on the same page;
he was obliged also to put in notes; but in these he has confined
himself to explanations of the manners and customs of the people.
He succeeded in obtaining the sanction of the Pope. This was
about twelve years since, when the Inquisition was in force and
in great activity; yet even then friends and enemies to the Bible
were anxious to have it in their hands, so the first edition was
very soon disposed of. He is now printing a second edition, and
has proceeded to the third volume. The Archbishop of Toledo,
and the Nuncio of the Pope, have made strong efforts to prevent
him, but he hopes to succeed in completing the work. The King
supports him in it. Amat is a man of liberal sentiments; he
wishes for unrestricted liberty of conscience: none but the Lord,
he says, has the authority to control it; he knows several persons

in Spain who are like-minded with himself. He much wished that we could see the Archbishop of Mexico, who has lately written a book setting forth, with much clearness and force of argument grounded on Scripture, his Christian views; demonstrating that none but those who build on Jesus Christ as the sole hope of salvation, are members of the true Church; and that no observances of forms and ceremonies, or the precepts of men, can give a right claim to this membership in the Church of Christ. The Bishop told me that the day before yesterday, as he was walking on the public promenade, between the Governor and the Chief Magistrate, he stopped them suddenly, as the thought came before him, and said to them, 'What do you think the people will say if they see me walking between the two Quakers shortly expected here, as I now do with you?' 'We cannot say,' they answered. 'Well,' said he, 'I will tell you; they will say, that the strong walls of intolerance and superstition are falling down.' He tells me also that several priests of the order of the Oratorians (those among whom I received part of my education at the college of Lyons) fled among the mountains during the late persecution; he represents them as men of piety, and calculated to spread vital religion wherever they may be scattered.

"23rd. I felt much refreshed this morning, and had no return of fever last night. My gracious Master has helped me; blessed be his name! We have had a succession of visitors to-day, priests, canons, merchants, and persons of different ranks: among others several of the nobility, and the Regent and Chief Justice. We had free and full opportunities with them; we set before them what the religion of Christ consists in, and what are the fruits of the Spirit, contrasted with those of the flesh. The hearts of some of them appeared open to understand and to receive our testimony.

"25th. A number of seriously-disposed persons came to see us to-day. We had interesting and precious religious opportunities with them. Very earnest appears to be the inquiry of some of them, 'What must I do to be saved?' No better answer can be given to such inquirers, than the short but very comprehensive one given by St. Paul to the jailor at Philippi, 'Believe on the Lord Jesus Christ.'

"26th. We have prepared our report to the King, respecting

various subjects that have come under our observation since we left Madrid, and the abuses which we hope he may correct. We have also prepared an address to him and the Queen. We have much peace in this our last service towards them. We have also written to the Count D'Ofalia, to whom we enclose all these documents, which are written in French."

Being released from further service in the Peninsula, S. G. and his companions took their departure for France. Passing through Jonquières, Perpignan, Toulouse, and Bayonne, they arrived at Bordeaux on the 6th of Fourth Month. In the latter places they had some service, but did not make much stay; and they arrived in Paris on the 10th, where S. G. writes:—

"11th. We breakfasted this morning, by invitation, at the Duke de Broglie's, Prime Minister here. The Duchess's sister, the Baroness de Stäel, with whom we both have long been acquainted, is here also at present. They both are pious women. Guizot also, another of the King's ministers, was with us at breakfast. I had wished to see him, and thus an opportunity was given me to represent to him the sentiments contained in some of the books they have in their public schools, which are not in accordance with pure Christian doctrine. He promised to attend to this. He stated also, that he has taken measures to have the New Testament introduced in all the public schools, for which purpose he has ordered an edition of forty thousand copies. He meets with no obstruction to it from the Bishops, the greatest is from some of the priests. After he and the Duke had retired to go to the Chambers, we had with the two sisters a precious opportunity: they know the language of the Spirit. The Duke, wishing to have more time with us, pressed us to take a family dinner with him to-morrow. In the afternoon we had religious opportunities with several persons, both Protestants and Roman Catholics."

They did not long stay in Paris; and on the 18th of Fourth Month arrived, with grateful hearts, at Stoke Newington, near London, the home of his beloved friend William Allen.

CHAPTER XXXIII.

FOURTH VISIT TO EUROPE.

CONCLUDING SERVICES IN ENGLAND, SCOTLAND, AND IRELAND—VOYAGE TO AMERICA—VISITS TO OHIO, INDIANA, BALTIMORE AND NORTH CAROLINA YEARLY MEETINGS—EXTRACTS FROM LETTERS.

AFTER his peaceful return from the European continent, Stephen Grellet was not long before he resumed his Christian labours among his friends in England. He visited the meetings in and about London, as far as Buckinghamshire, which kept him closely occupied till near the time of the Yearly Meeting, which he attended; and then went through Yorkshire into Scotland, visiting the meetings of Friends, and having some large meetings with those of other denominations. He then went into Ireland and engaged in similar service there. On arriving again in England he writes:—

"Liverpool. Eleventh Month 11th, 1834. Here I am once more at my long-beloved and kind friend, Isaac Hadwen's, who is full of love and greenness in his old age. He proposes to be my companion for a while in the north of this nation."

Attended by this kind friend he went into Westmoreland and Cumberland, and returned to the Quarterly Meeting for Lancashire; and after visiting several of the meetings in those parts returned to London. Respecting these, his last services in England, Scotland, and Ireland, he says:—

" My concern has of late been principally for the members of the religious Society to which I belong, that those who have known the blessed Truth may keep under the power of it, watching unto prayer against every device and stratagem of the adversary. In many places it has been much laid upon me to draw the attention of Friends to Christ, the author and finisher of our faith; preaching Him in all his Divine attributes; what He has done for us without us, by the atoning sacrifice of himself for our sins; and what, through his grace and good Spirit, He would do in and for us, if we were obedient to his influence."

And he further observes:—

"I was greatly comforted in being again with my beloved friend William Allen; but I was not long permitted to have his dear company in and about London. My mind continuing under great exercise for Friends in various parts of this nation, I felt it to be my religious duty to be resigned again to visit a considerable number of their Quarterly Meetings."

After these visits he once more crossed the channel and attended the Yearly Meeting in Dublin, accompanied by his faithful friend William Allen, returning to London in time to attend the Yearly Meeting there, respecting which he writes:—

"The Yearly Meeting continued its sittings till the 30th. We had many seasons when our spirits were animated and encouraged to trust in the Lord for evermore; for when some of us were fainting under the load of exercise and fear, trembling like Eli for the ark of the testimony of God, the shout of the King eternal and immortal was heard in our camp, and the name of the Lord was proclaimed. He is the saving help and strength of his people. But we rejoice with trembling, 'for our enemies are lively and strong.' My deep solicitude and close exercise as I travelled over this nation, especially of late, were not without a cause. I have pleaded with all Christian affection and tenderness in private, and laboured also very fervently in some of the meetings, particularly at the close of the Yearly Meeting of Ministers and Elders this evening, which was a very solemn season. Parting with my friends is deeply affecting to me, for they are very dear to me in the Lord; close is the bond of fellowship that unites many of us. I have a lively hope that though we may never see one another again in mutability, yet our spirits being united by that blessed bond of Truth, which is indissoluble, we may be permitted, through the Divine mercy and love, to be joined together before the throne of God and the Lamb to celebrate his praise for ever. The parting between dear Allen and myself has been sweet and solemn ; we were very reverently prostrated together before the Lord."

There is something very touching in this simple record of the faithful minister of Christ, towards the conclusion of his Gospel mission in England and in Europe ; and the interest can scarcely fail to be deepened by turning to the memoirs of William Allen, and finding how he "went with dear Stéphen Grellet to Devonshire House, during the Yearly Meeting, as it was the last meeting for worship he was likely to attend ; when Stephen had an opportunity fully to relieve his mind ; and his communication was very remarkable, rising brighter and brighter towards the close ; Elizabeth J. Fry followed in supplication, and there was a very solemn feeling over the meeting." And afterwards in the concluding sitting of the Yearly Meeting, " when the business was over, Stephen rose and delivered a parting exhortation, which was remarkably solemn and impressive ;—to some he addressed the language of warning ; and he had sweet encouragement for the aged, and for tender, visited minds ; and in the silence at the close, there was a deep feeling of solemnity, and the Great Head of the Church, having granted some precious seasons, was pleased to confirm the faith of his servants in Him." And it is added, sorrowfully, respecting the Meeting for Ministers and Elders, " Dear Stephen Grellet was with us for the last time ; he spoke in a remarkable manner,—it was indeed a faithful communication. Several Friends were with us at our lodgings, and before we separated we felt the drawings of the Father's love, and after a time of silence, Stephen knelt in supplication. It was a favoured opportunity. We afterwards walked to Bishopsgate Street, to John Hustler's lodgings, and then I took leave of him."*

---

* *Life of William Allen.* Vol. iii. pp. 173 and 174.

Stephen Grellet proceeded towards Liverpool the same evening. Thence he writes :—

"TO WILLIAM ALLEN.

"Liverpool, Sixth Month 7th, 1834.

"My beloved Friend,

"I have no letter from my beloved wife, as I had fondly expected. This is a further opportunity for my will to bow down in submission. To have heard that my beloved wife and daughter were better would have been a great consolation previous to my embarkation.

"My mind is preserved in much calmness and sweetness on my approaching departure from a land where strong Gospel ties attach me to many dear friends, towards whom I have seldom, if ever, felt so much of what it was through the baptism of the one Spirit to become one body. I fully believe that it is in the Lord's pointings that I leave you, and I am thankful to be favoured, on this my last step in this land, to have the same evidence of my dear Master's Divine guidance, as He has so mercifully condescended to grant me in moving about from one nation to another people, and preserving his very poor, dependent servant."

Next morning, the 8th of Sixth Month, 1834, he embarked, on board the packet-ship *Pocahontas*, Captain West, for Philadelphia.

On his arrival at home, he makes the concluding record respecting this his fourth and last visit to Europe.

"We had a long but good passage, and arrived at Philadelphia the 21st of Seventh Month. That afternoon, I went to Burlington, and met my beloved wife and daughter. We united together in ascribing thanksgiving and praise to the Lord, our gracious helper, who has been with us during our long separation, and preserved us to this day—monuments of his Divine mercy. I travelled during this last European journey above twenty-eight thousand miles. We had many passengers both in the cabin and in the steerage, with whom, and the ship's crew, I had

several meetings during the voyage. These were held mostly on
deck, when the weather allowed of it ; where all on board could be
better accommodated than below in the cabin. The Lord very
graciously owned some of these meetings, and some other religious
opportunities I had with the steerage passengers and the sailors.
I had many seasons of retirement in my private room, my soul
being frequently poured forth in prayer unto God for the people
of the nations I have visited, and also for the members of the
religious Society of which I am a member, both in England and
America. They are a people very dear to me, strong are the
bonds of Christian fellowship that unite me to many of them.
There is among them a very goodly company to whom the Truth
is precious, and who, by the power of the Truth, and their faithfulness in it, are made well qualified instruments in the Lord's
hand to advocate the blessed cause of the Redeemer. I am permitted also to have a cheering hope that the departure of some
from the purity and simplicity of our Christian profession is,
through the Lord's blessing, made a means of bringing many
others deeper to the root of religion ; so as to become more firmly
established in the faith of Christ, and the knowledge of those
· principles and doctrines on which our primitive Friends built ;
and which they did not flinch from maintaining before the world,
though the loss of their property, imprisonment, and death, were
the consequence of their faithfulness. To my great comfort I
have seen clear evidence of this manifested by some dear young
Friends."

————

Stephen Grellet had now arrived at the close of his varied
" missionary labours " in distant nations. Rescued by the
power of the Spirit from the meshes of infidelity, he had been
enabled, in the vigour of early manhood, to enter in by Christ,
the door, into the sheepfold ; rejoicing in the salvation of
God, he had gone in and out and found pasture ; dedicating
himself unreservedly to the service of the Redeemer, he had
known that when He, the good Shepherd who laid down his

life for the sheep, putteth forth his own sheep, He goeth before
them, and the sheep follow Him; *for they know his voice.*
That voice he had heard thirty-six years before, when, as he
thought, he was about to breathe his last, and seemed already
to have gained a foot-hold in the heavenly places, and saw
and felt things that cannot be written; it proclaimed the
word, "Thou shalt not die but live—thy work is not yet
done," when distant parts of the earth over seas and lands
were set before him, where he would have to labour in the
service of the Gospel of Christ.   Under a marked coincidence between the openings of Providence and the leadings
of the Holy Spirit, he had for many years been diligently
occupied in a long series of religious engagements; which,
in accordance with the clear intimation given him in the early
part of his ministry, had been gradually unfolded as the
requirements of his Lord; and he had now been brought
back in peace from his last visit to Europe.   The Saviour's
words, "My sheep hear my voice, and I know them, and they
follow me; and I give unto them eternal life, and they shall
never perish, neither shall any pluck them out of my hand,"
had been beautifully illustrated and confirmed in his experience.
Had he followed a delusive guide, or a true one less faithfully,
the issues of his life, thus far, must have been very different
from what, as it has been seen, they were.   He would not
have so distinctly borne upon him "the marks of the Lord
Jesus;" he could not have given so many proofs of the
reality of the direct influence and guidance of the Holy
Spirit, and of the safety and blessedness of following his
leadings in the path of holiness and duty—whilst resting
upon Christ alone as the foundation of his faith and hope.
Henceforward, returned to the bosom of his own beloved
family, and a large circle of friends, it was in the land of his
adoption that; during the residue of his years, he walked
humbly with his God, and exhibited a bright example of
Christian simplicity and faithfulness.

He thus briefly sums up the account of several years immediately succeeding his return from Europe :—

"I continued pretty much at home, except attending some of the neighbouring Yearly Meetings, till the year 1837, when I went to Ohio and Indiana, attended those two Yearly Meetings and a number of the meetings composing them. I had sweet peace in that engagement. Many of the meetings I had in those States were attended by a considerable number of those who have separated from us. I was thus introduced into close exercise and labour, but in some places a hope was given that with many of this class, particularly of the young people, an earnest inquiry after the Truth was the motive for attending these meetings. May the Lord cause the light of his glorious Gospel to shine upon them !"

In the spring of 1837, Stephen Grellet received the affecting intelligence of the decease of his "beloved and honoured mother," an event which took place on the 20th of Second Month, and was communicated to him in a letter from his brother Joseph, who, with many of her descendants, was present on the peacefully solemn occasion. She was in her ninety-fourth year, and it was a great comfort to Stephen Grellet to think of her as " full of love to the dear Saviour, weaned from a dependence upon priests or outward observances, with her heart fixed,—trusting in the Lord alone."*

---

* There are many letters from this excellent mother, and from other members of his family, all expressing the warmest affection and strongest interest. It is difficult to select,—they all breathe the same spirit. One, received soon after his return from his third visit to Europe, is very characteristic :—
" What delight thy letter gave thy mother, my tenderly beloved son ! After many dangers thou art at last restored to thy fireside, to thy dear wife and child, whom thou hast found in good health. What thanks should we render to the Lord ! I had received thy letter from England. I knew thou wast on the sea,—my spirit was near thee,—I felt every danger. Thy dear letter has removed the painful load from my heart. Thou left me in great anxiety, but not on my own account,—that troubles me the least. But other trials awaited me, and I have needed to recall to my mind very often thy tender advice, to bow in entire submission to

2 E

A few extracts from letters will show that S. G.'s health was beginning to fail; but his Christian zeal remained unabated, and his consolations in Christ abounded. To William Allen, he writes under date, Burlington, Eighth Month 11th, 1837 :—

"My health has been but feeble lately ; for some days I have been confined to the house ; but with a little care, and especially with my dear Master's help, who has never failed his poor servant, however feeble and impotent of himself for any service whereto He has called, all will be well. We have, my dear friend, great cause unitedly for praising and exalting the great and good name of the Lord; yet how can it be that at seasons clouds are intervening so as to bring doubt and fear ? Well, these, perhaps, are permitted to lead us to increase in watchfulness, and to be more frequent in the house of prayer."

TO LYDIA NEILD.

"Burlington, Twelfth Month 16th, 1837.

"I was favoured by my good and blessed Master with help to accomplish the little service He called me to in the West. I had some solemn satisfactory meetings among Friends and persons of other religious denominations, when the power of the glorious Gospel of Christ, the Lord of all, appeared to have dominion over all.

"The Yearly Meetings of Ohio and Indiana were considered by Friends there the most solemn they had had for many years ; blessed be the Lord ! from whom the life flows and the power is ; it is He that doeth the work ; and his works only can praise Him. These are two large Yearly Meetings, Indiana especially. There are valuable friends in that body ; and the visita-

---

the will of the Lord, and as thou hast told me, to be fully persuaded that our crosses, and our afflictions, are given us by the hand of the tenderest Father. Always remember me before the Lord. When I call to mind thy patience, thy resignation, thy advice, I feel strengthened.

"I wish you, my dear children, the Lord's blessing. Remember me in His presence and love, as she loves you, your mother.

"GRELLET."

tions of heavenly love have evidently been extended to many of the young people. I am comforted also in believing that some of them have received the Truth in the love of it. In the reports of the Quarterly Meetings on the state of their schools it appears they have among them six thousand four hundred and twenty-nine children of an age to go to school. O ! what a field in those young plantations for labourers. Our beloved friend, Joseph John Gurney, attended these Yearly Meetings and had a very acceptable service in them, and in other meetings."

TO L. NEILD.

" Burlington, Fourth Month 28th, 1838.

" Our dear friend, J. J. Gurney, has spent a considerable time in Philadelphia, visiting the families of three of their Monthly Meetings, besides attending some very large meetings, where his Gospel services have been extensive and attended with much evidence of Divine unction.

" My health has been feeble for these months past, yet I hope to regain my late standard, which will not rank me among the mighty ; but, if we have sufficient ability to perform the residue of the service that the dear Master has for us in the militant church, it is enough."

TO ANN ALEXANDER.

" Sixth Month 23rd, 1838.

" I must, however, tell thee that my days during this sickness have been among the most happy of my life—so much of the comforting and refreshing presence of my blessed and adorable Redeemer, that my cup has run over. Never before have I felt, Him so fully, so sweetly in his blessed character of a Redeemer, a Saviour. O how lovely He is in every part of his humiliation of his sufferings and the agonies of his death ; and that for the salvation of sinners ! To sinners it is given to know Him, to feel Him, to love and adore Him in the character and under the blessed name of Jesus. ' The angels desire to look into these things.' "

CHAPTER XXXIV.

HITHERTO Stephen Grellet's health had not been seriously impaired. His strength of constitution had been tested by his many and arduous travels in different climes; and his well-developed and hardy frame had seemed to resist with unusual tenacity the encroachments of disease. But the time was now approaching when his physical powers so far gave way, as no longer to allow him to undertake any distant journeys.

In the summer of 1842 he attended the Yearly Meetings of New York and New England, and soon after his return from these engagements, he was seized with an alarming complaint. His illness was of several months' duration, and his medical attendant repeatedly thought that he was near his end. Though his bodily sufferings were often great, he was enabled to bear them with his accustomed fortitude and patience, in cheerful submission to his Heavenly Father's will; —prayer and praises frequently ascended to Him whom he loved to serve even in the furnace of affliction. In reference to the final issue, he said that "the love of his dear Saviour was very near to him; his dear Master was very good, and did not forsake him in his extremity; all would be well, whether in life or in death; Christ was ours, and He would fulfil the promise: 'I will never leave thee nor forsake thee.'" Again he exclaimed, "Do not think that He who gives strength to suffer, does not give love to endure: we must bless the Lord, not by the measure of affliction, but by the

measure of comfort and love!" He spoke touchingly to his
beloved wife and daughter, and earnestly gave them his
blessing. He tried to utter some lines of a hymn, and on
his wife repeating them :—

"There is a land of pure delight," &c.

he bowed his head and said, "Out of the depths hast Thou
answered me." Again he remarked, "My Saviour is my
joy, my salvation, the rock of my strength, my Redeemer,
my song, my hope for ever and ever." "He is my rock and
my refuge, but I am very poor—utterly unworthy. I am but
a child; I wish to be but a child. We are very mercifully
dealt with; my dear Master is very near me; I feel his presence to be staying my soul; I can do nothing but bless and
adore his Divine name!"

Much more might be added from the family record of the
precious words of counsel and encouragement, and of Christian love, which flowed from his lips during this season of
confinement; but enough has been said to show how the exceeding great and precious promises of the Gospel, which in
health he had so often proclaimed to others, were now the
rejoicing of his heart, when apparently near the portals of
eternity. His end, however, was not yet; and on his recovery from this illness and a relapse he had in 1843, it is
interesting to notice the characteristic manner in which he
speaks of this portion of his life in the following extracts
from his correspondence.

On the 22nd of Tenth Month, 1842, he writes to his beloved friend, William Allen; and after expressing his great
concern on hearing of his illness at Lindfield, and his earnest
desire and prayer that, "for the Church's sake and that of
the blessed cause of righteousness in the earth," his life
might yet be prolonged, he continues :—

"I am persuaded that thy blessed Master and beloved Lord has
supplied all thy wants—has encircled thee by his presence, and

given thee richly to feel the joys of his salvation ; even when thou
mayest have pretty much concluded that the spark of animal life
was near being extinguished. Good, very good indeed, is the
Lord ; when afflictions abound, consolations by Christ abound
much more. Thou hast heard how very ill I have been myself.
It is three months since I was taken down, but am now recovered
to a considerable degree. Thou hast been these many weeks past
in my very sweet but very anxious thoughts, so that I often
spoke to my beloved wife of my anxiety on thy account, fearing
thou wast sick. Is it not remarkable that we who, in company
together in distant lands, have shared many trials, exercises of
mind and perils, should now also have walked together, at the
same time, through what appeared to be the valley and shadow of
death ? As under the former we were raised above fears of any
evil, our blessed Lord being with us, his staff supporting and
comforting us, so likewise in this latter He has been in a marvellous manner near us. Truly I may reckon these last three
months, though passed under such bodily suffering, among the
most blessed and precious of my life ; for by night and by day
my dear Redeemer and his Spirit were near me ; and at the same
time that the good remembrancer has brought to mind the various
portions of my life, my soul's travails and exercises, the state of
the churches past and present, yet it has been in a way wonderful
to describe ; for no painful consideration attended, no hard
thoughts against the troublers in Israel, but love, Divine love,
was as a garment, or diffused like oil over all. In my sleep, in
my waking hours—even under what, through the violence of the
fever, might be considered a delirium, the thoughts of my heart
were unto the Lord, sweet and refreshing. Oh I have had very
full confirmation of the rectitude of our Christian profession—
faith, doctrines, and hope being truly grounded on the foundation on which the Apostles of our Lord Jesus Christ did build ;
and that faith in Christ is that through which his redeemed and
sanctified ones have obtained the victory. Surely that Christian
hope which felt so clear, so sweet, when apparently having
already a foot out of time into eternity, giving to feel the joys of
God's salvation, through the redeeming love and mercy in and
by Christ, is a religion fit for a man to live by ; yea, a hope
springs from it, that has on no occasion made ashamed those

that have maintained it well. My much beloved friend, whilst giving thee a concise statement of the Lord's tender mercy and very gracious dealings towards thy poor and very unworthy brother, I have a steady eye to what I apprehend have also been thy blessed Master's dealings towards thee ; so that we may well unite in the adoption of the language, 'Bless the Lord, O my soul,' &c. And now, may the residue of these feeble lives, thus prolonged by the Lord's power, be employed in showing forth his praise. My wife desires her dear love to thee and dear Lucy, and our precious daughter joins : and in gratitude, at the prospect of thy restoration to health, although we cannot expect to hear of thy rising again to thy former vigour.

"Farewell, my much beloved in the Lord. It is He who is thy buckler, thy shield, and finally thy ' exceeding great reward.'

"STEPHEN GRELLET."

In the autumn of 1843, Stephen Grellet was so far recruited as to be able to attend the Yearly Meeting in Baltimore, but his health continued liable to great interruptions. He was "deeply affected by the accounts he received of the reduced state" of his beloved friend, William Allen, and "the prospect of a final separation on earth from that dear one ;" and when, in the early part of 1844, the intelligence arrived that "his redeemed spirit was gently released on the 30th of Twelfth Month, 1843," he keenly felt the bereavement, both on his own account and for the Church's sake ; whilst he thought "there was great reason to apprehend that he should not tarry long after him."

Some months later, on reviewing the last few years of his life, having nearly completed his seventy-first year, he makes the last record in his Autobiography : —

"With reverent gratitude I record how mercifully my good and blessed Master now peacefully releases me from the weight of religious service abroad. Good indeed is the Lord ! When He called me to labour in distant nations, or nearer home, He gave strength for the service required. Now, that bodily strength faileth me, nothing is required but what I have ability to perform ; and, through adorable favour, the same mercy and goodness that have followed me all the days of my life, continue to be with me in my advanced age and feebleness of health. Blessed and praised be his glorious and excellent name !"

Though thus "peacefully released" from active service in distant parts, the veteran "soldier of Christ" did not cease to feel the need of *keeping on* "the whole armour of God, that he might be able to withstand in the evil day, and having done all, to stand" *unshaken*. He continued to cherish a lively interest in all that related to the advancement of the kingdom of Christ at home and abroad ; and, with lively zeal, chastened by knowledge and without guile, he was quick to discern and faithful to bear his testimony against everything which, however specious in appearance, had a tendency, as he believed, to dim the brightness, to mar the beauty and to retard the progress of the Truth as it is in Jesus.

His health was still feeble ; but on the approach of the Yearly Meeting of New York in the spring of 1846, he felt well enough to yield to "an apprehension of religious duty, once more to mingle in Christian fellowship and love with his brethren of that portion of the body." It was the last time ; and he had much satisfaction in meeting so many of his beloved friends on such an interesting and important occasion.

Not long after this visit, adverting to the "love and meekness" which should prevail among Christian brethren, even when they may differ in their views, he remarks in a letter

TO JOSIAH FORSTER.

"The fruits of the Spirit, how precious ! May they abound more and more ! O that by these fruits *we* might more fully evince that we walk in the footsteps of our ancient Friends ! This is what gathers to Christ ; it convinces gainsayers. It may be very proper in its place, to *contend* for the truth ; but it should never be forgotten that 'the servant of the Lord must not strive.' The mind of Christ should be in us. What an attainment ! To press after it is surely our duty; and the more sensible I am of my great shortness in this attainment, the more earnést ought this to render me in pressing after it. On this, and many other subjects, I often think of the words of the dear Redeemer, 'The things which are impossible with men are possible with God.' Thus He may overrule for good all the present trials of our Society, and our every affliction."

A little later he writes :—

TO LYDIA NEILD.

"Burlington, Seventh Month 27th, 1846.

"The number of my correspondents in England has greatly lessened ; the undeniable messenger of death has opened the way for many of these to pass into a better world, even into the kingdom of everlasting blessedness and glory. Some very dear and beloved ones still remain, like myself, a short time longer inhabiters of this world of probation, wherein, however, we occupy a very important station ; for on the proper occupation of it, be the time longer or shorter, greatly depends our well-being.

"O for an increase of faith on my part, and a more steadfast abiding in watchfulness and prayer ! May I be preserved now in my advancing years, through grace and mercy unmerited, but on which alone my hope centres ; and be favoured in the end, through the merits and intercession of the blessed Redeemer, to be admitted among those who have come out of great tribulation, and have washed their robes in the blood of the Lamb !"

In the early part of 1847, having heard of the death of Clarkson, he thus alludes to that great champion of negro freedom, in a letter

TO ANN ALEXANDER.

"I have thought several times how much you must miss our late valuable friend, Thomas Clarkson ; you had so long enjoyed his interesting and instructive company. Is it not very sweet and precious to contemplate how many of those beloved ones we have known are now inhabitants of the celestial city with saints and

angels? Yet a little while, my dear sister, and I have a joyful
hope that there also thy habitation shall be."

From long and intimate acquaintance with Joseph John
Gurney, he had justly appreciated his Christian character,
and the value of his services as a devoted minister of the
Gospel in the religious Society of Friends; and he had
become closely attached to him in the bonds of Christian
fellowship. The intelligence of his unexpected removal on
the 4th of First Month, 1847, to the land "of rest, and
peace, and everlasting love," awakened deep and intense feeling throughout a widely extended circle, in which S. G. largely
shared. In reference to this event, he writes:—

TO ANN ALEXANDER.

"Second Month 19th, 1847.
"We are greatly obliged to thee for giving us, so early, so full
and detailed accounts of the last days and moments of our much
loved, and so much valued, departed friend, Joseph John Gurney.
As there was mourning in Egypt at the death and burial of Jacob,
so it may be said to have been the case on this solemn occasion:
rich and poor have partaken of the same feeling, which will long
remain in the breast of many of us; for it is no common loss that
the Church, those deeply concerned in every act of benevolence,
the poor, his numerous friends and relatives, have sustained; and
especially dear Eliza, his mournful and *indeed* bereaved widow.

"The dear departed has now entered, as we firmly believe, into
the enjoyment of the blessings pronounced on those that die in the
Lord; who have ceased from their labours, and whose works follow
them. This hope respecting the beloved departed one is confirmed
in that he so sweetly appeared to be engaged, day by day, to walk
with God under the guidance of his Holy Spirit; therefore, whilst
feeling and mourning our own loss, we must rejoice with and for
him."

In allusion to the same event, and the removal of others
to their "final rest," he writes a week later:—

"Burlington, Second Month 26th, 1847.
" My beloved Friend,

" I share with thee and deeply feel the great stripping of the
Church among you. We can truly rejoice in that there has been
an enlargement of the Church triumphant, in heavenly places, in
Christ Jesus. But the militant Church, how greatly reduced !
among us here especially. In ancient days, 'The Lord added to
the Church daily such as should be saved.' So was it also in
former years in the borders of our religious Society ; many of
those, thus added, have become of the saved of the Lord. In my
days I have seen in divers parts of this land, how in several
sections, ten, twenty, and more, were month after month added to
our number, on the ground of convincement. But I have lived
also to see many of these scattered as to the four winds, instead
of becoming of the saved of the Lord. This scattering seems to
have so completely stopped the tide of convincement in others,
that now year rolls upon year and not one instance is found
recorded of any increase by convincement ; whereas many are the
testimonies of disownment issued. This, together with the steady
work of mortality, opens the prospect of a waste, howling wilderness. Nevertheless, when I consider whence sprung the multi-
tudes of Israel, and wherefrom also our Society sprung and grew
up ; amidst what trials and sufferings they became instruments
by which such excellent principles and testimonies to the blessed
Truth were held and maintained—and which, in the present day,
are highly appreciated by many who do not go under our name—
my little portion of faith reaches to the fulness of hope that the
Lord will continue to work for his great name's sake ; for the end
for which the Redeemer has come, has suffered, and ever liveth,
will and *shall* be accomplished in his time. I shall not see it. But
the time for it is progressing—it is drawing nearer and nearer.
Methinks, sometimes, that through the thick clouds that pass over
our horizon, a view of this is permitted. Not one jot or tittle
of the divine promises but what shall be accomplished ; for the
Lord God Omnipotent reigneth, and his power is over all. But
why have I entered upon the expression of such solemn things ?
Dear friend, whatever gloomy things may at seasons appear to us,

let us trust in the Lord, and not be afraid.   He will work—*even in our Society*—and who shall let Him ?"

Writing to the same friend, a little later, he adds :—

"I shall die in hope that better days will come, and that the Sun of Righteousness will yet arise with healing in his wings. O then, what virtue ! what blessed efficacy will flow !   Our wilderness shall then flourish, and our desert shall become as the garden of the Lord. In his time, He will do this, and glorify his name."

There was at this time something peculiarly bright and searching in S. G.'s Gospel ministry in his own Meeting. At one time he rose with the Saviour's query to his disciples, "Where is your faith?" and reminded his hearers that this was not addressed to strangers or aliens, but to those who are frequently spoken of as the disciples of our Lord, and who had given evidence of their faith in Him, by having left all to follow Him : but who, in their frail bark, when the wind and the tempest beat high, whilst the dear Master was asleep in the midst of them, and they seemed as if they were actually sinking, gave vent to their fearful anticipations in the cry, "Master, we perish." Many, in the present day, whether they looked to themselves, the Church, or the condition of the nations of the earth, were ready to adopt the same language.   But, discouraging as might at times be the view of some whose life could not be much longer lengthened out, yet he believed the power of the Most High could breathe even upon the dry bones, as Ezekiel saw them spread forth in the valley ; so that at his word, bone should come to his bone, &c.—And happy would it be for those who, though dead in trespasses and sins, should hear this quickening word and be saved through the Redeemer's grace; and, obeying His voice, be enabled to bring forth fruit to the glory and honour of His great name.   "But where is the faith which will cause the young man and the young woman to bud and blossom continually, as did Aaron's rod ; or that

will make them as a green olive branch? Be watchful,
therefore, lest, having been quickened unto repentance, for
want of faith thou be cast forth and be withered!"

Speaking of the merciful dealings of Christ with sinners,
he said—"And when the shepherd findeth the lost sheep,
after leaving the ninety and nine in the wilderness, how does
he bring it home? Does he whip it? Does he drive it?
Does he threaten it? No such thing! He carries it on his
shoulders, and deals most tenderly with the poor, weary,
wandering one!"

CHAPTER XXXV.

FOR more than fifty years Stephen Grellet had laboured diligently in the service of the Gospel in various parts of the world. Gradually as the sphere of his active exertions in the Redeemer's cause had been lessened by the state of his health, he had still been able occasionally to go from home for a short time; and in the Fourth Month of this year, 1847, he went to Philadelphia to attend his own Yearly Meeting. After being present at the Meeting for Ministers and Elders he was taken ill during the night, and obliged to return to Burlington the next day; and from that time he did not again leave home even for a single night.

He was now in his seventy-fourth year, and when thus wholly deprived of the power of going abroad by a disease which subjected him for the rest of his life to frequent paroxysms of acute pain, he bore the trial with meek submission, and often praised the Lord for his goodness and blessed help in the hour of need. His mental faculties and his spiritual perceptions remained unimpaired; the love of Christ, and that rejoicing in Him, so often the privilege of the believer, seemed to form almost the hourly and familiar habit of his soul. Though sometimes prevented from worshipping publicly with his friends, he was able, at intervals, to attend his own meeting, where he was often engaged in the ministry of the Gospel, to the edification and comfort of his hearers; whilst those who were privileged to come within the circle of his daily influence, under his own roof or when he mingled with his friends in social intercourse, could not fail to be interested and benefited by his conversation, when, as the scribe well instructed unto the kingdom, he brought forth, out of the good treasure of his heart, things both new and old; and they would often be edified by the solemn silence that ensued—broken by words of comfort, of counsel, or encouragement, that seemed like refreshment drawn from the "nether spring" of the Saviour's presence and love, peculiarly adapted to the need of the hour.

The characteristics which had marked his earlier days, and largely attended his Gospel labours among all ranks and conditions in the many nations he had visited, shone with undiminished brightness in the evening of life, when entirely confined to the precincts of home. The warmth and ardour of his affections, his truly Christian cheerfulness, blended with a quiet, unaffected, unassuming dignity of manner, at once humble and self-possessed, gave the impression of no ordinary person. A true Frenchman in politeness, he was quite a model of the courteous and affable, without the fawning flattery of the world. Christian simplicity, sincerity, and truthfulness, marked his words and actions:— "his look was love,—his salutation peace." *

Whilst in the retirement of the home circle, the graces of the spiritual life were thus daily manifested; although his memoranda now cease, his letters manifest in a lively manner the experience of the aged Christian during the seclusion of his latter days.

His correspondence with Ann Alexander, the daughter of his "beloved and valued friend, William Dillwyn," had been so constant and long-continued, that a few extracts from his letters to her will from this time materially aid in exhibiting the different phases of his inner life. To her he writes:—

---

* To those who had no personal acquaintance with him, it may be interesting to know that he was about the medium height, erect, and rather slender.

"Sixth Month 14th, 1847. I have gratefully to tell thee that my own health, though still feeble, is much improved of late, so that I am able comfortably to resume all my religious meetings. I feel it a great privilege and consolation to be able to unite publicly with my friends in waiting on and worshipping our great and gracious Lord. He has indeed very mercifully condescended to be ever near his poor servant in my approaches to Him, when necessarily detained at home in my chamber or bed : so that I can reverently proclaim his goodness and tender mercy, as being extended both in the closet and in the congregation of his people. I am sometimes lost in wonder and amazement, under a sense of the marvellous provisions that an Almighty Father and merciful God has provided for the sustenance and the renewal of the strength of the weakest and poorest of his flock. They that wait upon the Lord shall renew their strength."

"First Month 14th, 1848. This last year, like some of the preceding ones, was marked by some pretty deep sufferings and conflicts of flesh and spirit ; yet in the end of it I see it crowned in such a manner with goodness, mercy and truth, that I must inscribe on the memorial of it these true testimonies of gratitude and praise, 'Hitherto hath the Lord helped me,' and 'Mercy and truth have followed me all the days of my life.' O ! that I may properly bless and adore his holy name !"

On the expected opening of the Crystal Palace in London he writes :—

"The congregation of so many persons from so many nations that are expected to be then in London, has brought me into very serious and solemn consideration, and perhaps thou wilt, and may indeed smile, when I tell thee that I, poor I, like an old worn-out race-horse, which, on hearing the sound of the horn or trumpet, is all animation, ready to start ; so thy poor, old, feeble friend has felt so much of the love of Christ and his Gospel towards such an expected multitude, that he thought, should the command be given, there would be a willingness to try, at least, to limp or creep, though not to run as formerly."

Speaking of afflictions and sufferings, after recovering from a severe illness, he adds :—

"I have compared them to a rough diamond,—very rough and unsightly in appearance,—nothing in it appears desirable ; but remove some of the crust from that rough stone, and then what a bright gem is discovered ! So, when, through the eye of faith, we are enabled to see into the sufferings allotted to us, what a glory is unfolded ! Yes, we behold how these afflicting dispensations work for us a far more exceeding and eternal weight of glory ! Then, in this very particular of our beloved Lord's dispensations, we see what grateful cause we have to break out joyfully with David and say, 'Bless the Lord, O my soul, and all that is within me bless Him for all his *benefits* :' for we see, we *feel* all these to have been to our benefit, and to bring a blessing with them.

"Twelfth Month 19th, 1851. I am under the necessity to abstain from reading *writing;* and even print, unless it be large, which is a great privation. I have, however, the Scriptures in large print, which are my welcome and constant companion. Should I be permitted to become deprived of this privilege also, may not my good and blessed Lord be pleased to bring to my remembrance, as need may be, portions of them suitable to my condition ?"

A painful inflammation of the eyes had almost deprived him of the power of using the pen, and when nearly blind he writes :—

"First Month 13th, 1852. For the first time I attempt to write, though I am not able to read my own writing, and possibly thou mayest not be able to do it ; but my good-will will be manifested, and thou wilt make every allowance for a brother's infirmities. I know not what will be the result with regard to my sight ; the dimness, independent of the inflammation, continues or increases, but no apparent defect in the eyes is yet observable : perhaps it is only an attendant on the feebleness of the whole of my outward man. Thanks, however, to the Lord, I am still able to see the excellency of the Truth, and to love and adore my blessed and glorious Lord and Redeemer ; also I am able to join my friends in publicly worshipping Him, and sometimes also with the voice of thanksgiving to proclaim his name, and rehearse his praise and his works."

2 F

In these extracts—embracing a period of several years, till
he was nearly fourscore—Stephen Grellet may be said still
to be his own biographer, and there cannot well be a nobler
sight than a Christian patriarch " having served his generation by the will of God," thus enabled to show how he was
strengthened to " hold fast the confidence, and the rejoicing
of the hope firm unto the end," giving all the glory to Him
to whom alone it is due.

———

The last two or three years of his life were, like some of
the preceding ones, attended with much physical suffering :
but he had not followed cunningly-devised fables in believing
in " the power and coming of our Lord Jesus Christ ; " he
knew Him in whom he had believed—he endured as seeing
Him who is invisible.   Remarkably applicable to his own
experience were the words of comfort addressed by himself
to a beloved friend in an hour of conflict :—" Trials and
afflictions are, to those who have known the Lord and
the power of his redeeming love, like the pressing of an
aromatic plant ; the more it is under pressure the stronger
and sweeter does the scent thereof arise ; well, therefore, may
we say, in all our tribulations, ' Awake, O north wind ; and
come thou south ; blow upon my garden, that the spices
thereof may flow out.' "
Whenever his health permitted, he seemed to forget his
own sufferings, and still went from house to house, visiting
the flock in their retired abodes ; and with tender sympathy
imparting the word of counsel, of comfort or encouragement,
where it was needed.   From the family record, and other
sources of information, it is evident that, as a father in the
Church, he was still fruitful in the field of offering, and joyful

in the house of prayer, and that his ministry continued to deepen and brighten even to the end.*

In the summer of 1853 he was again very ill—so ill that it was not thought possible he could survive many hours. This attack continued for some days, and several weeks elapsed before he was able to go out again. During this period the state of his mind was quite heavenly, and, with a countenance beaming with love, he would very often praise and glorify his blessed Lord and Saviour,—praying earnestly for his beloved family, and those who were about him. Once,

---

* See the Testimony issued respecting him, by Burlington Monthly Meeting.

His fellow-citizens of other denominations were not slow to recognise his worth, and in various ways manifested the estimation in which he was held by them. The following is an extract from a brief notice of his decease, which appeared in the *Burlington American :*—

" As a citizen he has been long known to the people of Burlington, and we may safely quote the Apostle's appeal: ' Ye are witnesses how holily and justly and unblamably he behaved himself among you.' A heart of larger sympathy we have never known, or one more ready to comprehend and to minister unto afflictions which were carefully concealed. His Gospel preaching was of a character rarely equalled, and probably nowhere surpassed. Its chief characteristic was its wonderful *vitality*. Perfectly free from every trace of egotism, he preached ' Jesus Christ, and Him crucified.' The sufferings of his Lord for the sake of sinful man deeply and abidingly affected his soul. His sermons manifested an extraordinary originality, scope of thought, and spiritual wealth. With demonstration of the Spirit and with power, he illustrated his subjects with passages brought from various parts of the sacred volume, and which the hearer found presented in a light in which he never saw them before. Holding all mankind as his brethren, his public ministry and prayers evinced his large-minded sympathy with the whole human race, and his deep interest in the movements among the nations. To him it was a *present* sorrow, if famine stalked through foreign lands,—if pestilence wasted distant cities,—if in any part of the earth the sword devoured men for whom Christ died.

" There was an unmistakeable halo of good to be felt about him, by which even the irreligious were impressed: but of his personal traits those best can speak who were privileged with his close friendship.

" His gentle, kindly, and true heart has for ever ceased its beating; and it remains for those who mourn his loss to bow in resignation to the will of his rich Rewarder, to rejoice in the perfect joy of his salvation, and carefully noting his shining footsteps, to follow him as he followed Christ."

on being asked whether he had slept during the night, he
replied, " No, except a little after four o'clock ; " adding,
that he had been in the house of prayer for a long time,
pouring forth his fervent supplications, even to wrestling,—
for himself, for his beloved wife and daughter, for his sister
Le Clerc, in her advanced age, and for his brother Charles,
and other members of his family in France ; then for those
who had unhappily been drawn aside from the right way of
the Lord, mentioning some of these by name ; for the Friends
of his own meeting ; and for the multitude of sinners who
were groaning in bonds and misery of their own procuring.
Whilst thus interceding for different classes of his fellow-men,
a bright view, he said, opened to his mind of the unspeakable
mercy of God in Christ Jesus, and of the virtue of his atoning
sacrifice, which seemed to be a resting-place to his soul.
Sleepless nights were often his portion, but he frequently
remarked that " he had that which was better than sleep."
After a time of much pain he. looked up to his Heavenly
Father, and said, " I pray Thee, not for a mitigation of my
sufferings, but that the full end may be accomplished !   Thy
mercies are great ; they proceed from an everlasting fountain !"

On reappearing amongst his friends at their meeting, about
two months after, he spoke very impressively on the words of
the Apostle : " Blessed be God, even the Father of our Lord
Jesus Christ, the Father of mercies, and the God of all comfort ; who comforteth us in all our tribulations, that we may
be able to comfort them which are in any trouble, by the
comfort wherewith we ourselves are comforted of God."
Though at home he could hardly speak above a whisper, on
this occasion his voice was strong, and he spoke with much
power.

During the remainder of the year, though often very feeble,
and suffering much from the inflammation of his eyes, S. G.
was generally able to attend his own meeting, and was
frequently exercised in the ministry of the Gospel.

In the beginning of 1854 he was again brought so low by another attack of illness that his life was despaired of. As usual, not a murmur escaped his lips, and he often numbered his blessings and gratefully acknowledged that "he was peaceful, rejoicing in the Lord, and in everything giving thanks." He again recovered for a time; but in the autumn his sufferings were renewed, and there seemed but little hope that his days would be lengthened out. One day, after having spent much time in quiet retirement of spirit, he remarked that it was not from suffering that he had kept silence, but that, during the solemn feeling which was granted him, the song of praise which had filled his heart had been wonderful, adding, "If I had the pen of a ready writer I could fill pages with the Lord's merciful dealings with me." He then very sweetly and encouragingly addressed his little family, reminding them how wonderfully the Lord had helped them, thankfully acknowledging that it was His doing. Thus days of bodily affliction were, through abounding mercy, times of much spiritual refreshment; and on his being raised up again, seasons of religious communion with his friends frequently occurred, when the venerable patriarch would pour forth the message of the Redeemer's love with an unction that bespoke the source from which he drew his supplies.

In the course of 1855, Stephen Grellet was generally able to meet with his friends when assembled for the worship of God. He continued to give evidence, amidst all his bodily infirmities, that his delight was in the Lord; and, having been "allowed of Him to be put in trust with the Gospel," he was often enabled, "so to speak, not as pleasing men, but God who trieth our hearts," that his preaching was in the life and power of the Spirit.

Clothed with humility, the nearer he approached to the source of infinite purity, the more deeply he seemed to be prostrated in self-abasedness; and if, rejoicing as he did in "the light of the knowledge of the glory of God, in the face of Jesus Christ," he had, during a ministry of nearly sixty years, laboured more abundantly than many to bring others to the same blessed experience and to win souls to Christ; he reverently acknowledged that it was *not he*, but the grace of God that was with him; he well knew—he deeply felt and was not slow to confess, that he had his treasure in an earthen vessel, that "the excellency of the power might be of God" and not of man.

But the time of his departure was at hand. In one of the last meetings he attended, he enlarged in a very striking manner on the words of Paul, "I have fought a good fight, I have finished my course, I have kept the faith. Henceforth there is laid up for me a crown of righteousness." Eight days before his decease he was present at his own Monthly Meeting, where he dwelt with much unction on "the joy of believing;" telling his friends that it might probably be the last time he should plead with them. And such was the case, for never again was his voice thus heard amongst them. A paroxysm of pain obliged him to retire from the meeting before its close—the only time in his life that such an emergency had occurred.

He was from this time confined to the house, suffering extreme physical anguish, in the midst of which he desired his friends might be informed that, though tribulation abounded, consolation did much more abound. Remarking that he might yet have to suffer much more, he added, "I desire not only to do so submissively, but cheerfully. These sufferings are indeed agonising; but in this my hour of extremity, my Heavenly Father has not forsaken me, but is comforting me. I have had to advocate his cause, and now am I called to serve by patiently suffering, and to glorify Him even in the fires." On one occasion he said, "There is not only peace, but peace and joy in believing—great joy!" And when, in the extremities of tried but not tired patience, he would pray for a little mitigation of his sufferings, he invariably added, "Not my will, but Thine be done."

On being asked how he felt, though he could not tell of any lessening of his pains, he simply answered, "My dear Master is very good to me." Again, "I cannot think that I shall be forsaken; He that careth for the sparrows will surely remember me." "My heart and my strength faileth, but"—and a radiant, expressive smile told the realisation of the remainder of the text, which he had recited a short time before—"God is the strength of my heart, and my portion for ever." In a severe spasm he meekly said, "Do not be discouraged; it is only the flesh." The two succeeding days were attended with almost constant agony, but each groan was turned into a prayer, ending with "Not my will, but Thine be done." Towards evening, on the 14th, he submissively petitioned for a little relief from suffering, if consistent with his Heavenly Father's will. Very soon the pain appeared finally to cease; and, while he took no notice of external things, the reverence of his countenance indicated a peaceful communion with his God and Saviour.

He slept sweetly during much of the following day; and a little before noon on Sixth-day, the 16th of Eleventh Month, 1855, with his family around him, the beloved and honoured servant of the Lord gently breathed his last, full of days and full of peace.

FINIS.

PRINTED BY R. BARRETT AND SONS, MARK LANE, LONDON.

www.ingramcontent.com/pod-product-compliance
Lightning Source LLC
Chambersburg PA
CBHW020858130726
47900CB00014B/1017